D1093953

Primordial Resurgence: Origins

By Dr. Philip Fico

DORRANCE
PUBLISHING CO
EST. 1920
PITTSBURGH, PENNSYLVANIA 15238

Dorrance Publishing Co
585 Alpha Drive
Pittsburgh, PA 15238
Visit our website at *www.dorrancebookstore.com*

ISBN: 978-1-6376-4076-0
eISBN: 978-1-6376-4919-0

Primordial Resurgence: Origins

Chapter 1

Sir Ethan Barnes sat in the empty conference room; his hand shook slightly as he sat there nervously awaiting a phone call. He'd known this day was coming, but damn if it didn't come too soon. Ethan had run out of time. Investors, he scoffed as he sat in silence thinking to himself, they're always looking for results. Always looking out for their own necks was more like it. They couldn't possibly understand his vision.

"Ethan," a voice interrupted his thoughts, "the board needs something concrete. It's been more than five years, and your lab has yet to produce a viable embryo. We are not going to keep sinking money into a lost cause."

He glared at the phone in front of him, not quite knowing what to say. His watch glared back at him from his aged hands. What a waste of time these phone calls were, he thought. These investors had no idea what he was trying to accomplish or how hard it was. Their complaining never got anything done; he just got complaint after complaint based on the lack of tangible research breakthroughs.

"Howard, how many times must we go over this? There's so many finite details, my scientists are still working out the kinks." He sighed. "We're hopeful this next batch will yield the results we're looking for. No one has ever done something like this before. We are in complete control. We just need more time."

Howard hesitated. "There's already another egg group? You have another set of embryos incubating?"

"Yes, we're working around the clock to get results. We just need more time to refine the process. Figure out some little odd and ends, that sort of thing."

He could hear Howard calculating on the other line. Fingers smashed calculator buttons quickly and fiercely.

"All right, I'll let the rest of the team know. But Ethan," he warned, "I can't imagine the board will wait much longer. My guess? You have until the end of the year and then your little project is cancelled."

The line went dead before he could respond.

"Blast," Ethan cursed, slamming his hands onto the table as he rose to his feet.

Deadlines. Who the hell put deadlines on scientific research? Grumbling, he packed his loose papers into his briefcase. What his scientists were attempting had never been done before: attempting to decode heavily decayed dinosaur DNA to revive the prehistoric creatures. He shook his head as he left the conference room. Many failures had been created, none viable. His investors had been antsy for a while now, but considering the monumental task they were undertaking, failures were to be expected! He hurried out of the facility, checking his watch as the muggy summer air hit him. He would get Archosauria up and running if it was the last thing he did.

Archosauria's scientists prided themselves on their advancements in genetic engineering, but arrogance and pride would ultimately be their downfall. Sir Ethan Barnes and his partner Ryo Sana were billionaires who made their fortune in genetic research and consumables. They had no idea how the field of medicine worked, let alone who to turn to for veterinary care for their creations. In these early stages of the park, they had not accounted for how hard bringing back an extinct life form would be. What they were attempting was so novel and cutting edge that there was not yet a branch of medicine capable of handling these accomplishments. Sir Barnes had succeeded in his goal to reanimate long extinct animals that predate history. The problem was that neither Sir Barnes, Mr. Sana, nor their geneticists knew how to take care of them. They needed help, and they needed it quick. Ethan Barnes' anxious investors were threatening to pull their funding if he couldn't produce results soon. Sir Barnes' scientists began their venture in the beginning of 1976. The more time passed without a viable clone, the more volatile the board became. Ethan and Ryo were getting increasingly desperate for a solution.

The first problem with scientific discovery is that one often finds that the most ground-breaking advancements never go according to plan. Discoveries often times happen by accident. There are plenty of trials and tribulations. Bringing back the dinosaurs was proving to be more difficult than they had anticipated. Animals that have been absent from the food chain for millions of years have no natural immunity to any of the various bacteria, viruses, parasites, or prions that inhabit our world. As life on Earth evolved without the dinosaurs, so too did these pathogens. This left their creations at a terrible disadvantage for survival in the 20th century. Even feeding these animals would prove to be a dangerous process for them. Bacteria that modern animals are unphased by could cause horrible outbreaks of dysentery or crippling skin infections that would leave the animal unable to walk from the pain. Sir Barnes would soon learn the frustration involved in trying to play God. Try as they might, Sir Barnes and his team were unable to find a solution to this blaring issue. Ethan was in charge of the genetics team while Ryo was focused solely on the investors and dealing with board meetings. Their group of geneticists were so preoccupied with the task at hand that they had not thought anything could go wrong once they succeeded compiling a complete genome.

Ethan had sent his dig teams to sites where the most marketable species' remains lay. The plan was to bring back species like Tyrannosaurus Rex, Apatosaurus, and Triceratops, as these were instantly recognizable animals. There was no point in spending millions of dollars in bringing back species that no one had even heard of. This would not draw the crowds that Archosauria needed to survive. Their company, Revolutionary National Amalgamations (R.N.A.), wanted to make as much money as possible on this venture considering how much money they had to pony up in order to get it started. People would be drawn more to a park with animals they knew from pop culture. They had to come half-way around the world to get there after all. His scientists had no idea what species' genetic codes they were working with initially. It was all chance in the early stages of the game as genetic sequencing was in its infancy, and no one had ever sequenced the genome of a dinosaur before. They would collect fossils in order to extract what little DNA they could get from them and then run these samples through the super computers. The computers would then catalog similar lines of code and began building DNA libraries. This, however, did not work well at first. The half- life of DNA (the amount of time it takes for half of a DNA sample to break down) was nowhere near the millions of years that had passed since the last dinosaurs lived. The material extracted from these raw materials was more like a bunch of puzzle pieces with no picture to use as a guide. The problem was this puzzle was trillions of pieces. It was a daunting task to say the least.

In order to get around this problem, R.N.A. began to train the program with extant or living species. This involved them mapping the genomes of modern animals on their own, as no one was doing this kind of work in the late seventies. This was long before the human genome project and other projects like it. In order to train the program to map genomes on its own from DNA fragments, they would then feed partial genomes into the sequencer and allow it to map out the complete code. R.N.A.'s scientists would then compare the end results and make sure the computer was accurate in its reconstructions. As the software adapted and learned, it was able to recreate genomes reliably with less and less genetic base material by filling in gaps with sequences from its data banks. This was the greatest accomplishment of Archosauria. Their work in genome mapping and genetic code reconstruction was nothing short of miraculous. Dr. Jin Moon Bai was the genius behind this of course. In order to protect his work from falling into the hands of rival companies, R.N.A. would tell the public a different story of how they accomplished this feat. This half-truth about finding large amounts of genetic material frozen in amber was invented by Dr. Bai himself. People loved believing pseudoscience and would never do the research on their own.

After years of sample collecting, genetic code compiling, and sequencing, the first full dinosaur genome was created. The gaps in the genetic codes were large due to decay of the source materials. In order to fix this, Jin Moon's program would insert completed genes from it's database to complete the code and create a functional genome. This led to his animals being pseudo-hybridized, but this was something that no one would care about once the finished product was in front of them. Who would care that the Tyrannosaurid in front of them used an inserted gene from the computer's database for protein synthesis at the cellular level when the forty-foot animal was roaring in front of them? Dr. Bai and his team called their main investor, Sir Ethan Barnes, to give him the great news upon the creation of their first viable embryo. They were successful! For the first time, man would be able to create life on his own. Man had conquered extinction. They would begin by inoculating an ostrich egg with their embryos and see what species they had uncovered. Dr. Bai used plasmids to hijack a developing ostrich egg and implant a dinosaur genetic code where an avian one should have been. Plasmids were small loops of genetic material that could be injected into a cell in order to change its DNA. They expected a gestation of about five months with the accelerated growth factors they planned on giving the embryos. No one knew how long dinosaurs gestated for; they could only surmise approximate times based on extant life forms. Sir Barnes was ecstatic and planned to fly down to his small island chain in the South Pacific to be there for the first hatching of a dinosaur in sixty-five million years.

The helicopter ride from Samoa to Protogonus was a tough one. Ethan had a penchant for Greek Mythology and had chosen to name his island chain accordingly. Hours of rough air and cramped seating made the experience almost unbearable. This was not the luxurious way of travel that Ethan was used to, but he would endure it for the sake of his creation. Upon arrival the hot jungle air felt like it was slapping him in the face as he disembarked his helicopter. He had forgotten how hot these islands could get. All manner of flying insects seemed to assault him as he climbed out of the helicopter. The landing pad was about a half hour drive from the worker village. Ethan was afraid the noise of the helicopter would disturb the animals that he was trying to create. He had wanted to keep everything on Protogonus as natural as possible. This would be until the animals were moved to Dionysus where they would be showcased to the public and put on display. Ethan was imprisoned by the forest due to this decision. Two vehicles sat about a hundred feet from the helipad. The blades of the helicopter caused a fierce wind that gave life to the surrounding brush. Trees and grass swayed to and fro like people jumping about in a mosh pit at a concert. Standing there waiting for him was Dr. Bai accompanied by two drivers waiting to take Ethan and his servants to the worker base. Sir Barnes never went anywhere without his chef and two butlers. The butlers helped Ethan down a large metal staircase to the vehicles below. Once on solid ground, Sir Barnes locked eyes with Jin Moon. The two men rushed to each other to embrace, both ecstatic over their accomplishment.

"It's so great to see you, Jin! I can't wait to get to the compound and see our new little ones!" exclaimed Ethan.

"Well, there are no little ones as of yet, but in the week or so, that should change," said Dr. Bai.

"You know what I mean, stop being that way, Jin," said Ethan as he approached the two vehicles that would take them to the main compound.

"I love the new logos," Sir Barnes yelled over the sound of the powering down helicopter as he got into one of the two cars.

This was his first time seeing the logo for Archosauria. There was a royal purple circle outlined in gold with a large egg inside. Encapsulated in the egg was the silhouette of a DNA helix. Towards the bottom of the circle were the words "Archosauria." This was the result of weeks of arguing amongst the marketing department over what a good name for the dinosaur island theme park would be. Ethan didn't have any desire to be involved in any of those meetings. He felt that these meetings were a bunch of grown men arguing with each other over trivial nonsense. All that mattered to Ethan was the finished product. He knew his target audience would drag their parents to his park no matter what it was called. The committee had settled on Archosauria after three weeks of debate because some board member felt it "sounded hip" and "cool." This name also paneled well amongst survey audiences; little did these random people know, they had chosen the name of the most ground-breaking wildlife preserve of the 20th century.

The dense jungle seemed to whiz by as they drove down the dirt road towards the worker village. This would all be paved of course as production time got closer and the work on Protogonus finished. Protogonus was not meant to be a tourist spot initially. As they expanded, it wasn't out of the realm of possibility for Ethan to imagine having people tour the island where it all started. After all this wasn't going to end with one island. Ethan had big plans to place Archosauria parks around the world. His partner, Ryo, wasn't so venturous. Mr. Sana felt that multiple parks would be too difficult to control. He was a shrewd Japanese businessman who was not one for taking risks. This was a point of contention between the two men. Ethan was always the dreamer of the two, while Ryo was the more practical partner. The two complimented each other well. Protogonus was the site where it would begin. It would be the site where the animals would be bred and raised, away from the viewing guests. No one was to know about R.N.A.'s hidden secret until they wanted them to. This would also allow them to experiment with new species as the park grew its roster. Mr. Sana had even had members of his team spread rumors amongst the neighboring islands about the haunted *Isles of Olympia*. They were a set of six islands (Protogonus, Aion, Erebus, Hemera, Nyx and Chronos) that Ethan and Ryo had chosen to set up shop on. Protogonus was the largest of the six and thus was a natural starting point. Ethan had named each island after one of the main Greek gods of creation.

The problem was that these islands were located near common local fishing spots. Mr. Sana had rumors sent out amongst the communities in the hopes of keeping these local fishermen and the prying eyes of rival companies away. Fishing boats that went near the islands stopped coming home. Men mysteriously vanished if they approached this island chain. All of the workers on these islands were also sworn to strict secrecy, being barred from telling even their closest loved ones what they were working on for fear of word getting out. Workers who did leak information were known to disappear along with their families, never to be seen again. R.N.A. also paid very well for the work they required, giving the locals good reason to keep their promises. Ethan wanted a big public reveal. He relished in the thought of how the world would react to his Archosauria. Sir Barnes purposely turned a blind eye to how his partner helped make this happen and tended to ignore these darker parts of this business venture.

Long before they arrived at the clearing where the worker village lay, the men could hear clanging iron and men shouting in Spanish. Construction was near completion on Protogonus. As they rounded a small bend, there was a break in the jungle. Huge cranes were hoisting large concrete pillars into the pre-dug holes of the foundation. Large holding pens could be seen towards the back end of the facility in preparation for the park's first arrivals. As their vehicles pulled up to a large wooden gate, the word "Archosauria" could be seen to already be in place. A crane carrying a gigantic pillar creaked forward as men worked on the perimeter fencing. The sight of this filled Ethan with pure ecstasy. The gates lurched open, and the two cars passed through. Ethan would have a similar gate installed on Dionysus. Two rows of hotel style buildings were present on either side of them on the main road. Ethan could see men playing basketball on one of the courts behind the worker's quarters. This little village was the home of all the construction teams, electricians, chefs, and essential personnel. The scientists had their own quarters closer to the laboratories. Sir Barnes had a small mansion built for himself, so that he could visit his creations any time he saw fit. This is where he was headed.

The whole camp was surrounded by a large metal fence with five-inch diameter rods placed horizontally between reinforced steel columns, ten inches in diameter. These were to be electrified for extra protection once Protogonus was in full operation. They had extrapolated how powerful some of the more aggressive animals may be using the known strength of a bull African elephant. Dinosaurs would be several times larger than this, so containment was a top priority. To say this was dangerous guess work would be putting it lightly. Apatosaurus, for example, was estimated to weigh as much as seven elephants. Keeping an animal like this contained was going to be a challenge. An animal of this size would have destructive power that was unimaginable. The task of containment went to Archosauria's game warden, Nalani Mwangi. She had been around dangerous African predators her whole life, and thus in Ethan's eyes was the perfect person for the job. Sir Barnes' containment team was hoping that electric shocks would be enough to deter the animals from getting too close to the fences. They wanted the animals to be visible to the public as tour vehicles drove by the fences. This safari was to be one of many attractions they would open with. This meant that safe concrete walls or pits were not an option as the animals would not be able to be viewed from the height of the vehicles.

R.N.A had the generators placed underground. All electricity would ultimately be powered by the island's own geothermal energy. Sir Barnes had overspent his budget in powering his baby. The project was meant to be self-sufficient and function without need of much from the mainland. He would have food and toiletries delivered via cargo ship twice a month along with any other essential supplies. Eventually all food for both human and dinosaur was to be grown on Protogonus. He had recruited local shepherds to tend to large herds of goats and cattle in order to feed the carnivores that he planned on bringing to life. The less he had to have delivered, the fewer questions he would have to deal with. Ethan did not want anyone looking into his venture before it was ready for visitors and the mainstream media.

The car pulled up in front of a two-story building with a large marble staircase. On either side of the railing were miniature Tyrannosaurus Rex skeleton replicas. His compound was surrounded by its own electric fence that was hooked up to its own set of back-up generators. Sir Barnes did not want to take any chances with his own life. He was not willing to risk himself if anything escaped the holding pens. Ethan walked down the long corridor and arrived at his quarters. He began unpacking and settling in for the night. He wanted to be present for the birth of the very first dinosaur. Based on their growth, activity, and hormone levels, the first clutch of eggs was ready to hatch at any moment. Sir Barnes had flown in, so that he could be available to witness the fruits of their labor. Days seemed to drag as he waited to be called to the labs with news of the eggs hatching. It was 3 A.M. when Ethan was jolted from his slumber by the sound of his room telephone ringing. He picked up with anticipation.

"Sir Barnes, it's happening!" exclaimed an excited Dr. Jin Moon Bai.

Chapter 2

Sir Barnes walked down the hall as fast as his legs could carry him. Age had left him with creaking joints and horrible arthritis in his lumbar spine. He hobbled down the long corridor followed by an entourage of individuals. Dr. Bai, walking alongside him, was eager to please his boss and mentor. Jin Moon was a tall, attractive young man that Sir Ethan had pulled from South Korea. Ethan had agents around the world scouting for promising young individuals. Over time Ethan had become like a father to Jin Moon. In the beginning, before he got high on himself, Dr. Bai was all about succeeding and the task at hand. Later he would develop a bit of a god-complex as success after success rolled in. The eggs were set in a small incubator with grasses and brush around them to mimic a nest as closely as possible. UV lights and space heaters were set to closely regulate the temperature and environment of this clutch. Incubation temperatures were set to parameters that one would need to hatch an ostrich since it was likely the closest animal to what they were trying to create. Each egg was worth millions, more if they hatched viable organisms that grew to adulthood. This was a momentous occasion. Sir Barnes and his team gathered around the eggs like a line of people around a buffet. The first egg began shaking and rocking slightly, a small crack visible at the apex. As the crack began to spread, faint honking noises could be heard coming from inside. The noise was unlike any animal that they had ever heard before. It sounded almost alien; a mixture of a goose honk and the bellow of a cow. This was the first time anyone had ever heard the call of a dinosaur. This would be the first time that man and dinosaur would ever interact outside of Hollywood.

Fluid began to ooze from the hole that the creature had created. None of those in observance for this event knew what was about to hatch from this egg. Holding the eggs to light revealed those embryos would be quadrupeds of some variety, likely herbivores. Sir Barnes had not thought to have an X-ray machine or advanced medical imagining equipment flown to Protogonus initially. The anticipation was killing them. They knew it would be an animal from the Late Cretaceous period based on the bone beds that the DNA had come from. This was all that they could tell. A small piece of shell tumbled to the bedding and a bird-like eye stared back at the group of men, blinking rapidly as it adjusted to seeing light for the first time. The pupil constricted in the radiating light from the incubator. A beak with an attached egg tooth became visible, breaking down the shell as the animal began to free itself from its white prison. The small head was visible pushing against the top of the shell. The egg membrane was trying desperately to hold the egg together against the baby's will. Just then the egg membrane tore, and a large chunk of shell fell to the ground. The baby paused for a second, panting from all of the effort. It became clear to the men what species this was at first glance. *Triceratops horridus.*

Sir Barnes, Dr. Bai, Dr. Sung, and Arthur Williams all stared in awe at the small creature. Above each eye was a small, soft-looking horn bud. There was a third horn bud just above the large parrot-like beak. Wrapped around the back of the skull was the famous bony frill adorned with horn buds around its perimeter. The baby bellowed and used its front legs to kick away another part of the shell. She then fell forward on the bedding covered in a thin layer of mucous and blood. The baby tried to get to its feet while the remainder of its clutch began to hatch. Attached to her toes was a yellow eponychium. Horses and other hoofed animals had this soft layer of deciduous hoof used to protect the mother from the fetus' sharp feet. Similarly this small creature had eponychium on her toe claws to prevent her from damaging her shell before she hatched when she moved. The men stared in complete awe and wonder. They were going to be rich beyond their wildest dreams!

As Jin Moon viewed the hatchling, he couldn't help but be annoyed that he didn't know what species he had brought back before watching it hatch.

The randomness of it all bothered Dr. Bai. He had to correct this as soon as possible; his perfectionist nature could not stomach producing animals at random chance. He would rectify it immediately, but first he had to tend to his infants. He had the babies tagged and moved as soon as they were all hatched. The first clone was designated TRC001. She was to live in a small enclosure with her four siblings. All five animals were designated in a similar fashion with TRC and a corresponding number given to them in the order that they hatched. Their enclosure was a small, fenced in area just outside of the lab. They were enclosed by a chain-link fence. At first there was nothing but celebrations and excitement over what they had just accomplished. This was world changing, Nobel Prize worthy to say the least. Dr. Bai and his team were patting themselves on the back for their accomplishments. This was his crowning achievement. He could not wait to start experimenting with other genomes and build his library of de-extinct species.

Only a few days passed before trouble began to set in. It started with the hatchlings developing diarrhea. They had only been alive for a few days, and they were already sick. Sir Barnes' chief paleontologist, Dr. Richard Bramme, had picked several plant species that were descendants of those most likely to have been present in large numbers during the Late Cretaceous to plant in the hatchling's enclosure. The issue was none of the infants would touch them. They showed no interest in eating any of the plants in their habitat. Without a mother to guide them, they seemed to have an issue with deciding what was food and what wasn't. It took a long time to find plants that the animals would eat, leading to them having to be tube-fed electrolyte solutions and dextrose (oral sugar) to prevent them from becoming malnourished. Keeping this small clutch alive had become the focus of their venture and was quickly becoming a tiresome task. Teams were scheduled around the clock to feed the babies every few hours since they would unreliably eat on their own. Work halted on completing other genomes and shifted to bringing back some Late Cretaceous flora. It made no sense to produce more animals if they couldn't keep the animals they had alive. Their resident paleontologist seemed to be no help in the matter. Bramme had his theories, but he was not a medical doctor. He did not know how to care for infant animals, let alone infant dinosaurs.

As time passed, the babies finally seemed like they were beginning to flourish. They were already four to five-hundred pounds apiece at a month old. Their growth rate was impressive. The animals had formed a very clear social group with TRC002 as the matriarch. It wasn't long before one of the babies had developed a small rash behind her frill. The lesion was small at first and barely noticeable as these animals were the size of a small cow at this point. One of the boys that cleaned out the pen happened to note it while playing with the animals. They were surprisingly docile and friendly in demeanor at this stage of their lives. The stall cleaners were often seen romping around with them during the day. Dr. Sung and his team ran a few initial tests on the animal's skin but did not come up with any cause for alarm when it was brought to their attention. He had reasoned that the birds that would often ride on the animals were pecking at their skin and causing damage to them. A tarp was placed over the open enclosure to keep any stray birds out. Within forty-eight hours' time, the rash had spread down the back of the affected baby. Scales were peeling off revealing red, raw tissue underneath. The infant was horribly pruritic; she would spend her day rolling on the ground and up against trees in her enclosure, trying to get some relief from the horrible itch. The animal's intense bellows could be heard from the outside of the hatchery building. TRC003 was separated from her siblings until the pathogen could be identified for fear that this rash may be contagious.

The animals were all brought indoors, and TRC003 was isolated from the rest of the herd in her own enclosure. Contact with her was limited to try to maintain isolation protocol. No one could interact with TRC003 unless they were in a hazmat suit. All suits were to be decontaminated with harsh chemicals to try to prevent the spread. TRC003 had also become very irritable. She would charge anyone entering the enclosure and resented any touch of her painful skin. It came to a point where she would have to be heavily sedated just to have any interaction with her. Her entire demeanor had changed. Isolation came too late, however, and the other animals soon developed a similar condition. Dr. Bai had workers applying cortisone creams and were administering sedatives around the clock to try to prevent the animals from ripping their own flesh off on the trees in their enclosures. The dinosaurs would spend most of their days gouging out chunks of flesh trying to get relief. Sedation and heavy narcotics were the only thing they could do for them until they could find a treatment. Dr. Ernie Sung, one of the park's bioengineers and a bacteriologist, had cultured the wounds and identified a

Staphylococcus species. He reasoned that this Staph infection was the cause of the animal's persistent rash. He quickly rushed to tell Dr. Bai of his findings, so that they could find a cure. Jin Moon was not a medical doctor and had no idea what to treat a Staph infection with outside of the lab setting. Dr. Bai knew vaguely of antibiotics that would kill Staphylococcus in a petri dish but had no clue how to dose it. The same was true for Dr. Sung. Jin rushed to consult the island physician for advice, hoping to get an answer on how to remedy this issue. Dr. Bai was soon at the door of the clinic demanding to see Dr. Eric Harper. He didn't care about his appointments with the various island workers, this was a priority.

"I need you to tell me what antibiotic to use to kill this Staph infection," grunted Dr. Bai. He was barely in the door of Dr. Harper's office when he accosted him.

"I mean I have no idea, Dr. Bai. This is not something I was trained to do," said Dr. Harper

"I don't give a shit what you were trained to do! I need a dose, or you are out of a job. I will see to it that you are blackballed in the medical community. Do not keep me…do not keep Sir Barnes waiting. Our funds are limitless! You will never work again," yelled Jin Moon. He had little patience at this point and was feeling the pressure to get the animals treated.

"Listen, Jin, threats are not needed here. I have no clue how to dose a dinosaur. If it were a 500-pound person, I would probably give it three grams of Ampicillin IV every eight hours. But there is no way of knowing what their metabolism is and if that will even be enough," warned Dr. Harper as he ran his fingers through his blonde hair.

"Thank you for your time, doctor. Where is it?" said Jin Moon curtly as he stormed out of the office and into the clinic pharmacy.

"But Jin, you have no idea what you are doing!" yelled Dr. Harper as he got out of his office chair to follow him.

"Ah, here we go. Is this the stuff?" questioned Jin Moon as he pulled a box of vials off a shelf.

"Well, yes, but …" said Dr. Harper, quickly checking the label on the box in Jin's hand.

Jin Moon wasted no time. Before Dr. Harper could finish, he had grabbed a box of the antibiotic vials, needles, and some sterile saline to make up the medication. He didn't care what Dr. Harper had to say at this point. He wanted to get back on track.

Dr. Bai drew up a dose of Ampicillin as soon as he got back to the lab taking care to mix the right amount of saline with the white powdered antibiotic. He was going to be the one to fix this. If Ampicillin treated Staph infections, then Ampicillin it was. What could possibly go wrong here? All Jin Moon had to do was kill this skin infection and then he could continue on his journey towards fame. He would be the top geneticist on the planet once Archosauria was open to the public. Dr. Bai could see it now, he would have all the money and fame he could ever dream of. Jin Moon approached TRC003, who at this point was unable to walk. The rashes on her legs made it too painful for the animal to move. She lay there pitifully moaning, staring at Jin with saddened eyes. A single tear ran down the side of her scaly cheek as she lay there in pain. The animal looked almost like a puppy who had done something wrong. The sadness and pain in her eyes were so apparent that even with his hardened heart, Jin felt sorry for her. Teams of men had to flip her every few hours to prevent her from developing bed sores. She was on high doses of sufentanil, a high-end pain medication, often used in large wildlife. If Jin didn't act soon, he knew that these animals were not long for this world. He feared how Sir Barnes and Mr. Sana would respond if he lost these creatures. He had to fix it. He had to be in control again.

Two hours after the first doses of Ampicillin, the animals began experiencing drops in blood pressure and racing heart rates. TRC005, the least affected of the group and the last one infected, collapsed in her enclosure. All of the infants were unresponsive by the evening. They appeared as if they were going into septic shock, all of them developing intense diarrhea and vomiting before collapsing, and slipping into a coma. Jin Moon was panicked. What was happening, he thought?! He had Dr. Harper rush down to the holding pens to try to help guide the treatment for the sick babies. TRC003 was the first animal to die, being the first infected and the most seriously ill. Within forty-eight hours, all the animals had joined their sister in extinction. What had happened?! Dr. Bai's face was crimson, a single vein bulged in his forehead. He was gritting his teeth, and his eyes were wider than dinner plates. The antibiotic should have worked. Failure was not something that Jin Moon handled well, nor was it something he was accustomed to. He began to throw anything within arm's reach as he screamed at everyone in ear shot. A coffee mug shattered into pieces as it hit the wall nearly missing a computer monitor. What was Sir Barnes going to say when he found out? This was unacceptable! Dr. Harper stood over the corpse of TRC005, the last animal to pass, with his head hung in defeat.

"I want these animals necropsied as soon as possible! We have to know why they died! We have to fix this!" Jin Moon screamed as saliva spurted from his mouth.

"We don't have a pathologist on staff, Dr. Bai," said Dr. Ernie Sung sheepishly.

"Well, get one! Our funds are near limitless, get one now," Jin Moon screamed at the cowering Dr. Sung.

"I warned you, Jin! I told you that you had no idea what you were doing," screamed Dr. Harper as he hovered over the body of TRC005. His stethoscope was almost falling off his shoulder, and his blonde hair was disheveled.

"Shut up! I didn't ask you for your opinion. I asked you to treat the infection, and you failed miserably at that! What kind of a doctor are you anyways if you can't treat a simple Staph infection?" screamed Dr. Bai.

"You medicated these animals without any guidance…with a medication you didn't even know the dose of! Don't you dare try to put this on me, you spoiled little shit!" screamed Dr. Harper.

Dr. Ernie Sung broke the two men up. He had managed to just barely calm the tensions in the room. This was bad for all of them. They had killed their success, and they had no idea how they had done it. Sir Barnes would not take this well, and all of their jobs were on the line.

"We need answers. Phone the mainland, get Mr. Sana on the phone, and let's get to the bottom of this," Jin Moon said, directed at Dr. Sung.

Ernie was a man of small stature to begin with. Jin Moon seemed to tower over him much in the way a mad scientist would tower over his minions when they had failed him. Ernie's glasses were falling off his face as he cowered away from Dr. Bai. He pushed a small strand of black hair out of his eyes as he recovered and ran out of the room. He didn't know what had happened. Ernie was accustomed to working with organisms in a petri dish, not playing veterinarian to zoo animals. This was way out of his comfort zone. Ernie's first thought was to contact Arthur Williams. He would have a direct line of contact with Mr. Sana and thus their resources on the mainland. He rushed to Arthur's lodgings and feverishly knocked on the door. It was seven in the morning. Ernie prayed that Arthur would come to the door soon. He was terrified of Dr. Bai and did not want to fail him again. After all it was his idea to treat the Staph infections in the first place. The crickets and crowing tropical birds seemed to build up a sense of anticipation as Ernie waited for the door to open.

"It's 7 A.M.!" exclaimed Arthur Williams. "What the hell do you want, Ernie?"

"They're all dead! I need Mr. Sana now! We need a pathologist…" cried Ernie feverishly.

"Woah, woah, woah, who's dead? What are you talking about? Come inside and let's talk," said Arthur, wiping sleep from his eyes with a yawn.

Ernie sat and discussed what had transpired with the sick triceratops. Arthur was in shock. He knew they had not told Ethan and he knew that this was going to be bad. They had to get an answer as soon as possible. Arthur ran his fingers through his red hair repeatedly as he tried to come up with some sort of a plan. He knew he had to tell Mr. Sana and Sir Barnes, but he didn't know what he was going to say.

"Good morning, sir, you just lost forty million dollars, and we don't know what happened" did not sound like a good way of starting a day. Arthur did his best to calm down Ernie. He called Mr. Sana as soon as Ernie had left. It would be an early morning call, but he had to get this over with.

The phone call went about as well as he had expected. Mr. Sana was livid about the loss of their investment and what he felt was obvious incompetence on the part of the team. He did not like the idea of starting from scratch, and he knew that this was going to make the board question their investment. Ryo had to keep this as quiet as possible. He instructed Arthur to tell Dr. Bai to immediately refrigerate the animals and get samples ready for transport to San Diego. He would deal with getting them analyzed. He also instructed Arthur to get Jin Moon to immediately begin work on the next iteration of triceratops. The investors had been asking for pictures of the animals, and he was going to need something to show them. Mr. Sana would have to have it out with Jin Moon and Eric Harper later. Right now damage control was the focus. He had to find a pathologist that he could swear to secrecy. The more people that had to be involved with this, the more money had to be shelled out. The long term pay-off of this venture would be astronomical. It would be worth it, he kept telling himself.

Mr. Sana knew his son's friend was a veterinarian in the San Diego area. He had watched this young man grow up with his son. Dr. Scott Harmon was also an expert in avian and reptilian medicine. As luck would have it, this would make him perfect for the job. Mr. Sana also knew that Scott had recently gone through a rough divorce. This would be perfect as he would likely need the money. Mr. Sana obtained the extension to Dr. Harmon at a large zoo in San Diego from his son. He immediately passed this information to Arthur Williams. Mr. Sana was not about to do this dirty work on his own. This is what Arthur was hired for. He gave him a timeline of two weeks to rope Dr. Harmon in. If he couldn't do this quickly, then Mr. Sana told Arthur he would be without a job. He gave Arthur the green light to offer Dr. Harmon as much money as it took. Every man had a price, and one way or another, Dr. Harmon would be the veterinarian for Archosauria.

Chapter 3

Dr. Scott Harmon had graduated top of his class. As a Los Angeles native, he had grown up on the beaches. One of his fondest memories as a child was sitting on the shore with his parents watching the various shore birds fly overhead and fight with each other over food. This is where his fascination with birds began. He would spend plenty of weekends going to the local library to read anything he could get his hands on pertaining to birds and wildlife. Scott had always wondered what it would be like to be able to fly. In his adult life, he would become recognized as an avian specialist before it would become recognized as its own specialty.

Dr. Harmon would go on to work at a large zoo in San Diego, taking care of their raptors and various exotic birds. He preferred the predatory birds or raptors above all else. There was something so majestic about them. He would often spend hours observing their behavior. He wondered if they missed the open skies and thought about how it felt criminal to him to keep them captive. Unfortunately it was a necessary evil. These birds were either reared in captivity or had been placed in captivity following an injury that would not allow them to hunt normally in the wild. They could not be released and survive. Dr. Harmon knew this, but it didn't stop him from daydreaming about releasing these animals. His fascination and dedication to his job had cost him his marriage. He had spent most of his time at the zoo and not enough time honoring commitments to his family. He couldn't count all the missed school plays, birthdays, and social functions that he had not been present for due to work. Deep down he knew it was a problem, but veterinary medicine was his first love. He couldn't help himself; veterinary medicine was his passion and his life. This was something his wife would never understand.

Scott would get visitation rights to his children, Erica and Ashley, every other weekend. When he split with his wife, Dr. Harmon felt like he had lost a part of himself. He never intended for things to go the way they had and missed his family dearly. Harmon had a hard time leaving work and would often come home late after his wife and children had gone to bed. This behavior did not end when his marriage fell apart. On weekends where Ashley and Erica were supposed to come by, Scott would very frequently cancel plans or have them stay with a sitter while he worked. One of the most painful memories for him was Christmas the previous year. He was supposed to have the girls come over to his place on Christmas Eve for dinner and a gift exchange. Scott could not wait to give them the gifts he had picked out and secretly hoped they would make up for some of the lost time. When he called his wife to set up the final details, he heard his daughter Erica asking her mother if she had to go. She whined to her sister about how he never spends time with them anyway and how they did not want to see him. Scott tried to act like he didn't hear this, but it hurt him more than anything else could. This wound never seemed to heal, and Scott thought about it often. Even still, he could not seem to change his habits. Like most addictions, admitting there is a problem doesn't always resolve the issue.

It was a typical September Monday for Scott. He arrived at work at 7:30 A.M. to start his morning rounds. He would start with the Amazonian birds of paradise, walk through the aquatic bird enclosure, and end with his favorite, the birds of prey. During his walk through, he would make sure that everyone appeared healthy and was behaving normally. Any animal that appeared lethargic, had feather loss, was limping, or appeared visibly ill would warrant an immediate check-up. The remainder of his day would consist of examining anyone whom the keepers were concerned about, working on diet plans for the new arrivals and coordinating with other zoos to try to establish his California Condor breeding program. Nothing was out of the ordinary.

Dr. Harmon took his lunch break a little early that day. He had no idea that a life-changing event was about to come knocking on his door. As he arrived back to his office, his secretary, Margret, flagged him down. Scott had always had a thing for Margret. She was a young twenty-something with curly brown hair and a pin-up model body. She was too young for him, and Scott wasn't at all ready for another relationship. He was still reeling from his recent divorce and was hung up on his ex-wife, Emily. But even still, some companionship might be nice.

"Dr. Harmon, some guy named Arthur Williams called for you. It sounded pretty urgent," said Margret.

"Well, what did he want? Did he say where he was calling from?" asked Scott.

"Some company called **Revolutionary National Amalgamations**. He wouldn't say what it was about and said it was imperative that you call him back. Something about an opportunity of a lifetime," Margaret said. "I mean he was really annoying and adamant about speaking to you. If I were you, I would probably return his call."

"Leave the call back number on my desk, and I will get back to him as soon as I look at the sick eagle that Roberts brought in," said Dr. Harmon.

"Whatever," Margret said indifferently as she went back to her desk. She quietly muttered under her breath as she sat down.

Scott had heard of **Revolutionary National Amalgamations** before, but he couldn't remember where or why the name of this company sounded familiar. He pondered for a bit over the course of the day and thought he had seen the name in one of the science magazines that he had subscribed to a while back. What would a company like that want with him? He did not have a background in genetics, nor was he at all interested in becoming a lab rat. The more he thought about it, the more he came to the decision that he was going to ignore this call as he had ignored many others trying to reach him at work, including his family. Once he got to his desk, he crumpled up the small note that contained the number for Mr. Williams and threw it in the trash. He didn't have the energy to be bothered with this. He had sick patients to attend to, and this "job opportunity" did not interest him. Little did he realize how wrong he was.

As the day ended, Scott packed up his bag and set off for his home. Once he arrived, he thumbed through a pile of take-out menus. His small San Diego apartment had become littered in clutter. His wife had gotten the house in the divorce. The court awarded her primary custody of their children and felt that the children needed a home to finish growing up in. Scott was never one for cleaning, although even he had to admit the quality of his living space was poor. A thick layer of dust coated the TV screen before him. His walls were completely bare, and there was very little in the way of decorations. His living quarters resembled a morgue; devoid of any life or character. Too tired to cook, he ordered dinner from one of the menus he picked from a huge stack on the table. Take out had become a big part of his diet now. Scott had to admit that his days post-divorce had become very mundane. He would wake up for his morning run, go to work, order dinner, sleep, and repeat the cycle. The only time his routine varied was when it was his weekend with Erica and Ashley. Having his daughters would mean trips to baseball games, museums, and other social hot spots. This of course was when they would show up. As they had gotten older, these weekend outings became less and less common. His girls would often choose to stay with their mother rather than come visit him. Otherwise this was Scott's life. He told himself he was content, but he felt like he was missing something. There was a distinct purpose that was no longer present. His purpose had been his role as a father combined with his career; now all he had was his job. Scott stood up, picking up the pizza box on his lap, and threw it into the back of the fridge. Now he had a meal for tomorrow, or maybe a post-run breakfast. The refrigerator was empty besides a few bottles of condiments and a large brown stain on the bottom shelf. Scott quickly went to bed so he would be refreshed for tomorrow. This day that would be just like any of his other days. But, like many nights prior, he lay awake in his bed instead of sleeping.

Business as usual commenced the following morning. Dr. Harmon sat down at his desk and began to prepare for his morning rounds. Papers littered his desk and tumbled onto the floor. Every one of his patients were surprisingly healthy today. This was an unusual occurrence as usually at least one of the animals needed his attention. When you're responsible for a few hundred souls, there is always something to take care of. Today, however, he may get out early. This thought annoyed Dr. Harmon; he had nothing to do when he got home and there was nothing to go home to. He decided to throw himself into some calls he had been ignoring from earlier in the week. While on the phone with the director of a major zoo in New York, Margaret interrupted him for the second day in a row.

"Dr. Harmon, Arthur Williams again. This man has called fifteen times today to speak with you. I can't keep putting him off, it's getting annoying," said Margret with a tone of disdain in her voice.

"Tell him I'm busy and I will call him back later this afternoon. I don't care what you tell him, but I'm not talking to him," said Harmon, covering the receiver with his hand.

Margret left the room defeated and in a huff as Dr. Harmon continued his conversation. She was tired of this Mr. Williams and his constant calls over the past two days. She felt she did not get paid enough to take this kind of abuse. When she got back on the phone, she explained that Dr. Harmon was in a procedure and told Arthur to not call back for the rest of the day. She told him that Dr. Harmon would get in contact with him when he was available. Margret had taken this job, so that she could use it as a stepping block to apply to veterinary school. Suddenly it wasn't seeming like it was worth it. Dr. Harmon had become moody since his divorce. What was once a fun job where she learned a lot as the assistant to one of the zoo's veterinarians was now a secretary job answering phones. Dr. Harmon no longer seemed to have any interest in teaching or taking her on his morning rounds. In fact he almost seemed like he resented her for some unknown reason. She wrote up another message for Dr. Harmon and decided to spend the rest of her day playing games on the computer.

Scott saw the message Margret had left for him at the end of the day. It made him angry that this man was bothering him. He was busy and had no time for this. He felt that this was some kind of scam, and he wanted no part of it. The note was written in a very snarky manner. Scott had become accustomed to Margret's new abrasive nature, and quite frankly he could not find it in himself to care. The next two days went in a similar fashion. Workwise his days were uneventful, but the phone calls from Mr. Williams were unending. Arthur was calling Dr. Harmon more than even the most persistent of telemarketers. This of course annoyed Margret more than anyone else as she was the one on the phone constantly trying to put him off. She began picking up the phone and hanging up on Arthur when she heard his voice. She was annoyed that Dr. Harmon wouldn't even entertain the idea of calling this guy back to end his assault on her ears. Scott continued to be stubborn and continued to ignore any and all efforts of Mr. Williams to contact him.

This of course did not sit well with Arthur. He was on a time crunch, and his job was on the line. Arthur also had Sir Barnes and Mr. Sana breathing down his neck. It wasn't enough that they had decided failure would cost him his job, but they had also decided that they were going to hound him every step of the way. Ethan seemed to ask Arthur every chance he got if he had gotten in touch with Dr. Harmon. Arthur knew he had to fly to San Diego to settle this, as phone calls were not cutting it. The plan was going to be to fly to San Diego after forty-eight hours of no response as it would take him that long to get a flight. Sir Barnes had nipped this in the bud by saying that he would go with Arthur in person for this task. The issue now became working around Sir Barnes' busy schedule, so the flight to San Diego had to wait for the time being. This restricted Arthur to calling insistently in the hopes that Dr. Harmon would speak to him. He had to get Scott's attention one way or another. Arthur had come up with a fool proof plan of catching Dr. Harmon's attention. As far as veterinarians went, Harmon was at the top of the field for avian and reptilian medicine. No one else would do the job better than him. Arthur got the flight cleared with Ethan on his private jet that was camped at the Samoan airport. Ethan had a certain finesse about him when it came to convincing people, which is why he made Arthur wait until he was free to join him once it was clear phone contact would not work. The two took the long, uneasy flight to San Diego with the hopes of acquiring the talents of Dr. Harmon.

Back in San Diego, Dr. Harmon had decided to go out for lunch. He did not want to eat what he had brought and was feeling like he needed a change. His life had become about small, trivial pleasures. When he arrived back at the office, he felt refreshed. As he opened the door to his office building, he noted two men standing at the edge of the hall. They seemed to be watching him. Stepping inside the office, he immediately noticed that something was different. Margret was not at her desk as usual. It was a bit atypical for her to go on lunch at the same time as him as this would leave the office unattended. It didn't make sense, but it also did not bother him for very long. Maybe now that she was gone, he wouldn't have to deal with ignoring any unwanted phone calls. When he got into his office, he noticed a package tied with a rope. The package was wrapped with brown paper and had a note fixed to the top of it. The envelope was addressed to him. Should he open it? Who was it from? All of these thoughts rushed through his head. Curiosity got the better of him, and he decided to open the letter. Inside there was only one sentence written, "Welcome to pre-history." It was written in block lettering in a very interesting font. What the hell did this even mean? Who had sent this to him? Dr. Harmon was extremely confused. This seemed like a very elaborate prank, and he didn't feel like he was in on this joke. Dr. Harmon turned the card over a few times to see if there was a hidden message somewhere. He shrugged his shoulders as he found nothing. He tore through the wrapping.

Inside the box was a small case of microscope slides that appeared to have stained tissue samples on them. The slides were grouped, and each group had a different label, such as "stomach," "skin," etc. There was also a small photo book at the bottom of the box. Putting the slides to the side, Scott slowly lifted the photo album. He thumbed open the book and immediately stood frozen. His eyes were fixed on the photo, but his brain did not believe what he was seeing. Dr. Harmon couldn't seem to process the picture in front of him. It made no sense. He collapsed down into his chair, the photo book still in hand. It was…it was a dinosaur and a person. There were two men in white lab coats holding what looked to be a baby dinosaur. The men were smiling from ear to ear. A baby triceratops appeared to be struggling in their arms, unhappy with being held. It was pressing on one of the men's chests with its front feet. This had to be fake, but it looked so real. This photograph couldn't be real, it just couldn't be. Why would someone send this to him? Scott was looking for some indication that this was doctored. He then realized there were other pictures. The shock of the first photograph had made him forget this was an album.

The next photo was a picture of five triceratops grazing. It was clear as day; these dinosaurs were there. Each animal appeared to be the size of a small cow. A set of porcupine-like quills extended off of their hind ends. Their three-horned faces were instantly recognizable. The animals were walking together in a small herd. There was a chain-link fence visible behind them with a small white sign saying, "Danger Electrified Fencing." How could this be? Where was this taken? Scott's mind was going a mile a minute. Was this photo taken in some remote jungle? If it was, why was there a man-made electric fence behind the triceratops? Scott was so confused and excited. The next photo was of a dinosaur attached to several IV pumps with ECG monitoring. This was impossible! The thought of a dinosaur hooked up to medical equipment amused Scott. He smirked at the thought of treating a dinosaur. A very clear skin breakdown was present along the animal's back and legs. Several of the quills on its hind end were missing, and a few lay on the floor next to it. The ground was soaked in various fluids. This was an animal that was clearly very ill.

The final photo spot had a small hand-written note, saying, "Have we got your attention now, Dr. Harmon?"

He sat there dazed and befuddled. He kept thumbing through the photos over and over again. His brain was trying desperately to make sense of what he was looking at. There was no way that dinosaurs still existed. The last dinosaur went extinct long before people came about. Humans and dinosaurs never overlapped despite what Hollywood had portrayed in various films. Scott knew that computer technology could doctor photos nowadays, but who would go through such effort to produce convincing photographs of living dinosaurs? As he sat there questioning what was going on, his office door opened. In walked a tall, red-headed man with sunglasses, khakis, and a collared shirt. Behind him walked an older man, likely in his mid-sixties, with a bald head and glasses. They were the same men that had been watching him from the end of the hall.

"Hello, Dr. Harmon, you are a very hard man to get in touch with," said Arthur Williams.

"No, no, no, Arthur, let me do the talking," said Sir Barnes. "We have a lot to discuss and not a lot of time to discuss it."

"Who are you people? Did you send these photos? What is going on here?" exclaimed Dr. Harmon. His wonder had switched to anger at the intrusion.

"Ah, yes, I'm sure you are very confused as to what is going on and all. Where are my manners? My name is Sir Ethan Barnes, and this is my director of public relations whom you've been ignoring, Arthur Williams," said Ethan.

"Ethan Barnes? The billionaire Ethan Barnes?" questioned Dr. Harmon. His anger now confusion as he recognized the face of Ethan from various television news stories.

"In the flesh," said Ethan, taking a half bow. "You are a very talented individual, Dr. Harmon. Your advancements in the field are well-known. We are in need of someone with your talents."

"Me? What do you need me for? I'm just a veterinarian working for a zoo. What does a billionaire need with…?" questioned Scott.

As he spoke, his mind thought back to the photographs and the slides sitting on his desk. There is no way, he thought to himself. Scott was beginning to put two and two together. Theories in paleontology had been changing on where dinosaurs fit in the phylogenetic tree of life forms. When they were first discovered, people thought that dinosaurs were lumbering cold-blooded reptiles not unlike giant crocodiles. More recently paleontologists had begun thinking of dinosaurs as warm-blooded animals. There were even some people saying that dinosaurs were the first birds. If those photographs were real and dinosaurs did really exist, then who better than an avian veterinarian to look after them. This was why they wanted him; this was why these men were here. This was impossible!

"Well, you see, Dr. Harmon; I have a set of islands in the South Pacific. We have embarked on a venture using cutting edge technology to create a biological preserve that is going to shake the world and blow the minds of the planet," said Sir Barnes.

"You mean to tell me the photos in that album, those tissue samples, this is real?!" exclaimed Scott.

"Yes, of course, this is why I have been hounding you," said Arthur somewhat bitterly, chiming into the conversation. "Would it have killed you to call me back?"

Scott could not believe what he was hearing. Living dinosaurs existed, and these men wanted him to take care of them. This was a dream come true. This could not be real, he thought to himself. Scott sat there for a minute with his eyes wide open. He realized he was panting as he thought to himself about the events that were unfolding; his eyes were darting back and forth as he processed what he was hearing. It didn't matter how he looked to these men. Nothing mattered at this point. Scott knew things were about to change for him. He had not felt this excited since getting his acceptance into veterinary school. This could give him a purpose, something to look forward to and live for.

"How many species? Where did you find them? How many are there? What..." Dr. Harmon asked in rapid succession.

"I'm sure you have loads of questions, my boy. All of these will be answered in due time," said Sir Barnes.

"We are willing to offer whatever you would like in terms of compensation. You will have to keep all of this strictly secret of course," said Arthur Williams, walking over to the desk and putting the photo album into his pocket.

"Now, now, we can talk compensation and secrecy in a second. Will you accept our offer, doctor?" asked Sir Barnes.

"I have projects here that I need to finish. I can't just leave my job," said Scott. The thought of relocating and giving up his life scared him, even though deep down he did not feel like his life was going anywhere.

"Don't worry about that, Dr. Harmon. Can I call you Scott? I will have someone take over your responsibilities while you are gone. I will also fully fund your condor breeding project for the next five years in addition to your salary," said Sir Barnes very calmly.

"Where do I sign on?" said Scott happily. He couldn't turn this down. This was too good an opportunity, and he was sold.

Sir Barnes had left Scott the task of analyzing the tissue samples on his desk. He excused himself from the room and told him that Arthur would take things over from here. Arthur began filling Scott in on what had transpired on Protogonus. He told Scott that they had lost their first five animals to disease. Dr. Harmon was brought up to speed on the details of the animal's passing and was told that there was a new clutch that was near hatching to replace them. Scott was instructed that he was not to discuss this with anyone under the threat of being financially ruined by R.N.A's big corporate lawyers. He was made to sign several legal documents forcing his silence. The samples were to be analyzed as soon as possible, and Scott was to report back with an answer as soon as he had one. Once he had a cause of death, Arthur and Ethan were going to fly with him down to Protogonus to have him meet the new iteration of triceratops. Dr. Harmon was to be the chief veterinarian of Archosauria. Arthur Williams instructed him that he would have any resource he needed, all he had to do was ask.

That night Scott didn't leave the office. He was too wound up to go home and just sleep. Scott began with the first set of slides marked "skin." He could not wait to look at samples of dinosaur skin and tissues. This was all exhilarating. Dr. Harmon placed the first slide onto the microscope. His heart was pounding as he turned on the light at the base and placed the low power lens over the tissue sample. He very gently adjusted the fine focus knob to bring the tissue sample into the focal point of the scope. As he adjusted the knobs, the tissue sample became visible. He scanned over the various cells colored purple and pink by the stain. Scott gradually increased the power of magnification as he scanned. He couldn't help but notice how reptilian the sample appeared. There was evidence of a secondary pyoderma or skin infection. The tissue was loaded with small circular bacteria or cocci. Dr. Harmon was told the animals had a Staph infection, but he would have to culture these bacteria to completely confirm that this is what they were. White blood cells were permeated throughout the upper skin layers. They had heterophils! This was a type of white blood cell that did not exist in mammals but was extremely common in birds. The new theories were right, he thought, dinosaurs were related to birds. This in itself was a scientific discovery that would make him famous. It was too bad that he could not tell anyone about this. He scanned the slide further to look for a cause of the rash that Arthur had told him about. Dr. Harmon came across something on the slide that shocked him, but it was something he recognized instantly.

Harmon was staring at a mite that was preserved within the skin sample that he was analyzing. The mite was a species that he was all too familiar with, *Dermanyssus gallinae*. This was a common avian skin mite that would cause intense itching and infection. They were extremely hard to get rid of as they could last for months without feeding. These mites could also infest humans, although only for short periods of time. Dr. Harmon had to combat this parasite many a time throughout his career. As he scanned the slide, he found more of the feather mites. He switched the slide to a different sample, and again he found evidence of the mites. Scott knew what had caused the skin infections, and it wasn't Staphylococcus. They had treated the wrong thing and jumped to conclusions, Scott thought. He had to tell Arthur immediately. The environment that the animals were in would need to be fumigated to remove any remaining mites. If they did not do this, then any new animals were sure to fall prey to them. This did not explain the cause of death. Feather mites could invade the respiratory system and were attracted to carbon dioxide and moisture. They would often congregate around the nostrils of affected birds and tended to be more active at night when the animals rested. The triceratops had no reports of respiratory distress though, so this did not seem likely. There had to be another cause.

The samples of the lungs and heart were interesting to look at but were normal. There was nothing exciting about them. Scott pulled out a set of slides marked 'GI system.' The stomach samples similarly did not show any evidence of pathology. He found it fascinating that they had a stomach similar to a person, with acid secreting cells and a thick mucus layer. This was not uncommon amongst herbivores. Animals that ate plants either had multi-chambered stomachs like a cow or had a specialized colon like horses or rabbits. Plant material is hard to digest, so specialized organs were needed to help them break down and process it. Given that the stomach tissue did not seem specialized, he assumed triceratops had a specialized colon like a horse. All of this was so fascinating to him. Dr. Harmon hadn't noticed that night had fallen while he was obsessing over the tissue samples and taking notes. The samples of the animal's colon gave him the answer he was looking for. Scott knew the cause of death of Archosauria's triceratops. He couldn't wait to call Arthur and discuss it with him. Even though it was 11 P.M., Dr. Harmon rushed to the phone to call Mr. Williams with his discovery.

"Hello, Arthur, I have your answers. I know what killed those animals, and you're not going to like it," said Scott.

"Well, out with it! Tell us what you found," Arthur said, placing Scott on speaker phone, so that Ethan could hear him.

"For starters your animals were infested with *Dermanyssus gallinae*," said Scott. "They didn't have a primary Staphylococcus infection. They also all died of dysbiosis and secondary sepsis due to the antibiotics that you gave them."

"English please," exclaimed Arthur. "We didn't understand a word you just said."

"Could you explain this to us in lay terms please, doctor?" asked Sir Barnes.

"Sorry, I was excited. I forget that people don't understand medical terms sometimes," said Scott, a bit embarrassed.

Dr. Harmon explained to the men that their dinosaurs had contracted avian feather mites. He explained that the bacteria they cultured had come about due to the wounds caused by the mites and the animals scratching themselves. Scott told them that they needed to clean the enclosures and sterilize them as soon as possible. He recommended they remove all birds and bird nests from around the dinosaur habitats. He also told them to look out for any people that were showing signs of infection and warned them to keep them away from the animals. The final piece of information infuriated Sir Barnes. Dr. Harmon told them that when he examined the slides of the animal's intestines, they were overgrown with bacteria. The tissue also had something known as villi blunting. Normal intestinal tissue had small, finger-like projections to help with food absorption. These projections were called villi. During times of severe illness and in certain viral infections, these villi would disappear and thus would prevent the animal from being able to absorb food properly. This would lead to nausea, diarrhea, vomiting, and severe dehydration followed by malnutrition, sepsis, and death.

"Your antibiotics killed the natural bacteria within the dinosaur's colon. This let bad bacteria take over and caused sepsis and enterotoxaemia," said Dr. Harmon. "It happens in rabbits and some other herbivore species with antibiotics like Ampicillin. This killed your dinosaurs, Ethan."

"Well, look at you," said Ethan. "We should have hired you from the start. You are sure of this?"

"I would have to take more samples and maybe culture the intestinal tissues, but yes, I'm pretty sure," said Scott.

"Fascinating. Seems like I will have to have a word with Jin Moon about this," said Sir Barnes. "He will have to consult you from now on before making any decisions about the animals' health. We will begin fumigating the pens as soon as possible."

"When can you fly back with us?" asked Arthur.

"Well, I will need time to pack and get things together. I also have to tell my job…" started Dr. Harmon before he was cut off.

"We have taken care of work for you, doctor. Everything you could need will be ready for you on Protogonus. Meet us at the airport tomorrow at noon," said Ethan.

Dr. Harmon could not help but feel like the men were rushing him. There was no way he could just pick up and leave in less than twelve hours' time. This was a huge opportunity though, and passing it up was not something he was prepared to do. Scott decided he did not want to make Ethan angry. He quickly agreed to be ready at noon the next day. The way home was devoid of traffic as Scott rushed back to his house. Shirts, pants, and clothing seemed to fly into his suitcases as he feverishly packed up his belongings. He grabbed a photograph of his daughters and carefully wrapped it in a shirt as he shoved it into his bag. Scott could not sleep at all that night. Tomorrow he would be in another country where dinosaurs ruled!

Chapter 4

The trip to Protogonus had not been not been an easy one. The three men took Sir Barnes' private jet to Samoa from San Diego. From there they had to take a small propeller plane flight to the island archipelago owned by Revolutionary National Amalgamations. The plane had no leg room. There was a cramp building in Scott's leg after the first twenty minutes of being in the air. Luckily, they were the only three people on this flight. The arm rest was flush with Dr. Harmon's ribs, and if there were someone sitting next to him, they would have been right on top of him. This was not the luxury jet that they had started the trip on, that was for sure. Scott hated flying, even though he loved animals that flew. There was something about the lack of control of flying that made him uneasy. The entire trip he fantasized about what he would see when he got there. What did dinosaur skin feel like? What did they sound like? He had so many questions about his upcoming experience. Scott felt a bit like a child on Christmas Eve; the anticipation of opening the coming gifts driving them crazy. The plane touched down on a small landing strip about a mile from the worker village. The plane jolted and bounced as it hit the runway. The cabin rattled and threw the three men about as the plane came to a stop. Dr. Harmon could feel his stomach being pushed against his spine as the plane came to a halt.

Getting off of the plane was almost as bad as being on the plane. Scott struggled to get to his feet on legs that were stiff. It felt as if his legs were made of plywood instead of flesh. A strong tingle ran from his left foot up through his calf. He limped down the aisle like a peg-legged pirate as he walked off the cramp in his right leg. Walking out of the small door, Dr. Harmon was hit with a wave of sweltering heat. He could hear various birds chirping and insects chattering. There was lush jungle all around them, like an envelope of green. He walked down a set of small metal stairs that now connected the plane to the firm ground below. The stairs creaked as he walked down them. This was certainly unsettling as Dr. Harmon felt as if he would fall through the rusted staircase. Thankfully the plane was not far off of the ground to begin with. Arthur helped Ethan down the staircase just behind him. Sir Barnes was having a hard time with recovering from the cramped plane as well. Scott couldn't wait to get off the plane to see the facilities. He could see a parked car waiting for them near the end of the runway. A fuel truck approached the plane, likely to refill the gas tank, so it could return back to the mainland.

"Don't wait for us, Dr. Harmon, go ahead and get in the car," Sir Barnes said from behind him. "Long journeys like this are tough for me. Don't get old, my boy!"

Dr. Harmon rushed to the car; his heart was pounding. This is the most alive he had felt in some time. The leather seats felt sticky as he hopped into the back of the vehicle. He was admiring the logo on the car by peering over the vehicle's side while he waited for Ethan.

"Archosauria," he read to himself. What a fitting name for a dinosaur island. The word Archosaur was part of the classification system that included dinosaurs, birds, and reptiles. Scott had to keep reminding himself that there technically were no dinosaurs at the moment. The pictures he had seen filled him with excitement. He couldn't wait to interact and study living, breathing dinosaurs!

Arthur helped Ethan get into the front seat of the car just before he got into the back with Scott. The vehicle jolted and then began lurching forward, slowly picking up speed as it went. Jungle seemed to whizz by them as their vehicle proceeded towards the compound. The breeze was a welcome change compared to the sweltering heat of the South Pacific jungle air. Scott caught a brief glimpse of some white-faced capuchin monkeys swinging from the trees overhead. Dr. Harmon never really liked primates. They had always creeped him out a little bit. Their little humanoid faces and hands made him uneasy.

He secretly hated walking by their enclosures back in San Diego. Scott felt like they were always up to something. You could see them thinking when you peered into their eyes.

The drive was taking forever. He was getting antsy and began to tap his right foot against the car floor. Scott then began to hear the sound of clanging iron and mumbled human speech. They were close! The vehicle pushed through a clearing, and suddenly a large metal fence appeared through the jungle. The fences were easily about thirty feet high and towered over their approaching car. Dr. Harmon questioned if this would be big enough for some of the larger species. No one really knew the maximum size of a dinosaur. Paleontologists were limited to the skeletons that had fossilized. There was no way to tell if these fossilized individuals were fully grown or if they had died young before reaching their maximum body size. Animals in captivity live longer than those in the wild, so it was reasonable to think that the animals of Archosauria would get larger than expected due to longevity, proper nutrition, medical care, and lack of predation. These factors would contribute to these clones living longer than their fossilized counterparts. Scott noted the white and red voltage warning signs on the fence as the cars approached. These were the same signs he saw in the photographs Arthur presented him with. Their car seemed to shoot through the big wooden gates, honking its horn as it proceeded. They were in a rush for some reason.

A loud beep and garbled voice became audible coming from the car's walkie talkie. Sir Barnes quickly picked up the receiver. He had been talking to someone for the duration of their trip back to the compound, but Scott had been tuning it out. Dr. Harmon didn't seem to care what they were talking about. Scott overheard someone talking to Sir Barnes about what Jin Moon had done. The voice stated that Sir Barnes should come to the lab before showing Dr. Harmon his quarters. Scott was focused on admiring the small village they were driving through instead of paying attention to Sir Barnes's conversation. All of the buildings had thick metal bars over the windows. This made sense, Scott thought. If something ever got out of containment, you wouldn't want easily breakable glass between you and a hungry predator. They came to a stop in front of a large white building. A large sign saying "Main Genetics Lab" hung over two large wooden doors. The doors looked very heavy and sturdy. The men walked up the stairs in a group. The large wooden doors creaked open as the men approached before they were close enough to touch them.

"We will show you your quarters soon, doctor. Looks like we got back just in time. Your patients will be hatching soon," said Arthur.

Dr. Harmon did not care; he was far too worked up to rest anyways. Ethan's men had taken his bags from him when they landed, and he was told not to worry about them. Scott wanted to see the dinosaur eggs. There was nothing that mattered more to him now than seeing these animals. He was so curious as to what species he would be interacting with during his stay. What would taking care of a T-Rex be like, or would they even have a T-Rex? Scott seemed to be on auto-pilot as he walked down the halls. This was sensory overload for him. He wasn't absorbing anything. It felt almost like his body was walking, but his mind was elsewhere.

Two glass doors automatically opened in front of them with a loud hiss. Scott was handed a white cover suit to go over his clothes by Arthur. Sir Barnes was already putting his on. Once he had the suit on, he placed light blue shoe covers on top of his boots and a blue surgeon's cap over his hair. Scott felt like he was scrubbing in to a procedure as he put on his face mask and goggles. Ethan mumbled something about taking no unnecessary risks with the animals this time as he put on purple nitrile gloves. Once they were in their protective gear, they walked through a second set of glass doors. A tall, handsome Korean man approached them. He seemed to walk with a purpose and had a very strong presence about him. This was not a man to mess with, Scott thought. Everyone around him seemed like they were afraid of him. Everyone, except for Ethan Barnes of course, who embraced Dr. Bai like a long-lost son.

"Doctor Harmon, this is my chief geneticist, Dr. Jin Moon Bai," said Ethan.

"A pleasure," smirked Dr. Bai as he shook Scott's hand way tighter than was necessary, crushing Dr. Harmon's knuckles against each other.

"Nice to meet you," said Scott. "So you're the mastermind behind this project?"

"Naturally," said Dr. Bai curtly, refusing to make eye contact with Scott.

Dr. Harmon could not help but feel like Jin Moon did not like him. Dr. Bai was very cold and responded only in one-word answers. This was not the type of greeting he had gotten from Sir Barnes or Mr. Williams. This bothered Scott a little bit; he didn't like it when people didn't like him. If he was to work with these people, he didn't want a sour work environment. Dr. Harmon was snapped out of his thoughts when they got to the incubators. There were twenty-five clutches of eggs with five to seven eggs in each clutch.

"This is not what we told you to do, Jin!" exclaimed Ethan. "This is way more than we accounted for. You were told to make another five triceratops infants. Are these all trikes?"

"Of course not, Ethan. Archosauria can't open with one species," said Jin Moon smugly. "Each of these is a different animal species. We have to deliver to our investors."

"Will we even be able to contain all of these?" asked Arthur Williams. "Do we know what any of them are other than triceratops?"

"Well, the eggs in banks four, eight, twenty, fifteen, and ten appear to be therapods of some kind based on their silhouettes," said Jin Moon. "The eggs in bank one are triceratops and should be hatching this week."

"Therapods, you mean like a T-Rex?" said Scott nervously.

"Yes, Dr. Harmon, a T-Rex is a therapod dinosaur after all," said Dr. Bai condescendingly. "Some of the genetic material we mined does come from the Hell's Creek formation, so it is highly possible that we may have a Tyrannosaurus."

The thought of twenty-five different species of dinosaur made Scott light-headed. His eyes saw twenty-five clutches of eggs. This was not an unusual sight to him being a veterinarian that focused primarily on birds and reptiles. The fact that these were very clearly not birds seemed to be something he could not accept. Scott wondered if he was truly cut out to handle this. This was not something he could have prepared for mentally. His brain seemed like it was having trouble accepting what he was being told. Dr. Harmon did not know what he was going to see when he got to Protogonus, but this far exceeded his expectations. If he was this worked up over dinosaur eggs, how would he react when he saw one in the flesh? Dr. Harmon approached one of the incubators. There was a large number one placed at the base just below a large glass dome. He watched a small mechanical arm turning the eggs. It seemed to cradle them gently as it moved them from one side to the next. Scott realized he may be too close to glass when his nose grazed the dome leaving a small smudge on the it. He backed away slowly, hoping no one saw, quickly clearing the smudge with his glove.

When it came time to leave the incubation room, Dr. Harmon did not want to go. He wanted to spend more time with the incubating embryos. Scott wanted to see them hatch and meet the animals inside. This would be a life-changing experience, seeing a living, breathing dinosaur! Arthur walked Scott into an apartment building about two blocks from the lab. The building was clearly still under construction. The floors were partially tiled, but even still patterns of different dinosaur species could be seen coming to life. The men climbed the stairs to the second floor. They walked through a maze of hallways. Parts of the hall had construction lamps hanging from open ceilings where the electrical components were exposed. Arthur came to a stop in front of room 2316. He opened the door with a small key card and then handed it to Dr. Harmon. Arthur held the door for Scott and then excused himself. The room was larger than Scott expected. There was a full kitchen, a bedroom, a living room, and a full bath with a walk-in shower. There were hints of prehistoric life throughout the furnishings of the apartment. Wooden carvings of dinosaurs and prehistoric mammals adorned the wall moldings. Scott found his luggage placed on the floor of the bedroom. He was wondering what had happened to his bags. There was a large glass sliding door behind a thick curtain on the left side of the room. Dr. Harmon pulled the curtain aside to reveal a small deck with two chairs. The deck was enclosed with thick metal bars. Scott felt like this looked more like a luxury prison cell than a luxury apartment. His deck overlooked a small courtyard. In the distance, he could see the holding pens behind the labs. His next stop was the refrigerator; it suddenly hit him that he was starving. Dr. Harmon found the fridge fully stocked. He quickly made a sandwich and opened a beer. Scott walked back to the deck to enjoy the sunset before trying to head off to bed.

Dr. Harmon did not sleep well that night. The bed was far more comfortable than what he had in his apartment. The sheets were softer than anything he had experienced. It felt almost as if they were caressing his skin as he tossed and turned. He spent most of the night staring at the dinosaur artwork on the walls. Dr. Harmon wondered if these paintings would turn out to be accurate. He didn't know much more about dinosaurs than the average person did, but he knew enough to know that opinions about how these creatures lived had changed dramatically since their discovery. Dr. Harmon stared over at his alarm clock on the night stand, noting that it was 5 A.M. He figured he may as well get up and try to get a quick work-out in. He wandered the halls of the building to see if there was a gym. After coming up short, he decided to venture out of the building to look for one. He came across a few Hispanic construction workers and decided to ask them where the gym was.

"Hola, como estas[1]?" said Dr. Harmon, suddenly realizing he had exhausted his Spanish. "Where...is...el gymo?"

"Um, there is one three blocks up to the right by the basketball court. Or you could go to the track behind that building over there," said one of the workers in perfect English.

Scott felt embarrassed, having patronized the workers. He could hear the men making fun of him as he sheepishly walked away. He didn't know what to say; he was flushed and could feel his face burning.

"Thanks, man," Scott said as he skulked away.

"Whatever, Gringo,"[2] said the worker.

The rest of the day was rather uneventful. Dr. Harmon was waiting for a call to be told that something was happening. Until the eggs hatched, there was really no place for him here. It was just like back in San Diego; there was no clear purpose to his life.

The call came at 4 A.M. that Friday ~~evening~~. *morning* Dr. Harmon was barely awake when he answered the phone. It took him a few sentences to realize that this was not a dream and that he was having a conversation with Arthur. Suddenly Scott shot up in his bed; it clicked why he was being woken from his slumber before his alarm. He jumped to his feet and immediately started combing through his drawers for a pair of pants. It was like he suddenly forgot where he had put all of his clothes. The layout of his hotel room had become a mystery to him. He grabbed a pair of khaki shorts and quickly pulled them on. Dr. Harmon shoved his bare feet into his shoes, thinking that he didn't have time for socks. He quickly brushed his teeth and ran to the door. He had rushed out of his room quickly, and he realized almost too late that he forgot his room key. Scott turned and shoved his hand in the closing door, just before it locked him out. That was close, he thought. Dr. Harmon rushed back into his room and just about ran into his nightstand before grabbing the key card and running back out of the door. Bolting down the stairs two at a time, Scott began to worry that he would miss the hatching. He was praying that the

---

[1]   Hello, how are you?

[2]   Whatever, foreigner

babies would wait for him. He didn't want to miss this. The two blocks seemed to take forever for him to transverse, when in reality he had covered them fairly quickly. A small group of construction workers stared at him strangely as he blew past them. Scott had gotten to the two laboratory doors faster than they could open. Scott hit the doors with a loud thud; they reverberated from the impact as he staggered backwards. As soon as there was an opening large enough in the automatic doors, he slid through and began to run to the incubation room. Sir Barnes and Mr. Williams were waiting for him just outside the airlock doors.

"Calm down, my boy, you haven't missed anything now," said Ethan. "They just begun hatching, calm down and relax."

"Oh, ok, I was so worried I wouldn't get here in time," said Scott, panting.

"Here, wipe your brow and have a seat. Jin will get us when the more interesting stuff starts. They've just begun rocking a bit," said Sir Barnes, handing Scott a white cloth from his pocket.

Dr. Harmon sat on a nearby bench and wiped the sweat off his face. His heart was pounding, but it wasn't because of his run. Scott had run similar distances and not had any issue many times in his life. He was worked up about seeing a clutch of triceratops hatch. Try as he might, he couldn't seem to settle. Even after he had stopped sweating, Scott could feel that his face was still flush and his heart was still pounding. Sir Barnes had asked him multiple times if he was alright. Scott brushed off the old man's concerns and continued to try desperately to get ahold of himself. He couldn't wait for Jin Moon. What was taking so long? After what seemed like an eternity, Dr. Ernie Sung came out and told the men to gear up and come inside. Dr. Harmon rushed to get his gear on. He ended up tearing a pair of shoe covers as he rushed to place them on his feet. Arthur forced him to put on a new pair, much to his dismay. As he approached incubator one, he felt light-headed.

The eggs were all rocking and shaking. Small cracks could be seen in the surface of two of the five shells. Dr. Harmon waited with baited breath for the dinosaurs to emerge. A foot burst through one of the eggs with a loud crack. Blood and mucus oozed from the hole as the baby struggled to pull its foot back into the egg. Dr. Harmon was shocked to see that they had eponychium on their claws like a baby horse. Once the infant got the foot back inside the egg, it quickly shot both front legs forward again, destroying the remainder of its prison. The infant fell forward and began to shake bits of shell off itself. It bellowed as it did this, making a noise that Dr. Harmon had never heard before. As he stared at the infant, it seemed to stare back at him. The baby had taken a pause and was gently panting from the effort of being hatched. Scott then realized the other infants were also hatching from their eggs. He was trying to focus on all five of them at the same time but was failing miserably. Their skin appeared to be similar in texture to a rhinoceros. It was more a leathery consistency than it was scaly. There were scales along the back of the animal with small osteoderms (boney plates embedded in the skin) in rows extending from the base of the frill to the tail. Even as an infant, they looked formidable. The infants were bellowing and struggling to get to their feet. They were clumsy and would often fall after a few steps. Each baby was about the size of a Chihuahua. It was hard to believe that something so small was going to grow into such a large, powerful animal.

"This…is remarkable, Ethan," said Scott, slurring his speech and stuttering.

"One of many miracles to come, I assure you, Scott," Ethan said placing his hand on Scott's shoulder.

"Can I examine them?" asked Dr. Harmon.

"Absolutely, doctor," Ethan said laughing. "That is what you are here for after all."

Dr. Harmon jumped a little as the glass casing of the incubator began to open. He asked Dr. Sung to grab a clipboard and the materials he needed to do a physical on the infants. Scott very gingerly reached for the first animal closest to him. He was almost afraid to touch it. It was like if he touched it, the dinosaur in front of him would disappear and he would wake up from his dream. The infant squirmed and squeaked while in Scott's grasp. He couldn't help but notice how warm the baby felt. Even through the gloves, Dr. Harmon could feel the smoothness of the animal's leathery skin. The baby kicked at his arms as he tried to examine it. Scott placed the bell of his stethoscope to the chest of the infant and listened carefully as he counted the number of beats per minute of its heart. The rate was faster than he expected, certainly faster than any reptilian heart he had ever auscultated. He passed the infant to a reluctant Ernie Sung as he jotted down the vitals. He was surprised at how high the infant's core body temperature was. Scott had just confirmed that dinosaurs were warm-blooded. This was something the scientific community had been debating feverishly. The infant was moved to a holding enclosure as Scott examined the next one. All five triceratops infants appeared healthy and happy.

"What are you feeding them?" Dr. Harmon asked.

"Well, the last time we had no idea what to feed them, so we ended up giving them daily fluids and dextrose solutions," said Dr. Bai.

"I'm willing to bet that their mothers pre-chewed their food for them. What plants were the previous clones eating?" Dr. Harmon asked.

Dr. Bai made a gesture to Dr. Sung. Ernie walked over to a door at the far east corner of the room. Upon opening the door, a small greenhouse was present with multiple ferns and cycads growing. Dr. Harmon was told there was a larger greenhouse elsewhere on the compound, but this one was specifically for the infants. Scott asked the men if they had a blender or anything to grind the plants with. Dr. Sung brought him a small mortar and pestle that had been used for grinding medications. Scott quickly picked some leaves after cleaning his mortar and began to grind them into a pulp. He took his slop to the small holding room with the infants and began to feed them the gruel. The babies began to eat it readily and pushed each other out of the way to get to him. Squeaks and honks could be heard as the animals vied for their turn to eat. Scott was filled with an immense joy as he fed the infant dinosaurs. He could feel tears welling up in his eyes. This was all overwhelming for him. He had gone from a lonely divorced father of two to the father of the first living dinosaurs to see the light of day in sixty-five million years.

Chapter 5

Months seemed to pass like hours to Dr. Harmon. He loved what he did before, but this was on an entirely new level. Scott would often wonder where his days went and why he never seemed to be tired. Back in San Diego, he always felt like he was out of energy and exhausted every day, no matter how much he slept. His routine in San Diego had become forced and more something he had to do than something he wanted to do. It was as if a huge black cloud had passed over him and his life was livable again. He was committed to the success of Archosauria and the survival of its inhabitants. Only ten of the twenty-five species had managed to survive past infancy despite his best efforts. There was a lot of trial and error involved in keeping these animals alive and disease free. It was not uncommon in the animal kingdom for large numbers of infants to pass. A lot of species' key to survival was a numbers game, producing more babies than could survive in the hopes that one or two would be strong enough to make it to adulthood. Dr. Harmon definitely had his hands full with all of these individuals to look after. Most of the species were currently herbivores, but Archosauria did have two carnivore species that survived. Jin Moon now had twenty-five genomes mapped and was determined to try again with the fifteen species that did not make it.

Dr. Harmon was gearing up to go on his daily patrol with Nalani Mwangi, the park game warden and head of containment. Today's patrol was slightly different than the usual rounds. Nalani and Scott were set with a task from Sir

Barnes. If there was anyone Scott trusted to be out in the field with, it was Nalani. She had spent most of her life in Kenya around Africa's deadliest creatures. She knew how these animals behaved and was accustomed to being around deadly predators. Nalani had had many a close call with Africa's big five; the five deadliest creatures in Africa consisting of the lion, leopard, rhinoceros, elephant, and cape buffalo. These were also the hardest animals to hunt on foot. She knew very well that the carnivores were not always the most dangerous animals on the savannah. The two had developed a fairly strong friendship during Scott's stay on Protogonus. They were the only two people on the island who had been around animals in an up close and personal capacity. They also seemed to be the only people on the property who truly understood the dangers of what they were dealing with. Sir Barnes and Mr. Sana were preoccupied with the dream come true aspect of this endeavor. The amount of money it would earn them was also a big factor in their thought processes. For Scott and Nalani, they were well aware of how dangerous these animals could potentially be.

Nalani Mwangi was carrying her usual air rifle to dart any animals that got too close to the vehicles or that got out of line. She also carried a small handgun on her person regularly. Today was no different for Nalani. Although the clones were young and nowhere near full grown, they were quickly learning how dangerous they could be. Scott and Nalani were planning on observing the Triceratops herd and were tasked with drawing a few blood samples. They currently had thirteen Triceratops cloned of various ages and sizes. Surprisingly the Triceratops had formed a tight-knit herd, even though they were all from different egg groups. The older individuals would circle around the younger ones to protect them when the park vehicles approached. Scott was taking out twenty men with him, including Nalani, and divided them amongst five cars. The plan was simple, dart the oldest five individuals, including the matriarch, and draw blood from them before the others intervened. Archosauria was set to open in the next three years, making sure the animals were healthy and ready for display by that time was paramount.

"Alright, men, remember to stay close and shoot your targets as soon as possible. We may not get more than one shot at this," said Nalani.

"Drivers, if your shooters miss their target, drive off to a safe distance," said Scott. "They can't outrun the vehicles, and we don't want anyone getting hurt here."

"They will charge if startled or threatened, particularly the big one," said Nalani. "You don't want to be on the receiving end of her charge."

The men all nodded as they checked their equipment. There was a symphony of clicking firearms and stomping boots. The men began to pair off into groups and load up into their respective cars. Scott had the task of going species by species to make sure they were healthy enough to transport. Archosauria was slated to open with eight species initially. More animals would be cloned and filtered in as the park grew and attendance rose. Mr. Sana had suggested that they wait until some of the larger predators had been successfully cloned before deciding which species to move to Dionysus. This was something that the board had approved as well. Scott was tasked with making sure these original ten species were viable before more were added to the roster. Currently their lot consisted of Triceratops, Brachiosaurus, Parasaurolophus, Gallimimus, Compsognathus, Herrerasaurus, Stegosaurus, Pachycephalosaurs, Edmontosaurus, and Microceratus. Despite their successes, R.N.A. seemed to want more. They just simply didn't have enough teeth to open with and be successful. Nothing would wow an audience like a large carnivore. The animals were to begin shipping to Dionysus over the course of the next two years. Sir Barnes wanted to make sure they were full grown or as close to full grown as possible for the park opening. Construction was set to be mostly done on all opening attractions by early 1991. The second phase of construction was to begin in 1994 after the park had established itself.

Scott and Nalani were in the lead car. As the car creaked forward, Nalani waved her arm over her head several times to signal that it was time to move out. The sun gleamed off of her shaved head as the vehicle moved forward. One by one, the cars pulled out of the garage and drove towards the back gates of the compound. The garage was situated near the infant holding pens where the animals were kept to grow before being moved to their more permanent enclosures. This was done to ensure they were viable and capable of surviving without human aide. The vehicles pulled up to the perimeter fence and came to a halt one behind the other. Two park workers dropped their rifles to their sides and rushed to the first door. As they did this, a third worker flipped a power switch, which cut the power to the bars on the perimeter fence doors temporarily. There were two sets of handles that each man grabbed respectively after being given the go ahead from the man at the control panel. They used the handles to pull back a large metal rod. Once the rod was pulled from the locking mechanism, the door was opened. The first vehicle drove slowly through the first door and came to a stop just before the second. The park workers shut the first door behind them, and the power was rebooted with a zapping sound. Once the first door was electrified again, the worker operating the control panel pressed a second button, which allowed the second door to open and the vehicle to leave the compound. This double door system was designed to prevent any animal that may have escaped containment from entering the worker village while the vehicles entered. The process repeated for each of the remaining vehicles. It was a pain, but it was worth it to keep them all safe, thought Scott.

Once all the cars had passed out of the main perimeter fence, they began their trek to the triceratops paddock. The vehicles drove along a dirt road sandwiched between two parallel electric fences, each about thirty feet high. The animals were in adjacent enclosures set in two long rows. At the moment, all species were kept separately with plans to mix them at a later date in order to develop a more realistic environment on Dionysus for the tourists. The Triceratops were currently kept about four enclosures down from the perimeter fence. The animals tended to not hang around the fences as they had all learned that touching them meant a painful shock. They passed by empty jungle on their way to their destination. Scott happened to get a glimpse of some of the Brachiosaurs wandering towards the pond in their enclosure for a drink. Each animal was currently about the size of a giraffe, varying from about sixteen to twenty feet tall. It was remarkable how fast they grew. The animals had started out the size of a Shih Tzu, and in five months, they were now the tallest land animal on Earth. Eventually they would get to be about forty feet tall. Scott was wondering what that would even look like as they drifted out of sight. Nothing on Earth currently grew to such a massive size on land.

Finally they had reached their destination as the vehicles stopped in front of the entrance to the Triceratops paddock. The man next to Dr. Harmon, Stephen, jumped out of the car and walked up to a small panel next to the gate. He lifted the metal panel covering and pushed a few buttons on the console. The red alarm lights on the top of the door began to flash, and the warning buzzer began to go off. This process was automated, to prevent people from having to be so close to the animals on a regular basis. Stephen quickly hopped back into the car next to Dr. Harmon with a small nod. The process to enter the enclosures was similar to leaving the perimeter fence. The only difference was that it was on a timer instead of being manually activated. Once all of the vehicles were in, they paused to check the motion sensors to determine where in the enclosure the herd was positioned.

"They are toward the back of the enclosure near the hills," said Stephen as he looked at the motion sensor.

"Alright, men, let's roll out," yelled Nalani.

The enclosure was mostly open plains. Dr. Harmon had surmised that these animals were the grazing buffalo or antelope of the Cretaceous, preferring open plains and grasslands to forests. When they were infants, they would spend the majority of their time in the open and would tend to avoid the more forested portions of the enclosure. Scott's job was to make sure these animals remained happy, and providing them with the most accurate habitat was part of this. Nalani had the vehicle follow carved out paths in the areas of long grass to try to prevent them from getting stuck. The Triceratops had already done the job of carving these paths out for them. Their large bodies had flattened out clear trails large enough for the vehicles to pass without issue. The vehicles passed over a large ridge, and the herd became visible in the distance. Several animals lifted their heads from the ground to stare at the vehicles. They had been spotted, and now the herd was on high alert. Harmon noted an increase in their vocalizations as the vehicles got nearer; they were talking to each other. When these animals were infants, they were friendly and playful. As they got larger, they seemed less and less tolerant with human contact. The closer the vehicles got, the more agitated the animals became. Vocalizations became louder as they approached the herd. Some individuals were throwing their heads from side to side and stomping their front feet into the grass, kicking up dust as they did so. The quills on their hind end shook and clapped together as they did this.

"Slow down!" Nalani yelled. "Stop the vehicles!"

"This is a threat display," Scott said. "Let's give them a moment to calm themselves before we get in range."

"They do this all the time," said the driver, Reginald. "Why is this time any different? They'll stop."

"Just trust my instincts here," said Nalani. "This time is different."

The vehicles came to a halt once again about 100 yards from the herd. Scott watched as the larger animals began to form a circle around the smallest individuals of the group. This was a phalanx of horns and shields. The beasts bellowed and continued throwing their heads from side to side, stopping only to let out loud snorts or bellows. They were out of range for their rifles as they could only get a clear shot at about fifty-five meters. With the animals so worked up, it would be impossible to get any closer without getting charged. This would be a waiting game. Scott told Reginald to put the vehicle in park with the hopes that by not moving, the animals would settle down. The third vehicle in the line went so far as to cut his engine. The largest member of the herd and matriarch stood five feet tall at the shoulder and weighed about 6,000 pounds. The quills on her back were longer and more densely packed than her siblings. A white rhinoceros would be a good contemporary size comparison for her. Rhinos were extremely dangerous and could make short work of a car. This animal was slightly larger than a rhinoceros and no less dangerous. Scott looked behind at the other cars, taking his eyes off the herd. He was wondering if they should just try another day and go to a different enclosure. The sounds of yawns and groaning stretches from other vehicles were clearly audible. They had been waiting for what seemed like an eternity with no change in the animal's demeanor. Scott was lost in his thoughts and suddenly was startled by Nalani's scream.

"EVERYBODY SCATTER!" yelled Nalani.

The matriarch had gotten tired of waiting for this threat to leave her territory and decided to charge the vehicles at full speed. She was going to defend her family from these intruders with force. Her head was so low that her beak was brushing the blades of grass as she darted forward. Her horns were facing the cars, and her shield was sitting at the level of her shoulders. The ground seemed to shake with each impact of her large clawed feet. Blades of grass and dust was flung into the air by her locomotion as she barreled towards them. Scott could see the driver of his car panicking and fumbling to get the car back into drive. The drivers of the vehicles behind them were in similar situations. The car at the rear managed to back up and peeled off at top speed. The driver of car three fumbled with his keys as he tried to get the car to start again. Time was running out; she was closing the distance quickly despite being such a large animal. The trike had to be moving thirty miles per hour, thought Scott. Nalani raised her rifle; she was going to try to put her down before she could get to the line of vehicles. Nalani stood on her seat with one foot on the car door. Her rifle was pointed at the charging Triceratops. The car directly behind them pulled off from the line and drove away. Car four was similarly making its way away from the charging beast.

"Don't you dare drive off, Reginald," Nalani said. "She's going for car three, not us. I'm going to take the shot before she gets there."

A loud crack sounded as Nalani fired a dart at the charging animal. Scott felt sick to his stomach as he saw the dart bounce off her frill with a loud clinking sound. Her frill was mostly solid bone. There was no tissue for the dart to take purchase in. Being struck with a dart didn't even phase the charging Triceratops. Nalani may as well have shot her dart into the ground. She was aiming for her back behind the frill, but the animal happened to lift her head at the wrong moment and blocked the incoming dart.

"God damnit!" Nalani exclaimed as she began to reload. "I missed!"

"Shoot it again!" screamed Stephen.

It was too late; she was too close. Nalani would not get another shot off in time. The driver of car three had frozen, the employee in the passenger seat was trying to help him get the car out of park but was making things worse. Their hands fumbled over each other as the two men fought for control. One of the men in the back seat jumped out and decided to run for it once he realized that the car would not be able to get away in time. The matriarch hit the vehicle with a loud crash, throwing it into the air and sending the three men inside it flying in different directions. Shards of metal and glass flew off the car from the force of the impact. The vehicle began rolling across the terrain, throwing up dirt and debris as it barreled along the ground. The passenger side door opened in mid-air and tore off as the vehicle hit the ground again and continued to roll.

"Circle over to where the men flew out," said Scott. "We need to pick them up and get out of here."

"I'm on it," said Reginald in a determined tone.

"Holy shit!" cried Stephen. "Did that really just happen?"

The car finally came to a stop on its driver's side with a loud thud, rocking slightly as it came to rest. The matriarch let out another bellow and lowered her head again. She charged the vehicle a second time. The front axle snapped from the second impact, and the engine block bent from the animal's sheer force. A piece of metal from the front wheel well was stuck on her horn. She shook her head, sending her horn through the underside of the car, crunching through the floor and tearing the seat in half. The horrible sound of crushing metal could be heard for miles as the animal began to destroy the vehicle. At one point, the car appeared stuck on her horns, and she was carrying the vehicle for a few short steps before lowering her head and smashing the car onto the ground again. She charged with the car still attached to her. The vehicle drug along the ground with a loud crunching noise, the driver side tire ripping off and rolling away right before the vehicle collided into a nearby tree with a large thud, almost uprooting the tree in the process. The metal was being bent and twisted with what seemed like minimal effort. She backed away slowly, the car sliding off her brow horns with a loud screech, as she bellowed and snorted leaving the car pinned to the tree. The power of this animal mesmerized Dr. Harmon. He never worked with large herbivores but knew he would not want to mess with a rhinoceros or a hippo.

Reginald pulled up to the driver of car three. The man was lying unconscious on the grass. Nalani and Stephen quickly jumped out to grab him and place him into their vehicle. They had to move quickly as there were twelve other trikes that could charge them. The injured man came to as he was being picked up. He panicked slightly and was mumbling a mix of gibberish and Spanish. A wave of pain seemed to snap him out of it, and he began to scream. His screams seemed to echo across the enclosure. Car two and four had joined Nalani in the recovery effort. The fifth car had headed back to the gate and was racing to exit the enclosure. As they recovered their men, the matriarch continued to maul the car. The remainder of the herd stayed gathered in a tight-knit circle. A few of the larger individuals began to mock charge. They would dash forward a few feet before returning to the safety of the group. These individuals did not seem as intent on aggression as the matriarch had just been. They needed to leave, and they needed to leave quickly. Once the injured driver was in the back seat, Dr. Harmon began to assess his injuries. The man had a broken right leg. His knee was bending in the opposite direction with his foot twisted in an un-natural angle. He had deep lacerations on his left forelimb from where he had tried to break his fall. The tendons were visible, and Scott could see the man's muscles twitching as he moved his fingers. There was a lot of blood soaking his shirt and khaki shorts. The man was in pain and had lost a decent amount of blood, but he was alert and seemed otherwise fine. Nalani grabbed her rifle and began to head towards the angry Triceratops on foot.

"What the hell are you doing?" yelled Scott as he ripped the sleeve off his own shirt to tie around the injured driver's arm as a tourniquet.

"She's gonna block our retreat," said Nalani. "She is standing between us and the gate. We may have issues getting enough speed to get past her at this distance."

"Are you crazy?!" exclaimed Dr. Harmon. "You're going to try to tranquilizer her on foot."

"I got this, man," Nalani said as she raised her rifle slightly and began to creep towards the rampaging beast.

"Be careful, Nalani," said Reginald.

Nalani walked slowly towards the triceratops. She was very used to scenarios such as this. Nalani stopped about forty feet from the animal's backside. She was downwind of her, and as long as she remained reasonably quiet, the dinosaur wouldn't notice her. Nalani felt the closest thing to a triceratops that she had dealt with was either a rhinoceros or a hippo. These animals were normally docile, but if pissed off, could become your worst nightmare. Dr. Harmon and the members of car one sat tensely as they watched Nalani approach the animal. All three cars were in drive this time and awaited Nalani's signal to peel away and rush to the exit of the enclosure. Nalani got down on her right knee and raised her rifle as she looked through the scope. Her finger clutched the trigger as she lined up her shot. Nalani knew one dart would likely not be enough; especially since the animal was so worked up already. Her adrenaline would keep the sedatives from kicking in immediately. Nalani knew this wind-up effect all too well. The more agitated the animal, the longer it took the sedative to work. There was also a chance that it would not work at all and would just make her more aggressive. She would only get one chance at this, and if she missed again, the dinosaur would likely kill them. A loud crack sounded as Nalani pulled the trigger. The dart made contact at the base of the animal's tail with a loud thud. She jumped, and her skin shuddered as the dart hit; her quills clacking together as her skin contracted. A loud scream came from her as she turned to look at what had just hurt her. Nalani began to reload; she was worried this would be the case as the animal faced her.

There was a tense staring contest between the dinosaur and Nalani. She was slowly reloading and was taking care not to make sudden movements or startle the matriarch. Nalani got to her feet in a very robotic fashion. The animal snorted and let out a loud bellow. The shock of the dart seemed to snap her out of her rage regarding the vehicle. She began to stomp her feet and then headed directly to Nalani, a small piece of scrap metal still hanging from her right brow horn. Nalani stood there trying not to move, standing her ground. The triceratops came to a stop about ten feet from her. She snorted, and Nalani could feel her warm, wet breath on her skin; her shirt rippled from the force of the dinosaur's expelled breath. The matriarch shook her head and shoulders and seemed to walk off with a nod of respect towards Nalani. She trotted calmly away back to the herd, leaving Nalani standing in place. Nalani let out a sigh of relief. She was surprised that her gamble had worked. Standing her ground had caused the creature to back off. She decided the small woman was not a threat, and after having expended so much energy on the vehicle, she had no desire to expend anymore. Nalani walked silently back to the car, hopping over the side and into the front seat without opening the door. She banged on the vehicle door and motioned for the caravan of vehicles to leave.

"Dude, you're a badass!" Stephen exclaimed.

Nalani smiled and motioned for the vehicles to move out again. Most modern animals would eagerly chase anything that decided to run from them. Nalani had enough wits to know that she couldn't have run from the dinosaur. She would never outrun her anyways. Her hope was that by standing her ground, the animal would decide she wasn't worth it and would back off. Sure enough she had guessed right. She was proud of herself. How many of her buddies back in Kenya could say they had stared down a dinosaur and won?

The drive back to the compound was a very tense one. Car five was waiting for them outside the enclosure when they reached the exit. The four remaining vehicles drove back to the compound as quickly as they could. Dr. Harmon was doing his best to try to keep the injured man comfortable, but his broken leg bounced with each jolt as the car traversed the dirt road. This sent intense waves of pain through the man, causing him to scream and moan as they drove. Scott didn't even know his name and felt terrible that there was nothing more he could do for the injured worker. All of his medical equipment was back at the compound over five miles away. He was able to make out the name Juan on the man's name tag after rubbing some dirt off him. The name had been a bit obscured in the man's blood, dirt, and grass stains. He could hear Juan mumbling in Spanish to himself. Scott did not know what Juan was saying but imagined that he was trying to tell himself they were close to the compound in order to help endure the pain. It was either that or he was praying. Scott looked to the vehicles behind him, trying to comfort Juan as much as possible. The two other injured men did not seem as affected as Juan. Juan had the unfortunate luck of being in the driver's seat when the animal had hit the vehicle. He had taken a good portion of the animal's initial impact. Reginald had grabbed the radio and was feverishly screaming into it as they rushed back to the compound. Trees seemed to whizz by as they drove, the fences on either side created the illusion of being in a tunnel. Rain began to beat down on the men. It was a freak tropical sun shower that soaked the men in the open top cars.

"We had an incident, three injured, one is really bad, over," said Reginald into the vehicle's radio system. "Have medical assistance ready and the gates open, over!"

"Repeat that page," said a voice on the other end. "Medical attention?"

"We were attacked by the damn dinosaurs!" screamed Reginald into the receiver. "Have Dr. Harper on standby at the gates when we get in in ten minutes, over!"

"Attacked?! Oh, Jesus," said the voice on the other end. "Roger that."

"What a bunch of idiots," said Nalani with disdain as Reginald put down the receiver.

The perimeter fence and rear gate became visible as the cars progressed. Reginald began to honk his horn feverishly as he approached to announce their arrival. He was hoping that this would send some sort of signal to the gate-keepers to open the gates, so the vehicles could just drive through instead of having to go through the usual opening protocol. He didn't trust that the men on the end of the radio had heard him correctly. Radio signals on the island were patchy at best. They got worse with inclement weather. This light storm was not helping them at all. Reginald picked up the receiver again and shouted that he was only five minutes away and the gate was in sight. He told the dispatcher to have the rear gates open for them as they needed immediate medical assistance. Reginald felt he needed to reiterate his initial words in the hopes that they would sense the urgency of the situation. Juan began to squirm as the vehicle jumped over a small ridge and the car crashed back to the dirt road.

"Ah Dios mio!" shouted Juan. "Coño! Baja la velocidad que me vas a matar[3]!"

"It's okay, calm down," said Scott. "We are almost there."

"Cállate!" screamed Juan. "Voy a demandar[4]!"

"Think about suing Sir Barnes and it won't go well for you, amigo," said Reginald.

Reginald began to talk to the man in Spanish as they neared the gate. Dr. Harmon was so happy someone in the car spoke Spanish. Reginald was a tall Dominican man who had done a lot of conservation work in the Dominican Republic. He had happened to become a member of R.N.A. through his brother's financial connections to the company. He jumped at the chance when he heard about what Ethan was doing on Protogonus. As he calmed Juan down, Reginald began to wonder if he was in over his head. They hadn't even cloned a large carnivore yet. If the prey animals could do this, what would the larger predators be like? The predators on Protogonus now were laughable compared to how big some of the more notable carnivores could get. Reginald did not know if he wanted to be around when a T-Rex was roaming the forests.

Reginald drove the car through the perimeter fence as quickly as he could. A wave of water shot up around the vehicle as it drove through a large puddle. Nalani called out to Dr. Harper, motioning for him to start with the injured man in their vehicle first. Dr. Harper rushed to car one, his stethoscope flopping on his shoulder as he ran. Dr. Harper's feet splashed through the puddles as he drew nearer, muddy water staining his already wet lab coat. He carried a large black bag in his right hand. He was accompanied by one of the nurses from his clinic. Several other nurses rushed to car two and four to attend to the wounds of the less injured workers. Dr. Harper was running as fast as he could, his heart was racing. He did not know what to expect when he got to the car. The rain began to let up as he got to the vehicle.

"What happened?" Dr. Harper asked. "How did this happen?"

"We got charged by one of the Triceratops," said Nalani. "She destroyed the car he was in like it was made of paper. This unlucky bastard happened to be in the driver's seat of the car that she slammed into."

---

[3] Oh my God! Damn! Slow down, you're going to kill me!
[4] Shut up! I'm going to sue!

"He's got a deep laceration going down to the extensor tendons on the left forelimb. None of the tendons look torn," said Dr. Harmon. "His right leg is trashed…torn ligaments in his knee and likely a compound ankle fracture. He may have head trauma, too, given the scleral hemorrhage in his right eye."

Dr. Harper pulled out a pen light and began to assess Juan's pupils. The white of his right eye was blood red. Juan was having issues focusing on the pen light; his pupils were not the same size and did not respond normally to the pen light. The pupil of his right eye remained constricted, even without the light being shown into it. Dr. Harper was impressed by Dr. Harmon's assessments. He began to shuffle through his bag for morphine and a syringe with which to give it. They had to move the man, and it would not be easy. Dr. Harper screamed for a spine board and immobilization equipment. He pulled out a syringe and put it in his mouth cap first. He was holding the needle cap firmly between his teeth as he dug through the drug bottles. Scott could hear the bottles clinking as Dr. Harper sifted through them. He had finally found the morphine and drew it up as quick as he could. Dr. Harper flicked some air bubbles out of the syringe.

"Stick out your arm please, I need to give this IV," said Dr. Harper.

Juan looked at him confused. He didn't understand what was being asked of him, and he was beginning to feel a bit dazed and foggy. His vision in his right eye was blurry. Juan could make out figures but could no longer see faces or any fine details. Scott was motioning for the man to stick out his arm in hopes that he would understand. Nalani tried to grab Juan's right arm in an attempt to speed things up. This resulted in Juan beginning to panic and struggle against them.

"Levanta el brazo, hermano," said Reginald, finally chiming in. "Deja que te dé algo para el dolor.[5]"

Juan looked at Reginald, calmly nodding, understanding that Dr. Harper was trying to give him pain medication. His head was bobbing a little from side to side, and he could not seem to focus on anything for more than a few seconds. Juan looked from face to face of the people in the car with him pausing for a moment before moving on, much like someone who had had too much to drink. His adrenaline had worn off, and he was beginning to feel the effects of his injuries. Juan stuck out his right arm shakily. Dr. Harper passed Dr. Har-

---

[5] Raise your arm, brother. Let him give you something for the pain.

mon some gloves and antiseptic. The two men put their gloves on, and Scott prepped the site for injection by rubbing off the dirt with alcohol. He placed a rubber tube tourniquet on Juan's arm and held it out for Dr. Harper. The needle easily pierced Juan's skin, and Dr. Harper injected the contents of the syringe into Juan's arm. Harper passed Scott a bandage to apply to the injection site. Nalani helped Scott and Harper move Juan from the vehicle to the spine board that was laying on the floor next to the vehicle. Stephen paused for a second before getting out of the car to stare at the huge blood stain that remained where Juan had sat. Reginald was speaking to Juan in Spanish the entire time, telling him to try to stay awake and focus on his voice. He was telling the man what Dr. Harper was doing every step of the way. Nalani and Scott picked up the spine board and rushed after Dr. Harper to the main clinic. Reginald ran alongside them, talking to Juan. The other two injured men walked to the clinic on their own power accompanied by nurses.

Sir Barnes was not on island for this little attack. It just so happened that his partner, Ryo Sana, was. Arthur had rushed to Mr. Sana's room to tell him what had happened to the men today. Ryo slowly lifted his head from the book he was reading and stared at Arthur for a few seconds before slowly rising to his feet. He remained silent and stared at Arthur with a piercing gaze. Mr. Sana was equal parts angry and upset. These kinds of things were not supposed to happen. He had to keep this from Ethan and the investors. Mr. Sana knew that Ethan was a bit of a bleeding heart at times and often felt bad for people. Knowing that there was one critically injured man and two others hurt would potentially make him want to slow down their timeline. This was something they could not afford. He also did not want the investors to know because they may get cold feet and back out of their contracts. There were accidents at zoos all the time, Mr. Sana thought, they just had to be more careful next time. Ryo was similar age to Ethan. He was slightly taller and had jet black hair. His peppered eyebrows were thick, and he had almost an evil look to him at baseline. He rushed with Arthur to the clinic to assess the damages.

Ryo walked into the back of the clinic with Arthur, completely bypassing the front desk. He walked straight to the back in the same manner as Dr. Bai had done months earlier when he looked for antibiotics. He began screaming for Dr. Harper. One of the nurses approached the two men and told them that she would take them to Eric Harper. Everyone on site knew who Ethan and

Ryo were by this point. Similarly they all knew not to cross Mr. Sana. The group walked through the halls with a purpose before stopping at the bedside of Juan. Dr. Harper was attending to the broken man as he lay motionless in bed. Tubes and wires were attached everywhere to the point where it appeared as if he was being slowly eaten by the monitoring equipment and IV lines he was attached to. Ryo watched as Dr. Harper began to wave an open palm towards Juan's right eye. He then repeated the process on the left eye. Mr. Sana cleared his throat, causing Eric to look in his direction in a startled manner.

"What happened here, doctor?" asked Ryo. "Bring us up to speed."

"Well, sir, things are bad," said Dr. Harper, motioning for the men to follow him away from Juan and towards a back room. He continued to talk as they walked. "The other two men have minor cuts and bruises, a few broken ribs, nothing…major. One of them I discharged moments before you arrived. This man is not doing so well."

"What does that mean exactly, what are we looking at?" asked Mr. Sana.

"Well, he is on the border of needing a blood transfusion, which we simply can't do here at this clinic," said Dr. Harper. "We don't have a blood bank, although I suppose we could test people on the island in a pinch if we had to."

"Okay…" said Ryo in a questioning tone.

"More seriously is the man's leg," said Dr. Harper. "We do not have the equipment to fix it here, and I am not an orthopedic surgeon. He also may lose sight in his right eye. I'm going to have to recommend that he be flown to the mainland for more intensive care."

"What, how come you can't do this here?!" screamed Ryo. "You're a doctor, aren't you?"

"I am an ER doctor who is doubling as a generalist for you, Mr. Sana," said Dr. Harper annoyed. "This man needs a specialist and is beyond my expertise. Your options are you fly someone down here to fix him with the needed equipment or you fly this man to a specialist."

"Ugh, this is not part of the plan," said Ryo exasperated. "Get me a list of what you need and who you need. Surely you must know men in the field that can fix this. I'll take care of the rest once you give me the names and contact info."

"I'll get on it right away," said Dr. Harper.

Ryo walked away slowly from Dr. Harper. Spending time and money to fix this was the least of his concerns. They had to be as discreet as possible and handle this delicately. Mr. Sana would not have word of this getting out to the mainland under any circumstances. He looked at Arthur Williams calmly, waving his hand in the same manner as someone would when they were trying to shew away a mosquito. This was a look and gesture that Arthur knew all too well. He was being asked to perform his usual duties when there was a mishap like this. Arthur, in addition to being an excellent publicist, had another job at R.N.A. He was tasked with calling the right people to make certain undesirable situations vanish. He pulled out a small notebook from his breast pocket and began to thumb through the pages. Arthur was looking for numbers of the people he needed to start the process of erasing this misstep. He would have Juan and his family paid off to keep them quiet. Juan was from a poor section of Puerto Rico. A large check and some benefits to retire with would keep him from ever becoming an issue for the company. Especially once the medical bills were handled. Arthur Williams was used to covering up things for Ryo and was just as accustomed to keeping these things from Ethan.

Chapter 6

Sleep had once again become a fickle mistress for Dr. Harmon. The ceiling of his bedroom was like an old friend. He would return every night from work to his bed and stare at the ceiling. Seconds would tick by like hours before he was finally able to drift off. There were 184 tiles, but this did not stop the nightly counting. When sleep did come, visions of his divorce hearings plagued him. Sometimes there were dinosaurs chasing him in the courtroom, and sometimes it was Juan in the prosecutor's corner instead of his wife. Guilt for the injuries that his team had sustained from the rampaging Triceratops dominated his dreams. He had led them into the paddock, it was his fault this happened. To try to make up for it, he visited Juan in the clinic daily to bring the man food from the cafeteria. The two could not talk to each other, but Juan seemed to appreciate the gesture.

He would smile and nod all while repeatedly saying, "Thank you, my friend" when Scott presented him with these gifts. It had been six days since the Triceratops attack. Scott had tried to get an idea from Eric Harper as to how Juan was doing medically, but Dr. Harper was always very vague. Dr. Harmon began to develop a mistrust of Dr. Harper due to his reluctance to answer simple questions.

Scott walked into the clinic to see Juan right before his morning duties only to find that his bed was empty. His head was darting back and forth like the metal balls on a Newton's cradle. Scott's eyes scanned his surroundings like a gazelle on the savannah, searching for the hiding lion. Juan had to have been moved to a new bed, Dr. Harmon thought to himself. He began to wander the halls, pulling curtains back as he walked the length of the make-shift clinic. Scott found himself disturbing multiple people and interrupting the nurses as he continued. Multiple people began to stare at him as he continued to search. Judging glances followed him down the hall as he walked.

"Can I help you?" asked a young nurse stopping Scott.

"Ah, yes, I'm looking for my friend Juan. He was in bed number fifteen," said Dr. Harmon.

The nurse seemed confused and looked at Scott with a perplexed face. It was as if she was questioning what he had said. She narrowed her eyes while tilting her head slightly like an inquisitive puppy.

"Hispanic man…messed up leg…attacked by a dinosaur," Dr. Harmon said.

"I'm sorry, sir, I don't know who you're talking about," said the young nurse. "Bed fifteen has been empty since late last night."

"There was someone there just yesterday morning! I saw him, he was here. Where is Dr. Harper?" asked Scott.

"Dr. Harper is in an appointment, but I'm sure if you just make an appointment for yourself…" said the nurse.

"I'm not making an appointment with Harper, I know him. I'll be waiting in his office; I know where it is," said Scott curtly, cutting her off. "Tell him I'm here waiting for him."

"But sir…." the nurse said in protest. She walked after Scott as he headed to Harper's office.

Scott stormed off to the back of the clinic in a frantic rage. The young nurse abandoned her pursuit and rushed away to get Dr. Harper. Scott's feet hit the ground with a loud clapping noise as he charged to the back office. He came to the door of Harper's office and went inside, slamming it behind him. The wall shook a little bit as the door slammed, and the various degrees on the wall inside the office shifted position slightly. Scott couldn't get over how crazy this all was. Did they really expect him to think that Juan had just disappeared, he thought. As he waited for Eric, he began to realize that none of the nursing staff today looked familiar to him. He had been coming to see Juan every day for almost a week and had seen many of the same faces on a daily basis. Scott thought it odd that today, there was not one familiar face. He was snapped out of his thoughts by the office door creaking open. The young nurse was standing behind Dr. Harper defiantly with her arms folded across her chest. She looked like a child who had just gotten her parents to intervene in a dispute with their sibling. Eric dismissed the young nurse as he stepped into the office and locked the door behind him.

Eric glared at Scott like a disappointed mother would glare at her child who had just brought failing marks home. He proceeded to sit behind his desk and kicked his shoes off after collapsing into his chair. The leather crinkled slightly as he leaned back into it. The two sat in awkward silence, staring at each other. Scott could hear the ticking of the clock on the wall. He began to count the clicks in his head as he tried to think about what he was going to say. His heartbeat seemed to line up with the incessant clicking of the clock. Scott was never good at confrontation. He tended to avoid arguments and very rarely stood up for himself.

"What is this all about, man?" asked Dr. Harper, breaking the silence.

"Juan, the man who was attacked by the triceratops, he's gone….vanished. No one seems to know anything about him," said Scott.

"Listen, you saw how mangled his leg was. I'm not an orthopedic surgeon. He had to be flown to the mainland," said Dr. Harper. "I'm sure he's fine. They flew him out at midnight. He's probably in surgery as we speak."

"That makes sense I guess," said Scott sheepishly, his face was bright red. Blood rushed to his cheeks and forehead.

"He's fine, we have all the resources in the world," said Dr. Harper in his best Ethan Barnes voice while using air quotations.

"But how come none of the staffing seems to know about his case? Why was he flown out in the middle of the night?" asked Scott.

"Sir Barnes felt that in light of recent events, we needed more experienced people on the floor," said Harper. "He flew in some new faces to be ready in case there were any more….er, mishaps."

"What happened last week was not my fault!" exclaimed Scott, clenching his fists.

"I never said that, geez, man, you're wound tight. Calm down," said Harper as he twirled a pen between his fingers.

Dr. Harmon sunk into his chair a little bit. His stomach began to ache as this interaction continued. His thoughts jumbled, and he was at a loss for what to say next. What Dr. Harper was saying made sense on the surface, but the sudden change in staffing and Juan being flown out in the middle of the night with no notice was suspicious. Scott did not know much about how human hospitals were usually run, but he did not feel that disappearing patients was standard protocol. All these new faces seemed like a good way to erase the memory on the island of what had occurred. The chair creaked as Dr. Harmon pushed it back and stood up. He stared at Dr. Harper silently as Eric returned his gaze with a smug smile on his face. The two shook hands as they said good-bye. Dr. Harmon headed for the door with a sinking feeling in his stomach. He had gotten his answers, but they did not feel right. He kept playing the conversation over in his head. The more times the scene replayed, the fishier things seemed. What could he really do about it? Scott plodded down the central isle of the clinic with his head hung low. Things that he felt he should have said began to pop into his mind like kernels of popcorn finally exploding as they reached the right temperature. He scuffed his feet as he walked. Several times he almost bumped into stationary objects on the way out the door. Scott made his way out of the clinic back into the tropical heat. He had work to do, he always had work to fall back on.

Later that afternoon, Scott met with a young man named Pedro at the perimeter fence. Pedro was fifteen-years-old with long, straight black hair in a bowl cut. He had a medium build and was wearing old, torn clothes. There were dirt smudges on his face and grass stains on his knees. Childhood innocence seemed to radiate off of him despite being a teenager. His father usually delivered the goats to Dr. Harmon, but today he had sent his son to do the job. The young man had a rope in his hand with three goats attached to it; it was feeding time. The animals fidgeted as they walked, teeth gnashing at their cud and ears flicking at the ever-present flies around them. Nalani and Reginald joined them as they did every day for these activities. Nalani grabbed the lead line from Pedro, and the two of them walked the goats to a large white pick-up truck. The hooves of the animals clanked on the wooden ramp as they made their way into the back of the pick-up. Soft bleating noises came from the animals as they boarded the truck. The goats were calm and blissfully unaware of what awaited them on the other side of the perimeter fence. Pedro sat on the pick-up's flat bed with his goats as the others climbed into the front of the truck. The four adults shared the cabin of the truck as it was a short journey. The carnivore species were kept about a hundred yards from the perimeter fence to make feeding the animals easier.

Passage through the perimeter fence was as painfully slow as always. The vehicles made their way away from the worker village to the enclosures. It did not take long for the rows of electric fencing to become visible once they left the compound. The pick-up pulled up to the first row of enclosures with a screeching noise that echoed through the jungle as it came to a stop. The vehicle shifted forward slightly and then backwards, causing the goats to slide and the men to jerk rhythmically with the motion of the car. Dr. Harmon hopped out of the pick-up, jumping down to the ground below. Dust stirred under his feet as his boots hit the ground. He walked to the first enclosure on the right side. The electric fence hummed like a swarm of bumblebees as he approached the loading door with Nalani and Reginald. The dense jungle of the enclosure hid its inhabitants from view.

"We haven't seen the little buggers in a while, huh?" said Nalani.

"I know, they never come to say hello anymore," said Reginald. "They must be getting big and fat back there."

"Probably for the best. They are pretty terrifying for little ones," said Nalani.

"Seriously, when Jin Moon finally creates a T-Rex, I don't know if I'm going to want to be out here doing this," said Reginald.

"You ain't kidding, man," said Nalani.

The Herrerasaurus avoided the fences and tended to stay towards the center of the paddock, much like the other animals on Protogonus. They were very rarely seen when these daily feedings occurred. Dr. Harmon would sometimes go weeks without a sighting of them. He had packed their enclosures with dense vegetation based on the recommendations of Richard Bramme, their paleontologist. It was thought that they lived in jungles based on where their fossils were located. The animal's skin was camouflaged like a modern tiger, so jungle living seemed appropriate. Despite their small size compared to their later and better-known cousins, they were no less dangerous.

These carnivores were from a period of time known as the Triassic Period. They were some of the earliest dinosaurs on the planet and were brought back completely by accident. Sir Barnes had his teams searching for large carnivore species in Argentina, including the Carnotaurus and the Giganotosaurus. Both of these species would have been impressive additions to the park and were sure to draw crowds. A large, bipedal carnivore is what any park goer would be looking forward to as soon as they arrived on Dionysus. The Giganotosaurus was a largely unknown dinosaur to the public but was an animal larger than the Tyrannosaurus Rex. What better star attraction could Sir Barnes hope for than an animal that was more ferocious than the popular T-Rex? Unfortunately for now they were stuck with the much smaller Herrerasaurus. Dr. Bai was actively working to change this. The Herrerasaurus stood around two and a half to three feet in height and weighed up to 700 pounds. One of these animals would be more than able to take down an unarmed person, being very similar in size to a modern tiger. Because of this danger, care had to be taken when introducing food into their paddock. They could not afford to have something like this escape into the worker village.

The park workers had set up a system similar to the perimeter fences for loading food into the Herrerasaurus paddock. This two-door system would allow the goat into the paddock safely without having to leave the enclosure open to the outside world for the dinosaurs to get out. Sir Barnes was insistent on the animals being fed live bait as he felt this would make for an excellent attraction for the future visitors. Scott was not used to this kind of feeding protocol as most of the animals at his zoo were fed slabs of meat with different vitamins and minerals shoved into the flesh to balance out their diet. Live bait was a potential danger for the predators. Live bait could fight back and cause injuries. Scott initially opposed Ethan's instructions for this reason, but he was quickly overridden. Ethan and Ryo's word was law on this island, and there was nothing Scott could say or do to dissuade him. The first goat was loaded through the small, metal door at the front of the enclosure. To the left of the door at chest height was a small control panel for operating the entry mechanism. Nalani pressed a button on the console near the door with a loud click. The first goat was released into the enclosure as the second door opened. The animal ran off into the brush, snapping twigs as it forced its way through the thick underbrush. A loud beep heralded the closing of the cage-side door. Nalani pulled a small metal lever to open the door on their side of the enclosure. Pedro forced the goat into the small holding chamber between the doors with some help from Reginald. The goat's hooves tore up the ground as it started to resist being forced into the small prison-like cage.

Once the goat was inside waiting for the second door to be opened, all of the usual bird and animal noises were suddenly gone from the background. Nothing but cold, dead silence could be heard. Scott was able to hear himself and the others breathing. At that moment, Pedro's eyes became wide, and the small boy began to shudder. He was frozen with terror and could feel the warmth leaving his arms. A chill shot down his spine, and he could feel the hairs on his arms standing on edge. Reginald told him everything would be fine in Spanish, but everything was not fine. The boy looked to Reginald briefly and then his eyes darted back to the enclosure. He remained frozen as he stared at a demon crouching in the bushes. He was fixated, staring at something that his mind could not make sense of; this was no animal that he had even seen or heard of before. Pedro was usually at home tending to the flock; he had never seen what happened to the goats his father brought to these men. Pedro had caught sight of the Herrerasaurus. He stared at the large lizard-like animal crouched in the tall grass. Black stripes ran up and down its brown back from its snarling jaws to the tip of its long, stiff tail. Striped feathers covered its arms and ran down its tail. Small protofeather projections ran from the base of its skull down its spine. Resembling a large reptilian tiger, the Herrerasaurus sat patiently waiting for the goat to get in range. The dinosaur lay completely still in the grass. It sat back on the haunches of two large, powerful hindlimbs. Its feet looked like that of a large hawk or eagle, thick scales extended from its ankles down to the jet-black claws on its three toes. The animal flicked its wrists ever so slightly, brushing the blades of grass with the claws on its fingers. The feathers on its arms spread out like small wings as it readied itself to pounce. Large, ferocious jaws opened slightly with beads of thick, ropey saliva dropping from its mouth like rain drops. Triangular teeth glistened in the fleeting sunlight, and the lips slowly pulled away from each other. The dinosaur's pupils began to dilate as adrenaline flowed through its body in preparation for the hunt. Silence echoed through the jungle as the predator readied itself.

One of the goats came slowly into sight. It lowered its head to the ground to graze on the grass, its tail swishing slightly from side to side. Ears swiveled on the top of its head listening to the jungle around it as it grazed. Pedro watched as the goat lifted its head in a quick, jerking fashion while it seemed to poise itself to run off. It was apparent the goat knew something was wrong.

Suddenly a loud, deep roar, unlike anything Pedro had ever heard, filled the air. The dinosaur darted forward and tackled the goat with a thud that was so loud, Pedro could feel it. It tackled the goat much like a football player, grabbing the goat around its shoulders with the huge talons on its arms. Claws tore into flesh, spilling blood onto the grass like paint splashing on a wall. The goat screamed as the two animals rolled into the brush. Leaves rustled, and branches snapped as the pair rolled along the ground before coming to a stop with a large thud. Pedro saw the large, stiff, feathered tail of this monster waving from side to side as the vegetation around it shook like it, too, was scared of the beast. The goat was able to push the dinosaur off and got to its feet. It rushed the dinosaur with its head lowered, smashing into the Herrerasaurus' side. The Herrerasaurus fell backwards having been rutted by the goat. The poor goat emerged from the underbrush with a thrashing of leaves. Pedro could see the panicked look in the animal's eyes as it tried to run away from its attacker. Screams of terror emanated from the goat as it darted off, bleeding from the bite and talon wounds around its neck. A second Herrerasaurus darted from the brush and tackled the goat again. It pinned the goat down by placing its strong muscular leg on the goat's chest.

The goat flailed and cried under the Herrerasaurus' foot. It snapped at the goat as the goat tried to gore the dinosaur with its horns. The first Herrerasaurus scampered to its feet and headed over to help its friend. The dinosaur came in from under the goat's head and wrapped its long jaws around the goat's windpipe, crushing it. The goat kicked and thrashed under the weight of the two abominations that had it pinned down. Hooves flashed in a white blur as the goat struggled to get free. The large, clawed foot of the second Herrerasaurus was placed firmly on the goat's chest. Eagle-like talons dug into the goat's fur, causing blood to leak up between the hairs. After a few minutes, there was no more movement from the goat, no more noise or fuss. The goat lay motionless, and the victorious predators began to eat. They ripped off chunks of flesh with ease, making excited clicking noises as they feasted.

"Que demonios son esos!" exclaimed Pedro. "De donde vinieron estos demonios[6]?!"

Pedro backed away from the enclosure, his eyes fixed on the monsters eating his goat. He saw Reginald loading the last goat into the waiting area and rushed to grab the lead away from him. Pedro tried to push Reginald away

---

[6] What the hell are those? Where did these demons come from?

and wrestle the rope from his grasp. The two began to play tug-of-war with the lead line and exchanged words with each other in Spanish. The final goat stood unaffected by what was going on around it. He was blissfully unaware of the struggle for his fate that was occurring between Reginald and Pedro. Pedro held the rope so hard, the fibers had dug into his hand. He would occasionally let go to beat on Reginald's chest. Tears flowed down his face as he tried to protect the last remaining goat. Reginald tried to assure the boy it was okay, but Pedro was unrelenting. He refused to let go, wrapping the rope around his wrist. Pedro wrapped his arms around the goat's neck in protest, sobbing profusely as he hugged the animal.

"No te dejaré alimentar a estos demonios con mi rebaño[7]!" cried Pedro as tears streamed down his cheeks.

"What is going on, Reginald, what is he saying?" asked Nalani.

"He says that he's not going to let us feed his goats to those demons," said Reginald. "He doesn't realize that these are dinosaurs and thinks they're evil creatures."

"Well, tell him that everything is fine and let's get on with it," said Stephen impatiently.

"That's exactly what I am trying to do," said Reginald. "A little help would be nice, guys."

Scott approached the boy and put his hands on his shoulder. He grabbed Pedro's hands and pried them open, leaving the rope to slip to the ground. Once Reginald had the lead line, Pedro collapsed to his knees and began crying. Scott immediately hugged the grieving boy; it was all he could think of. Even though he knew that Pedro could not understand him, Dr. Harmon kept telling him that everything would be fine. As the last goat was loaded into the paddock, the boy let out a high-pitched scream in protest. He pressed his face into Scott's chest and wailed loudly over his lost goats. Scott looked towards the enclosure and began watching the Herrerasaurus eat. The animals would tear off a chunk of flesh with their razor-sharp teeth by quickly ripping their jaws to the side once their teeth had made purchase into flesh. Once they had a sizable chunk of meat, they would jerk their heads upward to throw the lump of meat to the back of their jaws. When it was lined up appropriately in their jaws, the head would get thrown back, and the lump of flesh would slide down

---

[7] I won't let you feed these demons with my flock!

their throats with an undulating motion of the neck muscles. The process was very avian in nature, like his birds at the zoo. They were almost like giant penguins in how they consumed their food. Scott helped the boy to his feet and climbed into the back of the pick-up with him as they drove to the Compsognathus paddock, their second stop. Nalani put her arm around Pedro in an effort to comfort the boy as they walked to the truck.

Feeding the Compys was much less eventful. These animals were not large enough to take down a goat. Dr. Harmon fed them much like he would feed any other birds of prey at his zoo. Buckets of chicken loaded with various vitamins were thrown over the small chain-link fence for the animals to find. Dozens of picked clean bones littered the front of the paddock, remnants of the creature's previous feasts. Nalani, Stephen, and Reginald took to the task of feeding the Compys while Scott sat with the boy. Pedro was no longer crying. He sat there sniffling, his face bright red and his eyes swollen. This was something that Dr. Harmon had just realized he missed. The sobbing boy had begun to bring back memories of his own children. Scott thought of his girls often. It killed him to know that they seemed to despise him.

He was no longer sitting in the back of a pick-up truck, instead he was on a baseball field. This field was where his oldest, Ashley, played her championship game. Pedro was no longer sitting next to him, his daughter Ashley was. She was crying to him about how he missed her game. This wasn't just any game, it was the championship. The most important game of the season, and Harmon had sworn that he would be there at all costs. He promised her this, swore it even. Now he found himself apologizing profusely as he had gotten caught up in a surgery that day. Losing track of time at work was a staple of Scott's life.

"But Daddy, I hit the single that got the winning run in," cried Ashley. "You missed it, why couldn't you be there?"

"I'm sorry, honey, I had a sick patient to attend to," said Dr. Harmon.

"You always have a sick patient, Dad, you're never here," cried Ashley. "This was the championship! You swore you would be here."

"I know, sweetie, I wanted to be, I really did," said Scott.

"You're a liar! I hate you!" screamed Ashley.

Scott could see the scowl on his wife's face from the bleachers as she sat there with their infant, Erica, in her arms. Her eyes pierced him like a thousand daggers shredding through his skin. He could feel the disappointment in her gaze. Scott had let his family down yet again because of work. He had failed. He could see Ashley storming to her mother's arms. His wife comforted the crying child and shook her head at Scott with a disapproving gaze.

Dr. Harmon was jolted out of his daydream by the slamming car doors as Nalani and Reginald got back into the truck. The car vibrated as the ignition started. Slowly the truck turned around to head back to the compound. As they approached the perimeter fence, Scott was hit with a wave of sadness that weighed him down like a half-ton. His chest felt heavy, and he was ready for this day to be over. Once inside the perimeter fence, the truck came to a stop. Pedro jumped over the side of the flatbed and ran off towards his home. Scott hopped over the side as well and began to rush after the boy.

"Let him go, Scott," said Nalani. "You can't talk to him anyways. I'm sure his dad will talk some sense into him."

"He's just a scared kid, Scott. He'll be okay," chimed in Reginald.

"I just feel bad…" said Dr. Harmon, his words slowly trailing off into a low mumble.

Nalani walked over to Scott and put her hand on his shoulder. She suggested they all hit the showers and grab a quick drink. Scott begrudgingly agreed. Alcohol may make this rough day a bit more bearable.

The genetics lab was bustling with activity. Men rushed back and forth like a time lapse video of cars on a freeway. Dr. Bai was pushing his men to create new species for the park and to refine the process of de-extinction. Jin Moon had his men working past the point of exhaustion. It had become common for people to be found sleeping at their stations. The process was now very slow-going. Gene sequencing went from a process that would take a few days to taking several weeks of more. Archosauria was having issues with computing capacity despite having the latest equipment and technology at their disposal. Each genome was trillions of strands long; this was more data than the system was able to handle. Storing that kind of data and still having processing capability to sequence genetic codes was pushing the limits of their technology more than was ever anticipated. Jin had become known for throwing tantrums when the computers would crash and lag. He could often be found cursing and screaming at his employees. No one working in the genetic lab wanted to be there anymore. The wrath of Dr. Bai had been something they had all been subject to. The work environment had become draining and unbearable.

They had just sequenced about 85 percent of a new genome when the monitors in the lab all simultaneously went black. The lights flickered, and all of the computers rebooted. All of the genome data had mysteriously vanished with the reboot.

"What is going on here?!" screamed Jin Moon. His hands slammed against the desk, shaking everything on its surface. "Why does this happen every time we get even remotely close!? I will not stand for this any longer!"

"Dr. Bai, we are doing the best we can, but the system can't seem to process new data anymore," said Dr. Sung sheepishly.

"Unacceptable! Fix it!" screamed Jin, punching his fist into the wall. A small strand of saliva hung in the corner of his mouth; his mannerisms seeming more animalistic than human.

"I don't know how," said Dr. Sung. "I'm not trained for this; I'm a bacteriologist and a geneticist, not an IT expert! None of us are trained for this. You need to calm down and let us do our damn jobs!"

Ernie was not usually one to talk back to Jin. He would often do as he was told and skulk back to his lab when Jin got like this. Even he had reached his limit. Dr. Bai paused for a second from his tantrum. He stood there staring like a child who had just been slapped by his parent. No one in this lab ever dared to stand up to him before. Jin snapped out of his shock and approached Dr. Sung, grabbing him by the collar. He placed his face inches from Ernie's; a large vein was throbbing on the side of his forehead. Dr. Bai's cheeks and neck were flushed. The two were so close that they seemed to blend together to those viewing the encounter.

"I know you did not just talk back to me," said Dr. Bai in a low, angry tone. "We are on the cusp of greatness, and you are telling me that you can't do simple tasks. Do I need to get someone else in here to do your job?"

"No...no, sir..." said Ernie, terrified. His eye squeezed tightly shut, and his shoulders trembled as he received the consequences of his actions. Ernie's sudden burst of courage was gone just as quickly as it had come on. "I'm sorry, sir."

"You better be," said Dr. Bai. "That goes for all of you! Back to work!"

"Is everything okay, Jin?" asked Sir Barnes, walking into the room.

"Sir…Sir Barnes, yes, sir. Absolutely," said Jin Moon in a sheepish tone. His demeanor immediately changing from menacing to almost scared. Jin Moon seemed to act innocent in front of Ethan.

"Good, good. Everyone here looks stressed and tired. Perhaps a tea break is in order," said Ethan.

"Yes, sir, I was just thinking this," said Dr. Bai. "Everyone, take off for the rest of the night. We will pick up tomorrow."

Jin Moon was a slave-driver when it came to those working under him. The lab technicians all stared in utter shock for a few moments, frozen in place. They were all uncertain what to do. Soft chattering filled the air as the workers all looked to each other for someone to take the lead. No one expected the abrupt change in demeanor and cadence. Dr. Bai had a lot of respect and admiration for Ethan. He aspired to be like him in some ways, and in others, the admiration seemed paternal. Ethan had recognized Jin's talents at a young age, taking him under his wing. Jin viewed Ethan as a father figure; he would never dream of talking back to Sir Barnes and certainly would never speak to him the way he typically spoke to his staff. As people filed out from the lab for the night, Ethan and Jin Moon began to discuss the issues that were befalling the creation process. Sir Barnes told him he would have his IT specialists on it tomorrow morning and urged Jin Moon to take care of himself.

Sir Barnes had enlisted the help of several IT workers for this venture. Selena Ortega headed the department on Protogonus, and Jayden Charles was her counterpart on the developing Dionysus. Selena was a thirty-something Costa Rican native. She got hired by R.N.A fresh out of school, working mostly in internet security for the company. She was medium build with long brown hair that she often wore up in a bun on top of her head. She had piercing hazel eyes and was almost always seen in business attire. Selena often wore a set of frames, even though she could see normally without them. She felt it made her look more professional. Jayden Charles on the other hand was an electrical engineer with a dual degree in programing. He was a tall man with a strong presence about him. He came to Revolutionary National Amalgamations from Washington D.C. He had a muscular build and smoked constantly. Jayden almost always had a cigarette or cigar in his mouth. He happened to get involved in R.N.A. through family connections.

These two were responsible for the state-of-the-art programing behind Archosauria.

Selena sat on the deck of her hotel room. It was early morning, and the sun was just coming over the horizon, painting the sky with a bright orange hue. A large, clunky computer sat on her lap. The machine was heavy and difficult for her to carry. It rested on her lap as she feverishly typed. The light from the monitor glowed in the early morning and lit her face from underneath. Selena was signed into the system on Dionysus remotely. Today she was trying to write the program that would play the audio for the tour vehicles of Archosauria. Jayden was signed in as well to help her with some of the task. With construction well underway, there was a lot of pressure for her and Jayden to get these systems up and running. She was completely lost in her work and almost didn't notice the phone in her room ringing. The ringing phone dragged her away from her work begrudgingly. She lifted the laptop off her lap with a grunt and placed it onto the table of her deck. Selena rushed inside to pick up the receiver, nearly knocking her chair over.

"Hello, this is Selena," she said.

"Ah, dear, it's Ethan. I know you're busy, love, but we need you to look at the systems of the genetics lab," said Sir Barnes. "We are having quite a terrible time with the sequencing computers, and I need you to take a look."

"Hello, Sir Barnes. Jayden and I are almost done writing the tour program audio for the resort. I can't leave this all to him," said Selena. "It's a lot of work, and that's not fair."

"There will be plenty of time for this, dear. It's kind of an emergency," said Ethan.

"Alright, I'll be right in," said Selena, knowing that Ethan would not take no for an answer.

Selena hung up the phone and walked over to her computer. She placed the computer back on her lap and reached out to Jayden via a small chat window on her screen. Selena told him that she was logging off as she was being urgently summoned by Sir Barnes. Jayden left her a passive-aggressive message in protest. He was very clearly not happy about having to try to finish this task on his own. Writing the code would now take twice as long with only one person working on it. It could not be helped; she had no other choice. The boss was beckoning, and when Sir Barnes beckoned, one did not say no. Selena rushed to get ready, taking a quick shower. She paced back and forth in her room, trying to pick out an outfit for the day. Selena liked to be put together, and she was not going to let today be any different. Hours seemed to tick by as she prepared to head to the genetics lab.

Selena walked down the front stairs of her hotel complex, her high heels clacking on the pavement as she walked. She put her computer bag on the pavement and began fixing the earing in her right ear. A few construction workers walked by her as she made her way down the path. Selena made it a point to tone out the catcalls that echoed across the street as she walked. There was no time for the trivial calls of immature men. A gentle morning breeze ruffled her skirt as she walked up the stairs to the genetics building. Selena's presence in the building was announced by the sound of her shoes hitting the ground. She saw Sir Barnes and Jin Moon talking at the entrance to the main computer server room; they were waiting for her. She waved hello to the two men but did not wait for an official greeting. She entered the room with the two men following her. Selena stopped in front of a large computer tower and opened a panel on the side. She bent down to open her computer bag and pulled out her laptop. A plethora of different colored wires now joined her machine and the mainframe of Protogonus.

"Well, have you figured out the issue?" asked Jin Moon impatiently.

"Now, now, Jin. Let the woman work, it's what I am paying her for after all," said Ethan.

Selena rolled her eyes at Jin and sighed briefly. She had no tolerance for Jin Moon and was not shy about letting him know she was not a fan of his. Jin and Ethan watched rows of green lettering scroll across the screen of Selena's laptop, and she furiously typed. She paused for a second and placed the index finger of her right hand to her lips. Her face twisted as she concentrated on the code in front of her. Scrolling through the lines of code, Selena began to scowl. Jin Moon was now anxiously tapping his foot on the floor with an annoying clapping noise. Ethan grabbed Jin's arm while shooting him a look, causing Jin Moon to immediately stop his anxious tapping.

"Well, the good news is I know your issue," said Selena.

"And the bad news…" asked Sir Barnes and Dr. Bai in unison.

"Well, you have reached the data capacity of your hard drives. The codes you are storing are too long, and the system is 95 percent full," said Selena. "That's why you can't store or process any more data."

"So how do we get more capacity, dear?" asked Ethan. He had a very concerned tone in his voice as he was not prepared for another setback.

"Well, you either need to buy more hard drive space, or you could delete some of the existing data," said Selena.

"I'm not deleting the twenty-five genomes we have! That is not an option!" screamed Jin Moon. "Is there any way to compress the data?"

"Well, that may be an option, but these files are huge. It would take a few months to maybe a year to figure out how to do that effectively," said Selena.

"We don't have a year, and we can't open with our current roster of animals, love. The investors want a T-Rex," said Ethan. "Is there any way to get this done faster?

Selena let out a long sigh and looked at the screen while silently nodding. She knew a man that could help with this task, and she knew he would get it done a lot quicker and more efficiently than she or Jayden could. The problem was that this man disgusted her, and it made her cringe just to think about asking him for help. Selena was dreading having to call Kyle Bergin.

Chapter 7

Kyle plopped down into an old torn arm chair that sat in front of the TV screen. Empty bags of potato chips and candy wrappers were piled on the table next him, surrounding a small lamp that was missing its shade. Piles of trash and pizza boxes littered the floor, and the paint was chipped off the walls in multiple locations. Kyle switched through half a dozen channels as he lounged in his Worchester, Massachusetts apartment. The flickering light of the TV screen lit up his face like a strobe light in various shades of blue and white. Kyle was a large, bulbous man with thick black rimmed glasses and unkempt brown hair. He had as many chins as he did fingers on his hands. Despite his unkept appearance, he was one of the most talented computer programmers of his time. He was the best at what he did. He worked for a tech company that he helped create. He was unappreciated and undervalued. Kyle wrote code and set up security protocols for multiple large companies around the world. Despite his success, Kyle could never seem to get ahead in life. He always felt like the world owed him something, and it reflected in how he treated those around him. There were very few people he cared about, and thus he lived the life of a loner.

Kyle lived in a small apartment with his mother, Rebecca Bergin, whom he cared for. Kyle's mother was fighting a losing battle with pancreatic cancer, and he had spent thousands on her care over the past year. Her diagnosis had hit Kyle extremely hard. He had gained a large amount of weight since his mother started treatment. Kyle had completely disconnected from society, pre-ferring to spend much of his life in his apartment with his mother. The fortune he had amassed with the success of his business ventures had slowly vanished into experimental treatments and medical studies. Every week a new doctor would come by to try an experimental treatment protocol for his mother's dis-ease. He lived his life travelling from specialist to specialist in a desperate at-tempt to keep the one person who cared about him alive just a little longer. Kyle spent the rest of his time at home, remotely logged into work in front of his television screen. When he wasn't working or eating, Kyle spent his time caring for his ailing mother.

Kyle shoved a slice of cold pizza into his face with his left hand while fu-riously typing with his right. Tonight's endeavor was setting up additional fire-walls for a Fortune 500 company in New York City. This was child's play for him. He became increasingly annoyed with his job as it bored him. His co-workers couldn't seem to take care of the simplest tasks on their own, so he inevitably would always have to get involved. Ticket after ticket found its way onto his desk, leading to late nights and weekend assignments. He wouldn't even get a break when he was on vacation as he would often be pinged to an-swer pages from his team. It took Kyle the better part of two hours to write the needed code before he shut his computer down for the night. Life had made him very bitter; he had not had it easy despite seeming successful on paper. Kyle Bergin longed for things to be different in his life, but he was very reluctant to change anything. He was comfortable at this job, despite its draw-backs. Some part of him felt that he would eventually hit it big if he continued to work for this firm.

The arm chair creaked loudly as he rose to his feet. Kyle stretched his arms above his head with a loud groan. His T-shirt rode up his body, exposing his large gut as he reached upward. He headed towards his mother's bedroom. He always checked on her before he retired to his own room for the night. As he entered the small bedroom, the sound of beeping monitors echoed in uni-son. His mother's room had been transformed into a small make-shift hospital bed. Monitors littered the tops of dressers where once there were family pho-tos. Instead of clothes on the floor, electric cords snaked around the room like jungle vines. Windows that once let in copious amounts of sun were now cov-ered in black-out curtains as light would agitate his mother. One of Rebecca's full-time nurses turned her head as Kyle entered the room. He had startled her as she was preoccupied with changing his mother's IV fluid bag. Kyle's mother was in hospice care and had round the clock nursing staff. He did not accept the inevitable, and deep down he felt that there was a cure out there for his mother. He just had to keep looking hard for it. If she could only hold on for just a little longer, Kyle would often think to himself.

"How is she doing?" asked Kyle sheepishly. He hoped to hear that she was cured every time he asked this question. He longed for an end to this year long nightmare.

"She had a good day today, as I told you earlier. Her pain is much better controlled on the higher dose of fentanyl. You should get some sleep and let her rest," said Kristin, the caretaker.

"Oh, okay. Good to hear," said Kyle, slowly turning to his mother. "I love you, Mom, sleep well."

A low groan was all he got in return from his mother as she shifted positions. He couldn't help but think how thin she had gotten. His mother was once a full-figured woman not even two years ago. Now she had wasted away to a frail shell of herself. Her eyes were sunken into her skull and shined a bright yellow when they were open. Skeletal fingers were clutching her blankets as she shivered. She couldn't have weighed more than eighty pounds at this point. Kyle turned and began to leave the room slowly. As he got to the doorway, he looked back at his mother one last time. He wiped tears from his eyes and headed to his own bed. Kyle stopped at the bathroom and pulled some toilet paper off the roll. He blew his nose with a loud snort and wiped his eyes. It wasn't fair, he thought to himself, no one should have to die like this. There had to be something more he could do for her, he thought.

Kyle laid down on his own bed. The frame creaked under his weight as he adjusted himself to get comfortable. He often slept in his clothes as sometimes he just did not have the energy to change prior to going to sleep. He pulled a knitted blanket over his body and stared at the ceiling. Thoughts of his childhood filled his mind as he tried to fall asleep. Kyle remembered his mother picking him up from school and comforting him as he cried over what one of the bullies at school had said to him. He longed for the days where his mother was taking care of him instead of how things were now. Kyle stared at the clock on the wall and listened to the gentle ticking sound as he drifted off to sleep.

A loud ring echoed through Kyle's bedroom. His eyes fluttered, and he groaned as he looked for the source of the annoying noise. His head was in a daze. Light flooded through his bedroom window, causing him to shield his eyes and blink rapidly. Kyle wiped away a strand of thick saliva from the side of his mouth as he got out of bed to answer the ringing phone. He repeated the words "I'm coming" over and over again as he rushed to ~~the~~ grab the phone. The floor boards creaked with each step as he plodded down the hallway to the kitchen phone. His bare feet made a clapping noise on the floorboards, and he waddled along. Kyle hoped it was the doctor with his mother's bloodwork results from last week. He hoped that he would get better news this time around.

"Hell...Hello, this is Kyle Bergin," he said, picking up the receiver nervously.

"Well, hello, old friend, this is Selena, how are you?" said a very familiar voice.

"Selena, what a surprise! I see you couldn't resist my charms for very long," said Kyle in a cocky tone. He was disappointed that it wasn't the doctor, but Selena was always a welcome surprise. The two had gone to school together and had worked together on a few projects.

"Hardly..." said Selena, annoyed. "I am only calling you because you are unfortunately the last person I could think of. My employer would like to make you an offer."

"Oh, really," said Kyle. "Don't lie, Selena, you missed me and couldn't resist contacting me."

"I'm not doing this; I knew this was a mistake. I'm not talking to this pig," said Selena, disgusted.

Kyle could hear a bit of a scuffle on the other end of the line. He heard a male voice talking with Selena and encouraging her to continue the conversation. There was a brief silence before another voice got on the phone.

"Hello, Mr. Bergin. My name is Ryo Sana, and we require your skill set as my gracious employee was trying to tell you."

"THE Ryo Sana! Revolutionary National Amalgamations Ryo Sana?!" exclaimed Kyle, confused. Kyle had not expected something like this to be happening to him. He had heard of Mr. Sana and his business partner Sir Ethan Barnes. Dollar signs filled Kyle's eyes as he realized what an opportunity it could be to work for such an illustrious company.

"Yes, the Ryo Sana. I normally do not do this kind of thing, but we need your help," said Mr. Sana.

"I'm listening, what can I help you with?" said Kyle, trying to muffle a squeal of pure joy.

"You see my partner and I are working on a project, and we have run into some snags with our technology. How comfortable are you with bit-rate compression technology?" asked Mr. Sana.

"I mean I practically wrote the book on it. How large is the data source?" asked Kyle.

"We need a system that can process ten exabytes or more," said Mr. Sana.

Kyle's jaw dropped, and he went silent for a moment. An exabyte was an extremely large unit of storage. He was being asked to design a system that could process ten quintillion bytes. This was military grade computing power and something that quite frankly no company in the private sector was dabbling in. What could he possibly need this much storage for? What type of project was this? All of these thoughts raced through his head as he sat silently. Kyle was at a loss for words, which was not something that commonly happened to him.

"Well, can you do it?" asked Ryo Sana impatiently. "I am a very busy man, and I am not one to waste time!"

"Of course I can; it's a piece of cake for someone like me. I have to ask, what is this for? This kind of job will take time, and it's not cheap," said Kyle. "I expect proper compensation."

"Don't worry about the money, we will compensate you," said Ryo. "The job has to be on site though, and you will have to sign non-disclosure agreements of course."

"I can't," said Kyle. "My mother is very ill. It's either a remote job or nothing. I don't travel."

"We will take care of your mother and her care," said Mr. Sana, getting impatient. "Are you in or out?"

"I'll have to think about it," said Kyle. "Give me twenty-four hours. I can't just up and leave my mother here with how ill she is."

"You have until 6 P.M. EST. We will contact you," said Mr. Sana, hanging up the phone.

Kyle knew how these big impatient business types worked. A man like Ryo Sana was used to getting things his way and in a timely fashion. If there was one thing a man like him could not stand, it was not being in control. Kyle knew if he played hard to get, it could mean more money for him. He was in control for the first time in his life. There were eight hours until he had to give his answer to Ryo Sana. Kyle knew that the type of code R.N.A. would need was not something just any IT guy could write. Kyle was filled with immense joy but was also questioning if he was able to take on a job like this. His thoughts quickly shifted to the finances again; he cackled to himself as he began to think of the number he would ask for. He whistled with a high pitch squeak as he laughed to himself, stomping his feet on the ground and waving his hands like a child at a birthday party who just opened their presents. This job was exactly what he needed to keep funding his mother's care. Fortune had smiled on him it seemed.

Kyle rushed to his mother's side, barging into the room with a huge smile on his face. He ran past her care nurse and kissed his mother on the forehead. His mother stared at him with a blank expression through glassy, sunken eyes.

"Good news, Mom, I just got a new job offer. Everything is going to be okay," said Kyle. "We are going to find a cure for you! I'm going to make something of myself, Mom, and make you proud."

His mother was unable to reply or form words of any kind. She forced a faint smile and nodded her head ever so slightly. A lock of gray, greasy-looking hair fell onto her forehead. Kyle lovingly brushed her hair out of her face and smiled at his ailing mother. He sat by her side for a few hours to keep her company, holding her hand as he spent time talking to her about how R.N.A. had reached out to him. He explained how they would be rich and how he would use the money to find a cure for her. Kyle fantasized about all the things he would buy with the small fortune he planned to ask for. He pictured himself driving a fancy sports car down Hollywood Boulevard. He pictured women swooning at his fancy car as he drove by. This was going to be a dream come true for him.

The phone began to ring at 5:59 P.M. Kyle had his speech planned and a number in mind. He was ready to do battle with Mr. Sana and win. He psyched himself up as he reached for the receiver.

"Hello, this is Kyle Bergin," he said confidently.

"Have you reached your decision?" barked Mr. Sana. There was an air of impatience and anger in his voice.

"Yes," said Kyle. He purposely paused after speaking for a few moments. The silence was deafening.

"Well…what have you decided? We are prepared to cover all medical expenses for your mother as well as offer you $250,000 for the year with a plan to renegotiate salary after that," said Mr. Sana.

"Um, you see I was thinking more along the lines of half a million for the first year. It's a big job, and there aren't many who can do it," said Kyle arrogantly. "In fact you reaching out to me tells me you can't find anyone else to do it."

There was a long pause on the other end of the line. Kyle could hear Mr. Sana grumbling under his breath to someone else in the room. Kyle began to tap his foot. He then began pacing obsessively like a dog on a leash. He twirled the cord of the phone in his chubby fingers as he awaited an answer.

"One hundred and fifty thousand up front, expenses for your mom, and the rest to be delivered in quarterly installments based on performance," grunted Ryo. "Do we have a deal?"

Kyle thought long and hard over what he was being offered. A lot of money was on the table here, and this was certainly more than he was used to being offered for a job. The thought of how much this would improve his situation made him nervous. An offer like this seemed like it was too good to be true. Ultimately the pot was too sweet for him to turn down. His heart raced, pounding against his ribs. Kyle's face flushed, and he could feel his breath getting a little shorter.

"You have yourself a deal," said Kyle joyfully. He laughed nervously as he accepted the offer.

"Splendid. Answer your door," said Mr. Sana.

Kyle jumped as a loud knock resonated throughout the apartment. The person on the other end of the door was knocking far harder than they needed to. Confused, Kyle dropped the phone and his hand away from his face. He stared in the direction of the door and the loud knocking. Kyle placed the phone receiver down on the nightstand and walked to answer the door. He began to open the door slowly but was pushed back as a number of people rushed into his apartment.

"What's going on? Who are all you people?!" exclaimed Kyle.

Two men dressed in lab coats rushed towards his mother's room like they knew where she was and were already familiar with the layout of his apartment.

Kyle initially went to stop them when he was cut off by a tall man with red hair and sun glasses. The man introduced himself as Arthur Williams. He told Kyle that the men in lab coats were two of R.N.A.'s best doctors. Arthur assured Kyle that his mother was about to get the best care money could buy. He motioned for Kyle to join him on the couch. Arthur looked at the couch in disgust as he wiped away several wrappers and bags with his briefcase. He sat down, placing his briefcase on the table, using it again to push away wrappers and trash. Kyle nervously sat down next to Arthur. The suitcase locks clicked as they were opened, and piles of papers became visible. Arthur sifted through the documents and pulled out several large stacks of paper. Each stack had yellow tabs sticking out from the sides. Arthur placed three stacks of papers in front of Kyle and handed him a pen from his jacket pocket.

"What is all of this?" asked Kyle.

"This is all standard non-disclosure agreements. Sign wherever you see a yellow tab," said Arthur.

"Okay…I need to read this before I sign," said Kyle defiantly.

"If you must," said Arthur. "We will be flying out in forty-eight hours. We expect you to be outside, waiting and ready at 7 A.M. this Tuesday with these papers signed."

"What about my mother?! She isn't exactly mobile," said Kyle.

"We will arrange her transport. She will fly down after us," said Arthur.

This all seemed very shady and underhanded to Kyle. This type of secrecy and quick paced talking was worse than anything he had experienced. Kyle had done some work on government projects, and the security was not this heavy-handed. As he read through the mounds of papers, the legal language was very thick and convoluted. He had read computer coding that was less detailed and confusing. Kyle looked up at Arthur with a questioning gaze.

"What the hell is Archosauria?" asked Kyle.

"You will only find out if you agree and sign. Do not keep Sir Barnes and Mr. Sana waiting any longer," said Arthur as he packed up his things and left the apartment.

Kyle put the papers down and walked in to see the two doctors examining his mother. They stared at her with intense gazes and made subtle adjustments to the equipment hooked up to her. Kyle didn't even think to question what they were doing. He was overwhelmed by all that was occurring. His homecare nurse did not seem to protest at all to the changes, so this made Kyle feel at ease. Martha was a good nurse, and he knew she had his mother's best interest in mind. If she was fine with these changes, then so was Kyle. The two men greeted him, and after some time, they left the room. They told him they would see him tomorrow and slowly walked to the door.

Kyle brought the paperwork into his mother's room. He pawed through the endless pages as he sat with his mom. He wasn't sure how his mother would survive the transport down to this island, but how could he give up this opportunity? He was torn on what to do. He would never forgive himself if something happened to his mother and he was not there. Kyle struggled with this decision. He would normally ask his mother what to do in situations like this, but as he gazed over to her bed, he saw she was fast asleep. He couldn't wake her for something like this. Sleep was not something that came easily for Rebecca Bergin. Kyle knew this and thus did not want to wake her. He would have to make this difficult decision on his own. He began to talk to his mother in a soft tone as she slept, not expecting any reply.

"I wish you were able to help me make this decision, Mom. This is a big move and could finally help me get what I deserve," said Kyle. "But the trip is going to be rough on you, I don't know if that's fair."

"She would want you to do what's best for you, Kyle," said Martha. "All mothers want what is best for their children. She loved you dearly."

"Loves!" shouted Kyle. "LOVES! She's still here, Martha, she's not gone yet."

"I'm sorry, I misspoke. I think you know what I was trying to say," said Martha apologetically.

"Yes…" said Kyle with a loud sigh. "This has all been so rough on me. I'm so tired."

"I understand, Mr. Bergin, it's okay," said Martha reassuringly. "These types of things are never easy. It's such a terrible disease."

"It is. I just wish it were easier sometimes. I'm going to head to bed. I need to sleep on this," said Kyle.

"Good night, Mr. Bergin," said Martha. "Try to get some sleep."

Kyle fell asleep faster than he had ever fallen asleep in the past year. Something seemed to be putting him at ease. As he slept, he began to dream. He was suddenly sitting in a jungle on a large log. A small waterfall flowed silently under his feet as they dangled off the log. Kyle looked around at the various trees swaying slightly in the jungle breeze. He turned to look to his right when he noticed he was not alone. His mother was sitting next to him, but she no longer looked sick. She had a smile on her face and looked as she did a year ago before her diagnosis. Kyle's eyes began to burn as tears welled up. He felt a large knot in his throat. He tried to talk, but his words burned in his chest, unable to leave to get to his mouth. It was so nice to see his mother healthy and no longer in pain. He was completely overcome with emotion.

He forced himself to talk, but all he was able to utter was one word, "Mommy."

His mother looked at him with a huge smile on her face. She mouthed the words, "I love you, Kyle" as she stared at him. He felt warm, and for the first time in a year, he felt happy and at ease. He felt like everything was going to be alright. He reached out to hug his mother, but his arms passed straight through her. Confused Kyle stared at the figure as it became less and less solid. His mother now seemed to slowly fade away.

"Wait, Mom! Come back, please don't leave me here!" Kyle screamed fruitlessly.

His mother continued to slip quietly from view and out of his reach. He shot to his feet and began to reach for his mother as she drifted off into the jungle. She quietly vanished with one last smile, looking back at her son. He stood in the cold, dark jungle when a loud voice began to call to him from amongst the trees. The voice was quiet at first but then slowly increased in volume.

"Wake up, Kyle!" screamed Martha's voice from amongst the trees.

He was ripped from his dream and back to his apartment. Confusion wrapped over him as he lay on his back, staring into the face of someone who was very clearly not his mother. Initially he did not recognize her, but as the daze of slumber left him, he began to piece together what was going on. He realized he was staring into the face of his mother's nurse, Martha. Panic swept over him as he began to fear for the worst. He could see it in Martha's forlorn face, he felt it in his bones; Kyle knew his mother was gone. He shot out of his bed and began to run to his mother's side, silently hoping it wasn't true.

"Wait, Mr. Bergin…" said Martha, sheepishly grabbing his arm. "I'm so sorry"

"No, that's not how this story goes. That's not how this ends," said Kyle, pulling his arm away and running to his mother's room.

He came to a stop at his mother's side. The ECG monitor read a flat line; her IV pumps were beeping rhythmically with a little sign saying "Occlusion" flashing with a bright green light. He grasped his mother's cold hand in his as he knelt by her side. He could see that the little bit of light that was left in her eyes was gone. Kyle could feel that her hand was lifeless. His vision became blurry as tears began to fill his eyes. He could feel his nose running but didn't care enough to wipe it. Tears and snot dripped down his face as he was overcome with emotion. He sniffled loudly as he knelt in silence. He knew his mother was dead, but he couldn't bring himself to say or think it. He knelt by her side, whimpering and sobbing into his mother's bed sheets, tightly gripping his mother's hand as he cried.

"She can't be gone. I was about to make her proud, I was about to be successful. She can't be..." said Kyle.

"Mr. Bergin, your mother was very sick. This day was coming. There is nothing anyone could have done to prevent this," said Martha comfortingly. Martha was no stranger to the denial that came with the loss of a loved one.

Kyle did not want to accept that his mother had left him. He felt that it was far too soon. He had hoped that he would be able to change her fate and that she would have hung on for just a little longer. He thought long and hard over the next few hours about what he was going to do. He sat in silence, trying to figure out how he would go on without his mother by his side, all the while clutching her cold hand. Kyle had never felt so alone and lost in his life. Longing for something positive, he decided he was going to call Mr. Williams. He needed to postpone the trip, so that he could bury his mother. Kyle knew he would need the money to cover his mother's final arrangements. All of this treatment had wiped out his savings, and funerals were expensive. He was pleasantly surprised in the answer that he got from Mr. Williams. Arthur had told him to take all the time he needed to grieve and that as soon as he was able, to get back to him. Kyle was happy with how accommodating R.N.A. was with his recent loss.

Kyle needed to get out of this apartment and away from his life. Every minute spent in his apartment was torture. The place that had once been a home was now an ever-present reminder that his mother was gone. He packed a picture of his mother into his suitcase right before closing it. He took care to wrap it in a T-shirt before placing it on top of his clothes. He walked slowly to the door, pausing to take one last look at his apartment before closing the door. Kyle was on to better things, and he planned to kill two birds with one stone. He had to make his way to the West Coast to get to Protogonus. He used the last of his savings to fly himself and his mother's remains to California. He planned to bury his mother at a high-end cemetery in California. His mother's favorite actor was buried there, so it seemed fitting that she be laid to rest next to her idol. Kyle was going to be rich thanks to this venture with R.N.A. He cannibalized the last of his savings, so that he could send his mother off the right way. His mother meant the world to him, and he was going to make sure she was sent off in style.

Chapter 8

Kyle's trip down to Protogonus was a solemn one. He was still reeling from the services and was not mentally prepared for the journey to the island. Kyle was also disappointed at the turn out for his mother's services. Any logical person would realize it was a last-minute event thousands of miles away from anyone who knew her. Kyle was not thinking logically at this moment. It angered him that a woman such as his mother had to be buried in such a rush without any celebration or adornment. He thought the world of his mother, and he felt that the world should think the same of her. As he climbed into his seat on the private luxury liner, he saw Arthur Williams reviewing the paperwork that he had handed him. It looked as if Arthur was holding a deck of overly large playing cards as he sifted through to make sure the signatures were all in the right place. He couldn't help but feel like he had just signed his life away to Revolutionary National Amalgamations. The terms of the contract were very strict, mandating his silence and threatening financial ruin and strict litigation if he did not comply. Kyle normally hated being around people, but sitting in the plane next to these random strangers was comforting. Being around someone outside the four walls of his apartment seemed to dull the loneliness that he was feeling. He needed some form of comfort; he needed something positive to hang on to.

Sir Barnes's private jet was stocked with all sorts of amazing treats, sweets, and alcohols. Kyle had gorged himself on all numbers of delicacies that he was offered. He did not even recognize half of the things he was being offered, but he gobbled them down as quickly as he could. His belly was full, and he felt a strong sense of comfort welling over him like a wave of warm water running up his back. Food had become a source of relaxation and goodness in his life. Kyle felt a lot better now that he was full. Tiredness rushed over him on the journey to Samoa after his large meal. This day of travelling was wearing on him. But with all this great food, how could he be upset? Kyle couldn't help but think about how this must be what the good life is like. He was well-off at one point prior to his mother's illness. He had forgotten what it felt like to be pampered. Kyle had forgotten what it was like to have money, but he had never had this level of wealth. Mid-flight he was awoken from his slumber and was offered a full pedicure from two attractive women. They had seemed to come out of nowhere, and Kyle did not even see them board the plane. There was no way he could turn them down; he could get used to this.

The plane landed on a small airfield in the Samoan airport. It skidded and popped as it hit the rocky runway jolting Kyle from his second nap. He shot up in a panic, his arms flailing in the air as he tried to rise from his seat, only to realize he was strapped in. Embarrassed he quietly tried to play it off as his face flushed red and his heart raced. The plane slowly skidded to a halt, pinning those aboard to their seats as it came to a stop. Getting off the plane was painful as Kyle did not want to leave the luxuries of this airliner behind. The hot Samoan sun began assaulting him as soon as he exited the aircraft door. Rays of sun beamed onto his face and glared off of his thick glasses. Walking down a large set of metal steps, Kyle felt himself begin to sweat. A small bead of sweat fell from his armpit and began to tickle him as it rolled over the skin of his left side. Arthur Williams had gone down the stairs ahead of him and was motioning for Kyle to follow. He was much faster than Kyle and handled the stairs with ease.

"But what about my luggage?!" exclaimed Kyle as he looked back at the plane.

"Don't worry about that; Sir Barnes takes care of his own. Follow me," said Arthur, half running to another portion of the airfield. "The servants will take care of getting your bags to our destination."

Kyle found it hard to keep up with Arthur. What was a normal walking pace for Arthur was a light jog for Kyle. He found himself a good twenty paces behind Arthur. Where is this guy running to, thought Kyle resentfully in his head. The sweat began to pour down his face and drip off his chin onto his shirt. He could feel his breath getting short as it burned in his chest. Kyle could feel the warm jungle air entering his airways and flooding his chest with every breath. Even breathing was uncomfortably hot. Kyle could see that Arthur had come to a stop in front of a set of helicopters parked at an airfield behind the airport itself. Each helicopter was white with green striping. The name R.N.A. was painted in light blue lettering along the sides of the helicopters with a small DNA helix next to the lettering. Kyle had never been in a helicopter before. This was equally exciting and terrifying for him. He could feel the hair on his arms begin to stand up and the muscles in his back shudder.

"We are going to your secret island in that thing?" asked Kyle.

"Sure are! Hop in and buckle up, big man. The ride can get bumpy," said Arthur, motioning for Kyle to climb in the open helicopter door.

"Um…okay," said Kyle in an unsure tone. "Are you sure this is safe?"

"Put this on before you get in," said Arthur, handing him a yellow pouch with a black strap. "Of course it's safe. I've done this trip dozens of times. Now put this on and get in."

"What is this?" asked Kyle as he turned the yellow pouch over in his hands and investigated it.

"A life jacket of course. In case of a water landing," said Arthur in a nonchalant tone.

"Okay…that's nice…" said Kyle, his voice wavering as he took the pouch. "That's… comforting…"

Arthur Williams had to show Kyle how to fasten the life jacket around his waist. The strap just barely clipped shut when the strap was opened to its maximum length. His stomach bulged over the strap and rested on top of the yellow life jacket pouch. Kyle grabbed onto a small handgrip inside the helicopter as he lifted his right foot onto a long foot rail that ran the length of the helicopter's cabin. Using his upper body, he heaved himself up into the cabin catching himself as he fell forward on the leather seat. As he regained his balance, he pulled himself upright and into the seat. Arthur hopped into the helicopter seat next to him. He helped Kyle put on his seatbelt, taking care to make sure it ran under the life jacket and not over it. Arthur handed him a set of large black headphones equipped with a microphone to put over his ears. Kyle could feel his heart pounding. The back of his shirt was soaked with sweat and was sticking to the leather seat of the helicopter. He nervously wiped his brow and tried to wipe the nervous smile off his face. Kyle jumped as the door of the helicopter was slammed shut by an airport worker. He could feel the helicopter begin to shake as the large metallic blades began to rotate. The helicopter slowly rocked back and forth as the large rotor blades slowly generated enough lift for takeoff.

"Oh, Jesus," Kyle exclaimed as the helicopter began to ascend!

The helicopter began to shake a little as it slowly began to lift off the ground. Kyle watched as the ground rotated beneath them. The helicopter turned 180 degrees as it gained altitude. Arthur seemed to find Kyle's terror amusing. Arthur kept smiling and telling him to calm down throughout the trip in a similar fashion to how you would calm a child about the boogeyman in their closet. Once in the air, the flight was a lot smoother than Kyle thought it would be as they headed out over open water. Kyle's fears began to subside as the land behind them began to disappear slowly. He was startled by the sound of Arthur's voice echoing through the headphones he was wearing. Arthur was speaking into a microphone attached to his headset.

"Now listen, Mr. Bergin, you are about to see things. Classified things that I want to brief you about before we get to Protogonus," said Arthur.

"I get that, the language in those documents you had me sign was very explicit and heavy-handed," said Kyle. "This project is a big company secret."

"No, I don't think you understand. What we are doing on these islands is going to be a bit hard for you to believe," said Arthur. "There are..."

"Okay...listen, buddy, I'm just here to do a job. I've worked for big companies before and dealt with strict compliance laws for multi-million-dollar organizations. I think I can handle this jungle of yours," said Kyle in an exasperated tone. He was tired of all the red tape.

"Alright, suit yourself," said Arthur in a mocking tone.

The rest of the flight was uneventful as the two men sat in silence. An island seemed to appear out of nowhere as a large cloud formation lifted out of view ahead of them. Large rocky pillars jutted out of the sea like turrets of a giant castle. These sloping cliff faces were covered in greenery, and a light fog seemed to roll off them. The tops of the mountains were hidden in the clouds just barely out of view. It reminded Kyle of something out of a story book. He began to amuse himself with thoughts of a castle on top of the mountains resting just above the clouds. He could see waves beating at the base of the mountains as they got closer. That's when the helicopter began to shake violently.

"Turbulence from wind coming over the mountains," the pilot said, echoing in his ear

As the helicopter tossed and shook, Kyle could feel his stomach flopping inside him. He was beginning to regret the large meal he had had a few hours earlier. He felt his stomach sinking into his pelvis with the constant up and down motion of the cabin. He felt pressure begin to build in the back of his neck as he began to hypersalivate. The color began to leave his face, and he began to rapidly search for something to be sick into. Luckily Arthur had noticed Kyle's distress and shoved a small, white paper bag into his hands. Kyle began to vomit violently into the bag as the helicopter continued to jolt up and down while passing over the mountains. This was not the ride that he had expected. Once they had passed through the mountains, the rough air had passed. Kyle still felt horribly nauseous and clutched the bag filled with his lunch tightly in preparation, in case he had to be sick again. The landing pad appeared in front of them. A large concrete circle with a giant red letter H on it emerged through the thick trees. Kyle caught a glimpse of what looked like buildings and giant cages as the helicopter neared its landing site. The helicopter slowly glided down to the ground. Kyle let out a long sigh of relief, puffing his cheeks with anxiety as the skids of the helicopter made contact with the hard ground below.

Once on the ground, a wave of relief washed over him. Kyle was ready to get out of this damn machine and get back onto solid ground. He unbuckled his seat belt with urgency and almost pushed Arthur out of the way to get out of the helicopter. He unclipped his life jacket and threw it aggressively back into the helicopter with an audible grunt. The life jacket bounced off the seat and onto the floor. Arthur calmly took the white bag out of Kyle's hands and handed it to the co-pilot. He apologized profusely for the rough ride and motioned for Kyle to get into a vehicle that was waiting for him about a hundred yards from the helipad. Arthur told Kyle there would be dinner waiting for him in his room if he felt up to it. He instructed Kyle that Sir Barnes requested to meet him before he settles in at the main genetics lab. As Kyle approached the car, he took note of the logo on the side of the car. Archosauria? he thought to himself as he pondered again what it meant. That name was littered throughout the legal documentation that he was forced to sign with no explanation as to what Archosauria was. When he tried to perform an internet search on the term, he had come up with nothing other than some pictures of reptiles and birds. Kyle even tried some channels that were not open to the unsuspecting public. It was as if this project did not exist. Kyle took note of the large egg on the logo. What was this place, he thought to himself. He couldn't help but ponder what kind of venture he had signed up for.

Kyle hopped into the car, the car rocking as he climbed into it. The heat on this island did not seem to be as bad as the airport in Samoa. The overcast nature of the day was preventing him from feeling the brunt of the sun's radiation. The car ride to the worker village was bumpy, but it was nowhere near as rough as the helicopter journey he had just taken. The minor rocking and jostling made those in the car jiggle as the vehicle bounced about. Kyle felt the waves of nausea subside and gradually began to feel more and more normal. He began to feel hungry again, having just lost his lunch. As they rounded a bend in the road, Kyle heard a loud, high pitched bellow. This was not a sound he recognized and sounded very alien in nature. It sounded almost like an animal cry, but what the hell kind of animal was this loud? Kyle wrote it off as probably coming from a machine of some sort as he could hear the sounds of construction equipment in the background. As Kyle wondered what Archosauria was, he felt he had put two and two together as he pondered it. Maybe this was some sort of animal theme park, he thought to himself. It would make sense with the name and logo. Why would they need such secrecy about a theme park with a bunch of animatronic animals? It's not like they were the only park with audio-animatronics that existed. Many others had already beaten them to it. These days there was a damn theme park in every state, Kyle thought. The fact that he was in the middle of nowhere also perplexed him; why would they need to set up a theme park in the middle of the Pacific Ocean? He began to get angry over the thought of being asked to program animatronics for a children's theme park. If this is what he signed up for, he was going to be livid. This was a total waste of his services and talents. There was no way they needed the kind of computing power they were asking for with a project so trivial. The vehicle pulled up and stopped in front of a large building labeled "Main Genetics Lab." Kyle could see what looked like animal cages behind the building in the dense jungle. There was another building adjacent to the genetics lab that obscured his view of the cages behind the lab.

As he got out of the car, he heard the bellow again. It was much louder this time, almost deafening and sounded almost like a high-pitched car horn. Kyle covered his ears as his knees buckled underneath him from the abrasive noise. A sharp ringing echoed in his right ear as he recovered. He searched fruitlessly for the origin of the sound when his eyes caught a glimpse of something moving in one of the cages behind the genetics lab between the buildings. He removed his glasses and cleaned them on his shirt. When he put them on again, he could no longer see the fleeting creature. He wondered what he had just seen. The figure in the shadows of the dense jungle was large and looked like no animal he could recognize. It had come into view only for a split second and was gone just as quickly.

"What was that...that...noise?" asked Kyle, getting a little concerned. "What are you keeping in those cages behind the building?"

"Ha-ha, I tried to tell you. I'm sure Sir Barnes won't mind you getting a sneak peek at our little babies before you meet him. Come with me," said Arthur, walking towards the gap between the two buildings.

"Babies..." Kyle asked under his breath, almost as if questioning himself if he heard correctly.

Arthur disappeared behind the adjacent building. Kyle was annoyed with how light Arthur was on his feet and how quickly he moved. He followed him behind the building and saw that Arthur had come to a stop where the building jutted out at a right angle. The fence continued back behind the building, but the gap between the back wall of the building and the fence was too small to pass through safely. Kyle furrowed his brow as he stared at Mr. Williams. He was confused, frustrated, and nervous about what he had just done to himself. Kyle followed Arthur down the rocky area behind the buildings. He kept staring into the cage as it came closer and closer to where Mr. Williams was standing. He couldn't see anything but trees and shrubs. Signs on the bars of the cage read "Danger, Electric Fence." Kyle was so confused; why would they need electric fencing here? When he got to where Arthur was standing, he saw a small clearing in the brush that Arthur was pointing to. Kyle was paying more attention to the electric fence warning signs than he was to what was in front of them. Arthur began to encourage Kyle to peer into what seemed to be an empty cage.

"Careful, don't get too close to the fences," said Arthur as Kyle leaned forward to get a better look. "You'll get a wicked shock if you touch those wires."

Kyle stared at a small pool of murky water surrounded by trees. The loud bellow sounded again, breaking the silence and startling Kyle. It was deafening! What the hell was that, and why was it so loud? He covered his ears again and stared into the cage. Leaves began to rustle at the edge of the watering hole. Kyle could hear something coming, and it sounded big. A large animal slid out from between the trees and walked towards the water in front of it. The branches lightly caressed the creature's skin as it emerged from the brush. It came to a stop at the edge of the water and lowered its head to take a drink. The sun glistened off the animal's scaly back in a similar fashion to the way light glimmers off a car window in summer. Kyle felt chills run up and down his spine; the hairs on the back of his neck stood on edge. His eyes widened, his pupils dilated like saucer plates, and his mouth gaped open as he stared at the creature in front of him. The animal walked on all fours like a deer or a cow. It's hindlimbs were large and powerful-looking. Its forelimbs were markedly smaller and thinner. On each one of its toes and fingers were blunt-looking brown claws. The animal had a long, stiff, thick tail that trailed behind it. A lengthy, elegant, swan-like neck carried a large head with a large brown crest coming off at the back of its skull. A stripe of bright orange scales ran along its green body down its spine on either side. Instead of a mouth, it had a brown, spade-like bill. This creature was about the size of a horse; it was massive. Four more animals appeared in order to join their friend, walking out of the jungle in a slow, lumbering manner. Loud bellows filled the air as the creatures socialized before continuing to drink. These were the most advanced animatronics Kyle had ever seen. They appeared so life-like. The sides of their chest rose and fell as they appeared to breathe. Eyelids fluttered seamlessly in a blinking motion just like any living animal. Under their skin, he could see their muscles moving pulling on joints for locomotion. Try as he might though, Kyle couldn't find any seams or wires.

"I think there may be a misunderstanding here," said Kyle. "I can't help you with robotics, it's not my field. Especially ones this advanced. These robots are the most advanced I have ever seen or heard of."

"Oh, those aren't animatronics," said Arthur, laughing.

"What...wait..." Kyle said confused and flustered. "Not animatronics... are you trying to tell me..."

"Yes, my friend, those are real living, breathing dinosaurs," said Arthur, putting his hand on Kyle's shoulder from behind.

He returned his gaze to the cage and watched the animals drink from the pool of murky water in their habitat. Kyle watched carefully as they moved around looking for some evidence that he was being lied to. This couldn't be real. He was not a scientist; he knew he didn't know a damn thing about paleontology. This couldn't be possible, there was absolutely no way!

"Mr. Bergin, these are Parasaurolophus," said Arthur. "A dinosaur from the late Cretaceous. I tried to warn you on the helicopter of what you would see here, but you wouldn't let me."

"No, this is impossible...extinct...what?" Kyle said, finding it hard to form sentences. He began to hyperventilate and shake.

"Come, let's not keep Sir Barnes waiting. He hates to wait," said Arthur, motioning for Kyle to follow him as he began to walk back to the genetics lab.

Kyle stood there with his mouth agape. He had heard Arthur saying they needed to leave and saw Arthur walking away, but he couldn't seem to command his legs to move. He was snapped out of his thoughts by the sound of Arthur clapping and urging him to move from his current location. This was not going to be a normal job.

The two men walked down a long white corridor with bamboo trimmings. Fluorescent lighting beamed down on them as they progressed through the building. Kyle was much more comfortable in this airconditioned environment than he was outside. This was much more his style than the beastly hot island jungles. On the walls hung murals of all forms of prehistoric creatures. Kyle stared briefly at pictures of long necked sauropods and spikey-backed stegosaurids. He saw a painting of a Tyrannosaurus and shuddered as he thought about potentially encountering one on this island. They walked by door after door as they proceeded to meet Sir Barnes. Rounding the corner, a large glass office door sat with the words "Main Office" printed on them. Arthur walked a few steps ahead of Kyle, reaching for the handle. He opened the door and held it for Kyle to walk through. The office was large, almost as big as Kyle's apartment back in Worchester. A large, fancy, wooden desk was placed in the center of the room with large glass windows overlooking the enclosures behind it. All sorts of papers and office supplies littered the desk. Large book shelves were placed on either side against the wall. Two fancy, high-backed arm chairs were perched in front the desk. Royal blue cushions adorned the chairs, which appeared more like small thrones than office chairs. Behind the desk sat an old man with a bald head and bright white eyebrows. He was clean shaven, and his white eyebrows stood in contrast to his black suit. He had thin-rimmed black glasses on his face, and in his hand he clutched the side of his desk.

"Welcome, welcome, Mr. Bergin!" exclaimed Ethan. "It is so nice to finally meet you."

"Likewise, Sir Barnes, a pleasure," said Kyle, rushing to shake Ethan's hand so as not to seem rude or unappreciative.

"I'm sure you are wondering why we asked you out here to the middle of nowhere. You see we are in the process of a scientific breakthrough that will shake the world," said Ethan energetically. "What we have done here is going to blow the minds of everyone! But we have run into a bit of a small snag."

"What kind of snag?" asked Kyle. "Where do I come in in all of this? I'm not sure I can help you with this…uh, project you have here."

"Ah, yes, you see we are having issues with our computer systems. Our system is having some issues with data processing. Genome data is very large, you see, and we don't have enough memory for it, even with some of the most advanced equipment money can buy," said Sir Barnes.

"Mr. Sana had mentioned something about data processing, but how… those are dinosaurs out there," Kyle said nervously.

"So you've seen some of the local wildlife already. Good, good. Splendid! Let's get you to your living quarters for the night, and tomorrow we can talk business. You must be exhausted from the journey my lad," said Sir Barnes in the tone of a concerned father.

"Oh…okay…" said Kyle. "I could use a rest. I have so many questions though and…"

"All in due time. Mr. Williams, show our boy to his room and make sure room service takes care of him," said Ethan

Kyle was exhausted, it hadn't really hit him until Ethan had mentioned it. The journey down to the island had been a long and eventful one. Kyle also felt he needed time to process all of this. Arthur nodded at Ethan and motioned for Kyle to follow him out of the office. Arthur once again held the office door open for him as the two men exited the room. Kyle's feet began to hurt as they walked down the long hallway. He wanted nothing more but to lay down at this point. The long hallway seemed to go on for miles. After what seemed like an eternity, once again, they were now standing outside. The clouds had parted, and the sun was beating down on them. Kyle felt like he had just stepped outside into an oven.

"How far is the hotel from here?" asked Kyle impatiently.

"Just a block in that direction. You'll be working out of this building behind us for now, so Sir Barnes wanted you close," said Arthur.

"Okay, I can handle that," said Kyle.

The walk to the hotel complex was short, but the heat made it almost unbearable for Kyle. He could once again feel droplets of sweat rolling down his back as he approached the hotel door. The two men walked through two automatic doors that swung open when Arthur hit a button on a panel on the wall. The doors were not glass but were a thick-looking metal. There were two armed guards standing on either side of the entry. Each man had an automatic rifle in hand. Dozens of pockets and pouches adorned their clothing with all manner of gadgets poking out in various directions. Kyle caught sight of a smaller sidearm weapon against each of their hips.

"Tight security," commented Kyle as they entered the building. He glanced back at the closing metal doors as they walked towards the stairs.

"We have to take precautions in case some of the more unfriendly residents escape their cages," said Arthur. "We take security very seriously here, so don't concern yourself with that."

"Lovely...." remarked Kyle sarcastically, wondering what he had just gotten himself into.

Climbing the two flights of stairs to his room was a chore. Kyle huffed and wheezed as he climbed up to get to his room. He paused at the top of the second flight to catch his breath. Arthur was waiting for him and seemed a little annoyed that Kyle couldn't keep up. Mr. Williams began to walk again and got to the third door to the right of the stairs. He swiped a key card and held the door open while he waited for Kyle to meet him. When Kyle got to the door, Arthur handed him the key card and wished him a good night. Kyle pushed his way into the large room, noticing his luggage positioned in the center.

"All the money you people have and you couldn't afford elevators?" said Kyle in a snarky tone.

"A little exercise never killed anyone," said Arthur, smirking.

"Cute…" said Kyle, annoyed as he pushed past Arthur to get into his room.

The next day, Kyle awoke to the sound of his alarm going off. He had slept better than he had in a very long time. The satin sheets on his bed caressed his skin like silk clouds. He stretched his hands above his head with a loud groan; his toes poking out from under the soft sheets. He put his feet on the hardwood floors. He rocked backwards and slowly shifted out of bed and onto his feet. His first destination was the refrigerator. Kyle pulled a carton of orange juice out the refrigerator and grabbed a large muffin off the counter. He placed the carton down on the counter and peered at his breakfast. He un-pealed the muffin with expertise as he took a large bite. Crumbs fell from his mouth, rolling down his shirt, hitting the floor. All of the food here was excellent, he thought to himself as he began to look for a glass. He relished in his breakfast and slowly got dressed to go to his first day of work. Kyle began to button his collared shirt as he stared at the clock on the wall. It was 9:05 A.M., he had time.

Dr. Bai was waiting impatiently in the computer room of the main genetics' lab. He paced like a caged animal, getting visibly more and more frustrated as time ticked by. He stared at his watch often as he waited. This new IT expert was supposed to be here at 9 A.M., it was now 10:45! Where was he, Dr. Bai thought, how dare he do this on the first day? The doors to the computer room opened with a whoosh, causing Dr. Bai's head to pivot sharply to see who had just entered. He was filled with disgust as he watched Kyle enter over an hour and forty-five minutes late. This was unacceptable! Jin Moon wanted to get back on track, and this inconsiderate oaf was holding him up.

"You're extremely late," said Jin in an audibly irate tone.

"Yea, whatever. I'm on island time, man. Where is the main server?" asked Kyle, unbothered by Jin's visible disdain.

"If you are going to do this job, Mr. Bergin, you are going to be expected to be on time," barked Dr. Bai.

"And who are you? You didn't hire me, so if you want me to fix your little computers, I suggest you back off," said Kyle with a smile on his face. He knew he was untouchable and held all the cards in this situation.

Jin Moon puffed his cheeks and forcibly expelled air from his nostrils. As mad as he was, he knew that he needed this man to get him back on track. His hands were tied, and there was nothing Jin hated more than not being in control.

"My name is Dr. Jin Moon Bai; I am the chief geneticist here, and you had better watch your tone with me," said Jin.

"That's nice, back to your lab you go, and let daddy do his job, will you, junior," laughed Kyle.

"You...I..." Jin said. He had never been brushed off in such a disrespectful tone. Jin Moon was used to being worshiped by those around him. Being treated like he didn't matter was not something he had ever experienced before.

"Either leave me to work or figure it out yourself. And get me a coffee while you're at it, will you, junior," said Kyle. "I'll handle this little job and have you making more creatures in no time."

Jin Moon's face was bright red, the vein in his forehead was pulsing in an almost cartoonish manor. The urge to punch this disrespectful man was overwhelming. His work was more important than getting vengeance for this disrespect. Jin slowly regained his composure and stormed off. He couldn't stand being in the presence of this disrespectful toad in front of him. He raced down the hall to retreat to his lab.

Kyle sat for a second with a smirk on his face. He got a sadistic pleasure from pissing people off and winning arguments such as this. Kyle knew men like Jin couldn't stand not being in control. They hated not having all the cards in their hands. He walked through the maze of server towers. A myriad of blue and red flashing lights surrounded him as he searched for a place to connect and set up his laptop. When he found the appropriate tower, he put his bag down on the floor and pulled out a large, bulky laptop. Kyle connected his laptop to the computer tower and began furiously typing as he sat on the floor with the laptop resting on his thighs. This code was very simple, as if it was written by a child. It was no wonder they couldn't progress anything further than they already had. He began working immediately on reprograming the systems of Archosauria to fix these inadequacies.

Chapter 9

Jin Moon hated Kyle with a passion for his blatant disrespect and failure to recognize his genius. He had to give the man credit though, even though it killed him to do so. He did not like Kyle personally, but he had to respect his work. Jin Moon admired how efficient this Mr. Bergin was, despite his appearance and slovenly manner. He had to respect a man good at his craft. Kyle spent all number of hours working on the computer systems of Protogonus; a process that would need to replicated on Dionysus when the big move happened. Kyle sat in the main genetics lab where he had carved out a station for himself. His desk was similar in appearance to his apartment, candy bar wrappers and empty bags of potato chips littered his desk and the surrounding floor. A trash can sat next to his chair and was overflowing with various leftovers from past meals. Garbage piled onto the floor below. Kyle sat there day in and day out furiously typing, pausing only to move and click the mouse. The opportunities here did not escape him. With writing their code, Kyle was free to write in whatever access level he deemed fit for himself. This was something Kyle did commonly. If he was in control, he could make his employers dependent on his services by creating back doors into the servers that only he could access. He went to work setting up his own VPN with private access as he re-wrote the code for the compound's security.

"Are you almost finished; it's been days since I have been able to make any sort of progress," whined Dr. Bai.

"Do you think what I'm doing here is easy? Because if you do, then feel free to have at it, junior," said Kyle with a large grin on his face. He really enjoyed annoying Jin Moon more than anything else.

"Stop calling me that," shouted Jin, clenching his fists and stomping his right foot on the floor.

"Absolutely, junior, so sorry," said Kyle, laughing slightly to himself. Being untouchable was such a good feeling.

The men were interrupted by Sir Barnes and Arthur entering the room. The two men immediately approached Kyle at his work station.

"Ah, Sir Barnes, nice to see you," said Kyle in a jovial tone. "I'm glad you came now. You are back online in three...two...one...."

Ethan could see a green progress bar completing on Kyle's screen. The screen went black, and an R.N.A. logo appeared on the monitor. Ethan heard a whooshing noise coming from the severs behind him as they all went black and then subsequently rebooted in unison. The computer screen in front of Kyle returned to its normal view with small icons lined up neatly to the left-hand side of the screen. The Archosauria logo was visible as the desktop background.

"So... that's it?" questioned Jin and Arthur simultaneously. The two men shot each other a look briefly.

"Your entire genetic library has been rerouted to several shared cloud servers that I created specifically for you. They are quadruple encrypted and firewalled to protect from hackers. This leaves all your servers open for processing instead of storage," said Kyle.

"Come again? What is a cloud? I'm confused," questioned Ethan.

"Long story short, your computer issues are solved. I even recovered that last genome that you were working on before the crashes started. So you should be able to pick up right where you left off, junior," said Kyle as he winked at Jin.

"My word, this is astounding," said Ethan. "Great work, my boy!"

"I aim to please," said Kyle, picking up a stress ball and squeezing it in his right hand over and over again.

Jin Moon just scoffed at Kyle through a scowl. He did not want to give him any sort of credit but was impressed at how expertly he managed to handle things. It made Jin angry to have to admit that he was happy Kyle had arrived on Protogonus.

One person was not happy about Kyle's arrival on this island paradise. Selena sat in her office at her desk with her legs crossed in front of her. She stared at her computer screen as she scrutinized the code. Selena never trusted Kyle. There were more than a few jobs that they had worked on where things would mysteriously go wrong. Unsurprisingly Kyle seemed to be the only person to know how to address the issue. She was never able to prove it, but she swore he had caused the same issues he fixed. Selena was determined to catch him in the act this time. She noted that Kyle had set up a private VPN. As she tried to access it, she noted that her access was promptly denied. Selena flagged the VPN and changes that Kyle had made. She was going to follow him very closely over the next few months.

There was not much time to get things in order for Dionysus to be ready for its 1993 opening date. September of 1991 had rolled around, and they were behind the eight ball. There was no star attraction to be had. Ethan could not open Archosauria without a large therapod. People didn't come to the zoo to see the foxes and jackals, they came to see the lions, tigers, and bears. It was do or die for Sir Barnes, as any further delay in opening Archosauria was going to have catastrophic effects on his future. He was running low on finances as he was way over deadline, and his investor's funds were running low. Ethan's fossil dig teams had been searching diligently for all sorts of new genetic material. R.N.A. had men at many fossil dig sites around the world stealing small bone fragments for the company's genetic library. They were using a mix of their own legitimate dig sites and poached fossil fragments to build their library. Stealing material was much more efficient than finding and excavating it on their own.

Dr. Bai immediately pushed his team back into overdrive. They very hurriedly picked up where they had left off. Within a few days, there were new embryos incubating under his heat lamps. Jin stared at a clutch of seven eggs being turned tirelessly by the robotic nursemaid of the incubator with pride. He still did not like the fact that he could not accurately determine what species he was hatching when he had sequenced a new genome. His CT scanner was about two months out from arriving on Protogonus. This machine would allow him to peer into the egg with x-ray radiation and reconstruct a picture of what was developing inside of it. As they began to produce new species, knowing what to expect was becoming a clear necessity, so that proper enclosures could be designed and the proper precautions could be taken. This new batch should be close to hatching, and he was highly suspicious that something good was about to come of this egg group. The genetic material had come from Montana's Hell Creek formation. It was the strand he had been sequencing just prior to Kyle Bergin's arrival on Protogonus.

Dr. Bai had invited Ethan and Dr. Bramme, their paleontologist, down to the hatchery to witness this new group hatch. Jin Moon watched the eggs intently; the glow of the UV lamps lit his face in a similar fashion to the mad scientists of a science fiction movie. His vigilance and guess work paid off as a small crack appeared across one of the seven shells. The egg began to rock lightly back and forth as the infant began to hatch. Quiet chirping squeaks could be heard echoing from the glass covered incubator.

"Sir Barnes, come quick," Jin screamed across the lab. "They are hatching finally."

Sir Barnes and Dr. Bramme rushed to the incubator as quickly as they could. The two had been discussing what roster of dinosaurs Dionysus would open with in the coming year. Ethan insisted on being present for as many of the births as he could, especially when it was a new species. He liked having Dr. Bramme around during the hatchings, so that he could properly identify what they had brought back from extinction. The men stared intently at the egg rocking slowly back and forth. Their faces were all illuminated by the thermal and UV lights of the incubator. Ethan had a slight glare coming off of his glasses and very slightly shifted his position. A small piece of shell cracked off and rolled onto the nesting material below. A viscous yellow liquid oozed from the egg as it hatched, dripping down the side of the shell slowly like a bead of opaque honey. A small, two-clawed hand emerged from the hole in the egg and gripped at the side of the shell. The infant's claws made a soft scratching sound as it curled and uncurled its fingers against the shell. Dr. Bramme could feel shudders running up and down his spine. Richard shook slightly as he watched in earnest. He had a feeling he knew what prehistoric creature this was right away; this was the apex predator they were hoping for. The infant used its clawed fingers to pull another piece of the ivory shell away. It withdrew its small hand and pushed its snout towards the opening in the shell. A small egg tooth became visible as the baby began to bite at the shell. Cracking and squeaking noises filled the room as the men watched the creature hatch. It tore ferociously at the shell with its teeth, biting off small fragments and widening the hole in the shell little by little. A large, three-clawed foot pushed its way through the center of the egg, collapsing the shell from the middle. The top and bottom sections of the shell slowly fell away. The infant stood on two powerful legs as it shook the reminder of its shell from it's terrifying yet small body. The infant was covered in a what appeared to be fluff. The strands of fluff were matted together against the infant's skin as she stood there trying to dry herself off. As she shook off the shell fragments, the baby stumbled forward and landed on its face. It grunted and positioned its laughably small arms under its torso. The right hindleg came forward next to the small arms and pushed the infant up as it placed its strong left leg underneath it as well. The infant let out an almost cute squeak-like roar, revealing a row of sharp, glistening, peg-like teeth. This baby was going to be the queen of the island.

"What is it, Richard?" asked Ethan. "It's obviously a predator of some sort."

"Ty...Tyrannosaurus Rex," exclaimed Dr. Bramme. Tears filled his eyes as he glanced at the previous ruler of planet Earth reborn in front of him. Richard had never imagined that he would see his childhood favorite dinosaur hatch before his eyes. He was surprised to see it covered in fluff as an infant similar to a chicken.

"Jin, my lad, you did it. You actually did it!" exclaimed Sir Barnes. "This is just grand!"

"Well, of course. There was no doubt it would only be a matter of time for us to succeed here," said Jin.

The remainder of the eggs slowly began to hatch. They were going to make a fortune off of these marvelous creatures. Dr. Bramme stared at the young Tyrannosaurus clutch as they began to try to learn how to walk. The infants clumsily stumbled about like a bunch of drunk sailors. As they dried off, the fluff covering their bodies began to puff outwards. Despite knowing what they would turn into, the men couldn't help but find them cute. One of the young Rexes walked towards the glass incubator and stopped to face Richard. It waddled rather awkwardly and in a very non-threatening manner. The baby turned its head slightly to the left side, paused for a second, and then tilted her head to the opposite side. She was looking right at them. The baby suddenly lunged at the glass head first, hitting it with a loud thud. She fell backwards following the impact and shook her head. Dazed the infant slowly got back to its feet. Richard marveled at how beautiful they were.

"Someone get Harmon, we need to inoculate and feed them at once," exclaimed Sir Barnes.

"Right away," said Ernie Sung from somewhere at the back of the room. He had been sitting quietly at his station almost as if he was awaiting orders from someone.

For Scott this was just another day in the park; his routine was very similar from day to day. Even though there were no major disturbances to his routine, he did not find himself bored like he was back in San Diego. He had just placed food into the Compsognathus enclosure and was patiently waiting for the small animals to approach, so he could do a quick visual exam. The usual jungle noises were interrupted by the soft chirping and squeaks of the approaching dinosaurs. Several small, feathered dinosaurs emerged from the brush with playful hopping. The Compys quickly descended on their meal and began to pounce on the chicken carcasses that Dr. Harmon had left them. These dinosaurs were small, a little larger than the chicken carcasses they were feasting on. They stood on two strong legs and had a long, stiff feathered tail that trailed behind them. Their necks and heads were devoid of feathering, unlike the rest of their bodies. As they scurried about, it was almost hard to tell them apart from the chickens they were eating. Dr. Harmon watched as they ate, using their swan-like neck to tear at their feast. With one foot on the carcass, one of the small dinosaurs lowered its head and grabbed a chunk of flesh from the bird's thigh. Using its long neck, the small Compy began to jerk its head to the side. The chicken's skin began to tear, pulling a large chunk of feathers with it. The Compys had learned to defeather their prey fairly effectively by ripping off the skin just prior to devouring the flesh. Scott glanced at another carcass to his right. Two Compys had opened up the abdomen of the bird and were playing tug-of-war with a segment of bowel. They grunted and squeaked as they fought over the meat. The bowel segment tore and both animals staggered backwards a step. They quickly jerked their necks backward to throw the morsel down their gullets before returning to the carcass for more. Dr. Harmon watched the pride of twenty-five animals share the ten-chicken meal. They ate in a similar manner to the much larger Herrerasaurus, using their necks to toss back food quickly before returning for another bite.

According to Dr. Bramme, these animals were scavengers. That is why Scott had chosen to feed them in this manner instead of giving them live prey like their larger cousins. Dr. Harmon took notes in his journal about the behavior of the animals as they ate. Scott was snapped out of his train of thought by the sound of an approaching car. He gazed down the road that lead to the worker village to try to find where the sound was coming from. A vehicle became visible in the distance and appeared to be approaching at quite a considerable speed. What was the big rush, did something happen, he thought to himself. Scott got to his feet quickly and thought about waking Nalani. Ultimately he decided to wait to see what they wanted as she could be grouchy when woken from her slumber. The car came to a screeching halt just behind his pick-up, stirring up a cloud of dust and small pebbles as it stopped. Dr. Sung got out from the driver seat in a hurried manner, jumping to the floor and speed-walking to Scott.

"Dr. Harmon, we have a new species at the genetics lab. Sir Barnes requires your presence urgently," said Ernie.

"Alright, let me pack up and I'll head back," said Scott. "Is everything okay?"

"Yes, fine. It's fine. Sir Barnes just wanted your help with the inoculations. Dr. Bai was very explicit that you come quickly," squeaked Ernie.

"This guy...alright," sighed Scott. "I'm coming."

Scott packed his journal into a beat-up brown backpack. He beat some dust off of the bag before slinging it over his shoulder. He hopped into the truck, causing the vehicle to shift from side to side, waking up a sleeping Nalani in the process. She grunted and picked her hat up off of her face to put it back on top of her head. Scott put his hand on the passenger side seat and turned around to get a clear view as he turned the truck. The tires crackled as they rolled over rocks and twigs. Scott was not in a rush to get back to headquarters. This was the second new dinosaur species that Dr. Bai had brought back since being back online. Dealing with dinosaurs was beginning to feel normal to him at this point.

"How was your journal club with the little chickens?" asked Nalani in a joking tone.

"Fine. Dr. Bai requests my presence in the lab," said Dr. Harmon in a mocking tone.

"Ha! Better you than me. Drop me at the dorms on your way back, will you. I have no desire to see that weasel," said Nalani.

"Sure thing," said Scott.

Scott walked into the genetics lab alone. He had dropped Nalani off at the living quarters as she had requested, having no interest in neonatal care or in seeing Jin Moon more than she had to. Dr. Harmon had walked down these halls hundreds of times by now. His body was on auto-pilot as he headed to the incubation chambers on sheer muscle memory. He was thinking about what he was going to have for lunch and began to plan when he would do his evening run around the compound. Scott had been meaning to call his girls, but he had been so preoccupied lately. He made a mental note to call them at some point this week. Scott stepped through the doors of the hatchery and immediately reached for the boot covers. When he sat down to put them on, he realized how dirty his boots were from being outside all day. Scott pulled his boots off of his feet and put the shoe covers over his socks. He donned a surgical cap and goggles. This process annoyed him, but it was necessary to protect the infants from the world outside until their immune systems were up to par. Scott approached the incubators with a mild sense of urgency. He wanted to see what Jin and the gang were fussing over. Scott could see small infants wandering around the incubator as he approached.

"Good morning, Dr. Harmon," Ethan said with a huge grin on his face. "Come meet your new patients."

"Morning, Ethan," said Scott. "What do you got for me?"

"Dr. Harmon...meet our new Tyrannosaurus Rex," said Dr. Bramme. Excitement radiated from his body. Scott had never seen Richard so animated about a new species.

"Nice shoes, doctor," said Jin, motioning to Dr. Harmon's boot covers being placed on bare socks.

"Well, it was that or I track dirt into your 'sterile' lab from the paddocks, Jin," said Scott quickly. Like everyone else on Protogonus, he had had it with Jin Moon and his attitude.

Scott peered down through the glass incubators at the infants below. Each one was about the size of a large Yorkshire Terrier. The infants were investigating the egg shells. They were sniffing them and pushing the fragments around the incubator with their snouts. They looked hungry, thought Scott.

"Richard, would you mind getting me five rats from the food storage unit?" asked Scott.

"Sure thing. I'll grab the vaccines and supplements, too?" said Dr. Bramme in a questioning tone.

"Yes, please," said Scott.

Dr. Harmon observed the infant Tyrannosaurs as they bumbled around the incubator. They were uncoordinated and awkward as they moved about on their two powerful hindlegs. Many infant animals were born without grace; it was only as they aged did fine motor control develop. Dr. Bramme returned with the rat carcasses as requested on a tray. There were seven syringes bundled together on the tray. Each syringe contained a pink liquid vaccine. Dr. Bai was rummaging through a cabinet in the background as Scott took the tray from Richard. He placed the tray down on a small platform on the rim of the incubator. Scott grabbed the first rat and began to pull it apart with his hands. Dr. Harmon took care to make sure that the carcass was torn into small pieces.

"What are you doing, doctor?" asked Ethan in a concerned manner.

"Many predatory birds will kill their prey and eat it before heading back to their nests. By pre-digesting the meal, they make it easier for the infants to eat. When they return to the nest, they regurgitate the food for their offspring," said Scott. "I'm making things easier for them."

"I see; that makes sense. There is a lot of debate over what nursing care dinosaurs gave to their offspring. Some think they just laid their eggs and left the babies to fend for themselves," said Dr. Bramme.

"Based on how awkward these infants are, I highly doubt any mother would leave them to fend for themselves," said Scott.

"So you're saying we may have just proven that dinosaurs cared for their infants," said Dr. Bramme, glowing. "I need to write this up! You're right, these infants would easily be picked off by predators."

"Here is the faux mother," said Dr. Bai, handing Scott a plastic Tyrannosaurus Rex puppet.

Scott put a slab of rat carcass into the mouth of the puppet, clenching his hand tightly inside of it to hold onto the slab of meat. Jin opened the incubator, catching the attention of the infants. They began sniffing the air; clearly they had caught the scent of a meal now that the incubator was no longer closed. To the surprise of everyone, the babies lined up and began to chirp and fuss.

Their mouths gaped open, and they began to bounce slightly while sitting back on their haunches. This looked like any other bird nest filled with chicks to Scott. The babies were begging him for food in a similar fashion to modern baby birds. He approached the first Tyrannosaur chick with the puppet. The infant quickly lunged forward to grab the meat from the jaws of the plastic mother. It then ran off to the back of the nest to eat it. He reloaded the plastic jaws with another bit of flesh and again approached the next infant. Before he could present it to the infant he had chosen, a different baby had jumped in. She pushed her sibling out of the way to grab the lump of meat and then ran off with it to devour her prize.

"We are gonna need more rats, ha-ha," laughed Dr. Bramme. "I'll get another couple."

"I'll get them, my boy," said Ethan, interrupting and putting his hand on Richard's shoulder. "You stay and help Scott."

After the infants had eaten, Dr. Bramme and Dr. Sung put on thick leather gloves with metal plating over the fingers and wrists. It was vaccination time. One of the lab hands almost lost a finger vaccinating the infant Herrerasaurus many months ago. They had learned from their mistakes this time. Dr. Bramme grabbed the first baby Tyrannosaur quickly as he could around it's hips. The infant began to scream and turned quickly to snap at Dr. Bramme's hands. Its teeth clanged on the metal plating of the gloves. Dr. Bramme winced, although the teeth were not piercing the gloves, the pressure of her bite still hurt. Even with the metal plating, the pressure was immense. The baby repeatedly bit the same place over and over as it tried to free itself. It's teeth repeatedly snapped and clanked on the metal plating of the glove. The infant growled and snarled as she bit at Dr. Bramme's hands. Dr. Harmon uncapped the syringe and quickly jabbed the needle into the muscle of the baby's thigh. It let out a squeal and tried to snap at Scott. Before it had a chance to turn on Scott, Dr. Sung had intervened. Ernie grabbed the infant by the neck and did the best he could to restrain it. She pushed at this hand with her small arms to try to pull her neck away from Ernie. The two men struggled against the small Tyrannosaur as it writhed in their grasp, trying to free itself. Scott pushed the plunger down and removed the needle quickly after injecting the content into the infant's right thigh.

"All done...just six more to go..." said Scott, breathing heavily. The men had a quick laugh over the ordeal.

Dr. Bramme carried the infant away towards a holding pen at the back of the lab. All infants were kept in these pens isolated from the outside world until they were at least eight-weeks-old. By that time, their vaccination protocols were complete, and they could be moved to the jungles of Protogonus. Dr. Bramme walked towards the pen while Dr. Bai held the door open for him. He walked along a catwalk to a small metal box at the end. He quickly shut the infant into the box and lowered her some six feet down to the pen below. After pressing a button on a small console in front him, the holding box clicked open. The baby Tyrannosaur ran out into the forest of the pen as quickly as her legs could carry her. Dr. Bramme pressed a second button to raise the holding cage back to his level. He then returned to help with the remaining six infants. After the last infant was in the holding pen, the men gathered on the catwalk to observe their new chicks. All were panting slightly, exhausted from the effort of wrangling the infant Tyrannosaurs.

"My God, if they are this strong at day one, what are they going to be like when they are full grown?" asked Dr. Bramme.

"I don't even want to think about it," said Dr. Harmon. "Are you sure we are ready for something like this?"

"Of course we are," said Dr. Bai without a moment's hesitation. "Have some faith in my design, Dr. Harmon."

"Don't worry, Scott, Nalani has already begun overseeing the construction of a suitable enclosure for our star attractions," said Ethan.

Dr. Harmon let out a sigh and turned his attention to the pen in front of them. Two of the Tyrannosaur infants were rolling around on the floor scuffling with each other. He had a feeling that this was going to be more dangerous than they had anticipated. Scott shuddered at the idea of having to do any sort of veterinary work on an eighteen-foot-tall, forty-foot-long T-Rex. It didn't seem to him that anyone else was even a little bit concerned for what the future could hold for them as they tried to take control over one of the planet's most notorious predators.

Eight weeks went by faster than anyone had anticipated. It was time to tranquilize and relocate the Tyrannosaur infants to their permanent home. The babies had grown faster than anyone had anticipated, quickly making their indoor enclosure appear overcrowded. The infants stood between three to four-foot-tall and ranged from 250 to 320 pounds. At eight weeks, the largest infant was already almost as large as the full-grown Herrerasaurus. As they grew, they had begun to lose the majority of the feathering they once had. Feathers still remained around their necks, down their spine, and over their arms. In order to be handled, they all had to be tranquilized at once. Dr. Harmon felt they were far too dangerous to approach on foot due to their size and strength at this stage in the game. Nalani had gotten a team together of two of her best snipers. Each man carried a long-range tranquilizer rifle by their side. Ethan had the indoor enclosure rooms purposely built with outdoor access at the back, so that the animals could be safely darted and transported. A cargo door large enough for a forklift to enter was at the back of the pen, so that the animals could be moved from the enclosure to their next destination. Seven specialized pick-up trucks waited to receive their own animal. Large metal cages protruded from the back of the vehicles where a pick-up bed would have been. Nalani had requested that the cages be built into the frame of the cars for added strength. Nalani and her men climbed a set of metal stairs behind the indoor enclosure to access a small catwalk attached to the back of the genetics building. The men lined up in front of small windows placed at eye level. These windows connected with a small slit in the wall of the enclosure that angled downwards to allow for them to take clear shots at the animals inside without having to lean into the room below.

Dr. Harmon was ready with several rabbit carcasses to distract the young Rexes with. He stood in the main genetics' lab facing the Rex enclosure. The dinosaurs were already making their way to him. They had very keen sense of smell and knew there was food close by as soon as Dr. Harmon opened the door. The baby Tyrannosaurs began to get excited and roared eagerly as they prepared to be fed. The plan was to distract the hungry predators with food to pull them to the front of the enclosure while Nalani and her team tranquilized them from the rear. Scott waited for her signal to drop the rabbits.

"Scott, Scott….this is Nalani, over," echoed a walkie talkie in Scott's right hand.

"Roger that, this is Scott."

"Go in three…two…one," said Nalani.

Scott lobbed the first rabbit over the railing. It hit the ground with a sickening plop. One of the Rexes rushed forward and snapped the rabbit in its large, powerful jaws. It jerked its head forward and back to throw the rabbit carcass down it's gullet whole. Dr. Harmon reached into the bucket, his hand covered in fur and blood. He grabbed another rabbit by the back leg and lobbed it over the railing. A blood trail followed the carcass, staining the floor below in a linear splatter pattern.

WOOSH!

A dart flew through the air and hit one of the infants as it ate in its right thigh. The animal's leg muscles twitched on the impact with the dart, and the rabbit dropped from its jaws. The Tyrannosaur immediately raised its head in a roar and lifted its right foot off the ground. It placed the foot down and stared at its flank. The Rex looked back at its kill and stared at it as if staring into space. Scott could see that its eyes looked to be glazing over.

WOOSH! WOOSH! WOOSH!

More darts in the air and more impacts. The first infant began to stumble as she tried to make her way into the trees of the enclosure. She took a step forward and froze. Her left leg began to slide outwards, and her head dropped. She then fell forward with a loud thud, causing some leaf litter to be thrown into the air from the impact of her body hitting the Earth. Slowly all of the infants began to hit the ground one after the other. The mission was a success. Reginald hit a large red button on the wall of the enclosure. A sign under the button read, "Danger: Live Animals Inside." Red warning lights began to flash as the cargo door slid open, the sound of metal clanking as the door lifted echoed through the jungle. Stephen motioned for several armed guards to raise their weapons.

"Be ready, men, just in case they aren't out fully," said Nalani over the railing of the catwalk as she headed to the stairs.

Once the gate had lifted, dozens of men rushed into the enclosure with metal stretchers. Two forklifts followed them inside as they headed toward the infants. Leaf litter and twigs snapped and crackled under the weight of the forklifts. A group of ten men gathered around the first infant, placing the metal stretcher adjacent to her.

"Be sure to get those muzzles on first before you touch them," shouted Dr. Harmon as he climbed into the enclosure to help.

One of the workers grabbed the large head of the infant Tyrannosaur, lifting it off the ground with a loud grunt. The other two slid a leather and steel basket muzzle over the creature's snout. Her eyes were rolled into the back of her head, and a thick strand of ropey saliva filled with twigs and leaves hung from her jowls. Soft grunts came from the creature as they fastened the muzzle behind her head. Once the muzzle was taught, the rest of the men rushed in. Three men grabbed her long tail, two men grabbed each of her strong legs, another two lined up along her back while the first two men held her head.

"Ready....LIFT!" said Dr. Harmon.

Scott watched as the 300-pound animal left the ground. He directed the men backward to the stretcher, motioning with his hands for them to keep backing up.

"Okay...and down," said Dr. Harmon. "Easy does it, lower."

The infant was placed down on the stretcher with a soft clunk as the metal buckled under her weight. As the men moved away, Scott began to motion to the forklift to move in. The forklift maneuvered itself, so it was perpendicular to the stretcher. The long forklift blades slid into pre-made slots on the metal stretcher. As the forklift pulled into place, Scott placed his hand on the chest of the infant to make sure she was breathing normally. He quickly placed his hand on the inside of her left leg to feel her pulses.

"Everything alright?" asked Reginald.

"Yes, just making sure," said Scott. It was Scott's job to make sure that these infants lived through this journey. He wasn't entirely sure how much Etorphine to give them as he had not studied their metabolism quite yet. Etorphine is a potent wildlife tranquilizer often used to sedate large animals.

"Alright, lift her and let's go," called Reginald to the forklift operator.

The forklift creaked and shook as it lifted the animal off the ground. When she was about at waist height, men rushed in to place large leather straps over her to secure her to the stretcher for transport to the truck. Scott and Reginald followed alongside the forklift as it headed to the pick-up trucks. Scott wondered if he had given the animals enough Etorphine to get them to their new enclosures. The worst thing that could happen right now would be seven awake, angry Tyrannosaur infants thrashing about the trucks. He had given seven of the team darts with the reversal agent, a chemical called Naloxone, to reverse the effects of the sedative if the animals seemed that they were getting dangerously sedate. Dr. Harmon wondered if they would even need it. Things were going smoothly, but he couldn't stop himself from thinking about the worst-case scenarios here. The first forklift reached the truck and lifted the infant into the cage. The forklift reversed, sliding the long blades out of from the stretcher and leaving it behind in the pick-up with the infant. Reginald jumped into the pick-up bed and attached the stretcher to the bed of the truck with metal clamps. They didn't want the baby moving much in transit to her new home.

Dr. Harmon oversaw the process with the remaining infants. The last two were currently being loaded into their respective trucks. Scott and Reginald began going from truck to truck to do one final check.

"We good, man?" asked Nalani, shouting at Reginald as Scott felt the pulses of one of the infants.

"Yeah, let's roll," shouted Scott back to her.

Dr. Harmon climbed over the sleeping infant and hopped out of the pick-up bed to the ground below. He landed with a loud crunch, stirring up dust as he hit the ground. The sound of closing doors began to echo through the air as they secured the cages. Scott hopped into the driver seat of one of the trucks. He waived to Reginald as he drove his truck away. The infants were to be held separately in pairs, all except for the largest one, which they referred to as Titan. The animals were all reportedly female, but Titan seemed like a fitting name for the largest of the infants. Dr. Harmon and Dr. Bramme figured they would likely begin to fight amongst themselves as they grew, so separating them seemed to make sense. The one they called Titan was the largest and most aggressive of the hatchlings, so it was decided to keep her separate from the others. Dr. Harmon had volunteered to be the one to offload Titan personally to her new home. He turned his engine over and took off for the paddocks. He kept looking back at the pick-up bed to make sure everything was okay. Scott had two men in the cabin with him and four more men hanging onto the sides of the cage, riding alongside of the car like men hanging on a sanitation truck. Forklifts were waiting at the enclosures to help with unloading the infants, but they would still need the man-power to unload her in case something went wrong. Scott saw the man next to him shaking, clutching his tranquilizer rifle like his life depended on it. The infant Tyrannosaur was small compared to how big she was going to get, but that did not mean that she couldn't be deadly.

Scott pulled up to the electric fencing of Titan's new paddock. Nalani had the paddocks designed with thick electrified metal bars instead of the electrified metal wires that kept the other animals in. This enclosure was on the outskirts of the camp overlooking a small cliff. Scott could see the scaffolding of the aviary being built from this point. The aviary was being built into the side of the cliff, overlooking a large river. Large curved metal beams jutted into the air, reaching towards the top of the cliff face. Scott could see sparks flying off the aviary support beams as men welded the enclosure together. The thought was that when they did bring back Pteranodons, they could eat the fish already living in the streams. This would cut down food costs and give the animals a more natural life-style. The metal doors of the new T-Rex enclosure swung open and Scott drove through, followed by the forklift. They drove through a small, narrow jungle path. Leaves and branches beat against the sides of the truck, as well as against the men clinging to it. Scott could hear them cursing as they swatted away at oncoming branches. He soon arrived at a clearing and slowly came to a stop in the middle of the field. He put the car in park and hopped out, leaving the car running with keys in the ignition.

"Alright, men, let's do this quick. Just like we practiced. No one gets hurt here today," said Scott.

The men jumped off the side of the truck and one of them unlatched the door of the cage. The cage swung open with a loud metallic creak. Dr. Harmon jumped up into the pick-up bed to check on the infant and make sure she was still asleep. He could hear the animal breathing in an almost rhythmic manner. The sounds of her breath seemed to echo in the dark cage of the truck's pick-up bed. Scott climbed over her limp body. She suddenly kicked one of her back legs out multiple times, startling him. She was dreaming, he thought to himself. Scott unclasped the stretcher from the truck bed and called out to the forklift to wheel in. He watched as the forklift slid the long metal blades under the stretcher. Scott signaled to the operator to lift the infant and then signaled again to tell him that she was in position.

The driver expertly backed the infant out of the pick-up without any issues. The tip of her long tail bent slightly against the side of the pick-up as she was taken from the back of the vehicle. He made a short turn and headed to a flat, open patch of grass to lay her down. The men stood, anxiously awaiting the creature to hit the ground. Emanuel, who had been sitting next to Scott in the truck cabin, held the tranquilizer gun on the infant. He was ready to dose her again with another hit of Etorphine should she awaken prematurely.

118

Scott worried a little bit about whether Emanuel would actually be able to hit the infant since he was shaking so much. Scott felt it looked as if Emanuel would more likely run if the infant began to show any signs of arousal.

"Easy, my friend, va a estar bien,[8]" said Scott, placing his hand on Emanuel's shoulder to reassure him.

Once the infant was on the ground, Dr. Harmon began to remove the muzzle. One of the workers held her head up as Scott slid the muzzle off of her snout. They lowered her head back down very slowly. Scott grabbed a thick brown towel from another worker and placed it over the creature's eyes. He proceeded to lay on her head to keep the towel on and to make sure she couldn't snap at anyone if she woke up. The other workers began to remove the leather straps to release the creature from the metal stretcher below her. Once she was free from the straps, the men gathered around her body to lift her off the stretcher and place her onto the grass. Harmon could feel the muscles of her face begin to twitch under his hands. They were not going to have much more time to get this done.

As they placed the creature on the grass, the forklift operator picked up the stretcher and began to head out of the enclosure. The operator was visibly nervous, as the forklift was relatively slow. If the Rex awoke too soon, she could very easily run down the slow-moving vehicle. The men all proceeded to jump onto the body of the Rex to hold her down. She began to slowly become aroused and wiggle underneath them. Emanuel raised the rifle to his face and pointed it at the back of the young Tyrannosaur. Scott slowly reached into his pocket to pull out a syringe with a clear liquid in it. He slowly uncapped the syringe, using his teeth to reveal the sharp, large gauge needle. The needle had to be thick in order to pierce the Tyrannosaur's scaly hide and not bend. Scott waited for the forklift to be out of sight; he was trying to give the operator enough of a head start to get out safely before he gave the infant the reversal agent.

"Everyone ready?" asked Scott in an almost whisper-like tone.

The men silently nodded and stared at Scott for the signal to get up and run. The sound of rapid breathing filled the air. All of the men were very visibly tense. Scott had warned them that the Naloxone could either take some time to reverse the creature or could cause her to snap up almost instantly. If

---

[8] It's going to be okay

the latter happened, they would not have much time to get to the truck and escape. The hope was that the second scenario would not take place, and she would be too dopey to give enough of a chase. Scott could hear hard swallows and saw that a good number of the men were shaking. He raised his right hand into the air with the syringe in tow. His hand fell quickly, hitting the Rex in her shoulder with the needle. The muscle twitched slightly as he injected the contents into her bloodstream. Dr. Harmon pulled the needle out of her skin and jumped to his feet, leaving the towel over the animal's eyes.

The men all simultaneously rose to their feet. Scott noticed that Emanuel was already getting into the truck. As the men ran to the truck, one of the workers slipped on the grass and fell face first. A loud grunt filled the air as the Rex began to wake up. The worker got to his feet almost in unison with the young Tyrannosaur. He bolted to the car and jumped onto the side as quickly as he could. The sound of the closing car doors caught the infant's attention. Her head was held low below her shoulders, and the towel hung from her head, covering her eyes. She turned her head to face the truck and began to shake. The towel slid off her face almost in slow motion.

The feathers around her neck ruffled as she stared at the strange metal animal in her enclosure. She let out a mighty roar as she freed herself, rapidly blinking her eyes as they adjusted to the harsh sunlight. Scott was happy he had left the car in drive and was already heading towards the exit. In the side view mirror, he saw the infant charge after them. Her mouth hung open, revealing large yellowed teeth glistening with saliva. Her feet pounded the ground as she chased after the fleeing car. Dr. Harmon could hear the men clinging to the side of the truck, screaming as the infant began to close the gap.

"Hang on, everyone!" Scott yelled out the window at the workers. "Get close to the truck, and hang on tight."

One of the workers placed his forearm through the handle on the side and gripped his wrist so tightly with the other hand that his palm began turning pale. He pulled his body close to the truck. The rest followed suit as Dr. Harmon placed his foot down on the gas. The car lurched as it shifted gears and blew forward. The infant was still in pursuit, but she was falling behind.

When they got to the tree line, the branches began to slap at the side of the truck and the men hanging onto the vehicle. Dr. Harmon held his breath and began to pray that none of them would fall off the side. With the Rex in pursuit, falling off of the truck would certainly spell disaster. Scott began to honk as he approached the gate of the enclosure. This was his warning signal to the men on the other side that he was being followed. The forklift operator and men waiting outside jumped to their feet and rushed to the cage door. They readied themselves to shut the gate as soon as Scott passed through. The pick-up whizzed through the gate moments later; a large metallic blur flew by the men outside the cage. Dr. Harmon slammed on the breaks as hard as he could. The tires dug into the ground below, stirring up rocks, dust, and twigs. Scott banked the car hard to the left in order to avoid an upcoming tree. The truck drifted slightly over the dirt in a semi-circular path. The truck bounced and shook as it came to a halt. The men on the side screamed the entire way, fearing that the vehicle was going to crash. Once he had come to a stop, Scott looked at Emanuel to his left and then out the window at the enclosure. No free roaming T-Rex, he thought to himself.

Scott began to laugh nervously and got out of the pick-up. He headed towards the enclosure and the men standing in front of the closed gate. The mission was a success. Scott let out a sigh of relief. He peered into the enclosure to look for the infant they had left behind. The men began to gather behind him as he peered into the cage.

"That could have gone better," said Dr. Harmon as he caught his breath. His heart was pounding so hard in his chest that it felt as though it may burst through his ribs. He was sweating like he had just run a marathon despite it not being that warm outside that day.

"It could have gone a lot worse. Great driving," said Emanuel.

Scott smiled at Emanuel and stared back into the enclosure. The baby Rex walked out of the brush and along the fence line in front of them. She stopped to face the men, staring at them through the bars. She tilted her head slightly to the right as she investigated the barrier between her and the men. A few of the workers had taken a few steps back. The infant lunged forward and grabbed the metal bar within her jaws. Sparks flew through the air, and a loud electric hum could be heard. The infant let out a loud squeak and fell backwards away from the cage. Dr. Harmon lifted his arm to shield his face from the sparks that filled the air. The baby Tyrannosaur got slowly to her feet, staggering slightly. She shook her head and stared back at the men. The Tyrannosaur let out a roar and walked off to the jungles of her enclosure. She's pretty intelligent, thought Scott as he watched the young T-Rex wander into the forests of her new domain.

Chapter 10

Mr. Sana slept soundly in his estate in Northern Oregon. He had spent the day in meetings and on phone calls with his partners on Protogonus. The move date to Dionysus was to happen in the coming months. Large freight ships would be needed to transport the heavy cargo from the Olympia archipelago to Dionysus. In addition there were enclosures that needed to be built, a tour program that needed to be set up, and countless buildings that needed to be constructed. It was all so exhausting, but the payoff would be immense once this project got off the ground. Ryo had fallen asleep almost instantly upon hitting the pillow. He was far too old for this kind of work. He was jostled from his much-needed slumber by an annoyingly bright light. Ryo squinted against the bright light, shielding his eyes with his arm. He began to vocalize unintelligibly as he awoke. He combed the room with his eyes, trying to piece together what was going on around him. Ryo noticed his attendant, Tomoko, was standing by his bedside. She was a woman of similar age to Ryo with curly black hair, thin glasses, and a serious demeanor. Tomoko was in her nightgown but still had her hair pulled back in a bun at the back of her head. Her eyes were red, and her cheeks were puffy. It appeared as if she had been crying.

"Mr. Sana, I need you to come downstairs, sir," said Tomoko; her voice was cracking slightly as she spoke.

"What...what is it? What has happened?" questioned Ryo.

Ryo stared at Tomoko for a moment, not knowing what to make of what was going on. Tomoko seemed like she wanted to talk but couldn't seem to get the words out. She stood there covering her mouth with her hand, tears rolling down her face. Ryo got to his feet, throwing the blankets off of him like flicking a cape. He sat up and put on his slippers as he got to his feet. He got to his robe and began to walk to the door. His stiff joints rebelled against him as he walked; his knees felt like they were creaking. Ryo felt like a rusted machine, desperately needing oil to get going. His age was becoming more and more apparent these last few years; this project seemed to be escalating his normal aging process. The doctors had told him he would need a hip replacement and maybe a knee replacement in the coming years. He would have none of this. This was something old people dealt with, and he was only fifty-six-years-old. Ryo felt there had to be some sort of medication he could take or some wholistic method he could go through in order to make his condition better. Surgery had to be the last option, he often thought to himself as he made another excuse to keep going through his daily routines.

When he got to the hallway, his heart dropped into his stomach. It suddenly became very clear to him what was happening. The hallway was ablaze with blue and red flashing lights coming from the stairwell downstairs. Fear overtook Ryo as a chill ran down his spine. He stood there with his mouth agape, frozen in place and unable to command his feet to move. Ryo jumped as Tomoko placed her cold, frail hand on his back.

"Let me help you, sir," said Tomoko, grabbing his arm and locking it with hers. She knew Mr. Sana was at his worst when he first woke up from rest.

The two walked down the hallway together. Normally this trip took a few minutes, but to Ryo, it felt like an eternity. He couldn't feel his feet as they struck the floor, he couldn't feel anything. It was as if he was watching himself move down the hallway from a far-off place. Once he got to the stairs, he gripped the railing to start his descent to the foyer. Tears began to roll down his face as he descended slowly down the large wooden staircase. As a parent, this was the visit that every father dreaded. Ryo knew why the police were at his door in the middle of the night, although he had hoped deep down that it was something else. There had to be another reason, he was over-reacting, he began to say to himself. But then why would Tomoko just not be able to tell him what was going on? Ryo shrugged off the bad thoughts running through his head as he approached the doorway.

Once at the door, Ryo saw two officers standing there facing the woods of his property. They were conversing with one another in a very nonchalant way, seemingly unaware that he was standing in front of them. Mr. Sana saw the police cruiser in his driveway resting on the gravel. The lights of the cruiser illuminated his entire driveway, foyer, and staircase. It was amazing how bright they were.

"Hello, officers, how can I help you?" asked Ryo, trying to sound unconcerned.

The two officers turned to face Ryo, and he could see their demeanor change almost instantly. They were no longer joking and nonchalant. Instead they had become somber and calm.

"Are you Mr. Ryo Sana?" said the nearest officer.

"I...I am. How can I help you?" asked Ryo.

"We are sorry to tell you this, sir, but there has been an accident. Your son was involved, and we need you to come down to the hospital with us," said the officer

"No, no! Is he okay?! Tell me if he is okay, damn you!" screamed Ryo.

"Mr. Sana..." said Tomoko sheepishly, trying to calm him down.

"No! They need to tell me he is okay! How can they show up here and not tell me he is okay?" screamed Ryo as his breath lay heavy in his chest.

The words of the officers had hit him like a hot arrow, piercing through his flesh and directly into his heart. His stomach sank and his heart burned. This was not happening, he thought to himself.

"I'm sorry, sir, your son was driving drunk and crashed into another vehicle. There were no survivors . We need you to come down to the hospital to identify the body," said the second officer in a cold, emotionless tone. "We are truly sorry for your loss."

"No..." Ryo stood there silently trying to process what he had just been told. His son couldn't have been drunk, thought Ryo. His son never drank, even when offered alcohol in celebration, he would always turn it down. Something was very wrong here.

Ryo felt his knees buckle. If this was a boxing match, the second officer had just hit him with a haymaker and knocked him out. He fell to his knees and began sobbing uncontrollably. Ichigo was his only child, and he was all Ryo had since his wife had passed away a few years ago. He was now all alone. Tomoko crouched down on the floor and put her arm around Ryo in an attempt to comfort him as he grieved. She had loved Ichigo as well. Tomoko had raised Ichigo with Ryo and his wife, becoming almost a second mother to the boy. She was equally as hard hit by this news.

"We will give you a minute, again we are so sorry for your, loss Mr. Sana," said the first officer with a bit more compassion than the second officer had spoken.

The next few hours were a blur to Ryo. He got dressed in a hurry, not remembering what he had even decided to wear. Tomoko had phoned for the driver to meet them out front. The drive to the hospital was a very somber one. Mr. Sana, who normally liked classical music playing in the car, had requested to sit in complete silence. He sat on the leather seat, staring blankly out of the tinted window. His mind was blank; he didn't know what to think at this time. Part of him wanted desperately to believe that this was a cruel prank. He kept saying that this wasn't real and that he was still asleep. He longed very much so for this to all be some twisted highly realistic nightmare. The limo pulled up in front of the hospital, coming to a stop right at the entrance. Ryo's driver opened the car door and helped Mr. Sana and Tomoko out of the vehicle. Tomoko told the driver they would call him when they were done and asked that he stay nearby. The driver nodded his head and drove off, leaving them at the entrance. Ryo began to feel nauseous as they approached the entrance of the hospital. He normally walked everywhere with a purpose, but now he walked aimlessly with no direction.

When they got to the check-in desk, Ryo opened his mouth but was unable to speak. He couldn't bring himself to say the words. Saying he was there to view his son's remains would make it real. Tomoko was equally at a loss. She sobbed silently, taking a moment to wipe the tears from her face with a white lace handkerchief.

"Ah, Mr. Sana," said the woman behind the desk, recognizing him from an old interview she had seen on the television. "Give me a moment to assist you. Please wait here."

The young woman got up from her desk and walked into the back of the hospital. She approached a young doctor and began to have a conversation that Ryo could not hear. The physician looked in Mr. Sana's direction and nodded his head. He held his hand up to the woman, as if dismissing her, and began to approach Ryo and Tomoko. As the young doctor approached, Ryo could feel himself drifting out of focus. He felt as if he were watching a blurry television screen showcasing the events of his life.

"Mr. Sana, I am so sorry to meet you under these circumstances. I am Dr. Carey, my sincerest condolences for the loss of your son."

"Just take me to him please," asked Ryo in a very low tone. His voice cracked slightly as he spoke, trying not to allow himself to cry.

"Yes, sir," said Dr. Carey. "Right this way."

The doctor led them down a long corridor. The fluorescent lighting and white paint gave off an emotionless vibe to the cold, sterile ambiance of the hospital. Ryo saw where they were headed. A sign on the wall caught his eye with the word mortuary printed on it. The arrow next to this offensive word was pointing the direction they were headed. Tomoko had noted the sign as well and began to sob loudly. Ryo grabbed her hand in his as the two walked down the hall together. Dr. Carey stopped at a door and held it open for Ryo and Tomoko. When they entered, two black body bags lay on the table in the center of the room. The doctor approached the first bag and grabbed the zipper in his right hand.

"I'm so very sorry, sir, but we need you to identify the remains of the deceased," said Dr. Carey. "I realize this is unpleasant, so if you need a moment before I open the bag, I completely understand."

Ryo shook his head and motioned for the doctor to proceed. He was having trouble forming words at this point. Ryo Sana was a proud man who refused to let his emotions show to anyone. Crying at this point, although a natural response, was not something he wanted to do. The body bag seemed to open in slow motion as the body within revealed itself. There he was, his son, laying on the cold metal table in a black bag. He was pale as the white hallways with no life present behind his large brown eyes. His black hair had some blood still clinging to it. The sight of his son's lifeless body was too much for Ryo to bear. He could no longer hold back his emotions and began to sob loudly as he shook his head in confirmation that this was indeed his son.

Sir Ethan Barnes sat at a large dining room table in his quarters on Protogonus. The room had a large, wooden table in the center in which Ethan sat alone. A large chandelier hung above the table, illuminating the room in the darkness of the early morning. Several large windows lay perpendicular to the table from which Ethan sat. This allowed him to watch the sun rise and set over his operation. Large metal bars slightly obstructed the view of the outside world, a necessary precaution. In front of him was a large breakfast spread with scrambled eggs, bacon, ham, sausage, and several types of juice. The buffet was enough to feed several people, but there Ethan sat alone as he started his day. He sipped on his coffee as he turned the page on a report he had just received from the engineering department. He stared at the building plans of the visitor center that would adorn the main hub of his resort on Dionysus. The building had a Greek architectural flavor to it and was set to look like the Acropolis of Athens. Ethan wanted to play up the Greek mythology theme for his prehistoric island getaway. He was in negotiations with a major museum for several authentic dinosaur skeletons for his lobby on Dionysus. The museum, however, was not returning his calls. Ethan sat and contemplated how visitors would feel walking into his visitor center. Suddenly the doors of his dining hall swung open, interrupting his meal. Arthur entered in a rather hurried manner. This was out of character for Arthur; Ethan immediately knew that something was wrong. Arthur was usually calm, collected, and level in his persona. Nothing seemed to shake the man, even in the most extreme circumstances. It was part of the reason he was so good at his job.

"Sir Barnes, terribly sorry to disturb your meal," said Arthur, his voice was clearly stressed.

"Not at all, my boy, what's going on? Hopefully no more major setbacks," said Ethan, laughing slightly.

"I'm afraid it's not good news. Mr. Sana's son was killed in a car crash," said Arthur, averting his gaze from Ethan.

"Oh...oh, dear...That is not something I was expecting to hear," said Ethan, bowing his head slightly. "Get Ryo on the phone for me, will you? I need to make sure he is okay."

"Right away, sir," said Arthur, leaving the room quickly.

Ethan let out a deep sigh and placed his hands on the table in front of him. He did not know Ichigo Sana very well, having only seen him on occasion over the years at various business meetings and company events. Ryo had made sure that his son never worked on projects out in the open. This was to allow him to live his life privately. He had never been to Protogonus, and as far as Ethan knew, was unaware of what his father was doing on these islands. Sir Barnes began to wonder if this would affect Ryo Sana's dealing and involvement with the park. He thought he may be able to go it alone from this point forward; he questioned how involved Ryo would be able to be with this current development.

Arthur returned to the room holding a large cordless telephone. This was a relatively new technology, and Ethan was of course one of the first to adopt it into his dealings. He approached Ethan with his hand over the receiver and handed the phone over with great care. The manner in which he handled the phone was similar to a mother holding her child.

"Hello, Ryo," said Ethan into the phone as he took it from Arthur.

"Hi, Ethan."

"I am so very sorry to hear about your son," said Ethan. "Do you need to take a few weeks off?"

"I…I think so," said Ryo very coldly. A stark silence filled the room after Ryo had spoken. "Ethan, I think he was killed."

"What do you mean by that?" asked Ethan. "Who would want to kill your son?"

"The doctor said his blood alcohol level was 0.2! Ichigo doesn't drink," said Ryo in a very concerned tone. "They also found traces of other illicit substances in his system."

"Well…Ryo he was a young man…" said Ethan calmly, trying to figure out how to say that maybe Ryo wasn't aware of his son's private life. "I mean who would want to murder him?"

"We will discuss this further when I am on a more secure line," said Ryo in a cold tone. "My son was murdered Ethan."

"Alright then…take care of yourself," said Ethan.

The conversation was very cold and robotic. Sir Barnes never knew what to say in instances like this. Ryo's insistence in there being foul play did not help the issue. It was very clear that he was upset by the tone of his voice, but Ethan did not know how to handle the situation. Emotions were never Ethan's forte. The conversation continued for another few agonizing minutes as Ethan attempted to comfort his partner to no avail. Ethan bid Ryo farewell and handed the phone back to Arthur, shaking his head as he did so.

It was mid-afternoon, and it was time for lunch. Kyle got up from his desk in a hurried fashion; he couldn't wait to get to the buffet. He quickly turned his work station computers over to a screen saver and rushed out of the computer lab. He walked down the long corridors to the exit of the genetics lab. Kyle hated that he had to go outside in order to get to his meal, but the intense jungle heat was a necessary evil. He shielded his eyes as he left the genetics lab. The sounds of the island's large herbivores almost didn't faze Kyle anymore. He was used to hearing the calls of the large Brachiosaurs and Hadrosaurs that inhabited the island. Kyle waddled across the village to the cafeteria. He had the number of steps counted between the two buildings. He knew the fastest route to get to where he needed to be. He wasn't going to waste any more time than he had to in the intense sun. Once he had gotten inside, he was instantly happier. Kyle approached the buffet earnestly, rubbing his hands together and smiling as he prepared to eat. He grabbed the nearest plate and began to stack mounds of food onto it. He grabbed a heap of mashed potatoes to top off his dish and rushed to take a seat, so he could consume his feast.

Breakfast had put him in a much better mood. Food was his drug of choice. Kyle was elated as he approached his work station. Even though he was not a fan of the intense heat on this island, he was happy with the pay and looked forward to how much he stood to make with this venture. He got back to his work station and quickly logged back into his computer screens. He began to go about his usual checks and system repairs when he noticed the indicator on his email showed that he had several new messages. Kyle had admittedly been neglecting his email since he arrived on Protogonus. He did not really see a reason to keep up with his inbox. Being thousands of miles away from home and having nothing back home to be concerned about had led him to ignoring the world outside of this tropical paradise that he was marooned on. Kyle decided he would check his email to get rid of the annoying red notifications. He opened his inbox and began to scroll through the messages one by one. He was amazed by how much junk mail he had gotten since he last checked his messages. As he scrolled through his inbox, one particular message caught his eye. The email was from the burial services department where he had laid his mother to rest. The subject of the email was final billing notice. Kyle paused for a second as he stared at the subject line. Why would he be getting a bill from the funeral pallor when all of his expenses should have been covered by R.N.A.? Kyle was confused and began to debate whether or not he should open the email or delete it. He hovered the cursor over the message and finally decided that he should read it.

Dear Mr. Kyle Bergin,

We would like to thank you for using our services for the final arrangements of your mother. We know the loss of a loved one is never an easy process, and we strive to help our clients say goodbye to their loved ones in an easy and honorable fashion. Thank you for allowing us to serve you. We are emailing you as our several attempts to reach you at your address in Worchester, MA have failed. We regret to inform you that you have a balance of $75,000 on your account after the initial deposit. Please contact us at your earliest convenience to settle up your account. You may contact the main office at (949)-532-7777. We regret to inform you that failure to pay will result in your account being sent to collections and legal recourse to the fullest extent as detailed in the contract that you signed.

Sincerely,

Gerald Roberts
Funeral Director

Kyle stared at the email for several minutes. Confusion began to turn to anger. He was told by Mr. Sana that the expenses for his mother would be handled as part of his contract. How did he owe a balance, he thought angrily. It was bad enough that he had to pay the $10,000 deposit out of pocket, which he had yet to be reimbursed for. Now he was getting emails about being sent to collections and threatening prosecution; this was unacceptable. Kyle could not afford this price tag. He had some savings in his account from his recent paychecks but not $75,000 worth! Kyle had blown a lot of his initial sign on bonus in moving expenses and paying off debt he had accrued prior to signing on to work for R.N.A. He had to speak with Sir Barnes or Mr. Sana as soon as possible. Kyle quickly clicked out of his email and rose to his feet. The chair he was sitting in rolled backwards away from him. He quickly put up his screen saver, angrily clicking the mouse. Kyle stormed off towards Sir Barnes' office. He had to get this sorted as soon as possible.

Kyle rushed down the halls as fast as his legs could carry him. His face was flush with anger, and a vein throbbed in his forehead. He began to converse with himself slightly under his breath as he walked down the hall. He was preparing what he was going to say to Sir Barnes before he got to the office. Even his feet seemed to clap angrily on the tile floors as he proceeded to the main office. When he got to the door, he quickly pushed it open as hard as he could. The doors slammed open, making a loud crashing sound as it hit the wall.

"Kyle, what the hell, man?!" said Arthur as he jumped to his feet from behind the desk.

"Where is Ethan Barnes?" screamed Kyle. "I need to speak with him right away."

"He is off-site, he flew back to San Diego earlier this morning. He is likely over open ocean at the moment, so you're not gonna be able to reach him for a few hours," said Arthur.

"Typical, just typical," screamed Kyle.

"What's gotten you so riled up?" asked Arthur "What the heck are you so upset for?"

Kyle raised his hand to Arthur as if to shush him. He had no time for this; dealing with Ethan's lackey was not going to get him anywhere. He was very clearly wasting his time with this "yes man" in front of him. He needed to go to the top; he needed to get either Mr. Sana or Sir Barnes on the phone as soon as possible. Kyle stormed out of the office as quickly as he had stormed in. He rushed angrily back to his desk where he would have access to a landline telephone. If he couldn't reach Sir Barnes, then he would have to call Mr. Sana. Kyle knew Mr. Sana was not as easy to talk to, but this couldn't wait. Kyle needed to get this settled as soon as possible.

When he got to his office, Kyle rolled his desk chair quickly back to his station. The chair slammed loudly against the desk. He rolled it around and plopped down in his chair quickly. Kyle began to dig through the papers and food wrappers on his desk. He was searching desperately for the phone list, so that he could contact Mr. Sana on the mainland. Potato chip bags and candy wrappers fell to the floor as he rummaged through the mess that was his desk. He grabbed a small, laminated sheet of paper, and a smile lit his face up. Kyle had found what he was looking for. He quickly picked up the receiver on his desk and began to angrily smash the phone keys as he dialed Mr. Sana's main number. As he listened to the phone ring, he tapped his foot rhythmically on the floor. With each ring, his anger rose, and the tapping became louder. By the third ring, he was tapping his hand in unison as well. The sound of Mr. Sana's voicemail notification was about the most infuriating thing that Kyle could have heard.

"Hello, it's Kyle Bergin. You need to call me back as soon as you can! This is very urgent, Mr. Sana; we have a BIG problem here," screamed Kyle into the receiver. "Call me back!"

Kyle slammed the receiver down. The audacity of these people, he thought. They refused to pay the expenses they promised him they would cover and then both conveniently disappear. This was infuriating; Kyle had never been so mad in his life. He began to think about how he had thought this offer was too good to be true. How could they betray him like this, he thought. As Kyle began to fester, he attempted to calm himself down by repeating that "it must be some kind of oversight." That had to be it, thought Kyle, they must have forgotten. It was hard for him to not panic as there was no way he could cover the expenses on his own at this point.

Dr. Harmon had several new species to care for at this point. Jin Moon had been busy in his lab since being able to get back online. Dr. Bai had refined his de-extinction process to an art form. Scott was finding it hard to keep up with all of these new arrivals. Nalani was driving him and Reginald to the enclosure of one of the latest species. Scott stared down at a piece of paper in his hands as the vehicle drove through the dense jungles of Protogonus. Gone were the sounds of jungle birds and animals. Now the jungle was filled with the cries of the large herbivore species that populated the island spattered with the occasional Tyrannosaur roar. Scott began to wonder what else Dr. Bai would cook up as he stared at the list of species currently residing on the island.

Species List

Baryonyx (5)
Brachiosaurus (15)
Carnotaurus (4)

Compsognathus (52)
Edmontosaurus (17)
Gallimimus (50)
Geostembergia (4)
Herrerasaurus (12)
Mamenchisaurus (8)
Microceratus (62)
Pachycephalosaurus (19)
Parasaurolophus (34)
Pteranodon (15)
Stegosaurus (25)
Triceratops (32)
Tyrannosaurus Rex (6)

They were currently in route to the newest species, Baryonyx, to catalog their habits and to determine if they would be a viable species for Dionysus. Dr. Bramme had left ahead of them with Stephen to observe the newest arrival. Scott was not a part of the relocation process for this species, so he had yet to see what they were like as subadults.

The car came to a halt on the gravel road, skidding slightly as the pebbles crunched underneath them. Dr. Harmon placed the list into the glove compartment of the vehicle, and the three others got out in tandem. With the newer species, Scott had asked Nalani to get the construction crews to set up viewing galleries onto the enclosures. This was to allow for better observation of the animals, so that behavioral patterns and habitat preferences could be established. This data was to help the construction teams on Dionysus better establish enclosures for the animals. Dr. Harmon walked up the small metal staircase, his boots clanging on the metal as he walked up to the small platform. He gazed briefly at the thatched roof of the small, elevated viewing gallery. The gallery was set up at the edge of a lake within the paddock. The electric fencing connected directly to the gallery and wrapped around the front end of it just below the elevated platform. This was to discourage the animals from getting too close to the viewing platform.

"Hello, Rich, how is it going? Tell me the details of this new species," said Scott quietly to the two men already standing in the gallery.

"Hey, Scott, keep it down a bit. There is one in the water pretty close to the platform," said Dr. Richard Bramme.

Scott gazed into the enclosure and skimmed it for evidence of the Baryonyx. He approached the glass and stared out into the vast lake and swamp that made up the habitat. Scott was at a loss as he could not seem to find it.

"Right there, man," whispered Nalani as she pointed towards a large mangrove tree in the water. "I'll be damned, it looks like a crocodile."

Scott looked in the direction of Nalani's extended arm and pointing finger. He skimmed the water and saw what initially he had thought was a floating log. Nalani was absolutely correct, the animal had a long, narrow snout with conical teeth protruding from its scaly lips and running up the sides of its leathery face. Yellow-orange eyes sat at the sides of its head, pointing forward. The animal had several osteoderms running along it's back in rows, similar to the protrusions of a Nile crocodile. It sat perfectly still in the water as if waiting for something to come its way.

Scott did not know much about this species and admittedly had not done any research on it prior to heading out here to meet Richard. He was hoping that Richard would just tell him what he needed to know about this creature.

"So they are aquatic?" asked Scott in a low whisper.

"Well, we didn't know for sure at first. Based on the shape of their teeth and snouts, it was assumed that they were piscivores as their teeth were perfect for catching fish," said Dr. Bramme. "We have been observing them for about an hour prior to you getting here, and they seem perfectly adept to a semi-aquatic lifestyle."

"I never would have imagined that there could be a dinosaur adapted to the water like this," said Stephen.

"There are quite a few actually. This animal is part of the Spinosaurid family, which all appeared to be adapted to a semi-aquatic life. We didn't know for sure until now," said Richard Bramme.

Scott watched the animal as it sat in the water quietly. As they observed, a cool breeze flowed through the viewing gallery, washing over the group and giving them some relief from the intense jungle heat. The Baryonyx flared its nostrils a few times, and then with a few flicks of its powerful tail, began to swim off. Scott could see it's large, powerful hindlegs kicking under the water's surface as it undulated its tail back and forth like a crocodile. Within minutes the animal was far in the distance and heading towards the shore.

"They are very powerful swimmers," said Nalani. "Just like a prehistoric salt water croc."

Scott was about to say something and then paused to think about what she had just said. Her comparison was very accurate. Salt water crocodiles have been known to swim out to sea on occasion surviving on fish and sharks as they travel. They very often swim amongst the islands of the South Pacific, travelling miles across open ocean to get from place to place. It was not out of the realm of possibility to think that an adult Baryonyx would be able to do the same should one ever escape its enclosure. The thought of a large therapod escaping onto the mainland was not something Scott wanted to envision for very long.

"Richard, if this thing ever got out, do you think it could swim its way to the mainland?" asked Scott.

"Well, the short answer is I don't know," said Dr. Bramme, taking a second to pause as he considered his answer. "Certainly they are good swimmers, but I have no way of determining based on the fossil record how far they could swim or if they would attempt to swim in a salt water ocean."

"Well, saltwater crocs often swim out to sea," said Nalani. "I bet this bloke would be able to do the same based on what I've seen here."

"So you think this thing would turn up on a beach in Japan if it ever got out?" asked Stephen, shuddering slightly at the thought.

"That is exactly what I am saying," said Scott. "I need to talk to Dr. Bai; we need to be taking precautions with what creatures we are cooking up in that lab of his."

Scott tapped Nalani and Reginald on the back as he began to exit the platform. He motioned for them to come with him as he exited and proceeded back to their vehicle. They all hopped into the car. Nalani turned the car over and backed away from the viewing gallery, turning the car as she reversed. She did a quick K turn and began to head back to the base camp.

Back at the lab, Jin Moon was busying over a few new genomes that he had discovered. Based on his genome library, he knew these three new species were therapods. Jin was looking to add more teeth to the roster of Archosauria, as the carnivores were going to be the main draw for visitors. People wanted to be scared; they wanted to be thrilled. Nothing was going to be more thrilling and terrifying than a predator that towered over them and could swallow them whole. A big smile lit Jin's face up like a ray of sunshine as the new genomes neared completion. He was going to go down in history for his work here. This was very fitting for a genius such as himself, he thought. As he stared at his computer screen, he heard the lab door hiss open behind him. Jin ignored the sound as he focused intently on his work.

"Dr. Bai, I need to speak with you a moment," said Scott as he approached Jin's desk.

Jin stopped typing on his keyboard and turned slowly and purposefully to face Scott. He was robotic in his movements and had a scowl on his face. He let out a long sigh and stared at Dr. Harmon for a moment before he replied. It was very clear he was annoyed about being interrupted.

"What is it, Dr. Harmon?" said Jin in an exasperated tone.

"We just came back from the Baryonyx paddock, and I have a few questions for you," said Scott.

"I don't have time to field questions right now, Dr. Harmon. You can direct any dinosaur questions to Richard; he is a paleontologist after all," said Jin Moon.

"I am well aware of Richard's line of work, Jin; this is a question for you," said Scott in an annoyed tone.

"Very well, what can I help you with?" said Jin as he got up from his station abruptly and began to walk away from Scott to another section of the lab.

"That animal out there, the Baryonyx, I notice that it is a very good swimmer and…" said Scott before he was cut off by Jin.

"Yes, it is semi-aquatic after all. Your point is?" said Jin, abruptly walking to another section of the lab to make some adjustments to a piece of equipment.

"If it ever got out of its paddock, I worry it would be able to swim to the mainland. What are we doing to ensure that this doesn't happen? I mean we should be considering this, as a dinosaur on the mainland would be disastrous," said Scott as he tried to keep up with the ever-moving Dr. Bai.

Jin paused for a second; this was the first time he had been still since Dr. Harmon had entered the lab. He was caught off guard by the question and did not seem to have an answer readily available.

"Fascinating," said Jin. "If you have issues with containment, I suggest you bring it up with Nalani. That is her job after all."

"Well, what is our course of action should any of these animals escape, Jin?" asked Scott. "I'm asking you for answers, and you are refusing to entertain my questions."

"Dr. Harmon, trust me here. We have put millions of dollars into containment measures for these animals. We do not pay you to ask these kinds of questions," said Jin confidently with a smile on his face.

"Jin, we need to be more careful here. Any one of these animals could cause major damage and loss of life if they were to escape. We need to be more responsible here," said Scott.

"With all due respect, doctor, you were not hired for containment. I kindly suggest you step back into your lane, or I will have you relieved of your duties and sent back to your dark cave in San Diego where we found you," screamed Jin, a vein throbbing in his forehead as spit flew from his mouth.

Scott stood there, stunned for a moment. He was not sure what to say in response to Jin's threat. Jin Moon was in very close with Sir Barnes; it would not be impossible to think that he could have Ethan relieve him of his duties.

"I also suggest that you keep your big mouth shut and pretend this conversation never happened," said Jin Moon in a much calmer fashion.

Scott immediately began to think about what returning to San Diego would mean for him at this point. He couldn't go back to that dark, monotonous lifestyle. He was finally happy here and had no desire to go back to his normal life back in California. Begrudgingly he conceded and bowed his head in defeat. Dr. Harmon left the lab with his tail between his legs; Jin had won, and there was nothing he could do about it at this point. Scott sighed, dropping his argument. He walked away sullenly, deciding not to fight this battle. He wasn't going to risk his newfound happiness to go to battle with Dr. Bai.

Chapter 11

Dr. Harmon reported to the genetics lab for an early morning hatching. His interactions with Dr. Bai had been strained at best at this point. Scott greeted Jin with a nod as he walked into the lab doors with his usual gear on. He approached the incubator with his gloved hands held high as he tried not to touch anything and contaminate himself before he handled the new set of infants. This was another new species that they did not mean to bring back. Dr. Bai was hoping to de-extinct a creature called Therizinosaurus. This was a large bipedal herbivore with eight-foot-long forearms. Each arm contained three fingered hands with meter-long claws on each digit. The creature had a small head perched upon a long neck and could grow up to thirty feet long. Therizinosaurus would have made an excellent addition to Jin's cast of creatures. Unfortunately the DNA samples for this batch of chicks came from stolen fossil fragments courtesy of one of R.N.A.'s many spy groups. Jin had not gotten the sample he had hoped for but instead had gotten an entirely unexpected species from a different time period in history.

The incubator contained ten small, bipedal therapods. A soft hooting sound filled the room. The noise got louder and louder as Dr. Harmon approached the incubator. Scott peered into the incubator through the glass at the animals below. They were tiny by dinosaur standards, only about the size of a small Chihuahua. The animals were a dark yellow in color with tan underbellies. Like the other therapod infants, they were covered with hair filaments. They had a black, mottled pattern extending from the tip of their snout to the end of their tail over the tops of their bodies. Each animal has two large half-moon shaped crests on the top of their heads. The underside of their necks were brightly colored red, and they had a lot of extra tissue hanging around the base of their jaws on either side of the head.

"What species is this, Richard? I don't know this one," asked Dr. Harmon as he prepared his set of vaccines.

"Um, Dilophosaurus. Early Jurassic period. It was thought to be a scavenger due to its delicate jaw structure," said Dr. Richard Bramme.

"Interesting; what are the crests for?" asked Scott.

"We don't know for sure; it's assumed they are for attracting mates. Similar to modern birds," said Richard.

Dr. Harmon opened the incubator and began to distract the infants with bits of rodent carcasses. Dr. Ernie Sung grabbed the first infant from behind, startling it. He was careful not to hurt it as it was noticeably smaller compared with other species that they had handled. The animal began to writhe in his hands as it tried to escape; soft hooting became replaced with a loud hissing and growling.

RAWWWWWWWWWWWWWWWWWWWRRRRRRRRRRRRRRRRRRR

The creature let out a loud yell, and the extra tissue under its neck expanded into a brilliant red throat pouch that had black speckling on it. The Dilophosaur held its mouth open as the throat pouch pulsated. The pouch extended from the bottom of the jawline to the animal's sternum. The Dilophosaur let out a terrible screech as it struggled in Dr. Sung's grasp.

"Holy shit!" exclaimed Ernie, dropping the animal on the floor.

"What have you done, you incompetent fool! You better not have hurt it!" screamed Jin. "Don't just stand there, catch it!"

Ernie ran off after the small animal as it bolted for the computers along the far wall. The young Dilophosaur hid behind a computer monitor and refused to come out. It sat behind the machine, entangling itself in the various wires protruding from the back end of the computer tower. Ernie got down on the floor and reached for the infant. He could feel it biting and scratching at him through his gloves. The young Dilophosaur let out another set of hoots and forced its way out from behind the tower, almost knocking it over. Ernie caught the falling computer tower and pushed it back into place. The infant ran across the lab floor, turning its head from side to side as it ran, looking for another place to hide. Dr. Harmon jumped out in front of the infant, holding a towel up like a barrier. The young dinosaur skidded to a stop, falling on the tile floor as its clawed feet scrambled to maintain balance. Scott threw the towel over the infant and quickly grabbed it through the towel with his gloved hands. The Dilophosaur's crested head could be seen imprinted through the towel tossing from side to side as it tried to get free. Scott got to his feet with the infant in toe with a loud grunt.

He returned to the now closed incubator with the infant and held it as Dr. Bramme gave the vaccinations. Scott walked slowly to the holding pen that would become the infant's new home. He placed the creature into its habitat and observed it as it wandered. He wanted to make sure there were no visible signs of injury before returning to the group for the remaining nine. The young Dilophosaur wandered around its habitat, softly hooting as it explored its new home. It almost seemed to bounce as it moved around its habitat. None of the other dinosaurs moved like this. It almost looked kangaroo-like in its locomotion. This truly was an interesting creature. Scott left the temporary habitat to return to the group.

"What the hell was that about?" asked Ernie Sung. "It scared the heck out of me."

"I don't know, that wasn't in the fossil record," said Dr. Bramme. "Certainly an unexpected finding. Excess skin like that doesn't fossilize. There was no way to know it would have a pouch like that."

"What do you suppose it is for?" asked Dr. Bai, visibly intrigued by this conversation.

"I don't know for sure," said Dr. Bramme. "I may refer to Dr. Harmon's opinion, he would be much better to ask about animal behavior."

"Well, it's a small predator, so maybe it's an intimidation measure," said Scott, placing his hands on under his chin and flapping them in an attempt to mimic the Dilophosaur. "It may expand the pouch to look larger than it actually is and scare off potential rivals or predators."

"I don't think that's right," said Dr. Bramme. "Dilophosaurus would have been one of the larger predators in the Early Jurassic. It has to be the former, where they used it to intimidate others of its species."

"Very unexpected indeed," said Jin Moon. "They are beautiful, aren't they?"

The men returned to their task of feeding and vaccinating the clutch of young Dilophosaurs. They found that placing a towel over their heads made them much less aggressive and aided in the process. It seemed that if they couldn't see what was going on, they were much less willing to put up a fight. This was very similar to a lot of predatory bird species. Covering the eyes would pacify many different hawk, falcon, and eagle species, so that they could be handled easier without tranquilizing them. Scott was impressed with how avian these animals were.

Kyle had worked himself up into a frenzy in his hotel room. He had argument after argument with himself in the shower, telling off Mr. Sana for his transgressions against him. Kyle left the shower feeling accomplished as he had just told off an imaginary Ryo during his bath. He was proud of himself for the tongue lashing he had just dished out. If Mr. Sana returned his calls, he would be ready for him. Kyle had left Ryo several voicemails with increasing aggression as the days had ticked by without a response. He resentfully returned to his desk to begin his work against his will. Kyle would spend his days watching movies in secret on his computer. He was losing interest in answering all of the IT tickets that piled up in his cue. He no longer cared to debug phones and security systems. He was content to get paid for doing nothing at this point as no one was over-seeing him anymore with Ryo and Ethan off island. Kyle was enjoying one of his favorite movies as he sat at his desk. Kyle was startled by the sound of his office door opening. He shot a glance at the door, seeing Arthur enter. He quickly turned back to his desk and fumbled with the mouse as he struggled to minimize his movie.

"Don't you know how to knock, Arthur?" said Kyle, trying to look as if he had been working hard.

"Mr. Sana is on the line in Sir Barnes' office. He is requesting your presence," said Arthur in a formal tone.

"It's about damn time he returns my call," said Kyle.

"I would tread lightly if I were you, Mr. Bergin. You have no idea what that man is capable of," said Arthur.

"Yeah, yeah, yeah," said Kyle. "Big mean boss-man, I got it. Try to wipe the brown off your nose before you talk about him next time."

Arthur shook his head and opened the door as he motioned for Kyle to follow him. The two walked to the main office in silence. Kyle had a purpose; he had had this discussion numerous times over the last several days in his head. He knew exactly what he was going to say. No one was going to take advantage of Kyle Bergin.

He walked into the large office on his own, not waiting for Arthur to open the door for him as he usually did. Kyle approached the desk and reached out for the receiver of the phone with out-stretched hand. He placed the phone quickly to his ear.

"Hello, Mr. Sana, you finally return my calls," said Kyle angrily.

"What is all this about, Mr. Bergin? Your messages were extremely aggressive and quite frankly; I do not appreciate your tone," said Mr. Sana.

"Now listen here, I just got a $75,000 bill for my mother's final expenses. You told me these things would be covered when you hired me," exclaimed Kyle, slightly losing his cool. This was not the calm discussion he had had with himself in the shower.

"I said we would cover your mother's medical bills, NOT her final expenses. That is on you, Mr. Bergin, and quite frankly no one told you to put her to rest in such an extravagant fashion," said Mr. Sana, audibly annoyed with this discussion.

"Are you kidding me?! Your exact words were 'We will cover her expenses!' That implies her funeral!" screamed Kyle.

"No, it most certainly does not! Medical bills and final arrangements are two separate things, Mr. Bergin. We graciously covered all of her remaining healthcare bills, including some of which you were behind on!" screamed Ryo. "This is on you, Kyle, end of discussion."

"This is not end of discussion; you hired me under false pretenses and lied to me about covering my mother's bills," screamed Kyle, turning red in the face. "You owe me $75,000! The work I do here saved your operation, do you really think you can afford to stiff me like this?"

"I am not stiffing you, you misunderstood the terms of our agreement, which has nothing to do with me!" yelled Ryo. "You chose to bury your mother extravagantly, thinking we would pick up the tab, which quite frankly is very insulting. Don't you dare threaten me and my company, you did the job you were hired for. This is the same job you are being generously compensated for! Your financial problems are YOUR problems. I just finished burying my son, I don't have the time or the energy for this, Mr. Bergin! GOOD BYE!"

There was a loud click followed by the sound of the dial tone. Kyle stood there with the beeping receiver in his hand. He was stunned by Mr. Sana's harsh tone and words. For one of the first times in his life, he was speechless. He stood there with his mouth open, stunned by what had just occurred. This is not at all how he thought the conversation would go and certainly was not one of the many iterations he had gone over in his head. Kyle realized he did not have the upper hand here at all. A wave of anger swept over him. He slammed the receiver several times on the desk before replacing it. Kyle stormed out of the office, slamming the door behind him. A small picture on the adjacent wall crashed to the ground behind him; the glass shattered on the floor as he stormed off.

Kyle rushed down the hall towards his office. He grunted and panted as he rushed back to his desk. Anger welled up inside him like bubbling surf crashing against the rock cliffs of Protogonus. There had to be a better solution here, thought Kyle. He wasn't sure his credit was good enough to take out a loan to cover the remaining costs of his mother's final expenses. What was he going to do? Kyle slammed his office door shut as he entered. He collapsed down into his office chair with a terrifying, exasperated grunt. He slammed his fist onto his desk multiple times, cursing as he did it. He was in trouble, and he did not know how he was going to get out of it. He stared at his computer screen as if he hoped it would give him a solution. The glare of the computer screen was reflected on his glasses, which were now crooked on his face. Kyle replaced his glasses to their proper position as he continued to stare at the computer screen. He pulled up his web browser and quickly opened an incognito window. Kyle pulled up a small black window on his desktop with green lettering. He began to type furiously into the box, encrypting his next steps so as not to be caught by any of the other IT people. Kyle had a feeling Selena was being paid by Mr. Sana to watch him prior to this. He felt she was surely going to be monitoring him now after this argument he just had. Kyle returned to his web browser and typed the words "Splice Genetics" into the search bar. He was going to make sure Mr. Sana and Sir Barnes would regret their betrayal. If they weren't going to appreciate him and his genius, then perhaps their rival company, Splice, would.

Weeks had passed, and the move to Dionysus was quickly approaching. The young Dilophosaur chicks now stood about two feet tall and were about eight feet long. They certainly were nothing like their larger cousins and seemed almost delicate in their mannerisms. Scott felt they resembled cranes; they moved elegantly as they hopped around their temporary paddock. Their final enclosure wasn't finished yet, and thus they stayed in one of the temporary enclosures behind the genetics building. This enclosure was very much like the enclosures back at Dr. Harmon's zoo in San Diego. It had a large outdoor area where the animals spent much of their time. The bars of the enclosure were electrified like the other enclosures on the island. At the back of the enclosure was a door that led to a smaller indoor enclosure where the animals could go to sleep. Scott found this species rather interesting. He would watch them puff their throat pouches up at each other in dominance displays. They would do a similar threat display to the park workers as they cleaned their enclosures. Dr. Harmon found himself captivated by their beauty. Scott could watch them for hours.

He wrote furiously in his journal about the behaviors and nuances of this species. Everyone on the island seemed to have their favorite species at this point. Dr. Bramme spent much of his time observing the behaviors of the island's Tyrannosaurs. For Nalani she seemed to prefer the Triceratops. Scott had become enamored with the Dilophosaurus. He would often drop by their enclosure at the end of the day to watch them frolic about their habitat. It was very relaxing for Scott to watch these animals for some reason. Something about their mannerisms reminded him of his job back in San Diego. He began to feel like he had a repoire with them as some of them would approach the fences when they saw him coming. Scott would often say hello to them and wave as if they could understand him. Visiting them had become the favorite part of his day, and he began to dread moving them further into the island as their enclosure got closer to completion.

It was the middle of November, and Thanksgiving was quickly approaching. Scott was thinking about Thanksgiving dinner as he threw chicken carcasses over the fence to feed the Compys. Once the operation moved to Dionysus, he was going to invite his girls to come down to see the dinosaur island. His youngest, Erica, would love it. Scott was desperate to get his daughters back, and what better way to do this than to give them a once in a lifetime experience at Archosauria? Scott continued to fantasize about his daughter's visit to Dionysus and began to imagine himself escorting them around the various Dinosaur paddocks. This was just a typical day for Scott; caring for his animals and being lost in a daydream were commonplace for him.

Back at the Dilophosaurus paddock, a young man named Russell approached the cage from the long employee corridor behind it. He pushed a large, black plastic wheelbarrow with a pitchfork in it. Various bottles of cleaning solution hung off the handle and clanked together as he walked down the hallway. Russell was in charge of cleaning the indoor habitats of the dinosaur infants while they were out on display in their outdoor enclosures. He was responsible for making sure that they returned to a clean quarters when they came in at night. Russel was running a little behind today as there was a huge mess in the young Triceratops enclosure. He had hoped to be done around 6 P.M., so that he could go home and shower before dinner. He did not want to go to the cafeteria smelling like zoo today. He had his eye on this girl who worked in IT and did not want to see her if he didn't look his best. Russell knew when she usually went to dinner, and tonight he was hoping to introduce himself to her.

Russell pushed his cart down the hall as he changed the tracks on his CD player. He began to bob his head to the bass of the new track he just put on. He got to the Dilophosaur enclosure and checked his watch. Only 4:30, he had plenty of time. Russell pulled a lever to the right of the enclosure door. This lever closed the cage door between the outdoor enclosure the indoor one, electrifying it in the process. He checked a monitor to the left of the door, circling through camera angles of the indoor enclosure to ensure it was empty of dinosaurs before entering. Russell had made the mistake of not checking all angles in the past and ended up getting trampled by some scared Gallimimus in the process a few weeks back. He wasn't about to make that same mistake with one of the carnivores, even though he was pretty sure he could take one of the Dilophosaurs. Russel was 6'3" and had a fairly muscular build. He wasn't afraid of these animals and had gotten quite comfortable around them. He pulled a second lever on the panel to the right side of the door. An alarm sounded, and red warning lights flashed as the metal door slid open. Russell entered the enclosure, pulling his cart behind him. He walked over to a small pond and hit a hidden button on the wall to drain it, so that he could scrub the concrete before refilling it for the night. Russell grabbed his pitchfork and began to scoop up the dinosaur droppings with large clumps of hay. For little guys, they sure did make a mess.

There was a foul odor coming from the entry to the outdoor enclosure. Russell approached the source of the smell, covering his nose with his shirt as he got closer. He began to shift the bedding around with his pitchfork as he looked for the source of the repulsive smell. A large group of flies filled the air as Russell sifted the hay. He discovered a decaying piece of meat that the animals had left behind. This startled Russell. He gagged as his eyes met the source of the odor. The chunk of meat was a yellow-green in color with maggots rolling over it like a lawn of pulsating flesh. He let out another gag as he speared the rotting flesh with his pitch fork and threw it into his cart. He got down on his hands and knees and began to scrub the floor where the rotten meat had been. Russell continued to stifle gagging noises as he cleaned. This was absolutely revolting. As he cleaned, he noticed that he had caught the attention of one of the young Dilophosaurs. It was standing behind the bars and watched Russell intently as he cleaned, as if it were wondering what he was doing. The animal hooted softly and cocked its head to the side like an inquisitive puppy.

"What do you want?" Russell said laughing. "I'm cleaning your mess, pendejo[9], ha-ha."

The animal continued to watch him and hoot softly as it investigated what Russell was doing. Russell shook his head laughing and jumped at the creature to try to scare it away. His gesture worked as the animal let out a high-pitched squeal and ran off. Russell laughed to himself and continued about his business. The young Dilophosaur's head became visible at the door again. It was hiding behind the wall and poking its head around the corner to spy on Russell.

Russell paused from scrubbing the pond and stopped to stare at the young animal. The Dilophosaur emerged slowly from behind the wall. It moved cautiously back into the doorway and began to hoot softly again. It tilted its head slowly back and forth from side to side. Russell laughed to himself and again approached the doorway to face the creature. He raised his hands above his head and let out a loud growl directed at the creature. The young Dilophosaur staggered back a few steps and then trotted forward to face Russell.

RAWWWWWWWWWWWWWWWWWRRRRRRRRRRRRRRRRRRR
RRRRRRRRRRR

---

[9] stupid

The young dinosaur puffed out it's red throat pouch. The pouch shook slightly, and a sound similar to a snake hissing began to echo along with the creature's roars. This was Russell's turn to jump. He had seen the creature's threat display before, but this had startled him. He knew this was a harmless threat, especially behind the electrified bars. It was time to play a little game, he thought to himself. He had plenty of time.

Russell got close to the bars and began to again taunt the creature with his hands above his head. The young Dilophosaur roared, and he roared back. Russell began to enjoy this little game, laughing to himself as he played with the young dinosaur. The animal inflated and deflated his pouch with a loud roar. Russell could see the muscles in the animal's neck pulsating slightly. The animal began to make a slight gagging motion. He had never seen the animal do this before. He paused for a second to examine the creature closer, bending over and getting closer to the cage bars to get a better look.

"Are you okay, boy?" asked Russell. "What's wrong?"

Russell had seen these animals inflate their pouches dozens of times before, and they had never done this. He would be in deep trouble if something happened to one of these creatures while he was in the cage with it. Especially if he was on camera messing with them prior to the animal falling ill. He turned to look at the door behind him, debating on if he should run to get Dr. Harmon or Reginald. When he turned back to face the creature, everything suddenly went black. The animal had projected a noxious substance from its eyes into his eyes and mouth. Russell fell backwards onto his rear end and immediately began pawing at his face. The pain! The pain was unbearable. It felt like someone had just poured hot lava into his eyes. Russell not only felt a strong burning sensation, but it felt as if his eyes were bubbling inside his head. There was a strange popping sensation in addition to the intense burning.

Russell began to scream uncontrollably and writhed on the ground like a worm whom someone had just cut in half. He pawed at his face aggressively, trying to pull a thick, viscous substance off. Try as he might, the goo would not fully come off; it was stuck to his skin! He began to feel as if his eyeballs were being boiled inside his head. There was a strong prickly sensation mixed with a burning pain. The water pool; he had to make it to the water pool to wash this noxious substance off, he thought. But how was he going to make it there if he couldn't see!?

"Someone please, help me!" he screamed in pain. "Hijo de puta, maldita sea! Ayúdame! Ayúda[10]!"

---

[10] Son of a bitch, damn it! Help me! Help!

His screams fell on deaf ears; there was no one around to help him, and the sounds of animal cries began to echo along with his cries for help. It was like they heard him screaming for help and decided to join him. Russell tried to get to his feet, so that he could attempt to make it to the water. He got into a push-up position, but as he tried to lift himself, he felt weak. His arms shook, and his shoulders began to tingle as he lifted himself off the ground. He felt the pressure of his hands being planted on the ground, but the sensation in his fingers and palms were dull. His sense of touch seemed to be fading, and all he felt was a prickling warm sensation in his hands and feet. Russell had done thousands of push-ups in his lifetime; this shouldn't have been a problem. How come it was so hard to get up, he thought. He was then gripped by intense abdominal cramping and nausea. He gripped his stomach with his left hand and moaned in pain.

Russell staggered to his feet after much effort. He was panting, and he could feel himself crying as his eyes produced tears to try to wash out the venom. He tried to rub his face, but it made the pain worse. He took a few labored steps into the direction of where he thought the water was. His legs felt like rubber and refused to listen to his commands. He could feel his right foot dragging as his ankle buckled under him. He tried to lift his right arm up in front of him but was only able to lift it half-way before it fell to his side. Russell's left leg then followed suit and buckled under him as well, his knee shook and the limb went limp. Russell fell forward again and attempted to brace himself with his left hand but again his muscles would not listen. He fell flat on his face with a thud; nothing but the bedding of the cage to break his fall. He spattered some hay and leaf litter out of his mouth and again tried to stand. This time though, none of his limbs listened to him. He couldn't move! Russell began to scream as he tried desperately to move. His body rocked slightly, but no coordinated movements followed. He was paralyzed. Russell began to scream as loud as he could. His speech began to garble as his tongue went numb. He thought about how this was not how he wanted to die. He did not want to die alone in the dark on a cold cage floor. It began to get harder and harder to scream. Russell listened as his screams became fainter and fainter. What was happening to him, he thought. He began to pant loudly as it slowly became a little hard to breathe. The muscles of his chest and diaphragm began to burn with the effort of trying to breathe. Each breath became more and more shallow. Russell slowly began to feel himself slip out of consciousness.

"Omg, Reginald, grab a stretcher quickly; we have to get him out of here," said a voice in the dark that sounded like Dr. Harmon.

Was he saved, or was this a final delusion before he died? Russell began to think about all the things he had wished he had done and all of the things he had wanted to accomplish. He felt his body being turned and then lifted. He could hear Dr. Harmon and Reginald screaming orders. One of the men said he was running to get Dr. Harper. Russell felt himself being lifted and carried out of the enclosure. Was this a dream, he thought. He felt as if he was floating in mid-air. Russell noted that his sense of touch also seemed to be affected all over his body now, as he knew there had to be a stretcher below him, but he could barely feel it. He felt something being placed on his face and down his throat but couldn't tell what it was. This was all so bizarre.

Dr. Harmon squeezed the resuscitation bag slowly as he ran alongside the stretcher carrying Russell. The boy was barely breathing when they had found him, and his lips had begun to turn a dark purple. Thank God he had come to the Dilophosaur paddock on his usual afternoon visits today. Thank God he had heard the boy's last few screams when he arrived, or Russell would have been dead, thought Scott. He carried a heavy portable oxygen tank in his right hand as he squeezed the resuscitation bag with his left. He had never intubated a person before, but he had no choice as Russell was seconds from death. The boy was hypoventilating (breathing too shallowly) and was clearly not oxygenating well. Reginald had placed an IV line in the boy and was holding a fluid bag above his head as he ran alongside the stretcher. Scott had given him a dose of two medications called Atropine and Epinephrine. These medications sped up heart rate and were commonly used emergency drugs in situations like this. He had no idea how to dose Russell but guessed based on an approximate body weight for the boy. The worst that could happen with an overdose would be death, but when you are already dying, it almost didn't matter thought Dr. Harmon in the moment. Scott looked over at Reginald as they rushed the boy to the island hospital. Reginald met his gaze and shook his head. He was clearly just as perplexed at what was going on as Dr. Harmon was.

When they arrived at the clinic, one of the nurses was already holding the doors open for them. They rushed the boy in past the front desk and into the main clinic area. They paused for a second, searching for a place to lay the stretcher down. People in the lobby stared with looks of fright at the sight of Russell on the stretcher. The reddish-brown goo was still covering his face. The scene looked like something out of a science fiction movie and was terrifying to behold.

"Over here!" shouted Dr. Eric Harper as he motioned for the men to bring the stretcher to him. "Bring the man over here!"

The men rushed off towards Dr. Harper and placed the stretcher on top of the hospital bed. A flurry of people surrounded Russell with all manner of tubing and wires from monitoring equipment. A nurse grabbed the IV bag from Reginald, pushing him out of the way as she hung it on a large metal IV pole. Another nurse rushed in and began to rip off Russell's shirt with a bandage scissor. Once the shirt was removed, she began to attach pads to his chest with wires attached to them. The various red, black, and white wires connected to an ancient-looking machine. The machine began to beat rhythmically as it read the man's EKG. His heart rate was slow, and he was having an occasional abnormal rhythm known as a VPC or ventricular premature complex. This was evidence that the venom was affecting his heart's normal electrical rhythm.

"All of you can go, except Scott," said Dr. Harper. "I may need another doctor here. And I need someone to tell me what happened."

The men began to disperse as Dr. Harper donned his stethoscope and began examining his patient. Reginald hung around as he felt Scott may still need him. A nurse was attaching a blood pressure cuff to Russell's left arm, and another approached him with a wet towel to clean the man's face.

"Wait, let me get a sample of that," said Dr. Harmon as he stepped in to cut the nurse off, pushing her out of the way.

"There are non-additive tubes in the second drawer down on the right," said Dr. Harper as he removed his stethoscope. "Good idea by the way."

Scott opened the drawer revealing various test tubes all organized by color. There were also various IV and butterfly catheter sets organized in a similar fashion. Scott grabbed a white top no-additive tube. He had quickly put on some blue latex gloves before he approached Russell. Scott used a piece of gauze to push some of the Dilophosaur venom into the clear tube. He capped the tube once he was sure he had gotten a good enough sample. He quickly removed his gloves and went to wash his hands. He didn't know if it could be absorbed through the skin, but he didn't want to take any chances.

"We found him like this in the Dilophosaur paddock," said Scott approaching as he dried his hands. "I have no idea what that stuff is, as we have never seen the Dilophosaurs project anything. When I found him, he was cyanotic, severe respiratory depression, and was bradycardic. I intubated him with what I had in my emergency bag. Technically that tube is made for a dog, but it was all I had."

"You probably saved this man's life, my friend," said Dr. Harper.

"BP is 70/30 with a MAP of 54," said a male nurse, interrupting them.

"Give him a 10 milliliter per kilogram fluid bolus and prep a NorEpi drip just in case that doesn't work," said Dr. Harper in return.

"Here, take this to the lab and have them tell you what's in it," yelled Dr. Harmon handing the vial of Dilophosaur venom to Reginald. "Go quickly! And put gloves on before you grab it from me."

Reginald rushed to put on a pair of bright blue latex gloves as he snatched the tube from Scott who was holding the tube in his rolled-up gloves. His hands fumbled slightly to don the gloves as he was clearly nervous to handle the noxious substance. Reginald rushed out of the hospital and headed directly to the genetics lab. The echoing sounds of his footsteps faded into the background. Dr. Harmon grabbed another liter bag of fluids from a cart and connected a long set of tubing to it. He opened a set of clips and let the fluid flow through the tubing and into a trash can. He then clamped the IV line and handed it to the nurse to hang for the young man as his current bag was running out. Scott stared at the young man for a moment, watching his vitals closely. A nurse came running back with a small strip of paper and handed it to Dr. Harper.

"Here is his venous blood gas, doc," said the nurse, handing the slip of paper over to Dr. Eric Harper.

Dr. Harper stared at the numbers on the paper intently and then looked back at the young man. He was clearly thinking about something, trying to put the pieces together. Scott walked over to Eric and took a glance at the paper. He could see there were several blaring abnormalities on the paper.

Russell's blood pH was very acidic, and his blood carbon dioxide level was through the roof. These were common changes when a person was not breathing appropriately. As you hypoventilate, or don't breathe adequately enough, carbon dioxide builds. This is an acid and will change the pH of your blood as it poisons your body.

"His venous CO2 is super high, and he is very acidotic," said Scott.

"Yes, he isn't oxygenating very well on his own at all. Even though he is breathing, it's too shallow and carbon dioxide is building in his system. Xavier, attach the resuscitation bag again and breathe for him for now," said Dr. Harper.

"So strange, what is in that stuff that would cause him to hypoventilate?" asked Dr. Harmon in a rhetorical fashion. "Do we have a ventilator on the island?"

"Sadly no, we are gonna have to bag for him and hope it's good enough," said Dr. Harper as he handed the blood gas back to the nurse.

The two men sat and thought about the case for a while. It was puzzling that the boy was unable to breathe on his own even after his airway was secured. Initially Dr. Harmon thought this was an anaphylactic reaction, which would mean that once his airway was cleared, he should be able to breathe on his own. This was clearly not the case. Something was impairing Russell's ability to breathe. Scott began to think about toxins that he knew various reptiles and insects produced, combing his brain for something that would cause the signs he was seeing.

When he found him, Russell was in a semi-comatose state and was taking very short, shallow breaths. Scott did not see the initial symptoms, but it was very clear that Russell was unable to breathe on his own. There were many potential toxins produced by various animals that could affect muscle activity. Some toxins would attack the nervous system and prevent you from being able to use your muscles by default. It had to be something that would attack one of these two pathways in order to prevent Russell from being able to breathe on his own. Dr. Harper seemed equally as confused. Having come from a hospital in New York City, he did not deal with very many envenomations in his practice.

"I think I know what this is!" said Scott. "Start that norepinephrine drip right away! Do we have any physostigmine?"

"Um, I think so..." said Dr. Harper questioningly as he motioned for Xavier to go check the stock room.

"Tetrodotoxin," exclaimed Scott. "It has to be!"

"Like from pufferfish poisoning?" questioned Dr. Harper.

"Exactly! Tetrodotoxin will cause muscle paralysis, including the diaphragm. It leads to respiratory failure, cardiac arrhythmias, and hypotension. The signs fit," said Scott.

"But why would a dinosaur make tetrodotoxin?" asked Dr. Harper. "I thought that was just a fish thing."

"Pufferfish, blue ring octopus, some newts, a species of snail; it's produced by a more diverse group of animals than you think. It's not just the pufferfish," said Scott.

"I hope you're right, man," said Dr. Harper. "Start him on 0.5 micrograms per kilogram per hour of Norepinephrine. I need to look up the dose of Physostigmine really quick."

The two men worked tirelessly for the next few hours, treating Russell for suspected tetrodotoxin envenomation. After several hours of treatment, Russell began to stabilize. His respirations slowly began to return to normal, and his blood carbon dioxide level began to drop. Scott stood over the young man, feeling very triumphant. It appeared as if he was right in his analysis of what composed the venom. He wanted to discuss this with Dr. Bramme as soon as possible. Scott needed to know what other surprises they should expect from these devilish little critters. He wondered what would be the paleontologist's take on this development. Before he did this, he had to talk to Nalani. They needed to put up glass shielding around the Dilophosaur enclosure as soon as possible to prevent any more envenomation. Scott took his leave from the hospital and went to seek out Nalani once he was sure Russell was in stable condition. As he left the clinic, he headed to Nalani's quarters. It was now dusk, and the sky was ablaze with various yellows, reds, and oranges as the sun set. The time sure had flown by. It was early afternoon when Scott found Russell, and now it was almost nightfall. He knew Nalani was not going to like this, but this had to get done as soon as possible.

As the days went by, Russell gradually recovered. He complained about a tingling sensation in his fingertips, toes, and mouth once he became conscious. He gradually regained the ability to move his limbs but was left permanently blinded by the encounter. This news did not go over well with the young man. He was very visibly distraught when Dr. Harper delivered the news that he was not able to save his eyes. Russell knew this meant that he was likely going to lose this job and thus lose the ability to send money home to his family in the Dominican Republic. He became quiet as he realized that he had likely lost the ability to ever work again. What was he going to do now, he thought. Most of the jobs that were available in his country were jobs he couldn't do without his eyesight. The thought of becoming dead weight for his family filled him with despair. His family had enough financial struggle, they didn't need this. Russell dreaded having to tell his mother who had warned him about taking this job when he signed up. She told him that these big corporations did not care about the little guy and did not take care of their workers. She had warned him to not take the job, fearing something bad would happen to him. Russell sat there with his head down as he began to struggle with what to do with his life now. This animal had ruined his life and the lives of his family in an instant.

The venom analysis had taken longer than Scott thought it would. The lab had confirmed that he was correct in assuming that tetrodotoxin was a part of the creature's cocktail. But there were other components to the venom that they were still working out. Either way it was a very nefarious mixture of chemicals that would easily immobilize even some of the larger animals if it ever got into their system. Dr. Bramme was fascinated by the news of the Dilophosaurs having venom. There had been a huge debate on the feeding habits of this dinosaur among paleontologists. The jaw bones of Dilophosaurus seemed far too delicate for a predator. Because of this, it seemed unlikely that it would be able to hunt down and kill prey without damaging itself in the process. A predator can't attack another animal if it is at risk for breaking its jaw by doing so. This is why it was thought to have been a scavenger and was fed carcasses like the Compys by the Archosauria staff. The ability to project a very potent paralyzing venom changed this. With this ability, the creature did not have to rely on strong jaws to bring down prey. Instead it could paralyze the target and eat at its leisure without worrying about the prey fighting back. This was an incredible discovery. They were learning so many things about these animals that could not possibly be determined from studying their bones.

The Dilophosaur attack on Russell bothered Scott. He was beginning to feel like they were in over their heads. This was now the second animal attack that they had had on the property since his arrival on Protogonus. It was very hard for him to protect his staff when there was so much unknown about these creatures. What bothered him most was how little Mr. Sana seemed to care about it. Ryo had gone so far as to bring up that animal attacks happened in zoos all the time. He said it was "par for the course" when dealing with captive wildlife. This was not what Scott had signed on for. He sat on a patch of grass overlooking the Brachiosaur enclosure. He watched the animals walk amongst the trees and marveled at their sheer size. Their small heads towered above most of the surrounding canopy of trees. They bellowed softly as they grazed, pulling branches off of the trees by the dozen as they fed. Dr. Harmon pulled out his journal from his bag and began to write.

November 10th, 1992

I spoke with Dr. Sung earlier today about the contents of the venom that Russell was hit with. The compound is horribly acidic, with a pH comparable to hydrochloric acid. This is what damaged Russell's eyes and why he will no longer be able to see. It also contains tetrodotoxin, which is a potent neurotoxin. This chemical causes muscle paralysis, preventing the victims from being able to escape and eventually killing them from asphyxia as they lose the ability to breathe normally. Once the diaphragm becomes paralyzed, it's pretty much over unless the victim can be intubated and manual or mechanical ventilation can be instituted. The epinephrine I gave Russell just prior to intubation may have helped to reverse some of the effects of the toxin before I intubated him by stimulating the body's natural drives. It gave him a chance. There are other components to the venom that we don't know just yet. Dr. Sung's team is still analyzing it. I hope this doesn't mean that there will be other long-term effects for the poor kid. He's only twenty-two, far too young to be blind and permanently handicapped.

I'm afraid we are in over our heads here. No one knew that the Dilophosaurs were venomous until it was too late. This is now the second animal attack that I have been witness to. No one seems to care. I don't think we should keep bringing back extinct wildlife until we are able to control the creatures that we already have. Juan has been missing for months since the Triceratops attack, and no one can tell me where he is or if he is okay. Russell is recovering but seems to be permanently blind. I worry that R.N.A. will have him disappear as well. I'm not okay with this! These animals are too dangerous, and we are not in control. I have spoken to Mr. Sana about this, and he brushed me off. He went so far as to say that this is "par for the course" when dealing with captive wildlife. And that accidents were bound to happen. I don't know what to do here anymore.

Scott looked up from his journal and continued to observe the giant sauropods as they grazed. They were beautiful, weren't they, he thought to himself. The Brachiosaurs were slow-moving and lumbered around the forests of their enclosure, feasting on branches as they foraged. The ground shook with each step that they took. Scott could feel the impact tremors of their steps, even from 200 yards away. He was one of the first humans to see a living dinosaur here on Protogonus. He couldn't help but feel special to be privy to these sights. His sense dread and angst faded a little bit as he observed these majestic animals. Scott did not know what his next course of action was going to be. He loved his job at Archosauria but began to struggle with the morale issues that were befalling the park. How was he supposed to keep doing this job when people were getting hurt? Scott needed to think about this. He let out a deep sigh and decided he was going to head to the aviary to see how construction was coming along.

Chapter 12

Ryo Sana was not on island when the attack on Russell occurred. When he got word of the attack, he instructed Arthur to handle it in a similar manner to Juan. He could not have these little mishaps panicking his investors at this stage in the game. He was far too close to success to have some little boy's carelessness ruin his ambitions. He was going to go down in history for one of the greatest scientific advancements of all time. Even still Ryo was losing some of his drive. The loss of his son, Ichigo, was a huge blow to him. He was beginning to find it hard to focus on his day to day tasks. As he sat in on his most recent board meeting, the speech of one of the investors began to dampen. He stared at his notebooks in front of him and began to slowly zone out. His leather briefcase on the table caught his attention. Ichigo loved his briefcase as a child. He would often hide it from him around the house. He would have to run around and search for where in the mansion he had hidden it. At the time, he had found this little game annoying and petulant. But now, after his death, he would have given anything for his son to hide his briefcase just one more time. Ryo began to feel emotions well up in his chest. He had entrusted his son to work on a side project for him prior to his passing. Ryo couldn't help but wonder if he had gotten his son killed. His eyes began to burn, and he sniffled slightly. As the emotions began to take over, he realized he needed to excuse himself from this meeting. He was going to lose it, and the last thing he needed was for his investors to see him crying. This would make him look weak and could cost him Archosauria if the investors at all felt he was unstable or unable to do the job.

"Excuse me, gentlemen, so very sorry. I have to address something urgently. I will be back," said Ryo, abruptly getting up from his seat and packing his briefcase up; he shoved all of the papers in hastily as he exited.

As he walked back to his office, he began to reminisce about his son again. This time he was thinking about all the times he would tell him he was too busy to play catch or wrestle. He thought about how he had missed stopping by his house on the off weekend for dinner more than once. If only there was a way to make up for lost time and do it all over again, he thought to himself. Ryo stopped suddenly in the hallway, causing the person walking behind him to almost bump into him. Do it all over again, he thought. That was it! He had the technology to do it all over again. He had to talk to Ethan about this at once. Ryo could bring his son back, and he could do it all over again. He would do it better this time! He would be more present and cherish every moment with him. Surely Ethan would understand and would agree. He could get a sample of his DNA from his belongings, a strand or two of hair would be all he would need to do the job. Ryo smiled and rushed off to his limousine where he had a private phone line. This could work, he thought.

Ryo rushed out of the office building, his dress shoes clapping on the concrete as he ran. His jacket flowed behind him like a cape. Ryo's briefcase beat against his side. He saw his limo driver standing in the parking lot smoking a cigarette by the car. Ryo hated when his driver smoked. It filled the car with the scent of ashtray, and this irritating smell made him angry. He had told his driver, Adam, to not smoke in his presence multiple times in the past. This had been a huge point of contention for Ryo and Adam. When Adam saw Mr. Sana rushing towards him, he panicked and threw the cigarette to the ground, quickly putting it out with his foot.

"Oh shit, Mr. Sana….I can explain…I…I…I…" stuttered Adam.

"I'll give you a pass this time," said Ryo, rushing into the back of the limo. "Put the heat on in the back, will you."

Mr. Sana placed his briefcase down and almost immediately grabbed the phone. The back of the car rocked slightly as he got comfortable. He began to dial the number to Sir Barnes's office furiously. His fingers hit the keys with a purpose as he smashed them far harder than was needed. Ryo tapped his foot and rocked a little as he waited for Ethan to pick up the other line. He knew Sir Barnes was currently on Dionysus and that phone service there was not always the best. But if ever there was a time for the phones to work, it was now.

"Sir Ethan Barnes's office, this is Amanda speaking, how can I help you?" asked a female voice on the other end of the line.

"Amanda, it's Ryo, Ryo Sana. I need to speak to Ethan at once," said Ryo into the phone loudly.

"Mr. Sana...yes, right away."

Ryo heard a click and then some annoying classical music. He must have them change this song, he thought to himself. It was such an obnoxious tune to listen to. Ryo continued to tap his foot on the floor and rocked slightly as he waited. He repeated the word "C'mon" over and over again as he sat. It seemed like he was waiting for an eternity. What could Ethan possibly be doing on Dionysus that it would take him so long to get to the phone. It wasn't like he was doing any of the manual labor himself in the fields, thought Ryo. Suddenly Ethan's voice interrupted his thoughts.

"Hello, Ryo, how are you doing?" asked Ethan.

"I'm fine, Ethan. I had an idea, and I have something I need to ask from you and the boys in the lab," said Ryo Sana. "As you know, I've been struggling with the loss of Ichigo, and I just thought of a way to fix things and make them right."

"Ah, yes, terrible occurrence. Such a tragedy to lose him so young. My heart goes out to you, my friend. I can't imagine what you are going through," said Ethan as sympathetically as he could.

"I want to bring him back! I want to use the technology we have to clone him and bring him back. It will be a shot at redemption for me, and it will be a chance to right a wrong in the universe," said Ryo.

The silence on the other end of the line was deafening. Ethan was not expecting to hear this. He was taken off guard and sat with his mouth open as he tried to figure out what to say in response to his partner.

"Now....now Ryo, this is the grief talking, and you know it. Even if you did clone your son, he wouldn't be your son. There are no do-overs, my friend. You know this," struggled Ethan as he spoke, trying not to sound too harsh.

"I...I just really miss him," said Ryo, choking back tears as he spoke. "I can't help but feel responsible for all this."

"Surely you know that this was not your fault, Ryo," said Ethan empathetically. "Perhaps you should take a break from the project...some time to grieve and recoup. I can hold down the fort from here on out."

"Perhaps you're right," said Ryo as he stared at his shoe. He wondered if he should tell Ethan about Ichigo's side project. He thought that this may be a conversation better suited for another day. Ryo had some investigating to do before he talked to his partner about this.

"Listen, Ryo, I got this," said Ethan confidently. "Take some time, go on vacation, get away. The last thing you need is the rigors of the job breathing down your neck. Take all the time you need."

"You're right," said Ryo after a long sigh. "You're right. Thanks, Ethan, I appreciate it."

"Any time, my friend," said Ethan. "Any time."

Ethan hung up the phone and sunk down into his desk. He was not happy about having to take on the remainder of this project by himself. There was nothing else that he could do, he thought. It sounded like his friend and partner was on the verge of cracking. Ryo needed the time off, and Ethan knew it.

"Is everything okay, sir?" asked Amanda as she sheepishly entered the room.

"Yes, yes, it is, my dear. At least I hope it will be...leave me be for a moment please." said Ethan.

"Yes, Sir Barnes. By the way, Mr. Bergin has called twice today asking to speak with you," said Amanda.

Ethan waved her off and stood in silence as she exited. Ethan spun around in the chair slightly as he let out another deep sigh. There was a lot of work to do before their opening this summer. He had a lot on his plate already; he did not need this. Things were not going well, thought Ethan. The moving of animals was to begin in the coming weeks, and they were having many internal issues. They were so close to completion, thought Ethan. Things just had to work out.

Dr. Harmon was gearing up to relocate yet another new species to a more permanent home on Protogonus. The animal they were moving was a medium-sized carnivore from North America. Dr. Bramme identified this species as Dakotaraptor when they hatched two months ago. Currently they stood about two feet tall and about six feet long, with most of their length being in a long rigid tail that trailed behind them. The animals were fully feathered from head to toe with the exception of their snouts, feet, and two of the three digits on their hands. Their plumage was similar in patterning to a kestrel. Grey feathers covered the tops of their heads and their small wings. Light brown feathers ran down their backs and tail with a fan of brown feathers at the tips of their tails. Their underbellies were white with black spots. A black ring of feathers ran around their bright yellow eyes. They stood on two powerful legs like all therapod dinosaurs and had long, thin arms that were well-muscled. Instead of the usual three-clawed feet that other therapods had, Dakotaraptor had a long, sickle-shaped claw on its middle toe that it could retract. It held this claw off the ground to keep it sharp, as this was the creature's killing weapon. Something about this species did not sit right with Scott. As he observed them, he noticed that their eyes and faces appeared very communicative. They hung out in a pack exclusively, unlike the other carnivores on the island. The Dakotaraptors would run around their enclosure as a group, led by a single individual. The group would move as a single unit like a flock of birds about their enclosure, changing directions with the leader's instructions. Scott would often see them chirping to each other and standing around in a group, almost like they were having a conversation. This almost human-like behavior reminded Scott of his dislike for primates. Dr. Harmon did not have any concrete evidence that they could talk to each other, but the thought of this made him uneasy.

Scott entered the enclosure with a bucket of rats, readying himself to play distraction while Nalani and her team darted the animals from behind. The bucket was filled with dead rodents that were fileted open to get the scent of blood into the air. One of the Dakotaraptors walked slowly out of the jungle, sniffing the air as she walked; she had caught the scent of blood. As soon as she noticed Scott carrying the bucket of food, she rushed forward and came to a stop just below the catwalk Scott was standing on. She then reared up and began to vocalize. The feathers on the back of her head stood up as she cried. Her loud barking call elicited a chirping from her kin. The seven other raptors came running out of the jungle and appeared to line up next to the first in a single file line at her left side. All eight raptors were now staring at Scott intently in a side-by-side fashion. They looked like grade school children lining up for the lunch buffet. Quiet chirping and the occasional barking noise filled the enclosure as the animals looked at one another and then stared at him. Dr.

Harmon threw the first rat over the edge, having gotten the signal from Nalani. The lead raptor leapt up and snatched the rat out of the air. Scott was amazed at how high she was able to get. Even though she was only two feet tall, she appeared to have almost a seven-foot vertical leap. When she landed, the rat was hanging out of her jaws perpendicularly. She jerked her head and snapped her jaws a few times to realign the rat. Once the carcass was in the right orientation, she lifted her head and jerked her neck back and forth to swallow the rodent whole. Scott readied another rodent and picked a different animal to feed.

WOOSH!

A dart flew through the air and hit one of the Dakotaraptors with a thud. The animal jumped, and her thigh muscles twitched as the dart made purchase. The animal let out a high-pitched scream and glared at its flank where the dart was protruding from her feathers. She almost immediately grabbed the dart in her jaws and pulled it out. All of the raptors averted their gaze from Dr. Harmon and turned their attention to their darted kin. They began to circle her, almost as if sensing something was wrong. Chirping and barking filled the air as the creatures tried to make sense of what was going on. Are they asking her what happened, Dr. Harmon asked himself as he observed the strange behavior. He had never seen animals react like this to tranquilizer darts. It was not something that he had expected to happen. If they were doing what he thought they were, this was a degree of intelligence that he had never seen before in the animal kingdom.

Another dart rushed through the air and missed its target. The dart hit a nearby tree with a loud thud; the dart shook a bit as it stuck out of the tree trunk from the impact. All of the raptors were now looking at the tree where the dart had hit. One of the raptors ran over to investigate the dart. She sniffed the tree and nuzzled the metal dart. The Dakotaraptor then began barking to its kin, almost as if trying to convey its findings to them. Scott did not like where this was going; he needed to get their attention again to get them to stop focusing on the darts. Dr. Harmon tried to get their attention back by throwing another rodent over the catwalk. To his surprise, the animals ignored the food and let it hit the ground without any reaction. The raptors didn't show any reaction at all to the free food; they didn't seem to care about the food at all. Carnivores did not behave this way when there was an easy meal involved, thought Scott. He began to call to them to see if he could get them to pay attention to the free food. Scott waved his hands above his head and began to tap on the railing, trying to make as much noise as he could. As he called into the enclosure, the darted Dakotaraptor began to drop its head and stagger. This elicited another very unexpected response from the rest of the Dakotaraptors. The other seven raptors began to gather around their sedated comrade. They nuzzled and sniffed her as they tried to figure out what was going on. Dr. Harmon noticed that several of the Dakotaraptors were exhibiting a behavior called eye pinning. Their pupils were rapidly dilating and constricting as they investigated their sedated comrade. This was a behavior that Dr. Harmon was very familiar with. Some modern bird species would start to have eye pinning when they were intrigued, excited, angry, or afraid. A loud scream came from a second raptor as she was darted as well. Similar to her littermate, she pulled the dart out almost immediately. When the first raptor collapsed from the sedatives, this elicited immediate aggression in the rest of the raptor pack.

All of the Dakotaraptors turned their backs to Scott and lowered their postures. They stood with their heads low, their jaws agape, and their arms spread open. The feathers on the backs of their necks were on end. The animals had their arms held open in an attack posture, spreading their small wings to look larger. Chirping and barking was replaced with high pitched screaming and growls. This was incredible; they knew they were under attack somehow. Another dart landed just short of a third raptor, throwing up dirt and debris as it hit the ground.

EEEK!

The alpha let out a loud, high-pitched scream, almost like a king announcing a call to arms for his soldiers to follow him. She darted off in the direction the incoming dart had come from, followed by the five remaining raptors that had yet to be darted. The animals grunted and growled as they ran to the back of the enclosure. Leaves beat against them as the pack rushed off straight in the direction of Nalani and her crew. Dr. Harmon stood, dumbfounded, holding a rat carcass over the railing in his right hand still. The rodent dripped blood down on the dirt below. What was going on here, he thought to himself. Scott immediately snapped out of it and grabbed his radio.

"Nalani, two are down, but the other six are headed to you, over," screamed Dr. Harmon into his walkie.

"Yeah, we see them, over," said Nalani.

Nalani stared through the lens of her rifle scope at the charging animals. They were fast, she thought. The enclosure was about fifty yards long and twenty-five yards wide. In a matter of minutes, they were already almost to Nalani and her men. They navigated the jungle expertly, jumping over logs and circumventing trees easily. The Dakotaraptors changed direction swiftly, navigating around obstacles with no effort. Nalani lined up her shot, taking care to lead the animal a little bit before pulling the trigger. Her rifle discharged, sending a dart flying through the air at the oncoming Dakotaraptors. The animal let out a screech and stopped running suddenly when the dart hit it. Dust and debris flew into the air as she came to a stop, skidding a bit as she deaccelerated quickly from a full charge to a dead stop. The dart had hit her square in the chest by her left shoulder. She reared up on her hind legs and tried desperately to bite at the dart to remove it. She tried to claw at the dart with her forelimbs as well. She was finally able to remove the dart by kicking at it with her right hindleg.

Nalani and her men were all trying to reload their rifles at this point. Nalani kneeled down to get another dart. She grabbed one from a metal box next to her, pulling it up by the puff of red fluff at the tail end. She placed the dart behind her ear as she opened the rifle chamber. She removed the dart from behind her ear and placed it into the chamber. She quickly locked the rifle chamber and stood up to take another shot. Nalani approached the slit in the wall to again insert her rifle. Before placing her gun in the opening, she leaned her shoulder against the wall next to the opening and took a quick look down into the enclosure only to be greeted by the snapping jaws of one of the Dakotaraptors. The animal had gotten about three quarters up the wall in one leap and scared the hell out of her in the process. Nalani staggered back a bit from the shock of seeing snapping Dakotaraptor jaws when she was not prepared.

"Be careful, they are jumping…" said Nalani, only to be cut off by the screams of Reginald.

"Get off! Shit, shit, shit, shit!" screamed Reginald.

Nalani immediately dropped her rifle and rushed to the far window to help Reginald. Reginald was holding onto the butt end of his gun and was desperately trying to pull it back out of the enclosure. On the muzzle of his gun was a Dakotaraptor. The animal had the muzzle of the rifle in her jaws. Her feet were planted on the wall, and she attempted to drag Reginald and his rifle into the cage with her. Nalani saw her sickle-shaped toe claw gripping onto their side of the wall. Her first response was to grab the rifle with Reginald to try to wrestle it back from the animal. Despite being small, she was remarkably strong. This wasn't going to work, thought Nalani. She stood in disbelief for a moment before instinctively grabbing a knife from her right hip. Nalani turned the knife around and smashed the butt end of it into the creature's sickle claw. A loud snapping sound filled the air as the metal knife broke the raptor's toe claw at the tip. Blood spurted out of the shattered end of the claw. The raptor let out a scream and let go of the rifle, falling to the ground. She landed gracefully and looked up at the window she had fallen from. She let out a few grunts, calling the other four raptors to her. All five raptors were now gathered at the same window. They began to leap vertically towards the window, taking turns as they did so.

"Reginald, get to the left window and try to dart them from there. Geoffrey, keep trying to dart them from your window. I'll stay here and keep them occupied," said Nalani.

Nalani stared down at the animals and began calling to them and rapping on the wall with her knife to keep them interested. Two scaly hands appeared through the narrow window, feathers extending off of them and towards Nalani, almost as if they were reaching for her. The raptor's three-clawed fingers glistened in the sunlight. She stuck her snout through the slot and began snorting and growling. Nalani staggered back a bit and fell onto the metal catwalk she was standing on. The box of metal darts immediately caught her eye. She grabbed one out of the box and rocketed to her feet. Nalani snatched a dart and jammed it into the raptor's hand. The dinosaur let go of the window with her foot and fell to the dirt floor of her enclosure. The raptor yanked the dart out of her wrist once she landed, pulling out some feathers with the dart. The dinosaurs paused and stared at their comrade; they then stared back to the window. Reginald and Geoffrey fired again, striking two of the remaining four animals. The two that had not been hit with a dart looked at each other and took off into the jungle. They were retreating, Nalani thought; it was as if they knew they were bested. Reginald and Nalani picked off the remaining two animals easily while they retreated. The two looked at each other with a long sigh of relief as the last animal got hit with a dart.

Scott came running to the back side of the paddock as Nalani and her team walked down the stairs from the catwalk. The group was joking and laughing as they walked down the stairs. They were commiserating over their stressful experience.

"What the hell was that, man?" asked Nalani. "They knew we were trying to dart them, and they figured out where we were. I've never seen an animal do that!"

"I know, they completely lost interest in me once the darts started to fly," said Scott, panting. "You guys didn't see their reaction to the first one getting darted. They were talking to each other like they were asking her what was going on."

"Talking?! Did you say they were talking to each other?" exclaimed Reginald. "That's impossible, they're only animals."

"Well, when the first one was hit, they all rushed in to investigate and were chirping. Once more darts flew at them, they put two and two together…" said Dr. Harmon, trailing off at the end as if the realization of what he had just said was hitting him.

"You saw it with your own eyes too" said Nalani, hitting Reginald in the chest with the back of her hand. "Think about what we just lived through, how they reacted to everything we did."

"You're right I guess," said Reginald.

"Well, let's get them packed up quickly and shipped off to their new home," said Geoffrey. "We don't need them waking up on us when we ship them."

The paddock door opened and then men rushed in to collect their sedated animals. They were small enough for two men to easily carry them out of their temporary holding pen. They loaded the young Dakotaraptors onto the trucks for transport as they headed off to the animal's permanent island home. Luckily for them, they did not have to go far, as their permanent paddock on Protogonus was reasonably close to the worker village.

Russell sat on his hospital bed lost in his own thoughts. He was wondering what he was going to do now that he was blind. He held his hands out in front of his face as if hoping to somehow see them, turning his palms over repeatedly. He then lowered his head and sulked, tears filled his non-functional eyes as he lost himself in his thoughts and grief. This was not how he thought he would have ended up when he took this job. When R.N.A. came to his village to recruit workers, they were promised steady work and opportunities to make some real money. Russell had jumped at the chance as there weren't many jobs available for him in his country. He had worked on some of the resorts in Punta Cana, doing construction work and manual labor jobs. These jobs were good but were inconsistently available, and he would find himself out of work for long periods of time. This R.N.A. gig paid way more than any of those other jobs did. Russell had never gone to school; he didn't have a trade per se. He was good with his hands and didn't mind hard work, but now he was useless. He dreaded having to call home to tell his mother what had happened. As he sat there, he began to hear footsteps approaching him. He turned in the direction of the sound, and within a few minutes, he felt a hand on his shoulder.

"There is someone on the phone for you," said Dr. Harper, handing him a large cordless phone.

"Hello?" said Russell into the receiver. He was unsure who would be calling for him.

"Hola, mi hijo, dime lo que pasó cochinito,[11]" said Russell's mother on the other line.

Russell paused for a second. He wasn't ready to have this conversation. His mother was asking him what happened, but what did she already know? She couldn't know he was blind as she was referring to him by his nickname, little pig. His mother had called him this for as long as he could remember. She would use the term mostly after he had done something wrong. Did she already know that he was blind? Russell struggled with what to say but knew he had to answer soon as his mother was asking if he was still there. He finally responded to her in Spanish.

"Yes, Mom, I'm still here," said Russell. "Listen, mami, I got hurt...there was an accident and..."

"The man with the sunglasses told me. I am so, so sorry, my love," said his mother. "These unfortunate things happen sometimes. Look at your uncle who lost his leg working construction. The man with the sunglasses told me everything and is offering us a lot of money for when you come home."

"Money? Mom, what did he tell you? What man with the sunglasses?" asked Russell, confused and aggravated that his mother was blowing off his injury like it was normal.

---

[11] Hello, my son, tell me what happened, little pig

"A tall white man with sunglasses came over the other day. He said you had gotten hurt and is offering us three million US dollars to take you home and never speak of it again," said his mother, almost sounding excited as she talked.

"Mami, did he tell you I'm blind! I don't know if we should be taking this money. Something doesn't feel right," said Russell.

"I know, I know," said his mother, sounding a little upset. "This is a miracle in disguise; with that kind of money, we can live without worry here. The Lord has blessed us!"

"I would hardly call being blind a blessing, Mom," said Russell, getting upset over how little concern his mother had regarding his condition. "I'm never going to be able to see again, I'm a cripple!"

"It will all be okay, my little boy," said his mother. "The Lord works in mysterious ways. This is the beginning of a good life for us, and maybe your sight will return in time. Come home soon. I have to get going."

"Alright, mami, I love you," said Russell, knowing any further arguing was pointless. He knew that when his mother made up her mind, there was no convincing her otherwise. He clutched the phone tightly and let out a deep sigh.

"Love you, too, cochinito,"[12] said his mother.

Russell handed the phone back to Dr. Harper in an almost aggressive manner. The large sum of money was comforting, but he knew it was hush money. They were being paid to keep quiet, so that the company would not have to face any consequences for him being attacked on the job.

"I just need you to sign this paperwork," said Dr. Harper placing a pen in Russell's hand and a sheet of paper into his lap. "It basically says that for the duration of your life, you agree to not speak of what you experienced here. It also states that you accept R.N.A.'s compensation for your injuries and do not hold them at fault for your accident."

"You know I can't see this, right?" said Russell. "This could say anything and you could be lying to me. I feel like I should have someone else read this."

"Now, now you have to have a little faith here," said Dr. Harper. "The company is offering your family three million US dollars as compensation, and the only way you get that money is to sign this form. Think about how life-changing that much money will be for you and your mother. Delay signing and they may change their mind about being so generous."

---

[12] Little pig

Russell let out a sigh and shook his head in agreement. He let Dr. Harper place his hand and pen in the right location and reluctantly signed his name to the paper. He was trapped, with no way to earn a living; it was better for him to take this deal than live poor and be a strain on his aging mother. There were no real options for him other than to sign this paper and take their deal. He was trapped by his circumstances and he knew it. He had no real power here.

Dr. Bramme sat on an uncomfortable bench inside a large metal cage. Large diameter rods were in front of him, casting parallel shadows on his face. These rods were not his only protection from the residents of the enclosure he sat inside. A chain-link fence stood in front of the metal bars with an electrical current running through it. The hum of the electricity filled the air. He was supposed to wait for Dr. Harmon to get here before they cataloged the island's pterosaurs, but he couldn't contain himself and had gotten there a bit early. Jin Moon had managed to bring back two species of pterosaur in the lab. The first species was the well-known Pteranodon. This was the flying reptile that every person would immediately think of if you asked them to picture a ptero-saur. This toothless flying reptile had a large crest on the back of its head and a wingspan of up to twenty-three feet. Seeing them fly was remarkable. These animals were awkward on land but extremely graceful in the air. The second species that Dr. Bai had created was a pterosaur known as Geosternbergia. This species was slightly smaller than Pteranodon, with a wing span of only twenty feet. It also had a distinctive square-shaped crest on the top of its skull, making it easy to tell the difference between it and its larger cousin.

The doors of the aviary opened and in walked Dr. Harmon with Reginald and Stephen. The three men were conversing about something as they entered the aviary. The conversation came to a halt when they noticed that Dr. Bramme was already waiting for them.

"You're here early," said Stephen. "And here we thought we were going to beat you here."

"I couldn't sleep last night for some reason, so I decided to stop by and observe our little friends here," said Dr. Bramme.

"Well, let's get started, shall we," said Dr. Harmon, motioning to the metal stairwell.

The men proceeded to walk down a long circular metal staircase to enter the aviary. The metal stairs clanged from the impact of the men's boots as they descended to the catwalks. The bars of the aviary catwalks were also electrified to repel any pterosaur who got too curious over the men walking through their enclosure. The men stopped at the first landing and walked down a large metal hallway with electrified chain-link covering it. The catwalk extended along the cliff-face and gave a good view of the valley and river below. A light mist was rolling over the surface of the river as the morning heat began to increase the temperature over the surface of the water.

The men came to the first observatory section of the aviary, which was a small platform that jutted away from the cliff-face and into the enclosure. They stood and waited for their first sign of the flying reptiles. The pterosaurs liked to roost in the crevices of the cliff-face at night and would often be most active during the day. They didn't have to wait long before a large shadow blotted out the sun over their heads. The men looked up and saw seven Pteranodons gliding over them in a V-shaped formation.

"Like a giant, prehistoric flock of geese," Reginald remarked.

"Well, that pattern is actually a very effective formation from an aerodynamic standpoint," said Dr. Harmon. "When they fly in that pattern, it creates extra lift and makes it easier for them to fly longer distances."

"What do you think would happen if they got out of here?" asked Stephen. "Also, why are they furry?"

"Well, based on their wing shape and bone structure, we assumed it flew in a similar way to the modern-day albatross. They do more dynamic gliding on gusts of wind than actual flying," commented Dr. Bramme. "As for the fur, those are actually pycnofibers. It's slightly different structurally than what mammals have but looks very similar."

"To answer your question, Stephen, an albatross can fly around the world without landing. So if they did get out, they could go wherever they wanted," said Dr. Harmon.

"That would be a huge problem! Imagine some lady walking her dog and these things swooping down and flying off with her Chihuahua," joked Reginald.

"Ha-ha, as crazy as that would be to see, let's hope we never have to think about it," said Dr. Bramme.

The lead Pteranodon folded its wings behind it and went into a dive, followed by the other six. The seven reptiles picked up speed as they got closer and closer to the ground, slicing through the air with ease. At the last moment, they opened their huge wings to slow their descent and plunged their beaks into the water. Four of the seven animals came up with fish in their beaks and flew to the rock cliffs with their catch. The remaining three ascended back into the air, circling around to repeat the process. Scott turned his attention to the Pteranodons on the cliff to watch them eat. They looked like scrawny but large pelicans as they threw their heads back to swallow their prey. More shadows passed over-head as the remaining Pteranodons and Geosternbergia joined the buffet line for breakfast.

"Richard, do you think it's safe to relocate these animals to Dionysus?" asked Dr. Harmon.

"Well, you can't have a dinosaur park without the famous 'Pterodactyls,'" said Richard as he made air-quotations when saying the word Pterodactyl.

"Yea, but I mean if they ever got loose or something happened in transit, they could wreak havoc on natural ecosystems," said Scott, clearly having some doubts about what they were doing at Archosauria.

"I mean anything we have brought back here would create a disaster environmentally if we let it escape. We just have to be extra-careful. I mean Jin had told me he wanted to make a custom Pteranodon with teeth initially. I told him we should stick to more fossil-accurate animals and not create crazy hybrids," said Richard Bramme. "We can barely control the animals we have, let alone having to deal with mutants."

"I understand that, but I just feel like we are dabbling in waters that may be too deep for us," said Scott.

"When this is all said and done, the world will remember and praise us for our work here. Just you wait and see, Scott," said Dr. Bramme. "Try to enjoy it a little more, will you."

Scott lowered his head and contorted his face a bit as he tried to think of a reply. Perhaps he was being a little bit of an alarmist, he thought. His own zoo had had plenty of animal attacks and accidents. There were also zoos around the country that lost keepers to their animals. Maybe Mr. Sana was correct and this was just par for the course.

"Besides, if you think these guys would be a problem, wait until Dr. Bai brings back some of the azhdarchids," laughed Dr. Bramme.

"Az...what?" asked Stephen.

"Az...dark...ids," said Dr. Bramme, speaking phonetically. "Picture these guys but the size of a giraffe and able to swallow you whole."

"Something like that existed?!" exclaimed Reginald.

"Oh, yes, and I would love to see one," said Dr. Bramme, smiling. "It would be the closest thing we could get to seeing a dragon. That is what the word 'azhdar' means in Persian."

"No, thanks, I'll pass," said Stephen, laughing nervously.

Scott turned his focus back to the cage as a Geosternbergia landed on a rock face about two meters from the chain-link. He stared at its large, brightly-colored head. She had a deep, turquoise patterning around her eyes and nostrils. Her beak was a bright yellow, which blended to a deep orange as it got to the tip. Her large, square crest had a pattern of oranges and reds. Each animal had a slightly different pattern on the crests, allowing them to tell the animals apart. Their bodies were covered in a bright white fluff with leathery, hairless wings. Scott began to think about how frustrated these creatures must feel. Modern day sea birds would live on ocean cliffs seasonally to breed and then would spend much of the rest of their lives soaring over the open ocean. These animals had spent their entire lives in a large cage. The aviary was big, but compared to what these animals were used to, it was small in comparison. This was always the dilemma Scott had with his zoo. Keeping animals in cages seemed wrong to him, but in this case, there was no way in hell they could release these creatures into the open.

Chapter 13

Christmas had come quicker than Scott had anticipated. This year had been an eventful one to say the least. The move to Dionysus was set for January 15th, 1993, and tensions were at an all-time high. Any interactions with Ethan had become strained and incredibly brief. Sir Barnes had become visibly disheveled in these last few months; his clothes were often wrinkled. Dark rings began to make an appearance under his eyes. He had become jumpy and was lacking his usual composure. Rumors began to circulate that Mr. Sana was no longer backing the project due to his noticeable absence. Ethan was struggling with the added workload. When asked Sir Barnes would brush all of it off as mere rumors. He would try to change the topic of the conversation and often would direct it to the future success of his business venture. It was all an appearance as Ethan was very much in over his head. The financial burden was ever present, and his investors were fed up. They seemed to be looking for a reason to pull their funding; the daily barrage of calls and office meetings were taking their toll on him. In his younger days, this would not have been as much of an issue, but at sixty-five, all of this pressure was overwhelming. Ethan had set up a Christmas party for the staff in the main hall. He planned to make several announcements at this event about how the move would look and set the tentative open date for Archosauria for July of 1993. He wanted his park opening to coincide with summer break, so that kids would drag their parents to his park on summer vacation.

Moving dinosaurs off this island was a thought that made Scott very uneasy. He had had one too many close calls and accidents to be excited about what was to come. Nalani Mwangi, who usually was insufferably calm, seemed to be jittery about what the future was to hold. Her experience with the Dakotaraptors had shaken her. She had never experienced an animal encounter such as this. The move also posed a huge challenge of how to move such large creatures from one island to the next. The sauropod species were going to be the most difficult to relocate. Ethan had selected the Brachiosaurus and the Mamenchisaurus for Archosauria, but this was not going to be an easy feat. Each animal was seventy-five feet long and over forty feet tall. With a body weight of eighty-nine tons, these creatures never slept more than an hour or two. Having such a large body mass meant that it was dangerous for these animals to lay down for too long. Due to this bulk, their own mass would cut off their circulation and potentially damage their own tissues if they laid down for too long. This meant that they would have to be transported awake in order to relocate them safely as there was no effective way to turn a creature that large in transit. The journey from Protogonus to Dionysus was a little over four hours long by boat. The animals would never make it to the island alive if they tried to cart them there asleep. Getting a vessel large enough to transport them awake was also an issue. These animals couldn't be forced to stay still, so multiple shifting bodies of that size would become an issue for any transport. Dr. Harmon realized this problem early on when Sir Barnes had told him that Protogonus was not going to be the showroom for the public. To get around this, Sir Barnes had Dr. Bai hatch a small herd of the animals on Dionysus back in late 1992 because of Scott's advice. They were currently the only dinosaurs on Dionysus as Sir Barnes did not want to fund the creation of any more dinosaurs at the moment due to cost constraints.

Scott was waiting on Sir Barnes to give him and Nalani an official list of the species he wanted moved to Dionysus. Sir Barnes had mentioned something to them about a safari-like tour in addition to the usual zoo-type attractions. Both Nalani and Scott felt this was a very bad idea. Putting civilians up close and personal with these animals was not going to end well. Scott and Nalani had to plan how to trap and house the animals for the move. They figured the Tyrannosaurus and Triceratops would be on the list of species and had begun work on how to trap and transport these animals. Nalani felt that darting the Tyrannosaurus from the safety of a helicopter would likely be the best way to go about it. Dr. Harmon felt it would be safest to move the smaller herbivore species sedated but not fully asleep, so that they would be calm on the boat ride to their new home. He planned on giving the animals just enough tranquilizer to take the edge off but not enough to make them sleep. He had to calculate how much Etorphine to give them to keep them sedated for the four-hour journey to Dionysus. Nalani and Scott had spent countless hours designing transport cages for the animals that were large enough to allow minimal movement and strong enough to contain them for the trip.

Scott woke up in the early morning hours and stretched his arms above his head. He let out a yawn as he stretched and slowly shot up to a sitting position. A ray of morning sun was shining through his deck window like the spotlight of a stage, warming Scott's face as he sat on his bed. He placed his feet on the cold wooden floor and walked over to his balcony. His bare feet plodded on the wooden floorboards as he made his way towards the morning sun. He opened the sliding door, and a wave of warm jungle air hit his face. He swatted at a small flying insect who used the opportunity to gain entry to his apartment. There was a stark difference in temperature between his air-conditioned apartment and the morning air of Protogonus. He walked to the railing and leaned out over his balcony, taking care not to get too close to the electrified bars encasing him. The sound of various dinosaurs echoed through the early morning air. Dr. Harmon could make out the distinct calls of the Brachiosaurs and Parasaurolophus. These were easily the two loudest animals on the island. They had discovered that the Parasaurolophus could be dangerously loud. Much of their communication was done at the level of infrasound and was not audible to the human ear. Their huge crests produced sound waves at such a low frequency that instead of hearing their calls, you could feel them. These animals were, however, capable of producing blasts of sound that could reach over 160 decibels. This was loud enough to rupture a person's eardrums if they were close enough to the animal when they trumpeted. Richard Bramme thought was likely a defense mechanism that they employed against predators. A blast of high energy sound could be a very potent weapon against an attacker. Ruptured eardrums could cause disorientation, nausea, and a temporary inability to walk. Dr. Harmon looked to the rising sun and saw a few Brachiosaur heads grazing amongst the trees. He marveled at their size and beauty for a moment before he began to think about his itinerary for the day, going through a list of his to-do items. Scott was going to call his ex-wife today to ask if she would allow his youngest daughter, Erica, to come to Dionysus to see his work in a few months. He figured Erica would be the key to get Ashley to talk to him again. If Erica was happy with him, then surely Ashley would come around as well. What better way to get to a teenager's heart than to show her living dinosaurs, thought Scott.

Scott turned away from the railing and re-entered his apartment, closing the screen door behind him with a loud whoosh. It didn't feel like Christmas was around the corner due to the lack of cold air. Scott was shocked at how fast the night of the Christmas party had come. He quickly put on his running clothes and grabbed his key card. Scott lifted his CD player and pressed play as he left the apartment. When he got outside, he began to stretch, reaching over to touch his toes. He let out a slight groan as he lifted his right leg onto a nearby fencepost, leaning over his leg and placing his chest to his outstretched knee. Dr. Harmon then repeated the process with his other leg. Scrolling through his CD player for the desired track, he began to hop slightly on his toes to warm up. He leaned forward slightly and took off. The wind blew his hair back as he raced down the sidewalk to the perimeter fence. Scott was running his usual course through the buildings of the island. He ran around the perimeter of the worker village, which came to about a four-mile course. Scott usually ran this route twice. He was currently on his second lap around the perimeter of the compound when he began to hear footsteps behind him. This alarmed him a little bit as he was usually alone on his morning runs. Work usually didn't start on the island until 8 A.M., and it was only five. Images of the running Dakotaraptors began to flash through his head as he ran, but part of him was afraid to turn around. If he was going to be attacked, he did not want to see it coming. Suddenly a figure blurred by his left side, lapping him. He jumped slightly and let out a quick grunt as he raised his hands slightly as if to protect himself. Looking forward he noted that the figure who had ran past him was a person. It was Selena, and she was sprinting about two body lengths in front of him. She looked back at him and smiled as she raced on down the sidewalk. Her brown hair was tied in a ponytail bouncing behind her.

"Sorry for the scare," said Selena as she increased her pace and disappeared around a building.

Dr. Harmon couldn't help but smile with relief that he was not being hunted. He found himself filled with a competitive urge. Scott wasn't going to be out-paced by some woman. He took in a deep breath as he increased his pace to catch up. He didn't know why, but for some reason he wanted to lap her the same way that she had done to him.

As he rounded the building, he could see that Selena was already halfway down the block. Scott took another deep breath and began to sprint full force forward. Buildings seemed to whiz by as he closed the gap between them. His legs were pumping like pistons, and his arms waved at his side furiously. Selena looked over her shoulder as she heard Scott closing in. She realized Dr. Harmon was challenging her to a race. She smirked slightly as she increased her pace; she had accepted his challenge and had no intention of losing. Dr. Harmon was shocked at how fast she was. Scott was going full speed and yet Selena was still pulling further and further ahead of him. He struggled to keep up, and try as he might, he was unable to close the gap between them. It seemed like no matter how fast he ran, she was still pulling further and further ahead of him. Dr. Harmon ran behind her for the remainder of his run and began to slow his pace as he got to the end of his usual route. He had lost this round. Scott came to a walking stop, placing his hands on his hips and panting heavily. He watched as Selena disappeared around a corner while he stood there catching his breath. Damn, she is fast, he thought to himself as he wheezed. Scott wiped the sweat off his brow and walked back to his room. He limped slightly as he walked; his shin splints had been aggravated by the sudden prolonged increase in activity. He quickly showered and geared up to start his day.

Scott met Nalani at the equipment shed as they began stocking up their pick-up truck for their morning rounds. Scott loaded two large white buckets of chicken carcasses onto the pick-up bed for the Compys. Blood oozed slowly down the side of the white buckets as he placed them down. Chicken feet and feathers poked out of the top of the buckets. Scott secured them to the pick-up bed with a thick but frayed rope. There was a small blood stain in this area of the truck from the repeated placement of bloody buckets in this location. Nalani was leading a small herd of goats onto the truck for transport to the other predator enclosures. Reginald was closing the door to a large trailer that contained several cows for the Tyrannosaurs. This was business as usual for the men. The goal of the day was to finish early, so that they could get home and get ready for the evening's events. The bleating of goats and bellowing of cows filled the air as they saddled up to leave. Their first stop was the Tyrannosaur enclosures. Nalani had designed an underground system of tunnels under the enclosures for the introduction of cattle into the cages. She felt it was too risky to feed them like they fed the Herrerasaurus, fearing that the T-Rex may attack the fences. The trucks made their way down the long winding dirt roads leading to the enclosures. They came to a stop in front of a large concrete bunker.

Nalani hopped out of the truck and propped the doors of the bunker open. She turned on the lights, revealing a ramp that led down into a large underground corridor. Reginald and Stephen got out of their truck and slid a long ramp out from the back, extending it until it almost touched the ground. Stephen locked it in place by pulling a lever on the side of the trailer. Reginald hopped up onto the ramp and walked to the trailer doors. He opened them with a large creak. A loud Tyrannosaur roar filled the air, and some of the trees in the distance began to shake. She knew it was feeding time! Reginald paused for a second after hearing the roar and let out a nervous sigh as he entered. He walked up to the first trailer stall and untied two of the cattle. The animals were blissfully unaware of their fate and stood there chewing on hay that was left in their stalls. Reginald grabbed their lead lines and led them down the ramp and onto the ground below. Their hooves clanked on the metal ramp as they proceeded. Reginald began to feel the ground shaking slightly as he walked; the Tyrannosaurus was approaching. He handed a lead line to Stephen, and the two proceeded to meet Nalani while Scott closed the trailer and raised the ramp. They led the cattle into the tunnel and down the declining ramp. Nalani shut the doors behind them with a loud creak. At the bottom of the ramp, they turned right down a long corridor. Piping and all sorts of cables ran overhead. A string of lights lit the corridor as they proceeded. The hallway smelled like a barn. No matter how many times they cleaned the area, the constant daily droppings of the cattle had permanently marked the area with a distinctive smell.

At the end of the hallway was a large, open service area that they loaded the cattle onto. Scott closed the gate to the elevator platform, leaving the cattle to wander about the small platform freely. One of the animals laid down to chew its cud. Nalani pulled a large lever causing the elevator motor to turn on with a loud whir. The platform shook a bit and creaked as it rose. As the cattle ascended, panicked vocalizations could be heard. It was as if the cattle had now realized something was wrong. As the platform neared the ceiling, a metallic clunking sound filled the air as sunlight began to beam down on them from the enclosure above. Large metal doors slid open as the platform passed through. The elevator clanked and creaked as the platform came to a jerky stop. Light from the surface no longer flooded in as the platform was now flush with the ground above. Scott heard a whizzing sound, which he knew was the sound of the fencing around the platform being lowered to allow the cattle to enter the Tyrannosaur paddock freely. Scott excused himself as he wanted to head to the surface to watch the Tyrannosaurus eat He had seen this before, but it still amazed him and was entertaining to watch.

Scott rushed up the hallway, power-walking as he went so as to not miss any of the spectacle. He pushed open the doors of the bunker and proceeded out into the jungle air. He rushed around the side of the bunker to a large viewing platform that had been placed there for just this purpose. He climbed up the stairs two at a time as he entered into the elevated viewing dock. Scott rushed to the window and began to peer out into the large clearing that the cattle were grazing on. He combed the tree line with his eyes, looking for the Tyrannosaur. Scott felt his heart beating in his chest. He could hear every one of his breaths and could feel the hair on his arms standing up. A door opened behind him, causing him to jump. He turned in the direction of the sound to see the others entering the gallery; they wanted to watch too. The four of them stared intently at the trees, wondering what direction the attack would come from. The Tyrannosaur knew they were there and knew it was feeding time. It was only a matter of time until she struck.

The sound of splintering wood filled the air as a tree at the far end of the clearing shattered and hit the ground with a loud crashing thud. The tree bounced slightly as it hit the ground and rolled. The head of the Tyrannosaurus rushed out of the tree line; the ground was shaking as she plodded full force forward. The feathers on her neck stood on end as she charged looking similar to the mane of a lion. The men were smiling and could feel waves of excitement flooding over them. They stood there like children, watching a magic show for the first time. The Tyrannosaur let out a loud roar, her huge mouth gaping open, showing her large railroad spike teeth. The sun seemed to glisten off her teeth as a small strand of saliva fell from the corner of her hungry jaws. The cattle let out panicked screams as they began to run away full speed from the charging Tyrannosaur. Dr. Harmon could see the whites of their eyes as they stampeded away from the hungry dinosaur. It was futile, the large Tyrannosaur covered far too much ground with each step; she was closing in on the first cow. The dinosaur lowered her huge jaws as she closed in. For a brief moment, her jaws hovered open around the hind end of the cow. She snapped her massive jaws shut around the cow, lifting her head as she did so. This picked the cow up off the ground from its rump as the Tyrannosaur took a few more steps forward before coming to a stop.

She lifted the cow up into the air as she stood at her full height, holding the poor cow eighteen feet above the ground. The cow's front legs paddled and thrashed as the poor creature struggled desperately to free herself. She jerked rhythmically in a circular fashion in the dinosaur's jaws, bellowing loudly from the pain and panic. Blood slowly streamed from her back end and down the neck feathers of the Tyrannosaur as her six-inch teeth dug into the cattle's flesh. A loud cracking sound echoed through the enclosure followed by a painful scream from the cow. The Tyrannosaur had chomped down on her pelvis, breaking bones in the process. The dinosaur raised its head backwards with the cow and slammed the animal down onto the Earth. Dirt and blades of grass were thrown into the air from the impact of the poor animal hitting the ground. Faint, muffled bellows could be heard still coming from the cow. The Tyrannosaur lifted her left leg and stomped down on the head of the cow. She grabbed the animal's hindlimb in her massive jaws and quickly jerked her head to the side, pulling the hindlimb and tail off in one fluid motion. She jerked her head and began chomping on the leg until the hoof was pointed directly down her throat. The massive Tyrannosaur then lifted her head, and with a few jerking motions, swallowed the large chuck of meat. Again her head lowered to the carcass as she grabbed the other leg. She pulled, but this time the flesh did not yield as easily.

With several tugs, the back end of the cow ripped away from her front end. Loops of bowel were now spilled onto the grass as the Tyrannosaur consumed the back end of the cow with one large gulp.

"Okay, I'm done," said Stephen as he cupped his hand over his mouth, turning away from the spectacle.

"Don't have a strong stomach there, aye, man. Ha-ha-ha," Nalani said, laughing.

"Look at how quickly it disposed of that cow. That's about a ton of meat she is downing," said Dr. Harmon.

"She must be hungry," said Reginald, nervously laughing. "It's crazy how bird-like they are. Like a giant chicken."

"This is the only place on Earth where the chickens eat you," laughed Nalani.

Scott looked back to the enclosure, seeing that the poor cow was mostly gone at this point. All that remained of the animal was her head, a front leg, and a small portion of her torso. The Tyrannosaur sure was efficient. Soon all that would be left of the cow would be a small blood stain on the ground. The way it ate was very similar to many predatory birds. Scott thought that this animal reminded him of a large prehistoric eagle. The Tyrannosaur grabbed the last bit of the cow off the ground and greedily swallowed it. Blood dripped from her massive jaws as she let out a roar. She shook her head and neck and lumbered off back into the jungle. The feathers along her back ruffled slightly as she plodded out of sight. The ground began to shake less and less as she walked further and further away. She was likely looking for a place to slumber as she digested her meal.

The men left the viewing platform and walked back to their truck. They had to repeat this process a few more times; this did not include feeding of the smaller carnivores. Scott had a smile on his face as he walked to his truck. What more could he ask for at this point, he thought. This was truly a dream job. He opened the door to his pick-up and hopped into the seat. Scott buckled his seatbelt and drove off to the next enclosure. They had several more Tyrannosaurs to feed before lunch. Scott did not plan on watching the others as he wanted to finish on time today. He was going to need time to shower and get ready for this gala that Sir Barnes was throwing them. He wondered what kind of show the old man would put on for them. Scott also began to think of what type of food would be put out. His mouth watered as he thought about what delicacies would be offered. He knew it was strange, but watching the Tyrannosaurus eat had made him hungry.

As lunchtime got closer, Dr. Harmon began to feel a bit jittery. He was planning on calling home from the landline in the supply barn. He wanted to get his wife's permission to allow Erica to come down to Dionysus. He wasn't sure how his wife was going to feel about this, but he had a sinking feeling that she was going to take a lot of convincing. He could not tell his wife about what he was working on, and trying to convince her to allow her eighteen-year-old daughter to come to a jungle in the middle of the Pacific Ocean to see a zoo was not going to go over well. Scott walked into the office in the back of the barn. The walls were supposed to muffle sounds from the outside to make the area workable, but the animals were too loud for this. Even in the office, the sounds of various dinosaurs echoed within the office walls. Dr. Harmon approached a small desk with a black phone resting on the corner. He stared at the phone and began to pace back and forth in the small room. He muttered words of encouragement to himself as he prepared to call his ex-wife. He then sat down at his desk and began to twirl the long, coiled cord in his fingers as he procrastinated. Scott took a quick look at the clock on the wall and continued to twirl the cord in his fingers. He was breathing slightly faster than normal as he looked back at the clock, realizing he hadn't registered what the time actually was. I have twenty-five minutes left to make this call, plenty of time, he thought. As he lifted the receiver, he paused for a second and let out a long sigh. Scott hated awkward conversations almost as much as he hated confrontation. He had gotten permission from Sir Barnes to allow his daughter to be one of the island's first guests. Ethan was curious to see how older children would react to his park.

Scott dialed the number quickly, knowing it by heart. He sat tapping his hand on the desk as he listened to the ringing. Part of him hoped that the phone would go to voicemail, so that he would not have to speak to his ex-wife.

"Hello," said a happy sounding female voice suddenly on the other end of the receiver.

"Hi, Emily, it's me. How are you?" asked Scott.

"Oh…hi…" said Emily. The tone of her voice abruptly changing to a somber, monotone cadence.

"How are things?" asked Dr. Harmon after a long pause.

"Well, Erica got suspended for smoking on school grounds again, but you would know that if you were around and not on some island somewhere doing God knows what," said Emily, taunting Scott.

"What?! Please don't blame this on me. I barely see the girls anyways because you never allow them to come by," said Scott.

"Do not try to pin this on me, Scott! It's not my fault the girls decide not to come visit you. Maybe if you actually made time for them when they came by, you would be more involved," said Emily scathingly.

"Listen, I didn't call you to have this argument again..." said Scott, being cut off by his wife.

"Then why did you call me?" asked Emily, sounding annoyed.

"I was calling to see if Erica wanted to come down to visit me here. We have been working on this project, and I think she will really love it."

"You want me to fly our eighteen-year old daughter to the middle of nowhere by herself to come visit you?! Are you high?" asked Emily, almost screaming.

"She wouldn't be alone. I'll be sending one of my men to meet her at the airport and take her down to the island on Sir Barnes's own personal jet," said Scott. "I really think this will be a good chance for me to reconnect with her and then maybe with Ashley as well."

"Personal jet? What is it you are doing down there that you have access to a personal jet?" asked Emily.

"I...I can't tell you that. But I can tell you that when you hear about it, it's going to be worldwide news," said Scott. "He would be able to fly her down in mid-June, after she is out of school."

"I'll think about it," said Emily. "But Scott, I don't want to hear that you left her with some baby-sitter down there to work all day."

"There is no way I would leave our daughter alone on these islands," said Scott. "Have more faith in me than that."

"I try to, but you don't have the best track record," said Emily. "Anyway I have to get going. I'll think about it. Have a good day."

"Goodbye," Scott said, hearing a click on the other end of the line.

Dr. Harmon put the receiver back down on the hook and sat back in his chair. He let out an indecipherable noise in his frustration. He placed his hands on his head and tugged slightly. Scott let his hands fall to his side and hang over the side of the arm rests. At least the conversation was quick, he thought to himself.

Scott got up from his seat and proceeded down a long corridor. His footsteps echoed as he proceeded. He had a few more rounds to take care of before the day was through. The large pipes overhead resonated with the sound of running water being pumped from a nearby river. Scott opened a large metal door, which creaked as he pulled it open. Upon entering the room, the smell of fish and the sound of running water struck him. Multiple large fish tanks lined the walls. The greenish-blue water undulated with multiple large salmon, perch, tilapia, and a variety of other fresh water fish. At the far end of the room was a large open loading area. The hot jungle air mixed with the airconditioned room. There were several trucks pulled out in front of the loading platform. A forklift was approaching one of the cars with a set of three large white barrels on a large wooden pallet. Dr. Harmon could hear the water sloshing around as the forklift approached the pick-up bed. Water cascaded over the edge of some of the barrels as the platform made contact with the truck bed, spilling over the back end of the truck. The fish in these barrels were to be used to re-stock the Baryonyx and Pterosaur paddocks. Dr. Harmon and his team made sure the rivers were restocked at least once a month to ensure the animals had enough fish to feed on within their respective paddocks. Once the rivers were restocked, Scott would have some time to finish his paperwork and get ready for the night.

He greeted Nalani and Geoffrey as he walked towards the loading bay. Scott watched as they secured the barrels in their respective trucks. Nalani made sure to place an air hose into each barrel before sealing them for transit. Without this step, the fish would run out of oxygen before they made it to the rivers due to the hot jungle air heating the barrels. Dr. Harmon jumped onto the back of one of the trucks and peered into one of the barrels. One of the large fish panicked and began to thrash wildly, splashing Scott in the face with the murky water from the barrel. Reginald and Geoffrey laughed at him before throwing him a towel from one of the trucks. Scott chuckled a bit as he wiped his face. Aside from now smelling like pond water, it was kind of refreshing. He placed an air hose into the barrel and sealed it. Once all of the barrels were sealed and secured, the men drove off towards the Baryonyx paddock.

Nalani drove out of the compound and headed towards the nearest river. She followed the river upstream to get to their first stop. The jungle road was well-shaded by the local foliage. There was a stark temperature difference be-tween the open areas and the jungle roads. It was a welcome change. Nalani began to slow as she approached the first obviously man-made location along the river. There was a small concrete bridge traversing the river with a now rusted chain-link fence below it. The river was only about two feet deep at this section and did not flow very quickly. The chain-link below the bridge made sure that any fish added to the river would have to swim upstream and into the paddock ahead of them. The car pulled up to a raised area of the platform bridge that was flush with the height of the pick-up bed. Dr. Harmon hopped out of the pick-up and directed Nalani as she backed up to the platform. Reginald parked the second truck and walked over to a small work shed that lay just ahead of them, about twenty yards from the riverbed. He quickly unlocked it and opened the door. Shortly afterwards he returned wheeling a portable loading platform. Leaves and twigs crackled as he rolled the platform towards the bridge. Reginald rolled the platform up a small ramp to the right of where the truck was parked. The wheels made a soft drumming sound as they rolled over the concrete ramp leading to the platform.

Scott helped Reginald load the wooden pallet onto the portable loading platform. Reginald hit a small button on the handlebar, causing the loading platform to lift up off of the back of the truck and raising it a few inches into the air above the ground. He backed the barrels up to a section of the platform near the railing. Geoffrey pushed open the gate of the railing, so that there was free access to the river below them. The group worked together to open the barrels and dump their contents into the slow-running water. It was hard work as the barrels were very heavy and the fish flopped about inside, spilling water everywhere. By the time they got to the second barrel, all of them were sweating profusely and panting. They rolled the barrel about three feet from the edge and dumped it slowly onto its side to allow the water and fish to flow out. As they worked, the jungle began to become creepily silent. All of the usual jungle animal noises vanished and were replaced by a low rumble of approaching footsteps. Scott shot his head quickly to the left as he heard a loud snap. The men stared at the electric fence about forty yards in front of them where the noise was emanating from. Reginald was the first to spot the long, thin, hooked snout of the Baryonyx. Short whiskers on the front of their snouts glistened in the daylight. The animal was walking along the fence line and towards the river. Dr. Harmon couldn't help but notice it had a bright blue coloring surrounding its eyes and continuing onto its lower jaw. It also had a crimson coloring on the underside of its throat. This coloring was a curious sight; normally these animals were a dull gray color with a darker gray dorsum. They were also counter-shaded with a light beige underbelly. This bright coloring around the face was not something Scott remembered seeing before in these creatures. As he stared at it, he began to notice that the animal appeared stockier than the other animals in its habitat. The large sickle claw on its thumb was also noticeably longer and thicker than the other animals.

Another Baryonyx came from the opposite direction towards the river, confirming Dr. Harmon's observations. This animal was noticeably smaller and less well-built. The distinctive coloring of the first individual was also lacking.

"Hey, doc, why does that one look different?" asked Reginald.

"I don't know," said Dr. Harmon, staring at the animal just as perplexed as the others.

"If I didn't know better, I'd say he was a buck," said Nalani, wiping sweat off her head with a handkerchief.

"Yea…I think you're right. Dr. Bai said he wanted us to keep the female animals separate with the large predators for population control reasons," said Scott. "This is clear sexual dimorphism but…"

"I trust that guy about as far as I can throw him," said Nalani, laughing slightly.

"Agreed," said Reginald. "He seems like he is always up to something."

The animals waded into the river bed up to their ankles. The oddly colored Baryonyx tilted its head slightly to the left and stared into the water. Its pupils began to dilate as it exhibited the same eye pinning behavior that Scott had seen in the Dakotaraptors. It then lowered its jaws into the river water, keeping them wide open as it waited. He stood absolutely still; even his breathing was difficult to notice as he stood in the river. The men continued their work and unloaded the barrels into the river. Schools of salmon and perch seemed to group in front of the chain-link as if they knew what was upstream waiting for them.

A loud splash and the sound of a fish tail flopping in the wind began to echo through the jungle. Dr. Harmon watched as one of the Baryonyx chomped down on a large salmon that it had just caught. The brightly-colored Baryonyx lifted its head out of the water with a loud roar and charged at the individual holding the fish. River water splashed everywhere, throwing loads of white foam and sediment up in the air. The other animal turned as if poising itself to run from the aggressor, but it was too late. The brightly-colored Baryonyx lowered its head and hit its companion under its jaw, causing the fish to fly through the air and land on the river bed with a loud plop. The two animals were now in a stand-off with each other. They roared and snapped their narrow crocodile-like jaws menacingly as they circled each other. A small group of feathers on the back of their necks stood on end as they roared. After a few minutes of screaming and bravado, the individual who caught the fish lowered her head and walked further upstream defeated. The brightly-colored Baryonyx roared after it as it proclaimed its victory. It then headed over to the flopping fish and snatched it up in its long jaws. In a similar fashion to a pelican, the animal jerked its neck to line the fish up into the right orientation. It then swallowed the large salmon whole in one gulp. A large bulge travelled down the animal's neck as it turned to approach the river once again. There it stood with its jaws open in the river water again, waiting for another fish to swim by.

Scott got back to his apartment and paused for a moment as he realized he had opened the door a little harder than he should have. The door slammed against the wall with a crash. Scott quickly checked the wall to make sure he didn't damage anything. He walked past a small table in the foyer and dropped his keys and wallet onto it. He bent down with a groan and began to untie his dusty, mud-caked boots. Scott quickly kicked off the heavy work boots; they hit the ground with a thud as he removed them. Dr. Harmon then proceeded to his room in a slow, methodical manner, being driven by will only as his energy was spent. He peeled off his shirt, which was soaked in sweat, and let hit the ground. It hit the ground near his bed with a slight plop. Scott turned the shower on and proceeded to lay out his clothes for the night. He debated on whether or not he even wanted to go to this gala. Exhaustion was beginning to set in from his long day of labor. Aside from throwing a few beers back with Nalani and the boys, there was really no reason for him to go. He already knew when the move date was and had already begun prepping to move the animals that Archosauria would open with. Steam began to roll out from the bathroom door as he went about laying out his outfit. He rushed back into the bathroom and put his hand under the running water. Pulling his hand back, he cursed as the water was far too hot. Scott shook his hand as he pulled it back from the intense heat of the running water. He adjusted the temperature and then pulled back the curtain to jump in. Dr. Harmon let the water flow over him, as if to allow it to wash the stress of his day away. He quickly glanced at his watch and began to lather soap over his body. Dirt and dust ran off his body like rivers of grime; memories of the long day flowed down his drain.

Dr. Harmon dried himself off quickly and began humming the tune of a rock song as he got ready. The nights on Protogonus tended to be cooler than the days due to the nice coastal breeze. Even with the breeze, it was still hot out. The thought of walking outside in an uncomfortable suit made him cringe. He had to look the part though, so as to not look out of place. Standing in front of the mirror, he wrapped his narrow black tie around his neck. As he adjusted his collar, he smiled at himself. I clean up well, he thought. Dr. Harmon sprayed a little bit of cologne on around his collar. The smell stung his nostrils as he applied it; he had become unaccustomed to wearing cologne as of late. The strong smell would be picked up by the animals and cause agitation. Being in the field in the sun all day also made trying to smell good pointless. If the smell of sweat wasn't enough, the various scents of the animals would envelope him by the end of his shift. He quickly packed his keys and wallet into his pocket as he shut the lights systematically. Scott paused quickly to check his pockets once more for the necessary belongings before heading out of the door. Double checking the locks on his door, he meandered off down the hall.

Scott paused for a second as he walked out of the door and into the evening air. He stared at the sky, which was alight with various oranges, reds, and yellows as the sun was setting. This place sure was beautiful, he thought to himself as he headed to the party hall. The faint call of various animals began to echo through the night sky. Due to the intense heat, dusk and dawn seemed to be when many animals were the most active. His dress shoes clapped on the pavement as he proceeded down the sidewalk.

"Well, look at you," said a voice from behind him, startling him slightly.

He turned to face the direction of the voice only to see Nalani quickly approaching. He almost didn't recognize her. Nalani usually wore a khaki shirt and cargo shorts. Tonight she was dressed in a bright blue glittering dress. All manner of jewelry hung off her body. She had glittering earrings and a large sparkling necklace on. Scott worked with her so often, he seemed to have forgotten she was a woman. He paused for a second before realizing he was staring at her. He quickly complimented her on her appearance and headed to the gala with her.

When they got to the event hall doors, two men dressed in suits opened the doors for them in a very formal manner. Scott could see sweat rolling down their faces as they stood there and held the door for him. It was a strange juxtaposition to see the men standing there as if they were guarding the doors to an exclusive event in the middle of a tropical jungle. These throws of upper-class society seemed out of place with the rustic look of the compound and the lush jungles of Protogonus. They entered the hall to see tables adorned with fancy dishware and glasses. Dr. Harmon had never seen so many forks next to a dinner plate in his life. As he contemplated what he would use each one for, he was pulled by Nalani towards the direction of the bar.

"Let's get a pint, shall we," said Nalani, lighting up as she saw there was no line.

The two rushed over to the bar and through a small crowd of people who were gathered near the entrance. As they weaved through the crowd and maze of tables, Scott took note of a small podium with a projector screen behind it. A small projector was placed on a table with a fancy white tablecloth over it in an attempt to make it look glamorous. The bright white and blue light shown out of the projector, shooting the logo for the park onto the screen. Nalani got to the bar first and whistled to get the attention of the bar keep. She had both hands firmly planted on the wooden bar as she waited eagerly for the bartender to come by.

The bartender turned around slowly; it was very clear by his facial expression that he was annoyed by Nalani's whistle. He slowly approached Dr. Harmon first and asked what he wanted from the bar.

"I'll take your finest lager, man, and this guy here will take a Shirley Temple or something fruity," said Nalani, laughing at her own joke. "I don't know, what do ladies drink in America, ha-ha."

"Very funny, asshole. I'll take an old fashioned please," said Dr. Harmon.

"Oh, hey! The man thinks he can drink like a real bloke," said Nalani, patting Scott on the chest.

"I bet I'll out last you," said Scott with a smirk.

"You're on," said Nalani, laughing as she noticed the bartender rolling his eyes at them.

Scott turned around and skimmed the crowd to see who had shown up. He noticed Jin Moon standing towards the front of the room in a light gray suit. He was surrounded by his usual cast of characters. Dr. Sung cowered in Jin's presence like a child hiding behind his mother at a social event because he was shy. Scott couldn't help but think he looked like an evil villain surrounded by the minions he used to do his bidding. He continued to look around the small room for signs of people he liked. Kyle Bergin was standing by one of the servers and was piling multiple hors d'oeuvres off of the server's platter and onto his cocktail napkin. It was quite the cast of characters, thought Scott as he waited for his drink.

The bartender placed the drinks in front of them in an almost elegant manner. The glasses almost didn't make any noise when they hit the bar. Scott picked up his drink and clanged his glass against Nalani's. He took a quick sip and paused for a second as the alcohol hit his lips. Scott had had many an old-fashioned drink in his life but none that went down so smoothly.

"Even the beer here tastes pretentious," said Nalani, chuckling as she wiped her lip with a napkin. She seemed to be in an unusually good mood tonight.

Scott chuckled and almost spit out some of his drink. He picked up a napkin off of the bar to cover his face and continued laughing. Nalani gazed over Scott's shoulder and began waving and motioning for someone to come to them. Scott looked in the direction she was facing and noticed Reginald and Stephen approaching. Maybe this wouldn't be such a bad night out after all, thought Scott.

The group drank and joked about various things as the night went on. Jin Moon walked up to the podium in the middle of the room and asked them to all quietly find their seats as Sir Barnes had arrived and wished to begin. Commotion ensued as people seemed to struggle to find their seats. Picking a table seemed to be a more challenging process than they had thought.

"Let's sit near the back away from all the stiffs," said Reginald, taking a sip of his drink.

"Agreed, good idea," said Nalani.

The group picked a table towards the back of the room that was unoccupied by the rest of the crowd. The joking continued, and Scott had become engrossed by his conversation. The room gradually became more and more quiet as people found their seats. Scott was startled by a sudden hand being placed on his shoulder. It caressed his shoulder in such a soft manner that a tingle ran down his back.

"Anyone sitting here, slow poke?" said a distinctly feminine voice.

Scott turned to see who was asking and was surprised to see Selena standing behind him. She looked elegant with her hair pulled back into a tight bun on the top of her head. Her hazel eyes seemed to sparkle in the dimly lit room. A long, sparkling purple dress flowed over her curves in a very flattering manner. Scott was struck by how amazing she looked and didn't realize that he was staring instead of answering her question.

"The seat is open, miss. Feel free to join the cool kids table," said Nalani, motioning for her to sit and kicking Scott under the table to snap him out of his daze.

"Thanks," said Selena as she pulled out the chair and took a seat.

"If you stare at her any harder, you'll scare the lass away," whispered Nalani to Scott under her breath.

"Hey," Scott said sheepishly as it was all he could seem to get out.

"Hi," said Selena politely in return as she eased into her seat.

Scott was embarrassed by his lack of a prompt response. His face and chest began to feel warm as he began to blush. He began to consciously try to stop the wave of embarrassment flowing over him, trying to think of his daily chores to get his mind off of what he was experiencing. Suddenly Sir Barnes's voice came over the speakers, urging everyone to quiet down. He was saved, he thought. Now he didn't have to struggle to have an awkward conversation with Selena.

Ethan stood at the podium and greeted the guests. He thanked everyone for coming and raised a small little box in his hand to point it at the projector. After several minutes of smashing the button, he began to shake the pointer aggressively. It was clear he was becoming frustrated with the lack of response from the projector. A man rushed up from his table and took the box from Ethan, examining it closely. They had a quick, inaudible conversation before the man sat down, and Ethan triumphantly changed the slide. This victory made his face light up. On the screen was an overhead view of Dionysus.

"Ladies and gentlemen, thank you all again for attending tonight. This night is meant to celebrate each and every one of you. You are the true heart and soul of Archosauria. As we gather here tonight to enjoy a meal and some libations, let us not forget all that we have accomplished in these last few years. We stand now on the cusp of greatness as we prepare to reveal our achievements to the rest of the world. Here before you is our lovely Dionysus, the site of our showroom floor, the site of our Archosauria. We will begin moving animals over the next few weeks. Once we are set up on our new site of operations, we will begin cloning animals on both sites. The move date has been officially set for January 15th, 1993 as we plan to have a soft opening on July 15th. Our first guests will be able to tour our aviary to see our wonderful Pteranodons. We also plan to have a safari tour of sorts that will take guests on an adventure that defies time. This is in addition to the standard zoo-type attractions we will feature."

Sir Barnes continued to drone on and on about what was planned for the different phases of opening for his park. Slides of different attractions and animals flashed across the screen as he changed from slide to slide. Scott began to play with a small fork near his plate as he drowned Ethan's voice out. He gazed over to Nalani and noticed that she was bobbing her head, falling in and out of sleep. Scott couldn't help but smile as he noticed.

Dr. Harmon ran his eyes over the crowd to see what everyone's reaction to this speech was. Many were paying avid attention to what was being discussed, but there were definitely those that like him were occupying their minds with other things.

"Riveting speech, isn't it," said Selena in a light whisper as she leaned towards Scott.

"Yeah, no kidding, any more of this and we are gonna lose Nalani," said Scott as he motioned to the now snoring Nalani.

"I think his tour idea is terrible by the way; so many things can go wrong, and the programming is very glitchy," she said.

"Nalani and I already told him that but from an animal safety perspective," said Scott.

"I guess when you're as rich as these guys, no is not something you hear often," said Selena.

A man in front of them turned around and shot them a look as if to say "be quiet." Both Selena and Scott apologized for disturbing him. When the man turned back around, Selena gave the man the finger and shot Scott a quick smile. The two turned their attention back to Ethan again, who was now talking about utilizing Dionysus's large inland bay to bring back marine reptiles in the later stages of the park's opening. The ocean fed the bay directly through a small salt water river. Scott couldn't help but thinking this was also a terrible idea. If any of these reptiles ever escaped into the rivers, it wouldn't be long before they would return to the open ocean. A large marine reptile would not be a good thing for the already struggling whale population of the world. Scott lowered his head and shook it in dissent. Ethan was having delusions of grandeur as per usual.

The speech seemed to go on for ages. As Sir Barnes wrapped up his discussion of future expansions on different island archipelagos around the world, Scott could see that he had lost most of his audience. Ethan finished his long speech to the delight of everyone. As he concluded, he raised his hands and men flooded out from doors behind him carrying their dinner. A large plate was placed in front of him with a giant piece of juicy-looking steak, vegetables, and mashed potatoes. The group looked at each other with excitement in their faces. Selena, on the other hand, did not seem as happy. She grabbed the attention of one of the waiters before they had a chance to pull away.

"I don't eat red meat. Do you have a fish or vegetarian dish by chance?" asked Selena.

"Yes, of course, ma'am," said the waiter as he lifted her dish away and whisked off back to the kitchen.

"I'm surprised you eat meat as a veterinarian," said Selena to Scott as she placed her napkin onto her lap.

"Well, I mean, I guess I never really thought about it much," said Scott, stumbling over his words. He felt a little embarrassed that he didn't have a response prepared for her.

The waiter returned with a large plate of fish and vegetables for Selena and placed it in front of her. She thanked him as she picked up her fork, preparing to eat. Remarks of how good the food was echoed throughout the table. Nalani in particular seemed to enjoy her dish the most as she was already almost done with the large portion of beef.

The night began to wind down, and people slowly began to filter out of the event hall. Sir Ethan Barnes was talking with Dr. Bai and Kyle Bergin at the front of the event hall. The conversation seemed to be very intense as Kyle was waving his hands rather aggressively. This aggressive hand movement caught Dr. Harmon's attention. As he watched the events unfold, a man tapped him on the shoulder and told him that Sir Barnes was requesting his presence. He excused himself from the table, taking care to wipe his face one more time with his napkin before he approached the group. Scott weaved his way through the tables and small groupings of people before he got to Sir Barnes.

"Now, now, Mr. Bergin. Let's talk about happier things. Dr. Harmon is here," urged Sir Barnes. "We shall continue this little debate later."

"Whatever, this isn't over, Ethan. We need to settle this soon, or I'm not going to keep running this little show for you," said Kyle in a clearly agitated tone. He crossed his arms and scowled at Sir Barnes.

"Yes, we will settle this little financial debate once and for all, but for now let me talk to Dr. Harmon," Sir Barnes said as he seemed to try to dismiss Kyle.

"So sorry about that, Dr. Harmon. Now let's discuss a species roster for Dionysus," said Ethan. "I understand that you and Nalani have already begun preparations for the transportation of the Tyrannosaurus Rex and Triceratops."

"Yes, we figured they would be in demand animals that you would want for the showroom's opening," said Scott. "We were thinking eight species in total in addition to the Pteranodons."

"Oh no, no, no. Think bigger, my boy. We were thinking fifteen species for the initial tour," said Ethan very jovially. "Not to mention the other enclosures off the tour route."

"Fifteen?!" repeated Scott, sounding alarmed. "Sir Barnes, with all due respect, that is a lot of work to move that many of these animals in such a short time."

"Yes, double digits will go over better with the guests," said Dr. Bai. "Tyrannosaurus Rex, Triceratops, Gallimimus, Parasaurolophus, Brachiosaurs, Baryonyx, Metriacanthosaurus, Dakotaraptor, and Microceratus. I am currently working on Proceratosaurus and Iguanodon. I also think we should include Pachycephalosaurus, Stegosaurus, and Compsognathus. We will bring these animals over, but they will not be put on display until phase two. Then for the final species, we were torn between the Dilophosaurus and the Concavenator."

"I would argue very strongly against the Dakotaraptors, Sir Barnes," said Scott firmly.

"Now, Dr. Harmon, they are beautiful animals and will be very entertaining for our audience," said Ethan defiantly as he turned to notice Kyle was still standing with them. Ethan turned to Kyle to include him in the debate. "Mr. Bergin, what do you think would be best for our park?"

Kyle stared at the at Ethan menacingly with a very annoyed look on his face. His mouth was twisted, and his brow was furrowed. He appeared as if he was trying not to say something out of anger.

"Whatever, Ethan, I'm out of here," said Kyle, storming off in a rush.

"Right...." said Ethan as he tried to ignore Kyle's display of contempt.

"Ethan, again I must insist that we not move the Dakotaraptors or the Dilophosaurus off this island," said Scott. "It's far too dangerous."

"Nonsense, Dr. Harmon, we are in complete control here," said Ethan confidently. "These are beautiful animals that the public has the right to see. Begin preparations for relocating the animals Dr. Bai has mentioned, as well as seven of the Pteranodons as soon as possible. This is not a discussion."

"Yes, yes, sir," said Dr. Harmon as he sheepishly walked back to his table.

None of this set right with Scott. Scott felt very torn at the idea of what he was being asked to do. Moving the Dakotaraptors and Dilophosaurs seemed like a very dangerous venture. These animals posed more of a danger than your standard run of the mill dinosaur. It was as if Ethan had no idea how dangerous this was going to be.

Scott returned to his group defeated with his head hung low. He dragged his feet a bit as he wandered back to the table contemplating how cavalier he felt Sir Barnes was being. Scott did love these animals, and he was happy with his position, however, he felt that Sir Barnes and his team were throwing caution into the wind. To Dr. Harmon, it seemed as if R.N.A. cared more about getting these animals on display than it did about displaying them to the public safely. They had no contingency plans and seemed to be placing profit over caution. Scott also began to wonder if Dr. Bai was purposely trying to breed the animals to save the company money by mixing the sexes. Natural breeding was free, whereas cloning them cost a fortune. He was noticing male animals in all female paddocks due to their gender dimorphism, a difference in appearance between the male and female of a given species. There was something fishy going on here, and Scott did not like it.

Nalani was slightly red in the face with a smile from ear to ear. She jovially handed Scott another drink while mumbling something about Dr. Harmon not keeping up with her as promised. Scott took the drink and began to sip from it. He stood there quietly and stared into the bottom of his glass.

"What's the matter?" asked Nalani. "He isn't firing you, is he, ha-ha."

"He wants us to move the Dakotaraptors to Dionysus next month," said Dr. Harmon glumly, throwing back a large gulp from his glass.

Nalani and the rest of the veterinary team stood there silently. The laughing and joking that had been filling the table was now replaced with silence as they contemplated what moving these animals would look like.

"What? Is that bad?" asked Selena. "Isn't that what we made these things for, public display?"

"You have no idea what those things…" began Reginald as he was cut off by Dr. Harmon.

"The Dakotaraptors, well…they show a level of intelligence we were not expecting," said Scott. "They were somehow able to recognize our tranquilizer rifles as a threat and attacked the shooters as a group when we tried to move them the first time."

"Don't be ridiculous, they are just animals, guys. I mean we have a Tyrannosaurus Rex on this island for God's sake," said Selena, almost seeming to laugh at them. She stopped her giggling when she noticed no one found her statement humorous.

"You don't understand, miss, I've seen many animals hunt in my day. Been around predators my whole life in Kenya. These creatures, the Dakotaraptors…They are dangerously smart, and smart animals have a tendency to escape their enclosures," said Nalani. "Give these things enough time and they will be traipsing about Dionysus, munching on our guests."

"You guys are legit scared of these things," said Selena, laughing. "They are animals, I mean, c'mon. Plenty of dangerous animals live peacefully in zoos all over the world."

"Come by the enclosure sometime and you'll see why these things are so dangerous," said Reginald.

"Maybe I will," said Selena defiantly as she finished the rest of her drink. She slammed her glass on the table.

The discussion continued as the lights came on; it was clear that the party was over. People slowly began to shuffle out of the event hall as the loud conversations that filled the air slowly began to taper off. Dr. Harmon began to feel a wave of exhaustion wash over him; it had been a long day, and he had to do it all over again tomorrow. He muffled a yawn with his hand so as to not seem rude. Looking at his watch, he noted that it was after 11 P.M. Nalani was shockingly the first to excuse herself, saying she needed to turn in, or she wouldn't be able to work. The group all agreed and began to disperse.

Scott, Selena, and Nalani walked out of the building together as the last remaining stragglers of the party dissipated. Stephen and Reginald left as they came, together. Dr. Harmon wished them a good night and watched them walk off towards their quarters. There was a slight awkward tension in the air as the three remaining from the group stood in a slight silence.

"Well, I'm gonna head back to my room now," said Selena, breaking the silence.

Scott was quietly zoning out and had not noticed that Selena was still hanging around despite having just said goodbye. He winced slightly as Nalani stepped on his foot. At first he didn't understand why, but then it became obvious to him what Nalani's intent was as she motioned towards Selena with her eyes when Dr. Harmon looked at her.

"I can walk you back," offered Scott nervously.

"It's okay, I'm a big girl. I can walk myself home," said Selena confidently.

"Really, it's no problem, I'll walk you back. Wouldn't want you to get eaten by a stray dinosaur," said Dr. Harmon, embarrassed that he had just said something so corny. I couldn't think of anything better than that, he thought to himself. It was a poor attempt at trying to sound smooth.

"Okay, if you insist. Such a gentleman," Selena laughed and smiled at him.

The two said good night to Nalani and walked off into the night together. The sounds of various animals grew louder as they headed towards the dorms. Dr. Harmon began to rack his brain for something to say to her but continually came up blank. This wasn't exactly the suave move he had hoped it would be. A Tyrannosaur roar resounded through the night sky; the two could feel the sound waves in their chests as they walked.

"Being up close to one of those things must be terrifying," said Selena. "It's still very surreal to hear living dinosaurs, even though I've been on this island for a long time."

"Yeah, they are definitely intimidating," said Scott. "It's amazing how fast they grow. A few months ago, they were only about three feet tall. Now they are all over sixteen feet."

"That's crazy," said Selena, not knowing what to say to his comment. "So how did they get you down here?"

"They needed a veterinarian and, well, here I am," said Scott. He didn't want to tell her that he was a divorced father of two who struggled with depression and had nothing else going on in his life. Scott wanted her to think he was some badass, dinosaur veterinarian. He did not want her to know about his troubled personal life back home.

"Makes sense…" said Selena, pausing awkwardly at her door. "Well, this is me. Thanks for walking me back."

"Oh, okay. Good night," said Scott. "It was a fun night."

"It sure was," said Selena.

The two stood there for an excruciatingly long, awkward pause. Scott had realized that he had just frozen and had no idea what to do. Thoughts rushed through his head as he began to contemplate if he should try to make a move or not. Suddenly she leaned in slightly and kissed him on the cheek. A warm tingle rushed down Scott's spine as her warm lips hit his face. She opened her door with her key card while shooting him a flirty smile and walked inside, closing the door behind her. Scott followed her with his eyes, standing frozen with a dumb smile on his face. He felt his cheeks flush red slightly and become warm. This was the first time he had had a positive interaction with a woman in a long time, probably since his divorce, he thought. He turned and walked back to his room, almost bouncing as he went. Tonight was a good night, he thought to himself.

Chapter 14

Nalani sat on the edge of her seat with her air rifle held tightly at her side. A large set of headphones covered her ears and thick-brimmed sunglasses shielded her eyes. The sound of the helicopter's rotary blades blocked out almost all the other ambient sound. The helicopter jostled slightly about as it hovered just above the tree line, flying low so as not to miss its target. Today was the first stage of moving day. Nalani had instructed several teams on how to move the Parasaurolophus, Pachycephalosaurus, Gallimimus, and Triceratops. The plan was to move the larger animals in the first wave of the move and then come back for the rest of the smaller ones in the following days. Dr. Harmon and Nalani had thought it best to handle the Tyrannosaurus Rex personally, not trusting their teams with such a dangerous task. Nalani sat strapped into her seat and ready to dart the animal. Just behind them was a heavy lift cargo helicopter carrying a large metal cage underneath it. The cage swung very slightly in the wind as the helicopter advanced through the air. This helicopter flew at a slightly higher altitude, so as to not hit the transport cage on the trees below. If all went well, they would have the Tyrannosaur in the cage and on the cargo ship by lunchtime. The goal was to leave Protogonus by early afternoon, so that they could get to Dionysus before nightfall. Nalani could feel the hairs on the back of her neck begin to stand on edge at the words "she's just up over the ridge there," echoing through her headset. The helicopter banked over a small ridge, causing the canopy to ripple like the surface of a calm lake being struck by a stone. Branches fluttered and waved under the thrust of the passing helicopter. The sounds of cracking twigs echoed through the jungle below, and a few small birds took flight from their perches as the helicopter passed overhead.

A large field became visible with a lake in the center. Through this gap in the forests, their target became visible as a small bipedal object in the distance. The Tyrannosaur lifted her massive head from the pond that she was drinking from as she noticed the helicopter approaching. Water flowed from her massive jaws, and she rose to her full height. A loud bellow filled the air as water spewed from her mouth in a fashion similar to a dragon spitting fire. Her teeth glistened in the early morning sun as her terrifying jaws swung open. A mane of white feathers ruffled around her neck as she prepared to defend herself from the invaders. Nalani raised her rifle and looked down the barrel through her scope; they were still out of range.

"Bring the chopper around closer to her side, over," she said into the microphone attached to her headset.

"Roger that, swinging around closer," said the pilot.

The helicopter increased in speed and began to rush over the open field to flank the large predator. Despite being at a decent altitude, the grass below was fanning out in response to the down-draft of the helicopter rotor. The dinosaur kept her gaze focused on the strange flying metal animal. It seemed to Nalani that she was trying to decide if this strange object was food or foe. As they came in closer so that Nalani could take a shot, the Tyrannosaur stood there defiantly, refusing to back down. She faced the helicopter and bellowed loudly to challenge it. Her deafening roar echoed over the whirring blades of the helicopter and resonated in the chests of all on board. She lifted her right leg and slammed it down onto the ground as she bellowed. The impact tremor from this action could be heard by everyone in the helicopter, even though they were hovering about fifty feet over the ground. This invader was not going to be taken lightly by the animal.

Nalani looked through her scope another time; she was within range to take a shot, and luckily for her, she had a big target. She had six and a half tons of bulk to aim at. This was going to be easy, thought Nalani. She began to take aim at the Tyrannosaur's massive thigh. A large muscle group like this was filled with blood vessels that could carry the potent sedatives through her body and knock her out. Nalani had to be careful though, if she happened to fall as-leep in the body of water she was drinking from, they would never be able to get her out in time before she drowned. She was far too heavy for the men to move her quickly. This was not something she would want to try to explain to Sir Barnes. Nalani's finger hovered over the trigger as she readied herself to fire. Her line of sight bounced slightly with the motion of the helicopter. Hitting a moving target was bad enough, hitting a moving target while moving yourself was very difficult. Nalani pulled down on the trigger; she almost wasn't able to hear the sound of the rifle going off between the roaring Tyrannosaur and the whirring helicopter blades. The dart struck the Tyrannosaur in the thigh just above its knee. The quadriceps muscles of her thigh contracted, and her skin shuddered from the impact of the dart. Feathers along her back stood on end as she lifted her leg in surprise.

The animal let out a mighty roar as it tried to process what was happening to her. One dart was not going to be enough for an animal this large, especially not when it was so worked up already. Nalani opened a large metal case and pulled out another dart. The metal tip glistened in the early morning sun, and the pink fluff at the end of the dart bristled in the wind. Nalani took care not to grab the dart anywhere near the tip. Etorphine was a very potent opioid. She had lost a friend to this chemical. Her friend had a bottle of this drug on his dashboard. It would roll back and forth as his car moved about the savannah. He happened to place an apple on the dash one day without even thinking. When he began to eat the apple out in the field, he passed silently before he realized he had had an accident. If Nalani got just a little bit of this drug into her system, it would be enough for her to end up just like her friend. The danger of handling these darts was very real and was almost as dangerous as the creature she was using them on. Nalani opened the chamber of the rifle and slid the dart inside. She closed the chamber and raised her rifle again as the helicopter jutted forward. Nalani fell forward slightly with the motion of vehicle. She was then jerked back by the seatbelt across her chest. Thankfully she was strapped in, or she may have fallen out of the cabin. Nalani was about to complain when she noticed that the Tyrannosaur had decided to walk away from them while she was focused on reloading. They were now in pursuit of the creature as it rushed for the safety of the forest. Nalani had to hit her again before she made it to the tree line, or recovering her was going to be exceedingly difficult. She hung out of the side of the helicopter, leaning her torso out of the cabin. Nalani raised her rifle once more and aimed at the muscular back of the animal. Her line of sight wandered with the movement of the helicopter. Nalani began to feel anxious as the animal got closer and closer to the tree line. She squeezed the trigger and watched as the second dart hit the animal in the back, just to the left of her spine. The dart buried itself in the line of feathers running down the back of the massive predator.

The Tyrannosaur bellowed and banked off to the right hand side, away from the tree line. The helicopter pilot flew up along the animal's left side, placing himself between the T-Rex and the safety of the forest. The Tyrannosaur began to slow down and stumble slightly as she walked. Nalani noticed she was heading dangerously close to the shore of the lake again.

"No, no, no, no! Pilot, get to her right side and chase her away from the water, over," screamed Nalani into her headset.

"Roger that," said the pilot.

The helicopter cruised over the back of the Tyrannosaur and now placed itself between the dinosaur and the water's edge. Nalani pulled her handgun from her hip and fired several shots over the animal's head to startle her. The animal snapped at the air in the direction of the helicopter, as if telling them to stay away. Fortunately the helicopter was well out of biting range. She veered back towards her left-hand side and away from the water's edge. Her thunderous footsteps echoed throughout the enclosure in a rhythmic percussion. The Tyrannosaur slowly began to come to a stop and swayed slightly with each new step. She stood there, frozen on the open plains of her enclosure panting heavily. Her large chest rose and fell as her warm breath flowed from her nostrils like two air cannons. Dust and leaf litter stirred under her snout as she breathed. Her head hung low to the ground; she was clearly feeling the effects of the tranquilizer.

The Tyrannosaur lowered herself to the ground, sitting down on her muscular, powerful hind limbs. She held her head just above the Earth as her eyes began to glaze over. Her terrifying jaws swung open in a loud yawn, revealing a row of gigantic, yellowed teeth. She lowered her head towards the Earth and slowly closed her eyes. Nalani was equally happy about their success and terrified by the thought of getting on the ground with her. Her stomach began to sink as the helicopter began to descend to the ground below. The cargo helicopter that was following suit also began to descend. A metallic creaking sound echoed through the air as the cargo helicopter lowered the metal cage to the ground below. Once the cage was on the ground next to the animal, a series of ropes fell from an open door. Multiple men began to descend down the side of the helicopter and onto the cage below. Some of the men began to climb down the side of the cage while others disconnected the large cage from its attachment to the helicopter. The cargo helicopter again took off into the sky and proceeded to hover over the large animal. Men began to furiously work towards the back of the cage as they opened the large doors on top of it.

Nalani got out of her helicopter very tentatively. She was not excited at being on the ground with such a large predator. No lion had ever filled her with as much anxiety as this creature did. Nalani felt that she at least stood a chance against a lion. She could try to beat it off with a stick or could shoot it with a gun to scare it away or kill it. This animal would not care about either of those things as it would swallow her whole before she could even think of a way to fight back. She approached the Tyrannosaur slowly, partially hoping someone else would test to see if she was for sure asleep. As she looked at the other team members, she could see they were approaching the predator with the same level of caution. Men slowly advanced towards the animal as they whispered to each other. Everyone was very clearly uneasy about this.

"Unnerving, isn't she?" whispered Scott as he approached Nalani.

"Very much so…" said Nalani. "That has to be the understatement of the century."

One of the men creeped up close to the Tyrannosaur and paused a few feet from her. He gingerly extended his leg towards the animal's large foot. The tip of his boot barely touched her skin before he withdrew his leg. The man giggled nervously as he extended his leg one more time, kicking one of the large toe claws of the animal's foot. His boot made contact with a soft thud and elicited no reaction from the animal. He promptly kicked it a few more times before another worker stopped him. One of the men reached into a pouch and pulled out a small flare gun. He fired a red flare into the air to signal to the helicopter to continue with the second part of the capture.

Thick rubber bands attached to large diameter cables fell from both sides of the cargo helicopter. Men rushed to grab the bands after they cascaded onto the ground below. Now began one of the most nerve-racking processes that any human probably had to endure. The team of men began to attach the rubber restraints around the sleeping predator. A group of forklifts with a large wedge-like attachments over their blades advanced towards the animal. They lined up along her side and slowly slid their wedges under the animal. There were two forklifts on either side of the creature, poised to lift her massive body off the ground. A team of men stood nervously at the ready, holding the straps in hand. The forklifts creaked and shuddered as they picked the massive animal up off the ground. Once the animal was no longer being hoisted, the men then proceeded to crawl under her on their bellies. Their job was to thread the rubber straps under her tail base, chest, and abdomen. Terror filled their eyes as they army-crawled under the beast. Her large body radiated heat onto them. A few of the men pinched their noses from the foul odor emanating off of the large predator. The men paused occasionally to look up at the animal above them, realizing what their fate would be if the forklifts gave out. A loud metal creak filled the air as the animal shifted its weight slightly on the forklift beds. The men began to crawl as fast as they could, all fearing being crushed under the Tyrannosaur. Scott reached down and grabbed the hands of one of the workers to help him to his feet. The two of them pulled the rubber strap under the creature's massive bulk, so that she was now placed at the center of the straps.

Once all of the men were out from under the beast, the forklifts lowered the creature back to the ground. Her massive jaws were now suspended from a set of cables just a few feet above the ground as the rest of her body returned to the Earth. The forklifts backed away, leaving the enclosure while several men climbed on to the back of the animal. Scott swallowed hard as he felt a huge lump building in his throat. So far everything was going according to plan, but at any moment, this could go south very quickly. The men stood on the creature's broad back, struggling to keep their balance due to the uneven footing. They attached the two ends of the rubber straps to the cables they hung from to form a cradle for the huge creature. Scott motioned for all of the men to get clear of the Tyrannosaur on her left side while Nalani did the same on the animal's right. A green flare rose into the air, signaling to the helicopter that the animal was ready for transport. The rotary blades began to increase in their rotation speed as the helicopter attempted to climb. The rubber bands snapped taught, and the sound of them creaking filled the air as they began to bear the weight of the Tyrannosaur.

Slowly the large Tyrannosaur began to rise up into the sky. Its legs extended limply and were dragging on the ground underneath it. Slowly the animal's legs began to leave the ground with its large toe claws being the last thing to touch the grass before the animal ascended into the air. The helicopter climbed to about a hundred feet off the ground before it began to move towards the open metal cage. Men with red marshalling wands began to direct the motion of the pilot towards his destination. The helicopter began to slowly descend as it hovered over the open metal cage. Slowly the Tyrannosaur was lowered into the cage. Its feet made contact with the bottom of the cage first, her claws lightly scratching on the metal. Her long legs folded underneath her as her bulk descended to the ground. Her head was the last thing to touch the cage bottom. Men rushed into the enclosure with the animal through the bars to disconnect the rubber bands from the helicopter. The plan was to leave the rubber transport bands in there with her and have her sort out removing them when she woke up. Once all of the bands were disconnected, the men rushed out of the cage to close the doors on the top of the cage above the sleeping predator.

The helicopter again began to descend, so that the cage could be attached to the bottom. Men climbed up the bars of the cage like spiders climbing up a web as they re-entered the helicopter. Once the cargo was secure, the rotors of the massive cargo helicopter began to increase their rotation. Nalani hung onto her hat as a rush of wind blew across the ground. She stood there with Scott, watching the large Tyrannosaur ascend into the sky. The animal rose far above the tree tops as the helicopter pilot got to a cruising altitude, so that he could make the journey to the tanker waiting in the harbor of Protogonus. Scott patted Nalani on the shoulder and motioned for them to head to their helicopter. They wanted to check in on the other teams to make sure that the capture of the other animals had gone just as smoothly. Nalani and Scott broke into a light jog as they rushed to the helicopter. Scott put on his headset and called up to the pilot to head to the docks. He secured himself into his seat by clipping his seat belt. The helicopter jolted and rocked as it took off from the now empty Tyrannosaur paddock. Dr. Harmon could see a small indent in the ground once they were in the air that had been left by the sleeping Tyrannosaur.

The helicopter made its way over the enclosures and the worker village as it headed to the docks. Scott closed his eyes as their journey continued. He had some time to take a quick nap before they got to their destination. He was jostled awake after what seemed like no time at all by the helicopter coming in for a landing on a small helipad near the dock. Once the helicopter skids made contact with the ground, Scott and Nalani began to unbuckle their seatbelts and take off their headsets. Both were anxious to get to their team to hear how things went. Scott jumped to the ground as soon as the helicopter doors swung open. He walked off the helipad and down a small set of metal stairs. Scott walked a short path through some trees before he got to the docks. Trucks with cages attached to them filled the area. Various animal cries resounded through the air as Dr. Harmon approached. He passed by one of the trucks that they had used to transport Titan when she was small. Instead of a young Tyrannosaur in the cage, however, a trio of Gallimimus paced back and forth. Their high-pitched cries filled the air as the animals aimlessly wandered in their cage. As they walked in the cage, the car creaked under their weight, and the tires shifted in the gravel.

"Reginald, where is Reginald?" called Dr. Harmon.

"What's up, doc?" asked a voice from behind a nearby car.

"Why aren't these Gallimimus sedated, and why is there a pack of Microceratus in that car over there?" asked Dr. Harmon. "The Microceratus were scheduled to go Thursday, not today. And these Gallimimus are gonna stroke out if they keep doing this the whole four-hour trip."

"The Microceratus were close to the Trikes, and we had time, so we figured we would grab them and save ourselves a trip," said Reginald. "As for the Gallis, they burned through the sedatives we gave them and all woke up way sooner than we thought. We will get them re-dosed right away."

"I'll take care of redosing them," said Nalani. "You focus on getting these animals counted and onto the damn boat. We have three hours before we have to cast off."

"Yes, sir," said Reginald, running off with his clipboard.

Scott walked among the various trucks to observe the dinosaurs before they were placed onto the boat. He wanted to make sure every creature was properly sedated. He walked by a large vehicle with a Triceratops sleeping soundly in the back. Her breath echoed rhythmically as he walked past. Another truck contained about five sleeping Pachycephalosaurs. Dr. Harmon continued his visual role call as he walked among the trucks. A loud clanging sound coming from his left side startled him and caused him to jump back. A large Pteranodon had slammed against the cage bars; its long, sharp beak poked out of the bars as the animal screamed. It was trying desperately to get at Scott as he walked by. Soon two other Pteranodons were following suit and trying to get at him. Scott shook his head and took a deep breath. This was going to be a long boat ride, he thought.

Dr. Harmon climbed onto the boat through a ramp that was placed onto the dock. He paused for a second to marvel at how massive the ship was. Her large cargo bay could easily fit all of these animals and would likely have room left over. Scott saw a large vehicle at the very back of the cargo bay. The back of the vehicle was covered with a thick black tarp that was secured to the floor of the boat with large metal clips. A loud roar emanating from the vehicle told Scott instantly what was residing under the tarp. Their buddy from earlier had made it safely to the ship and was wide-awake it seemed. Scott placed his finger in his ears and began to twist them. The bellow of the Tyrannosaur echoed throughout the cargo bay. He was going to have to sedate her again, or her cries would terrorize the others on board for the whole four hours. The vehicle shook slightly as another roar resounded through the ship. Scott walked over to an armed guard who was standing watch near the Tyrannosaur.

"Do you have live rounds or tranquilizers in those rifles?" Scott asked one of the soldiers guarding the Rex.

"The rifles have darts, but we have live rounds in the automatic weapon on our backs," said one of the soldiers.

"I need you to tranquilize that T-Rex as often as needed to keep her quiet please," said Scott.

"You want us to what?" asked one of the soldiers, clearly very distressed.

"You heard me; if she keeps doing that, all of these herbivores we are going to load onto this boat are going to freak out," said Scott. "The last thing any of us need is a dinosaur stampede. Two darts should do it."

The two men looked at each other in shock. They each pointed at each other to nominate them for the task.

"It's in a cage, get it done," said Scott, walking towards the dock.

He walked back onto the ramp, stepping back onto the dock. Scott walked towards Reginald, who was standing at the front of the procession of vehicles with his clipboard.

Scott walked up behind him and tapped Reginald on the shoulder. Reginald wiped a bit of sweat from his brow and turned to face Scott. He shook his hand at his side to allow the beads of sweat he just wiped off his forehead to shake onto the ground below.

"Everything accounted for?" asked Scott.

"Yes," said Reginald. "Thirteen Triceratops, thirty-eight Gallimimus, forty Microceratus, ten Pachycephalosaurs, eighteen Parasaurolophus, seven Pteranodons, and one very angry T-Rex."

"Okay, good, let's load 'em up," said Scott.

"Got it," said Reginald, motioning to the first set of drivers to begin loading the cargo ship.

Vehicle after vehicle began to drive past them as they flooded into the cargo ship. Animals in various states of sedation passed by the men. Some dinosaurs were very clearly passed out and snoring while others were screaming and panicking in their cages as the trucks rolled into the bowels of the boat. This was going to be a long ride, thought Scott. The last of the trucks rolled past with a herd of Microceratus chirping inside it. Their bright red and yellow bodies stood out against the dull gray of their cage.

Nalani walked up to Scott with Stephen. Dr. Harmon took the clipboard from Stephen and boarded the vessel with Nalani.

"You two are in charge, and if anyone balks at that, tell them Nalani said you could shoot them," said Nalani as she boarded the vessel with Scott.

Stephen and Reginald were to stay behind on Protogonus to make sure the remaining animals were taken care of in their absence. There was a team waiting on Dionysus to help Scott and Nalani deliver these animals to their permanent homes. Nalani and Scott made their way through a maze of cages as they walked to the front of the boat. The large cargo door creaked and shook as it closed, slowly cutting out the natural light. Darkness engulfed the cargo hold as their eyes adjusted to the much dimmer fluorescent bulbs. They began to pick out animals that needed more sedation and gave orders to the men of the respective vehicles to sedate their cargo. As they approached the front of the ship, Scott saw the two R.N.A. soldiers from earlier. The men were sweating, and the color had left their cheeks. The Tyrannosaur was silent, so clearly they had done the job.

Dr. Harmon approached them with a smile on his face. They stared at him angrily, furrowing their brows.

Scott said, "Good job, boys" in passing and continued to walk towards the exit. Once his back was turned, one of the soldiers promptly gave him the finger. Nalani opened the door of the exit and held it as Scott passed through. The two walked up a metal staircase as they climbed up the bridge. The stairwell came to an end with a large metal door with the word Exit glowing red above it. Scott pushed the door open and shielded his eyes as he walked out into the sunlight. He walked over to the rails and leaned over slightly. He looked towards the stern of the massive boat to see Protogonus slowly disappearing behind them. It amazed him that it had taken him that long to walk the length of the boat and climb to the upper decks. Waves crashed against the hull of the large ship, but Scott did not feel any rocking. The ship was so large that the normal rocking of the ocean was muted. This was a relief as Scott was afraid that he would get seasick on this trip.

Nalani tapped him on the shoulder and motioned towards the bridge of the ship. They headed across the deck to another set of stairs that led up to their destination. Scott saw the R.N.A. logo emblazoned along both sides of the bridge. They entered a large room and saw various sailors walking about a large control room. Numerous instruments that Scott had never seen before littered the room on various control panels. It all looked so complicated. A tall man approached them. He was of thin build, had a dark complexion, and short black goatee. His shirt was littered with various emblems and medals, none of which Scott recognized. The man extended his hand to Scott and introduced himself.

"My name is Captain Isaac Espinosa. There are cots, beers, and some food in the quarters through those doors for you. Sir Barnes wants you well-rested for the relocation process."

"This is my kind of boat," said Nalani happily as she proceeded to the back room.

Scott followed Nalani after introducing himself. The introductions seemed pointless as the captain already knew who they were. Nalani wasted no time in opening a beer as she collapsed onto one of the cots. Even though there was nothing special about it, the cot was surprisingly comfortable. Scott sprawled out on the nearest cot and closed his eyes again. He wanted to rest before the long afternoon they had ahead of them.

Scott was shaken awake by an obviously impatient Nalani. He slowly opened his eyes as he groggily wiped some saliva from the corner of his mouth. He extended his legs and stretched aggressively as he woke. Scott looked around the cabin confused as he tried to figure out where he was. This was not his usual bed, and Nalani wasn't usually in his apartment.

"We are here, man, wake up and let's get this done," said Nalani.

Dr. Harmon shot to his feet as he realized where he was. He had completely forgotten about the move. He walked with Nalani out of the bridge and looked out from the deck towards the stern of the boat. The boat had already docked, and vehicles were beginning to exit the ship. Dr. Harmon could see that they were grouping into clusters based on which animals they were carrying. Two trucks with Microceratus were at the front of the dinosaur parade. A small cluster of trucks were gathering towards the left-hand side destined for the Triceratops paddock. Another cluster was forming towards the right-hand side filled with noisy Parasaurolophus. The lush jungles of the island swayed in the distance with the winds as they awaited their new inhabitants. A large set of gates were present at the end of the dock with the words "Archosauria" emblazoned above them. Scott could see the large wooden gates beginning to open as the first trucks approached. Torches flickered with the ocean breeze on either side of the dock's gates to the park. The gates were themed to the ancient Greece motif that Sir Barnes loved so much. At first glance, one would think they were entering a huge temple with the large pillars crafted in a similar fashion to other Ionic order Greek architecture. The pillars at either side of the gates stood on large bases. Huge columns extended sky-ward with spiral-like ornaments on the tops of them holding up the giant archways. A tall electric fence enclosed the dock to form a perimeter around the park's exhibits. Scott let out a sigh and began the descent below deck to reacquaint himself with the sleeping Tyrannosaur that he was going to transport with Nalani.

As he approached the large truck, he could hear the dinosaur's rhythmic breathing while she slept. The large black tarp over the cage billowed in and out with the animal's respirations. Her breath was foul, the product of months' worth of decaying flesh rotting between her dagger-like teeth. Scott covered his nose with his shirt as he peaked under the tarp. Flies circled her gigantic jaws as they flitted around her snout. The muscles in her nose twitched in response to the insects landing on her face, temporarily shooing them away before they found a new landing spot. Dr. Harmon pulled the tarp back over the cage and began to help disconnect the truck from the boat. The large clips creaked as they were released. The driver hopped in and began to drive the vehicle off of the boat. Scott walked with the truck as it slowly rolled onto the dock. The truck jostled slightly as it came off the ramp, causing grunts to spout from the sleeping Tyrannosaur. Nalani and Scott paused for a second to stare at each other when they heard the noise. Nalani made a slight grimace and shook her head; neither of them liked the idea of her waking up now as they were out of tranquilizers. The two men headed towards a parked vehicle on the dock that was waiting for them. Nalani threw her tranquilizer rifle into the back seat as she hopped over the side of the car and into the driver's seat without opening the door. Scott smirked and opened the passenger side while shaking his head at Nalani's showing off. The truck carrying the Tyrannosaur began to make its way towards the Archosauria gates. Nalani followed closely behind in her car. As they passed through the gates, Scott looked up at the giant archway. He stared back over his shoulder to watch the gates close behind them.

"I guess we are stuck in here with her," laughed Scott. "Not a fun thought at all."

"There are much better places I would rather be right now," said Nalani.

"Yeah, no kidding," replied Scott.

"Don't worry, I'll make sure to get you back to your lovely Selena in one-piece," said Nalani, patting Scott on the chest.

"Shut up and drive," said Scott smirking.

The car shot down a long winding jungle road; trees encased their car like a giant, leafy prison. They came to a rolling stop as the truck made a slow turn onto a slightly paved road. The road was cobblestoned and looked like it belonged in an ancient city instead of an island jungle.

This must be the track for the tour vehicles, thought Scott as the car's front tire climbed over a small metal rail and onto the road. Their vehicle rocked as they drove up onto the road. Nalani pulled the car into the center of the road. A large electric fence became visible on the left side; this was their destination. They had to get this animal to the loading dock for her paddock and then they were home free. A concrete archway appeared in the distance. Greco-Roman statues adorned the archway through the mountain pass. Even though there were clearly lights in the tunnel, it appeared to be very dark compared to the blaring tropical sun. It almost didn't seem like the truck was going to be able to pass through this cavern. Nalani followed closely behind the truck carrying the sleeping Tyrannosaur; her knuckles blanched as she gripped the steering wheel tightly. She did not like the idea of being in close quarters with this animal. This part of the journey began to make Scott nervous as well; he could feel a wave of anxiety building in his chest like a smoldering fire. He did not like tight spaces, and being in a tunnel with a sleeping Tyrannosaur was not helping. If she did wake up and freed herself from the truck, there would nowhere for them to run. Scott began to think about whether or not he could hide under their car for safety if she did break free. Along the sides of the tunnel were marble carvings of various dinosaur species that were lit from the top with small hanging lights. A few of the carvings appeared unfinished with tarps hanging over them. Various tools were strewn along the floor that the artists had left behind. Light flooded Scott's face as the truck pulled out of the end of the tunnel. He squinted his eyes and covered his face with his forearm.

The truck rolled past the fence and crackled over the gravel as it proceeded. Scott peered at the twenty-five-foot-tall electric fence; the electric current running through the thick wires wrapped around the fortified steel bars hummed slightly as they passed. They approached another smaller tunnel at the end of the road. The truck veered off to the left down a small jungle path off of the tour route once it exited the second tunnel. It rocked as it rolled off the smooth cobblestone road and onto a narrow dirt one, eliciting more grunts of resistance from the Tyrannosaur as it shifted in its cage from the bumpy ride. About two miles down this long jungle road, the loading dock for the enclosure became visible. Several vehicles were already waiting for them, including a trailer containing two large steers; these were to be the animal's first meal in her new home. Nalani pulled their vehicle up near one of the trailers. She jumped out of the car and began instructing men to get the cattle into the Tyrannosaur paddock before she woke up. Two men led the cattle off of the trailer and into a bunker. Their hooves clattered on the metal ramp as they were led down to the ground below. The food delivery system was similar to that on Protogonus. R.N.A.'s engineers had put two food delivery systems into this paddock. One lift was near the loading bay to facilitate getting the Tyrannosaur into the paddock. This lift would also bring her to the fence away from park guests, so that veterinary care could be administered behind the scenes if needed. There were two towers standing above the loading gate to survey and guard the paddock. Currently men were standing there with high powered rifles to shoot her if she breached containment. The second lift was near the fence on the tour route to lure the animal to the fences when the tour was in operation. This lift was for smaller prey, like goats, to give her a snack and wow the tourists.

Several men rushed over to disconnect and remove the large tarp over the cage. The sleeping Tyrannosaur lay curled up, blissfully unaware of all the tasty men surrounding her. Dozens of workers surrounded the truck with rifles at the ready. Scott pulled a large sixty milliliter syringe from his pocket filled with the reversal agent for the Tyrannosaur. Swallowing was very hard at this moment. It felt as if he had a golf ball stuck in his throat, and his mouth was dry as a desert. He uncapped the syringe and slowly reached into the cage towards the animal's large clawed foot. He jabbed the needle into the Tyrannosaur's clawed toe, just to the side of the thick scales covering the top of her foot. He injected the contents of the syringe and quickly removed his arm from the enclosure, jumping off the side of the truck.

"We need to move quick; she is either going to wake up slowly or she is…." said Scott before he was interrupted by the sound of the metal cage creaking and the truck shifting on its many wheels.

The men in front of him began to slowly back away from Scott as a large shadow fell over him. Scott stood frozen, afraid to turn back around and see what was happening in the cage behind him. He slowly turned around to see the Tyrannosaur on her feet, her head was hanging low as she slowly came to. The animal staggered a bit, falling back down hard on the cage bottom. She began to kick her feet and sway her head in a bit of circular motion. Soon she was back on her feet again; this time she was far steadier and shook her massive head as if to shake off the remaining pangs of the sedation.

"Move, move, move," yelled Nalani as she came out of the bunker where the cows were being loaded. She ran over to the truck as fast as her legs could carry her. "What are you doing?! Back that truck up now! GO, GO, GO! Before she completely comes to, you idiots!"

The truck driver began to slowly back up; his eyes were wide as dinner plates as he saw the mighty Tyrannosaur in his rear-view mirror. The truck lurched back to the loading dock, causing the Tyrannosaur to stumble forward; she wasn't quite awake yet. Men rushed to the cage entrance to open the large metal doors, so that the back of the truck could enter the enclosure. This was a two-step opening process. First a gate of electric bars had to rise out of the way in order to allow a second set of thick metal doors to open. The electric bars began to slowly raise up as the truck approached. One of the workers began to nervously tap his feet as he waited for this door to rise, so that he could open the enclosure to the oncoming truck.

The Tyrannosaurus slowly rose to her full height and let out a mighty roar. One of the workers who was standing towards the back line had reached his limit. He ran off into the jungle in a panic, screaming as he ran. The Tyrannosaur had seen this, and she decided she wanted to give chase. Sixty-five million years of animal instinct was kicking in, and she was hungry! She began to bang her head against the thick bars of the cage, causing a deafening metallic clanking sound to fill the air. The truck lurched and rocked as the animal tried to free herself. The driver stopped the truck as it was no longer safe to back up with the trailer being rocked so violently. It was going to tip over if she continued this. The Tyrannosaur bit onto the bars and began to tug at them. Her large railroad spike-sized teeth clamped around the steel bars. The truck lurched left and right as the Tyrannosaur tugged violently at the cage. The muscles in her neck were taught and could be seen contracting under her feathery mane as she pulled. She stood with her legs staggered, her feet sliding slightly on the metal cage bottom as she wrenched herself backwards. This was probably the worst thing that could happen, thought Scott as he stood there frozen.

"Oi!" screamed Nalani. "Knock it off! Look at me, you asshole!"

Nalani had grabbed a flare off of one of the workers and was waving it above her head. She began throwing rocks at the animal to get its attention. The small pebbles clattered against the bars and bottom of the metal cage. The Tyrannosaur stopped its assault on the cage bars and began to focus on Nalani. It stood there and cocked its head to the side as it tried to make sense of what Nalani was holding. She had gotten her attention. Her head swayed back and forth with Nalani's arm as she moved the flare above her head.

"What are you waiting for, you damn moron, back the truck up while she is distracted!" screamed Nalani.

At the cage entrance, the bars of the electrified door had been lifted. The second set of large metal doors began to creak open behind this first barrier to allow the back end of the truck to enter the paddock. Nalani followed the truck as it backed into the loading area, keeping the Tyrannosaur's attention fixed on her as she walked.

The back end of the truck slowly slid into the enclosure through a concrete archway. As the back of the truck entered the arch, a red light on the side of the archway lit up. The Tyrannosaur was now standing towards the front end of the cage, just behind the cabin of the truck towing it. She was very curious about the red sparkling object in Nalani's hand. As the back third of the truck entered the enclosure, the red light turned off, and a yellow light below it lit up. Scott watched as the cattle lift in the cage reached the ground level to release the two steers into the Tyrannosaur paddock. It was perfect timing, thought Scott. The Tyrannosaur paused and began to sniff the air; she had gotten the scent of her next meal. She turned and headed towards the enclosure, roaring furiously as she came to the locked cage doors. Now almost the entirety of the cage was within the archway with just a small part visible on the outside of the paddock. The yellow light had turned off, and a green light below it began glowing brightly. Everyone let out a long sigh as the truck driver pressed a button on his dash with great purpose. The truck shifted and shook as the doors at the back of the cage swung open. The Tyrannosaur wasn't about to wait anymore, and she smashed the doors with her skull to throw them open. The impact of the Tyrannosaur jumping off the back of the truck shook the ground. Nalani threw the flare into the enclosure through the electrified bars for good measure. It landed at the feet of the cattle, who seemed unaware of the danger they were in. The Tyrannosaur was standing behind the truck, sniffing the air and surveying her new domain. She turned to face the cattle and let out an ear-shattering roar. Scott covered his ears and watched in trepidation as the Tyrannosaur barreled towards the cattle at full speed. The steers took off into the brush with the Tyrannosaur in pursuit. The truck driver pulled the truck out of the archway as quickly as he could while the Rex was distracted. The large metal doors closed quickly behind him. The second, electrified cage door was pulling down over the first set of doors in a painfully slow fashion.

Scott walked over to Nalani and shook her hand. Nalani seemed to be completely fearless. She had no issues staring down an angry Triceratops, and now she had tamed the mighty Tyrannosaurus Rex. Scott wished he had the nerves of steel that Nalani had.

"You never cease to amaze me, my friend," said Scott. "You really have no fear of anything."

"Well, none of you pansies were going to do something, so I had no choice," laughed Nalani. "You'll grow up and become a man one day."

"Yeah, yeah, yeah," said Scott. "Always the tough guy."

"Damn straight," said Nalani triumphantly, patting Scott on the shoulder as she walked back to their car. "Never trust a man to do woman's job!"

The two laughed victoriously as they got in their vehicle. The rest of the crowd stood and stared at them in disbelief. None of the workers seemed to know what to do or how to process what had just occurred. They stood frozen as Nalani and Scott drove off.

Scott threw his beat-up backpack onto the floor near his bed. His luggage was already in his room and stood in the corner by one of the dressers. A large TV screen flashed images of coming attractions and dining options that did not yet exist. This room was bigger than what he had had on Protogonus, a sign of appreciation from Ethan no doubt. He walked around his new luxury room, pausing to admire the artwork on the walls and the craftsmanship of some of the wall carvings in the molding. His room was part of a large complex located on the far end of the island near what would be a paddock for the Iguanodon. This was a species whose genome Dr. Bai was currently working on. Sir Barnes had had this building complex built specifically to house the veterinary team on the far end of the park near the end of the tour route. This was to facilitate their ability to get to the paddocks quickly. It was one of three such facilities around the corners of the park. A knock on the door cut through the silence of Scott's room. He walked slowly to the door, putting down a shirt he was folding onto a small table. He looked through a small peep hole in the door and opened it.

"Hey, the boys and I are having a few drinks in my cabin as a night cap," said Nalani. "Do you wanna join us? We got another long day tomorrow, so might as well get in a little fun."

"Um, sure. Let me finish unpacking," replied Scott. "I'll be right down, get a drink ready for me."

"Alright, I'll save you a Shirley Temple," said Nalani, laughing as she walked away.

Scott shook his head as he closed the door. He grabbed the shirt off of the table and went back to his bedroom to continue to unpack. This was going to be his new home, so he might as well get comfortable while he had some time. Scott removed his shirt and quickly re-applied some deodorant. He pulled on an old T-shirt and left his room. He was on the second floor of the complex, and Nalani was on the first. Scott walked down a long deck that connected his room to the several others on the floor. It was similar to many motel complexes he had seen in other parts of the US when he travelled. Scott ran his hand along the metal railing as he went and gazed at the large complex; it lacked the gaudy decorum of the architecture around the rest of the park.

He walked down the metal stairwell, which curved around in a semi-circle as he got closer to the ground level. He stepped off the last step onto the gravel with a crunch. The small stones crunched under his feet as he walked towards Nalani's cabin. The dark jungle enveloped the small compound. The lights from the compound did not illuminate much more than the compound itself. Scott could see the beginnings of the narrow road that they had driven in on slowly begin to fade into obscurity as the sun went down and the sky darkened. He could only see a few feet down the road as darkness enveloped the rest of it. As he approached Nalani's door, the sounds of men laughing and glasses clanking could be heard. Scott knocked on the door of room 611. One of the workers opened the door to let Scott in. He walked through the apartment and grabbed a beer out of a cooler before heading out to the patio to join the rest of the team.

"Hey, he decides to join us," exclaimed Nalani as she noticed Scott. "Dr. Scott Harmon, gents, let's have a round of applause."

"Thank you, thank you," Scott said, taking a fake bow before opening his beer and taking a drink.

He leaned up against a railing and looked out into the dark jungle. The torches on the deck flickered and cast a glow onto a small open area in front of their barn. All of the equipment he would need for the coming months was resting in that barn. Scott took another sip of his beer and began to think about how much he was dreading the trip back to Protogonus to capture the remaining animals. He was not looking forward to having another encounter with trapping the Dakotaraptors.

Chapter 15

Nalani was not one to get nervous easily, but encountering these animals again was not something she was looking forward to. She stood there with two dozen men, all armed with a long-range rifle pointed at the cage in front of them. They were all dressed in camouflage so as to not catch the eyes of the incoming predators. A feeding platform rose from the ground, revealing an unsuspecting steer. The animal was laying down on its haunches while it chewed its cud. The poor creature was tethered to the base of the platform with a thick rope to prevent it from running off. Once the Dakotaraptors had begun to eat the animal, the men would try to dart all of the raptors through the fence while they were distracted. It wasn't a perfect plan, but it was the best they could come up with to get all eight raptors in the same place at once. Eight vehicles were parked outside the paddock with plated metal cages. These cages were just big enough that the animals could turn around. Comfort was not a concern as they would likely sleep for the duration of the journey once dosed with Etorphine.

The men stood focused on the cage with their rifles at the ready. A soft bellow came from the steer as he sat on the metal platform. He became silent, and his ears began to flutter. The steer got to his feet and began to scan the jungle with his ears, turning them in all directions. They moved like small satellites, scanning the area for any signs of danger. Scott looked to the men on the towers of the loading platform who were watching the cage with binoculars for the incoming targets. One of the men lowered his binoculars and gave the signal that he saw the Dakotaraptors approaching. Scott tapped Nalani on the shoulder, who silently gave another signal to the men to get into position. Scott hurried away to rush into one of the trucks, so he would not be spotted. The men dropped to their knees and rested their rifles on the concrete barrier just below the electric fence. On their helmets were all manner of twigs. Their faces were painted in camouflage patterns to hide them from the incoming Dakotaraptors. Scott knew that if these animals ran in to the feeding area and saw a bunch of men with guns, they would likely run back off into the jungle. This had to be a stealth mission; they were too smart for it to be otherwise.

The steer began to scream and tried to tug himself free. His halter dug into his face as he pulled backwards. His eyes were wide, and his neck was fully extended as he pulled rhythmically against the pole he was tied to. The pole clanged from the stress. Scott felt sorry for the poor animal as he seemed to know what was coming.

EEEK!

A Dakotaraptor screamed as it flew out of the jungle through the air and landed on the steer's back. As it flew through the air, it adopted a similar appearance to a giant hawk diving on its unsuspecting prey. Its toe claws dug deeply into the flesh of the steer's back. It tore through his thick hide effortlessly, exposing bits of fat and muscle tissue. Deep lacerations were being made in the animal's flesh as the Dakotaraptor rode on his back. The steer began to buck and jump as the raptor clung to his back biting furiously into the steer's nape. The scene was like a prehistoric rodeo with the Dakotaraptor taking the role of the cowboy. Blood and hair began to fly through the air as a second raptor leapt onto the back of the steer. It hung off of his hind quarters as it bit onto the steer's tail base. The steer shook violently and kicked his hooves into the air, throwing the second Dakotaraptor off of his back and onto the ground. The raptor rolled through the brush before jumping swiftly to her feet. Two more raptors joined the first as the three of them forced the poor steer to the ground with a thud. The steer's feet thrashed wildly as he desperately tried to kick at his attackers. One kick landed square in the chest of one of the raptors, causing it to squeak and bark as it staggered backwards. The rest of the pack rushed in and enveloped the steer like a pack of hungry zombies. Glimpses of the steer could be seen between the gaps in feathered

Dakotaraptor bodies. The raptors tore furiously into the steer as the cries of the animal slowly became muffled. Nothing but Dakotaraptor tails and bodies could be seen as the dinosaurs converged on the poor creature. Bits of hair and flesh flew into the air as they began to pull their meal apart. The raptors would throw their heads back to gulp down huge chunks of flesh and fat before returning to the kill.

Nalani raised her hand slowly above her head, so as to not attract any attention from the feeding raptors. Nalani's movements were very robotic in nature. Her ghillie suit slid down her wrist slightly as she held her arm up, exposing her dark skin. When she was sure that the feasting Dakotaraptors had not noticed her, she lowered her arm as the signal to fire. The air exploded with the sound of rifle fire as darts flew at the unsuspecting Dakotaraptors from all directions. The animals began to scream and panic as the darts made contact. They quickly abandoned the kill as if realizing it was a trap and ran off into the jungle in unison. None of them seemed to bother to try to remove the darts this time. They were all in shock and seemed confused by what had just occurred.

"Did we hit them all?" asked Scott as he approached Nalani.

"We'll find out very soon I'm sure," said Nalani as she removed her ghillie suit.

They kept their eyes on the tower guards as they waited for some sort of confirmation that it was safe to enter the paddock. Minutes seemed to pass like hours as they sat patiently in their vehicles. One of the tower guards walked over to the railing in a rushed manner.

"All eight of them down just due East about a mile and a half," screamed the guard.

The gatekeeper, Geoffrey, immediately began the paddock opening process. Engines began to turn over as the men readied themselves to go and retrieve the sleeping Dakotaraptors. Once the gates were open, the vehicles raced into the paddock.

Even though the sedatives should buy them hours of time, no one wanted to take any chances with these creatures. Nalani and Scott wanted to get this over with as soon as possible. The containment vehicles raced through the jungle and into a large open field. Blades of grass beat against the underside of their vehicles as they rolled over a large ridge. There in the valley laid the bodies of seven sleeping raptors.

"Where is the eighth one?" screamed a voice over the walkie talkie.

"I do not have visual either, over," said another panicked voice.

"Over there by the tree line, car twenty-seven will pick her up, over," said Stephen's voice.

Scott let out a sigh of relief as he heard this. He pulled his truck up to one of the sleeping raptors and came to a stop parallel to the animal's back. They had become massive, thought Scott. Each raptor stood between five and half to six feet tall and was about fifteen feet long from tail tip to snout. It would likely take several grown men to lift them as they topped out close to 700 pounds each. Scott pulled a large stretcher off the side of the truck and placed it near the sleeping raptor. She grunted in her sleep and kicked out one of her legs, causing Scott to jump as he laid the stretcher down. The men that were with him similarly backed away from the predator.

"It's okay, she's sedated," said Dr. Harmon. "I hope...."

He encouraged the men to line up near her abdomen to push her onto the stretcher. In unison they rotated the large creature onto the stretcher and began to strap her in with thick leather restraints. The group gathered around the animal bending over into a squatting position. They slowly lifted the Dakotaraptor off of the ground and began to walk to the back of the truck. Scott looked down at the head of the animal; he could see a large yellow-green eye staring at him as he moved her over to the vehicle. The Dakotaraptor was watching him it seemed. There was an odd intelligence behind the creature's stare, something Scott had never experienced before. He began to wonder if this is what human doctors experienced when they sedated their patients. It was almost as if the creature was questioning him about what was happening to it. Once the raptor was in the truck, Scott applied a sterile lubricant to its eyes to prevent them from drying out due to lack of blinking. Lifting her head to get to the second eye on her down side was difficult, and Scott ended up having another person hold her head up while he performed this task.

Scott hopped out of the truck and locked the doors. He double checked them multiple times to make sure they were secured. He shuddered slightly as he walked back to the driver's seat of the cabin. Scott picked up the walkie, pausing for a second as he watched the other trucks loading their raptors in their respective vehicles.

"Make sure you lubricate their eyes prior to locking them up, over," Scott called over the intercom.

"Yes, sir! I'll paint their nails and do their make-up while I'm at it, over," called Reginald over the intercom.

"How did luck have it that I got the one whose toe claw I broke?" called Nalani. "You guys planned this, didn't you?"

"Let's get to the boat and get this over with, over," called Scott.

He put the walkie back onto its mount and started his truck. Scott watched the other men pile into their respective vehicles as they prepared themselves to head to the boat. Voices began to echo through the cabin on the truck as the other vehicles began to radio in that they were ready to transport. Scott pulled out first and began to head to the docks, followed by the other seven vehicles. Scott hummed to himself as he led the caravan to the docks.

He pulled his vehicle up just behind the ramp of the boat on the dock. They were the first ones to arrive from their task. They were waiting for the rest of the crew to bring Dilophosaurs, Herrerasaurus, Baryonyx, Metriacanthosaurus, Stegosaurus, and the Compsognathus. This shipment was going to contain mostly predators, so containment was going to be very important. These animals were going to pose a much larger threat to the crew if they were to escape onto the boat. A truck became visible on the horizon rolling down the island road to the docks. Unlike the other trailers, there were no openings on the side of it. The only openings this trailer had were along the top surface. This had to be the trailer containing the Dilophosaurs, Scott thought. He was happy that the men had managed to capture them seemingly without incident. The openings at the top of the high trailer would allow them to gaze in at the creatures without risking envenomation. Scott wanted no more mishaps. Overall the day went relatively smoothly. Before Scott knew it, the animals were loaded onto the massive freighter, and they were en route back to Dionysus. Scott felt a pang of sadness fill him as he watched Protogonus disappear into the horizon. He was going to miss this island as it had become home to him in the last few years. Now it was time for him to begin his new life on Dionysus, and he was not ready for it.

Scott awoke to the sun beaming on his face through his deck window. The sound of construction off in the distance added to the background noise of birds and dinosaur calls. He glanced at his alarm clock to notice that it said

5:45 A.M. He had woken up fifteen minutes prior to his alarm going off again. Scott let out a loud groan as he stretched his arms above his head in protest. I may as well get up now, he thought to himself. Today was the day that Nalani and Scott were going to take the park tour to make sure it was safe for both the animals and the guests. Sir Barnes had entrusted this task to them as he knew that they would tell him honestly where the flaws were in the tour program. Scott was excited to play tourist today instead of going about his usual park duties. He was a bit relieved that he did not have to do any of the feedings or usual check-ups. His feet hit the cold wooden floor as he stood up. He walked across the room to his kitchen where he put on a pot of coffee before heading to the shower. If it weren't for the Brachiosaurus calls in the background, he would swear he was on some tropical vacation. This had all become so normal, that he almost never paused to process what he was hearing. Scott ate his breakfast and went about his normal routine as he psyched himself up for the tour.

He left his room and walked down the deck to Nalani's dwelling. In this complex, they were both on the same floor. Before he could knock, the door opened, revealing a startled Nalani. She had on a safari hat and her usual work attire. The two headed to their vehicle without a word. It was early, and neither of them were particularly chatty. The car crackled along the gravel as it pulled out and headed down the road to the visitor's center. As they approached the visitor center, the sound of construction became louder. They pulled around the back of the main hub of the park and walked towards the guest entrance. The water fountains in front of the visitor center were off as men busied about them to lay the plumbing. A large marble Tyrannosaur sculpture faced the stairwell in each of the two large fountains. The sculptures would be facing the visitors menacingly as they walked up the stairs to the visitor's center. Nalani was unusually tired today, despite having slept well the night before. She followed Scott up a large white multi-level staircase as they approached two large doors. The doors were covered in carvings of various dinosaur bones. Nalani pushed the large doors open to reveal more construction teams at work. They walked into a large rotunda with various information desks and restaurants being constructed in a circle around the main entrance. Scott could see several large Pteranodon replicas being bolted to the ceiling by various teams of men. The replicas did not look nearly as impressive as they used to given that he had seen the real things in action. Their plastic bodies gleamed unnaturally in the light of a giant circular skylight that capped the visitors center. He saw the men working on putting up panels of various prehistoric animals around the storefronts of the various shops in the rotunda.

Scott could see a large glass mural at the back of the entrance hall. On it was a jungle scene with various popular herbivore species. The mural looked like something that belonged in a church. Overall the entrance hall was fairly impressive. It was a little humid inside the hall as the walls of the visitor center were still open to the outside. Sir Barnes was planning to put several outdoor dining options in these locations, as well as an outdoor gift shop. Work on this portion had not yet begun, but tarps covered the holes in the wall where the entrances would go for these locations. Nalani headed instinctively to the upper level, walking up one of the two large wooden staircases around the back of the main entrance and led to the second level. Scott stared at the Pteranodons as he walked up the stairs and slowly came up to the sculpture's eyeline. He wondered how the public or even his daughter would react to seeing these animals alive for the first time. When they got to the top of the stairs, they walked to the end of the rotunda to a door marked "Staff Only." Nalani flashed a key card, and the two entered into a small hallway that led to the control room. They passed by the large circular glass windows as they walked to the control room door. Dr. Harmon caught sight of Kyle sitting at his desk furiously typing away, his eyes glued to the screen in front of him. The multiple monitors lit his face with a dull blue light as he stared intently at the characters flashing across his screen. Next to him was Jayden Charles, who was gazing at the one of the monitors on the far left of Kyle's desk as he typed. The two had an uneasy partnership, as most people did when they had to work with Kyle. Mr. Bergin was not the easiest of people to get along with.

Scott pushed open the control room door and held it, so that Nalani could enter behind him. Sir Barnes was sitting towards a set of television monitors in the far corner. He was watching his animals on the various closed caption television cameras placed around the park. Ethan clutched a cup of tea in his hands. A small wisp of steam rose into the air from the hot beverage. Nalani and Scott came up behind the old man and gently called out to him, so as to not startle him.

"Ah you're here! Marvelous, marvelous," said Ethan in an almost giddy tone. "The tour vehicles should be pulling up in about an hour or so. Have you two eaten?"

"Yea, I had breakfast. Thank you though, Ethan," said Scott.

"And you, Ms. Mwangi?" asked Ethan.

"I'm always up to eat," replied Nalani.

"Wonderful, I'll have them cook you some eggs and pancakes before your departure in the kitchen," said Ethan.

"Can you have them make me something, too, pops, I'm famished over here," called Kyle sarcastically.

Ethan nodded his head and let out a sigh as he brushed off Kyle's comment. He picked up the phone and began to place an order to the kitchen.

"Make sure you tell them extra syrup; I hate dry pancakes," called Kyle as Sir Barnes spoke with the kitchen.

Ethan begrudgingly asked for extra syrup and got up from his chair. He led the two out of the control room and back into the main rotunda away from Kyle. They walked down the wooden staircase, heading towards a door behind the stairwell to the right-hand side. They approached the fancy looking door near the stained-glass mural. Lobby music began to play throughout the main hall and then promptly turned off. They must be testing the speakers, thought Scott. Ethan led them into a large dining area with multiple long wooden tables. Buffet carts were wrapped in plastic at the far end of the room. Only about half of the tables had tablecloths on them. Tarps with multiple splotches of paint on them covered the floor as men furiously rolled paint onto the walls. The room was clearly not yet finished. Dinosaur skeletons were built into the moldings of large support columns throughout the hall. Each column was capped with a volute or a spiral patterned cap.

Towards the back of the dining room was a small gift shop. All manner of prehistoric memorabilia lined the shelves from lunchboxes to stuffed toys. T-shirts of all sizes covered with dinosaurs hung on clothing racks. A few creatures that were not dinosaurs were included amongst the roster of ancient animals on the shelves. Scott caught sight of wooly mammoths and saber-toothed cat plushies.

"Are we planning on bringing back more than just dinosaurs?" asked Scott as he pointed to the stuffed wooly mammoth plush.

"Well, my lad, every theme park has room for expansions," said Sir Ethan proudly. "We will address just that before your tour."

"You got some animals we don't know about?" asked Nalani, sounding concerned.

"Let's just say Dr. Bai has been busy on Dionysus with a few…projects," said Ethan with a smirk on his face. "Please have a seat."

Ethan directed them into a small conference room with a large table in the center. Several projector screens lined the room. This area was well-lit by large fluorescent bulbs hanging from the ceiling. The room had no windows but instead blank projection screens lined the walls, slightly reflecting some of the light from the ceiling light fixtures. Scott pulled out a chair and took a seat in front one of the empty plates. Men rushed over to him like ants rushing to a morsel of food on the ground in the summer sun. They removed the napkin from his glass to fill it with water, placed a plate of fruits in front of him, and handed him a menu in seamless fashion. Dr. Harmon was always impressed by the service at these events Sir Barnes put on for them.

Despite not being hungry, the food was too good to pass up. Scott found himself trying a little bit of everything. He scooped fork-fills of eggs into his mouth. He glanced over at Nalani, who was cleaning up what was left on her plate with a piece of bread. Ethan sat at the head of the table like a proud father, watching his children eat. He seemed to watch them with a sense of impatience as they ate. Ethan was tapping his fingers on the table and repeatedly checking his watch.

"Are you ready?" asked Sir Barnes. "The cars should be arriving shortly, and I have something to show you beforehand."

"Yea, let's go on this little tour," said Nalani, wiping her face and rising quickly to her feet. "I'm always up for an adventure."

"Marvelous, let's make a quick stop first," said Sir Barnes. "Our visitor center isn't without its own attractions of course."

Nalani and Scott looked at each other questioningly. Neither of them was aware of any dinosaurs within the visitors building. If there were animals in the visitor center, they were not from Protogonus. This was concerning to Scott as he wondered who was feeding these creatures and what precautions they were taking to protect the guests from them. Scott was supposed to know about all animals in the park, so that he could work on containment measures for them. They walked back out the way they had come, again walking into the shadows of the hanging Pteranodons. They trotted along the stained-glass mural. Ahead of them was a set of large wooden double doors with elaborate silver handles. The words "Paleozoic Era" stood over the doorway in big block letters similar to the letters on the park's archways. A fluorescent glow from this sign lit the entranceway with a dull red hue. As Nalani and Scott pushed the doors open, a slight hissing sound filled the air as a breeze from the room inside caressed their faces. Nalani held onto her hat as she entered, afraid the gust of air would blow it away.

On the wall to their right as they entered was a timeline of the Earth's history starting at the Proterozoic Era (2500- 542 million years ago) and extending to the present. The various eras of the planet were highlighted with a few animals present from each time period. Panels with information on the types of life from each of the periods were present. There was also details on various points of mass extinctions, including the event that killed the dinosaurs. On the left wall of the hallway was murals and plastic statues of what looked to be giant insects. A giant cockroach figurine appeared to be squaring off against what looked like a huge centipede. Nalani paused to look at a mural; she shook her head and shot Scott a confused look as if to ask what they were looking at. Scott was equally confused as he began to ponder what was behind the next set of doors.

"Wouldn't you want to meet this creepy crawly, huh, doc?" said Nalani, laughing as she pointed to the giant cockroach.

Ethan had a very suspicious grin on his face as they continued down the hallway, hobbling a bit as he walked. They pushed their way through another set of double doors and into a large theater-like room. To the left of the entry was a large glass wall separating them from a forest of cycads and ferns. On their right was a row of tiered seats that were covered with a red and yellow pattern carpet. Scott had a similar type of enclosure at his zoo where they would display various artic birds or animals that needed environments different than what San Diego provided. Scott walked over to the railing in front of the glass and stared into the enclosure. A loud humming noise could be heard throughout the room, along with a faint screeching sound. He leaned on the bar in front of the glass. Scott began to wonder if there was an electric barrier or some sort of other deterrent on the glass in front of him. The glass appeared to be thick, at least six inches or so. It was similar to the type of shatterproof glass he used in his zoo. Above the glass was a panel that was clearly supposed to hold an information card of some kind about whatever was inside this enclosure. The panels were currently blank. An annoying buzzing noise seemed to get louder and fade over and over, but Scott couldn't seem to find where it was coming from. Soon Nalani joined him as they stared into the odd-looking forest of ferns. After a few minutes of seeing nothing, they turned to walk away from the glass. Why was Sir Barnes having them stare into an empty enclosure, thought Scott.

"I would look a little harder into that enclosure if I were you," said Ethan as he clutched the bar in front of him proudly. Ethan had a smile on his face as he pointed to a small pond near the back of the forest.

Scott returned his eyes to the ground and began to comb it for signs of life. Sir Barnes seemed confident that they were going to see something if they kept looking, but Scott wasn't so sure. Nalani was looking down at her shoes and was completely ignoring what was in front of her. She was clearly bored. The buzzing sound returned and seemed louder than it was before.

Scott saw the small pond towards the back of the enclosure that Ethan was repeatedly pointing to. A rat ran out towards the water's edge and was scurrying about it. The rodent stopped just short of the shore line and sat up on its hindlimbs. Small paws began to comb over its head as it began to groom itself. The rat rubbed at its face several times before returning to all fours. It rummaged through the pebbles by the water as it looked for food. The humming sound returned again. What was that sound, thought Scott. The rodent took a few more hopping steps and then vanished in a blur as it was whisked up into the air. Something big had grabbed the rodent off the ground and was flying through the enclosure. It had moved so quickly that he had not gotten a good look at it.

"What is that?!" squawked Nalani as she pointed to a large fern directly in front of her. A look of pure horror filled her face as she took a few steps away from the glass.

Scott felt immediately repulsed by the sight of this monstrous creature. Perched on the top of a palm frond was a dragonfly, but this was the largest dragonfly Scott had ever seen. Since when were dragonflies large enough to eat rats, thought Scott. The gigantic insect held the squirming rodent in its forelimbs as its mouth parts tore into the rat's writhing flesh. The way it ate was almost mechanical, as the multiple plates of the insect's mouth parts slid past each other. They tore off chunks of flesh and fur from the now lifeless corpse of the rat. Blood quietly dripped onto the fronds below it. The creature's wings flitted slightly and glistened in the light of the enclosure. Scott could see the huge veins of its four translucent wings. The tips were opaque with a dark red coloring. Long hairs protruded from its shiny armored body. At the tip of its long tail were two large spikes. This was something out of a horror film.

"To answer your question, Nalani, that creature is called Meganeura," said Dr. Bramme's voice as he entered the room almost as if he was entering on cue.

"Mega what?" asked Nalani. "What's with the massive insect?"

"Meganeura, it's a prehistoric dragonfly from the period before the dinosaurs," said Richard Bramme. "Dr. Bai has managed to bring back several prehistoric insects. This set of enclosures is an homage to the past before our main attractions existed. It's a fitting start to the journey of the park tour."

"Ethan, insects like this can't be safe," said Scott. "Insects are very resilient and spread everywhere. Do you know how bad it would be if this thing were to fly to the mainland? That thing is the size of a damn hawk!"

"Not to worry, Scott; they need an oxygen-rich environment with concentrations twice what our atmosphere provides," said Richard. "That's why they are housed here and not out in the park. If they ever escaped, they would suffocate before they got very far. This whole rotunda is pressurized and oxygenated to mimic their natural environment."

"Come, come," said Sir Barnes. "Let me show you the rest of our creepy crawlies."

"Sir Barnes, you have to see the danger here, you just have to," said Scott. "We should have been consulted before Jin Moon did this."

"C'mon, Dr. Harmon, our target audience will love these creatures. Every young lad loves bugs, so what's better than giant ones?" said Ethan, lightly giggling to himself.

"I'm almost afraid to see what you have next in this little shop of horrors," said Nalani as they walked away from the feasting giant dragonfly.

Through the next set of doors, the enclosure changed from lush forest to a semi-arid area. Scott began to feel his skin crawl as he caught sight of the next creature. There was a small grouping of rocks forming a cave. The cave ran down to a burrow that had been cut in half by the glass, so that people could view the creature residing inside. A red heat lamp lit the small cavern, which was filled with all manner of twigs and branches in the form of a small nest. The bones of several rodents lined this den and rested alongside the creature resting inside it.

Sitting in the burrow was the largest scorpion that Scott had ever seen. It had to be over two feet long from the tip of its thin pinschers to the end of its long, thick, segmented tail. The tail hovered over the top of the animal's back, brandishing a spine at its tip that looked similar in diameter to a large bore hypodermic needle. Long hairs bristled from the animal's segmented body. Its armor-plated skin glistened under the infrared light of the nest it had made for itself in its burrow. Multiple large beady eyes stared blankly and coldly ahead of it, almost looking like ball bearings. Given how thin and feeble its claws looked, Scott knew this had to be a species that killed by envenomation. In general scorpions with thin claws were often the most venomous. That was just what they needed, more venomous animals on this island, thought Scott. The scorpion's long segmented legs were perched alongside its flat body. Scott could see hooks on its feet that it used to grasp and cling to surfaces. He slowly put his hand to the glass to try to get a size comparison for the creature. The animal was about as long as his arm and thicker around its mid-section. He shuddered slightly as he felt the hair on the back of his neck raise. There was something about these giant insects that Scott found more unsettling than the dinosaurs he had been dealing with for the last few years. It sat there motionless almost like a statue. Scott knew it was alive because he could see the small spiracles on its side opening and closing as it breathed. Nalani tapped him on the shoulder and pointed to a sign that read *Pulmonoscorpius kirktonensis*. Information on the panels talked of the animal's potent venom and how a single drop could kill an adult human. Nalani shook her head and motioned for them to follow Ethan and Dr. Bramme as they continued on into the next room.

Sir Barnes pushed them along into the next section of the walking tour. Scott and Nalani stopped in front of a large fish tank that was built into the wall on the left side of the room when they walked through the door. Various corals lined the enclosure that was set up to look like a large underwater cave. Rocks ran up from the floor to the ceiling in an arch. There were animals swimming in the tank, but they very clearly were not fish. Scott stared blankly at the strange creatures as they flitted through the water column of their tank. He tried to place the animals but couldn't come up with a modern relative for them in his head.

"What am I looking at here, Richard?" asked Scott, clearly confused by the animals in front of him.

"So the big guys swimming about with the long mouth parts are Anomalocaris, a prehistoric shrimp," said Dr. Bramme, pointing at the strange animals swimming through the tank. "And those horseshoe crab like animals swimming along the bottom are Trilobites."

Scott stared at the large, almost alien-like animals swimming in front of him. They had two large compound eyes on small stalks. The eyes were jet black and appeared dead. Protruding from the front of their head were two almost tentacle-like mouth parts lined with spikes of various sizes. These tentacles were curved slightly under the animal's body. Its trunk was plated with armor running along it's segmented back. On its side ran multiple fan-like projections that all fluttered independently of each other in an undulating fashion. It beat its powerful tail to gain momentum and then would glide through the water by slightly adjusting the projections on its side. They almost flew through the water instead of swam in a similar fashion to a stingray. There was something oddly majestic about these animals and not as terrifying as the other creatures had been. They seemed simple as they paced back and forth around their tank.

The next few enclosures were empty. Some had plant life and decorations within them, and some were just empty concrete cages. Clearly the animals for these enclosures had not been successfully brought back yet. As they walked into the final room, it was clear that Ethan had become more animated. They seemed to rush past a large room containing a small herd of Compsognathus. Ethan now had a pep in his step as he hustled through the final set of double doors. Ethan was excited about showing them what was in the next enclosure and kept referring to it as the ultimate finale. Nalani and Scott were almost scared to try to begin to imagine what he had in store for them next. As they walked through the doors, they found themselves in a semi-circular room. The glass ran from the ceiling to the floor and followed the semi-circular design of the viewing area. This enclosure was also a forest with a small stream running through it. The enclosure was noticeably larger than the others; whatever was in here was big. The bushes rustled at the far end of the enclosure as a hissing noise filled the air; something was coming. Nalani and Scott stared at the moving bushes intently as they waited for the creature to emerge. They didn't notice that one of the animals was heading straight for them. Scott jumped as he caught sight of what looked like a long moving tank. This animal was absolutely massive and didn't look real. But there it was, crawling in front of him. Two giant antennae waved to-and-fro as it propelled itself forward on dozens of jointed legs. Thick, plated armor covered its body, and large spikes jutted from its sides. It looked like a giant millipede, but it was much stockier and appeared to look much more threatening. Harmon could see it's giant mouth parts quivering as it moved along the ground.

"That's an Arthropleura," said Dr. Bramme. "It's one of the largest insects ever found."

"Aren't they marvelous!" remarked Ethan. "Terrifying to look at but completely herbivorous. No need to fear these guys. Absolutely remarkable creatures!"

"I think I'm ready to get back to the dinosaurs now," said Nalani, looking away from the enclosure. "These guys are a bit unsettling."

"I agree," said Scott.

"Fine, fine," said Ethan, sounding disappointed. "Let's get you two to your tour vehicles then, shall we."

Sir Barnes led the group out of a set of double doors that were covered with various large insects. Nalani hesitated as she went to open the doors. She was a put off by the insect carvings and did not seem to want to touch them. There was another loud hissing noise as they exited into the warm jungle air. A cobblestone path lay ahead of them that led around the back end of the visitor center towards the main entrance. Dr. Bramme excused himself and re-entered the building where they had just exited. He stated that he wanted to continue to study these prehistoric insects some more.

Scott shuddered slightly as they made their way away from the house of bugs and into the jungle. He could have done without what he had just witnessed. Scott wanted no part in the care of those animals, and as he glanced over, he could tell by the look on Nalani's face that she felt the same way. They made their way around the visitor center almost running instead of holding their usual calm pace. Sir Ethan began to lag behind them, hobbling as he struggled to keep up. Scott could see the main road that led to the tour vehicles through the trees. Parked in front of a small building in between a ticket booth and a restaurant were a set of large armored trucks. The fronts of the vehicles had large metal plating on them to make them appear to look like chariots. Armored panels ran along the sides of the trucks as well. The back of the trucks were open seating with thick metal bars encasing them. A large glass-domed roof covered the vehicles to allow the guests to look at any animals that would tower over them. A driver dressed in a toga sat in the driver's seat behind thick glass windows.

"Those are a little…loud. Aren't they, Ethan?" asked Scott.

"These are top of the line, fully protective vehicles with interactive CD-ROMs," said Ethan defensively. "Each one costs a small fortune to produce. Even got some of Hollywood's greatest to narrate the tour for us, personal favor of course."

"Impressive, I can't wait to see who we will hear, marked Nalani as she entered the back of the vehicle.

Scott climbed into the back of the truck through the large passenger door. He walked around the back of the vehicle searching for a seat. He came to a stop on the left side of the vehicle and hopped into one of the many booths that lined the back of the truck. Ethan walked up alongside him and leaned on the side of the truck motioning for Dr. Harmon to roll down his window. His demeanor suddenly changed to a sterner appearance.

"Remember, be critical lads," said Ethan. "You two are the first to take this tour. It runs about three hours total. I want to know all the weak points you find. You will be going on the full tour with animals that will not be on the opening tour until phase two."

"Oh, don't worry, we got you covered," said Dr. Harmon as he buckled his seatbelt.

Ethan tapped the side of the armored vehicle as if to send it off. The rings on his finger rapped against the metal plating. He took a few steps back and waited for the vehicle to roll off. Sir Barnes waved towards the cameras of the tour program entrance bay to signal Jayden to start the tour program. He had told Jayden to keep close eye on the security cameras outside the tour for his signal prior to them leaving the control room. Ethan stared proudly at the vehicle as they took off, like a parent watching their child graduate. Scott and

Nalani looked at each other and collectively let out a huge sigh in anticipation. They were obviously very familiar with these animals, but neither of them could believe that this day had come. The park was almost ready to open, and if this tour went well, they would be seeing guests flood through the park in the coming months.

The truck lurched backwards a bit and then began to propel itself forward. The driver waved at Ethan as he took off along the cobblestone road that led to the animal enclosures. Scott gazed out of the windows at the dense jungle surrounding them. The tour track cut through the thick forest as the main hub of the park disappeared behind them. Soon all Scott could see was the road in front of the car and the jungle enveloping them on all sides. It was a very claustrophobic feeling to be surrounded by nothing but forest. The tour vehicle rounded the corner as two giant wooden doors under a large concrete archway peered through the trees. Torches lined the sides of the archway, and the words "Archosauria" adorned the top of the arch. Large marble Tyranno-saurs stood on the tops of the huge support columns of the archway and faced the oncoming tour vehicles. The perimeter fence connected directly to this large gate that they were steadily approaching. A voice came through the speakers, suddenly breaking the silence as they approached the entry. TV screens embedded in the backs of the seats in the truck systematically turned on and began to broadcast a recording into the near-empty tour vehicle.

"As we enter these gates, we will slowly travel back in time to a world that pre-exists our species. On this tour, you will see amazing creatures that will astound you. Archosauria welcomes you to land that time forgot."

The doors creaked and shook as they automatically opened in front of them allowing the vehicle to pass through. Scott gazed through the large glass roof of the truck at the giant marble archway as it passed over their heads. The vehicle moved slowly forward through the gates at a snail's pace. Once the tour vehicle had passed through, the large doors slowly slammed shut behind them. The sound of them creaking closed echoed through the jungle around them.

It wasn't long before a small electric fence appeared off to the right-hand side of their vehicle. A large concrete sign had a skull imprinted in the center of a green circle that Scott recognized instantly. Two large crests sat atop the narrow skull of this animal. The sign read Dilophosaurus. Scott felt his mouth become a bit dry, and he began to recall poor Russell. Visions of him intubating the poor boy began to enter his mind as the car rolled forward.

"This species is one of the largest carnivores of the early Jurassic Period. Standing at just under three meters tall and at about seven meters long, this animal was a very formidable predator. We now know that they utilized a potent venom containing tetrodotoxin to paralyze their prey prior to eating it."

"Can't we mute this thing?" asked Nalani as she examined the monitor. She scrolled through the various options as she looked for a way to turn off the audio.

"I think it's part of the tour, I don't think so," said Scott. He turned his gaze to the electric fence and began to comb the area for the animals.

The audio droned on in the background as the two stared into the enclosure. Nalani noticed that there were no splash guards in front of the fence to protect the guests from Dilophosaur venom. She promptly began to roll down the vehicle windows.

"What are you doing?!" asked Scott in an alarmed fashion. "Have you lost your damn mind?!"

"What a stupid tourist will inevitably do," said Nalani as the window rolled slowly down. "He's got signs saying don't roll down the windows on that fence, but you know some idiot will try to roll the windows down anyways. We have to tell them to make sure they can't do that on their own. Especially not in front of this enclosure."

Nalani stared angrily at the now open vehicle window. She shook her head and began to roll the window up. She cursed as the window closed.

"Idiots!" Nalani exclaimed. "I'm so tired of rich people not giving dangerous animals the respect they deserve. Write this down Scott on our list. The windows should not be able to open at all during any part of this tour, let alone in front of the damn Dilophosaur cage!"

The bushes rustled as a Dilophosaur ran out into the open. The animal ran alongside the tour vehicle for a few feet. It stared at Nalani for a moment as it followed the car. She quickly veered off back into the jungle with a soft hooting noise. The bushes shook and settled quickly as the animal disappeared into the brush. All that was visible now were trees, bushes and red flowers. They were perfectly camouflaged against the brush of the enclosure as none of the rest of the herd were visible. The tour vehicle lurched onward, leaving the Dilophosaurs behind. Scott still found them to be captivating, even though he knew how dangerous they were. They were no less beautiful now that they were full grown. They weighed as much as a brown bear but were not as intimidating as their beautiful coloring made them seem elegant.

The tour vehicle began to climb a small hill, lurching slowly forward as it climbed up towards a small set of gates. As they approached the gates, large concrete signs became visible denoting that they were about to enter the Brachiosaurus and Parasaurolophus paddock. Loud cries began to echo through the air as they entered the gate. The electric fence here stood about thirty-foot-tall, likely to deter the massive Brachiosaurs from interacting with it. The track ahead of them rolled through the center of the enclosure with no barrier between them and the animals inside aside from some terrain obstacles. They rolled over a few sloping hills before they came to an overhang that overlooked a large lake. A herd of Parasaurolophus was drinking and socializing at the water's edge. Their loud cries filled the air as they honked and grazed along the lakebed. Scott estimated that they were about 200 yards or so away from the animals. Even from this distance, they could be clearly heard. The vehicle came to a stop at the edge of a large hill, and the audio track began to drone on and on about the Brachiosaurus. Scott could feel the ground begin to rumble a bit. Nalani smirked and pointed to the tree line. A group of four Brachiosaurs made their way out of the forests and were heading to the water's edge. The ground shook with each step the massive beasts took. Their cries joined the cacophony of the Parasaurolophus in a symphony, that even at this distance was akin sitting in a concert hall.

One of the Brachiosaurs paused at the water's edge. This animal was a different color than the ones Scott knew on Protogonus. She had a dark blue skin with a bright yellow underbelly. Black bands ran down the tail from its base to its tip. The animal splayed its forelimbs in a similar fashion to a giraffe and slowly lowered its relatively small head to the water. Its large tongue began to lap up water as she was joined by her sisters for a drink. The tour vehicle remained on the hill for about twenty minutes, likely to give the guests time to observe and take photographs of these majestic animals. Scott realized he had a huge smile on his face. Tears began to well in his eyes as he marveled at the majesty of these animals. Despite all the trials and tribulations that this job had put him through, this was why he had done this. He couldn't wait to take this ride with Erica in three months. She was going to absolutely love these animals. The car lurched forward and began to head away from the herd of dinosaurs. They came to a fork in the tour path as the car lurched to a stop.

"The left fork will be the tour that our first guests will experience. We are going to have you take the right fork to see the full phase two tour. Sadly the audio has not been programmed for this part of the tour just yet. Hang on while we have your car switch tracks," said Jayden's voice through the car speakers.

The tour vehicle rocked into motion and rode down the right fork. They headed through some dense jungle towards another gate in the tall electric fencing. The gate lurched open, and their vehicle passed through. They continued along the road for a few minutes before the next paddock came into view. A sign that said Iguanodon came into view as they rounded the bend.

"I didn't think Jin had brought this guy back yet," said Nalani. "Last I heard he was still working on it."

"He didn't; I think Ethan said this enclosure was empty," replied Scott.

Even still they stared into the forests as if they expected to see something. This area was all rather dark as the tall trees overhanging the area blocked out the sun. An odd screeching sound echoed through the trees, startling them. They combed the dense forest for signs of life but came up with nothing. The tour rolled unceremoniously by this enclosure and wrapped around a long bend. To their right was a large set of mountains covered in a lush forest. To their left was another enclosure. The bottom third of the fence was composed of thick metal rods that were wrapped in electric wiring. The rest of the fence was the normal electric fencing present throughout the rest of the park. Scott had a feeling he knew what was residing in this enclosure. His suspicions were confirmed by the concrete sign they approached, which was marked by the word Stegosaurus. Scott and Nalani peered across a large open field, scanning for the animals. A faint bellowing cry filled the air. Nalani examined the brush for signs of movement as they came around the basin that these animals were enclosed in at the southern tip of the island. The vehicle again came to a stop at the tip of the curved basin. Scott began to notice some movement at the very back of the field. The large back plates of the animal became visible over the horizon and then vanished just as quickly.

"Who knew something so big could hide so effectively," joked Nalani.

"To be fair, I wouldn't want to see you either if I didn't have to," joked Scott, slapping Nalani on the shoulder.

"Bugger off," laughed Nalani as she punched Scott repeatedly.

"That's for all the non-alcoholic jokes," retorted Scott as he returned fire, striking Nalani on the knee.

The car lurched forward again and came around the other side of the large basin. As they came around the paddock from this side, Scott caught sight of some more dorsal plates. Once again the animals ran off into the woods. The enclosure was a large semi-circle surrounded on all sides by large mountains. The tour track wrapped around the outside of the enclosure, giving the guests a full view of the open fields. The back end of the enclosure was covered in densely packed trees, which were now obscuring their view of the animals. It was a shame, as they were truly a wonder to see.

The tour continued on as the Stegosaurus paddock slowly rolled out of view. The vehicle climbed along a cliff face with the ocean beating against the shore of Dionysus on their right-hand side. Scott stared over the edge at the rolling ocean and the bright blue sky. There wasn't a single cloud out today. The sun beat through the glass roof onto them, warming them despite the vehicle's strong air conditioning. Scott could feel its warm glow on the back of his neck, right arm, and thighs. The vehicle veered left, away from the cliff face, and back into the jungles. A chain-link fence poked through the forest with an electric fence warning sign hanging on it. The fence was about ten feet high and circled around a densely packed jungle. A small breeze rolled through, causing the leaves to sway and beat against the fence. Sparks flew through the air, and the smell of burnt foliage began to fill the car. As the tour wrapped around the fence, a small river could be seen running through the center of the enclosure. A sign designated this the Proceratosaurus paddock. Scott let out a sigh, as he knew this paddock should also be empty.

"There is the little bugger," exclaimed Nalani, pointing to the riverbed.

A small bipedal animal stood by the water's edge. The dinosaur had blue-green plumage that blended in with the surrounding foliage. It was scrawny in its build, small wing-like arms tucked under its chest. On the top of its head sat a bright orange and yellow crest. It squawked as it stood by the river-bed and was joined by several more of its kind.

"This shouldn't be here, Nalani. Jin told me he wasn't finished with this one either," said Scott, annoyed. "First the bugs and then new dinosaur species we weren't alerted to. I'm concerned for what else Jin is doing behind the scenes."

"I guess he finished early?" said Nalani questioningly. "I've worked for these people for a while. It's annoying, but sometimes you just have to go with the flow."

"Makes me wonder what else he has been working on without telling us," said Scott as the car pulled away from the Proceratosaurus paddock. "We could have a very real security threat here and not know it."

Nalani shrugged her shoulders, knowing that there was nothing they could do about it. The tour rolled out of the jungle and onto a mountainous path. Carved into the mountain side was another enclosure. A herd of Pachycephalosaurus dotted the rock face in a similar fashion to a herd of mountain goats. They perched on various levels of the cliffs and called out to each other in their deep, moaning cries. Scott gazed over to the left side into the ravine. The top of the aviary and visitor center became visible through the tree line. They were heading back to the main tour route and away from the phase two part of the tour that the park's first guests would not see.

The vehicle rolled down off of the mountains and back down to the ground below. Scott watched as the aviary slowly got absorbed by the forest and disappeared from his view. He wanted to visit the park's multiple aviaries, but knew it was a separate attraction from the park tour. He had not had a chance to visit this part of the park since he arrived on Dionysus. Nalani pointed out several warning signs posted along the road warning guests to stay in their vehicles. The signs warned of a dangerous animal up ahead. Nalani got to her feet and walked over to the entrance at the back of the truck, opening the door and letting out an exasperated sigh as it swung open.

"God damnit! We need locking mechanisms on the vehicle door, too," said Nalani. "They really didn't think any of this through!"

"I agree, we don't want to go chasing children out into the park," said Scott. "Lord knows we may never get them back."

Nalani seemed like she was about to say something but paused. Her face became sullen as she pointed to the concrete marker in front of them. The color left her face, and her eyes opened wide as she registered what she had just read. The sign in front of them read Dakotaraptor. They looked at each other nervously. Scott gulped slightly as the vehicle made its way forward. He caught sight of the other track that they had skipped over, joining the track that they were on just ahead of them. They had made it back to the main tour route.

"Please stay in your vehicles as the next dinosaurs on our tour are extremely aggressive to park guests. Dakotaraptor is a bipedal pack hunter similar to today's modern-day wolves. They demonstrate remarkable intelligence and are formidable predators," droned the audio track.

"That's an understatement," marked Nalani, crossing her arms and sighing.

Scott could feel his heart pounding in his chest. His face began to feel warm and tingled as the color left his cheeks. He stared off into the enclosure for signs of the Dakotaraptors. He began to hope that they would just pass this enclosure like they did with the Stegosaurus and not see these animals.

The minutes began to feel like hours as the tour vehicle slowly plodded along. Scott looked into the enclosure with trepidation as he scanned the tree line for signs of the Dakotaraptors. He felt as if his ears were beginning to play tricks on him. The distinctive barking cries of the animals resonated through the air. They seemed as if they were coming from all directions simultaneously. Scott looked over at Nalani to see if she had heard them as well. Nalani remained silent but shook her head in acknowledgment that she had also heard the animals. A bright flash of light illuminated their faces as sparks rained down onto the tour vehicle. A Dakotaraptor flew backwards off the fence and rolled along the grass. Smoke billowed from the area of the fence that the animal was clinging to. The animal got slowly to her feet and shook her head. Suddenly another bright flash as a second Dakotaraptor leapt onto a different part of the fence. It hung onto the bars for a moment, trying to chew them in defiance as sparks shot out from the wires. A loud scream filled the air as it flew back off the fence and onto the ground. Before long the rest of raptors had become visible. They followed alongside the tour vehicle, barking and screaming as the car rode past.

It seemed as if they had learned their lesson, thought Scott. The lead Dakotaraptor began to chirp to the others who followed behind her. Scott and Nalani both let out a sigh and nervously laughed at each other. They were promptly interrupted by another flash of light and another rain of sparks. All eight of the raptors were now leaping up onto the fence. They would jump into the wires and begin to chew at them before succumbing to the electric shocks. Animal after animal would attach themselves to the fence, fall off, and then repeat the process.

"Are they are testing the fences?" remarked Scott. "Notice how they never attack the same place twice."

"We need to get the hell out of here before they figure out a way out," said Nalani.

Scott began to tap the glass separation between the driver and the tourist cabin, trying to get his attention.

"You need to get us out of here! Can't you speed these things up?" said Scott with fear clearly filling his voice.

The driver looked back in acknowledgement and put his foot on the gas. Sparks continued to pour down onto the tour vehicle, rolling along the glass roof and hood. The raptors were unrelenting as they systematically attacked the fence. The vehicle audio droned on and on about the origins of these animals and what their diet consisted of. It was almost comical, thought Scott, for the tour program to be talking about the diet of these animals when clearly they wanted to add *Homo sapiens* to their menu. The raptors paused from their assault and gathered in a small group. They chirped to one another and seemed like they had decided the vehicle was not worth the pain of electrocution. The lead raptor took off back into the brush with the remaining seven on her heels. The tour program dialogue cut out abruptly with the sound of a microphone feedback. The vehicle began to pick up speed and roll away from the aggressive creatures. Scott watched as the driver over-rode the program, so he could increase his speed and get away. Nalani glanced back to the enclosure and noted that the raptors were now running along the fence and keeping pace with their truck. This was pretty impressive, she thought as the vehicle was now rolling away at thirty miles per hour. The raptors came to a halt as they got to the end of their enclosure. They barked and cried in frustration as the tour vehicle rolled out of their view. Once the raptor enclosure was well out of sight, the vehicle began to slow down again, and the dialogue snapped back on.

Scott clutched his chest as he sat there panting. A bead of sweat dripped from his brow onto the collar of his shirt. Even Nalani, who was usually very composed, appeared shaken by this close encounter. She took off her safari hat and laid it on her lap as she wiped a few beads of sweat from her forehead.

"Those monsters can't be on this tour," said Nalani. "They are eventually going to wear the electric wires out if they keep chewing on them."

"Yeah…adding that to the list," said Scott, shaking his head.

The vehicle continued through the jungle and exited into a large swamp. Crooked, rotten trees covered the tour track, almost forming a roof above the cobblestone road. Their gnarled branches reached towards the heavens at various different angles. Large tufts of swamp grass and lily pads dotted the landscape. The electric fence of the next enclosure became visible on their left-hand side. The sand and gravel crackled under the vehicle tires as they journeyed onward. The sound of slow-running water became just audible over the tour program's babblings.

This was the Baryonyx paddock, thought Scott. It had to be with the drastic change in scenery, gone were the lush forests as they pressed forward into a much more foreboding swampy area. The Baryonyx was the only animal that lived a semi-aquatic lifestyle on the island. A sign up ahead confirmed Scott's suspicions. The tour track rose up over the swamp in front of them as it tracked over an enormous concrete bridge. Electric fencing lined the sides of the bridge, even though the bridge ran about fifteen feet above the water below. This put the tour vehicles well above the animal's heads as the water was ten feet deep at this section. Scott looked down at the swamp below as they passed over several Baryonyx. The dinosaurs were swimming peacefully below them, ignoring the vehicle that was passing overhead. Their similarities to a salt water crocodile were very striking. Their long, narrow snouts cut through the water as they propelled themselves forward using their undulating, powerful tail and muscular hindlimbs. Scott watched them intently as the tour vehicle came to a stop at the center of the bridge. There was something very relaxing about them, like staring into a giant fish tank.

"Baryonyx is a dinosaur from the early Cretaceous Period. It is a member of a family of dinosaurs called Spinosaurids. We now know that Baryonyx is semi-aquatic. It swims in a similar fashion to a Nile crocodile and eats a diet consisting mostly of fish and crustaceans."

One of the five Baryonyx plodded slowly out of the water, letting out a high-pitched roar as it got to land. The animal shook like a dog to dry itself off as it stood on the shore. Her large clawed feet crunched the gravel. Scott could see the webbing between their toes, even from this distance. The canopy of trees heavily shaded this area, adding an almost spooky feel to the enclosure. A constant croaking sound of mud frogs, mixed with the chirping of cicadas, further adding to the ominous atmosphere.

Nalani pulled a flask out of her pocket, unscrewing the lid, and offered some to Scott. Scott took a sip from the flask and promptly began to cough. He handed it back to Nalani, who was now laughing hysterically as she took the flask back. Nalani took a few large gulps from the flask before putting it back into her pocket. Scott wiped his mouth as he coughed a few more times. They had been driving along for hours it seemed with no sight of any dinosaurs. The vehicle was supposed to be in the Gallimimus paddock, but the animals seemed to be absent. As the tour vehicle rolled through the open fields, Scott stared at the large mountains running through the enclosure. The mountains stood like giant green soldiers lined up end to end, almost as if they were protecting this enclosure. Lush forests blanketed the mountains from their base to their peaks. A thick mist rolled over the top of the peaks, obscuring them from view. It almost seemed as if these mountains continued endlessly into the sky with their peaks above the clouds.

"Something moved over there I think," said Nalani.

Faint, high-pitched cries from the Gallimimus could be heard in the background. None of the animals revealed themselves, and the two stared aimlessly into the forest. The tour continued to roll unceremoniously through the open field. Scott let out a sigh and stretched his arms out above his head, placing his hands on the glass roof of the car. His hands left smudges on the glass. Scott shifted his hips slightly and slumped back into his seat.

The tour vehicle ran into the woods again and began to head towards the mountain range. A large concrete tunnel became visible as the vehicle looped through the trees; Scott immediately recognized this tunnel from his first trip to Dionysus. The tunnel swallowed their vehicle encasing them under thousands of tons of earth. The last time he was in this tunnel, he was escorting a sleeping Tyrannosaur to her new kingdom. Scott and Nalani began to blink rapidly as they adjusted their eyes from the bright island sun to the dimly lit tunnel. Even with the vehicle flood lights and lighting along the walls, this mountain pass was still dark. The marble carvings along the walls were completed now and were actually pretty impressive, thought Scott. He stared at the various animals depicted and began to count how many of these animals existed in their zoo. He couldn't help but notice that the artist who carved them had left out the feathers on many of the species. The wall was littered with inaccurate depictions based on old thoughts of how these animals looked. The vehicle rolled on at a snail's pace, triggering Scott's claustrophobia. He longed for the ride through this mountain to be over. I could walk faster than this, Scott thought to himself. Slowly they rolled towards the end of the tunnel. A banner hung near the exit reading "The Tyrant Lizard King."

"Ethan sure has a taste for the theatrics, doesn't he," said Nalani, pointing to the banner hanging from the ceiling as they passed under it.

"Let's just hope she is calmer than the last time we saw her," said Scott, smirking.

"She better be," said Nalani. "No one has bothered her in a few weeks."

The bright midday sun flooded through the car windshield, causing Scott and Nalani to shield their eyes with their forearms. Looming over them was the electric fence of the Tyrannosaurus Rex paddock. Densely packed forest filled the enclosure. The rolling mountain range they had just driven through framed this enclosure as well, acting as a barrier between the Tyrannosaurus and the Gallimimus for two thirds of the enclosure length. The tour vehicle rolled up to a section of the fence where there was a gap in the forest. A ditch that served as a terrain obstacle to prevent the animal from getting too close to the fencing could be seen from this vantage point.

They came to a slow, rolling stop at this section of the fence and listened to the tour program drone on and on about the Tyrannosaurus Rex in the background. A mechanical whirring noise broke through the silence as a small cage began to arise from the ground behind the electric fence. A brown, scruffy goat emerged tethered to a post with a thin metal chain. The cage bars fell back into the earth, leaving the goat alone and without any protection inside the Tyrannosaur paddock. Soft vocalizations from the goat caught their attention as they toned out the tour program. An eerie silence took over. The only sounds Scott could hear was the goat and his own respirations. There were no birds chirping, no insects chittering. All the normal jungle noises were noticeably absent. A small shockwave shook the vehicle as it rocked slightly. Then another one came shortly after. Scott and Nalani looked at each other and shared a collective moment of dread. The goat's ears began to swivel as it shot up to its feet. Scott could see the panicked look in the creature's eyes as it tried to make sense of the vibrations. It hopped a few times, trying to free itself from the chain that was holding prisoner. The impact tremors from the Tyrannosaur's heavy feet thundered closer and closer. Nalani and Scott sat in complete silence as they waited for what was going to happen next. The vibrations from the Tyrannosaurs footsteps shook the car and seemed to shake Scott's bones inside his body. His stomach sank, and he could feel his mouth becoming dry.

A large set of jaws rushed down through the tree line, whisking the goat off its feet and into the air with a thunderous crash of snapping wood. The thin metal chain broke easily as the goat rose off the ground in the Tyrannosaur's jaws. The Tyrannosaur began to shake her head violently from side to side, her massive teeth shredding through the goat's flesh like knives through a perfectly cooked steak. The goat thrashed around in the Tyrannosaur's jaws. The animal began to walk away from the fence with the goat. A trail of blood ran from its jaws. The Tyrannosaur threw her head back into the air and began to jerk her neck as she swallowed the poor goat alive. The quiet vocalizations from the goat disappeared as he slid down the throat of the dinosaur.

"That's going to give the kids nightmares," said Nalani, laughing nervously.

"Forget the kids, that's going to give me nightmares," said Scott as he stared at the massive dinosaur in front of him.

The Tyrannosaurus let out a deafening roar of triumph; blood dripped from her chin to the ground below. Her white mane of feathers was now spotted with blood. Scott and Nalani immediately covered their ears. Scott squinted and winced from the discomfort of the loud cry. The tour vehicle rocked slightly and slowly began to press forward once more as the T-Rex wandered back off into the jungles of her paddock.

Again the tour led them through a mountain tunnel, although this tunnel was not nearly as long as the previous one. Only three animals left, thought Scott. The Metriacanthosaurus was next up on the tour. Like clockwork the tour program chimed in as the paddock got closer.

"Metriacanthosaurus is a small therapod from the late Jurassic Period. She stands at about seven feet tall and is roughly about twenty-six feet long. Hailing from the United Kingdom, we now know that they were pack hunters like our Dakotaraptors."

A gurgling growl could be heard coming from within the enclosure. Palm trees gently swayed in the wind as the tour vehicle drove by. A small tropical bird flew past the car and landed on a branch within the enclosure. It hopped along the branch a few times, coming to a stop near some small berries. Using its beak, the bird pulled the berries from the branch. The small bird reminded Scott of his patients back in San Diego. His life was so different now than his life back home. His time in San Diego seemed like it was decades ago. Margret suddenly popped into his mind as he day-dreamed about his old office. Scott wondered what she was doing at this moment and if she was working well with whoever R.N.A. replaced him with. A pang of guilt washed over him as he remembered how rude he was to her during their last interactions. He would have to make it up to her by offering her a park pass or something, he thought. They used to have a good relationship, with him acting as her mentor. Surely a trip behind the scenes of this wonderful place would make up for how he treated her, he thought.

The tour vehicle rode away from the Metriacanthosaurus paddock and towards the Triceratops enclosure. The small bird disappeared from view, and Scott was slowly drawn back into the present time. They passed a large open field where the herd of Triceratops were clearly visible grazing on the long grass. Fencing in this area likely was not robust enough to stop a charging Triceratops, but these animals were generally docile. The electric shocks seemed to keep them in line, much like a herd of cattle. The tour vehicle paused at this point, so that they could get a good view of these large herbivores. Two of the animals began to bellow at each other. Breaking away from the rest of the grazing herd, they faced one another. They threw their heads from side to side and stomped their large feet on the ground. Dust flew into the air from the impact of their clawed toes striking the earth. These threat displays seemed to not work. The animals had lowered their heads and collided into one another. The two dinosaurs smashed their heads together with a thunderous crack as their horns locked in a similar fashion to fighting deer. They began to try to push each other back, digging their feet into the ground for traction. It seemed similar to a sumo match as the animals pushed each other around. A small tree smashed against one of the animal's sides, quickly snapping as she was pushed through it by the other animal. They bellowed as they pulled away from one another and charged again. Horns locked together as the animals continued their quarrel. Debris flew through the air from their massive bulk tearing up the terrain.

"I wonder who is going to win," said Nalani.

"It's interesting that they would fight like this. Usually these types of disputes are for dominance," said Scott. "Usually groups of female animals live in peace together."

"I wouldn't be surprised if Dr. Bai threw in a couple extra genes to make them more aggressive," said Nalani. "You know, so they would put on shows like this for the wealthy park guests."

"I guess so," said Scott. "I'll have to talk to Dr. Bramme. I guess we don't truly know how these animals actually behaved when they were around."

One of the Triceratops backed away and slowly trotted off into the woods of the enclosure. Its large head seemed to be bowed in defeat as it retreated. The victor of the scuffle began to howl and snort. She threw her head back and yowled as her long horns caught the tropical sun. Light reflected off the tips of her frill as well as the horns of her brow, almost as if the heavens themselves had recognized her victory. Scott caught sight of a small Microceratus herd running through the front of the enclosure along the fence line as they rolled away. They were likely fleeing the ruckus that was occurring further into the enclosure.

The Herrerasaurus paddock was the last enclosure before they returned back to the visitor's center. As they approached the fence, Scott could hear them calling to one another. These animals lived in harmony together for the most part but did not tend to hang out in groups. Each of them had claimed a territory within their paddock for their own. The only exception for this seemed to be feeding time. All of these animals would flock to the center of the enclosure to eat before they returned to their dwellings. The tour vehicle came to a stop in front of the enclosure, pausing for them to view its inhabitants. Scott peered into the cage, looking for evidence of the dinosaurs. Similar to their time on Protogonus, the animals were hiding in the brush and all but invisible to the naked eye. They should have been placed earlier in the tour, thought Scott. He did not feel these animals would make a good send off for the park guests, especially if all they were going to do was hide. They came slowly into motion again and began their return to the central hub.

Kyle knew that everyone would be distracted with watching Scott and Nalani's tour. The more eyes on this tour program, the less eyes on him. This was the perfect time for him to reach out to his contact in Splice Genetics. Kyle was tired of his role here; he had not been given what he was promised when he signed on with R.N.A. This company had left his mother's funeral expenses in his lap, expenses that they had promised to cover. He would not let this injustice stand, and he would make sure Ryo Sana and Sir Ethan Barnes rued the day they crossed him. Kyle glanced over to his left and saw that Jayden Charles and the others were thoroughly distracted. He pulled up a small direct chat window on his computer screen and immediately began typing away.

Kyle: I have been working on our little project as long as you can come through with the finances, I will deliver.

DinoRider0572: How long is this going to take?

Kyle: I wrote the programs, so not as long as it normally would. I am using my back door into their security to disable it.

DinoRider0572: That is not an answer.

Kyle: I should have it done before summer is over. I can have you caught up on decades of research. Not to mention the technology they used to make this place.

DinoRider0572: Hurry up. I don't like to wait.

Kyle: It'll get done. Relax. They suspect nothing.

Kyle waited for a reply, but after a few minutes, none came. He was not fond of his contact at Splice, but it was a means to an end. They were offering him a total of ten million dollars for this venture, as well as a key position in their company. He was not about to pass this opportunity up. Kyle glanced over at Ethan as he stared into the video surveillance screens on Jayden Charles' desk. These poor fools had no idea what was coming. Kyle smiled to himself as he closed out the chat window. No one crossed Kyle Bergin and didn't regret it!

Selena sat at her desk as she monitored the camera footage from Archosauria's first park tour. She stared at Scott and Nalani, watching their reactions as they rolled by the various animal enclosures. A small notification popped up on her screen as she watched. Selena ignored it at first, but her curiosity got the better of her. Clicking on the notification, she was able to see that Kyle had accessed his private VPN and was actively using it at the moment. She was glad she had flagged this when she first caught it.

"What are you up to, you little rat?" Selena asked herself as she leaned in closer to the screen.

Selena began trying to access the VPN that Kyle was using. She wanted to know what Kyle was doing secretly while all eyes were off him. She began recording what she was seeing on her screen as she attempted to hack into Kyle's encrypted server.

Chapter 16

Nalani stared at the weather forecast glumly as she sat at her desk in the control room. Her mouth twisted and contorted as she stared at the glowing computer screen. A tropical storm was heading their way, and this could mean disaster. Nalani knew from experience that inclement weather would cause anxiety in most wildlife. Stressed animals could mean escapes or worse. She radioed to Scott earlier in the day to discuss their plan for weathering this incoming storm. It would be all eyes on the Dakotaraptors as this storm rolled in. The worst thing that could happen was for the Dakotaraptors to escape their enclosure and traverse the island freely. Nalani picked her cup of coffee up off the desk and finished it in one large gulp. She strapped her rifle onto her back, throwing it over her shoulder and headed towards the control room exit. As she walked out into the main rotunda, she paused briefly to consider if she wanted breakfast prior to venturing out for the day. She decided against it and made a beeline to get to her vehicle, her boots crunching on the gravel lot as she walked. Dark clouds filled the sky and seemed to swallow the trees on the horizon. Nalani hoped the storm would swing away from the island at the last minute, so that they could avoid taking the damaging winds at full force. Nalani was nervous about what was to come if the storm did hit them. Several of the animals on this island would require extra security. Nalani did not trust the containment of the raptors to anyone other than herself.

Nalani rushed over the gravel parking lot to her car. She pulled the cloth cover of the vehicle to close the sun roof, tugging it the last few inches as the cover seemed to not be large enough. Nalani took care to zipper the clear plastic that would act as her rear windshield. She proceeded back to the front of the vehicle and opened the door. Nalani threw her rifle into the passenger's seat in a hasty fashion. The weapon bounced and rattled against the door as it settled into place. Hopping in the car, she promptly started it and slammed the door shut. Speeding along a service road that ran around the perimeter fence, Nalani checked her watch. She didn't have time to waste and circumvented the tour route to save time. She needed to get to the barns, so that she could organize her men for the coming storm. She was worried about how these animals were going to respond to this weather. There were a number of things that could go wrong, and Nalani wanted to be prepared for all of them.

She rolled into the lot of the veterinary complex rather quickly; her car skidded to a halt on the dry ground, stirring up dust as she came to an abrupt stop. Men were already scurrying about, being directed by Reginald and Scott. It seemed like Scott had taken the lead in organizing the men already. Nalani quickly grabbed her rifle and rushed over to Dr. Harmon's side. A loud thunderclap resounded through the air, startling the men. The sky began to darken even further as light grays and whites slowly turned to black. A light breeze began to blow through the compound, shaking the surrounding trees and bushes.

"Looks like you two have this under control," said Nalani, smiling. "Where is Stephen?"

"Stephen took a group of men to guard the Tyrannosaurus Rex," said Reginald. "We figure the T-Rex, Dilophosaurus, Metriacanthosaurus, and Dakotaraptors are the ones we would need to observe."

"What about the other predators?" asked Nalani.

"The Baryonyx is semi-aquatic, rain should not bother it," said Scott. "The other animals are in cages that should be strong enough hold them. I don't see a Compy breaking out of the thick glass in the visitor's center."

"Alright, men, I want four of you to go to the Dilophosaurus enclosure with Reginald. Dr. Harmon will take ten of you for the Metriacanthosaurus, and the rest of you will be on Dakotaraptor duty with me," called Nalani to her men.

Armed men ran about the complex sorting into their various groups. There was a clamor of boots hitting the ground as they prepared to head to their respective destinations. Nalani ordered all the men to carry live ammunition in addition to tranquilizers. The instructions were to put down anything that even appeared as if it were going to escape containment. She knew Jin Moon would not be happy if they killed one of his precious creatures, but Nalani was not about to risk the lives of her men for Dr. Bai's science projects.

Nalani led a group of twenty men in multiple vehicles down the service roads to the Dakotaraptor paddock. They were to form a loose perimeter around the enclosure with each man responsible for about two to three miles of fencing. Jayden Charles was using a team of men to monitor the security cameras. If he saw something suspicious, he would be able to alert them to the threat. Nalani figured that if anything would escape tonight, it would be the raptors. When they got closer to the paddock, the cars began to split up, so as to get to their respective parts of the enclosure. Nalani and Geoffrey were responsible for monitoring the segment of the fence along the tour route. She parked her car in front of a large tree and donned a bright yellow poncho. She threw it over her shoulders like she was putting on a cape. It had already begun to drizzle; this was going to be a long night. Geoffrey joined Nalani at the fence, peering into the enclosure for any signs of life. All she could see was an open field surrounded by trees. Their vision was limited, as the horizon was being shrouded by the pouring rain. It was a beautiful sight to see, thought Nalani. It almost reminded her of the plains down in Kenya. The rain drops beat heavier and heavier on them as they split up. Their feet began to slosh through the moist earth that was quickly turning to mud in the downpour. Nalani headed to the left of the fence, and Geoffrey headed to the right.

Nalani looked back at Geoffrey as he slowly disappeared into the distance. She clutched her rifle and took the safety off. None of these animals were going to get past her alive. Nalani hoped this would go smoothly and that it wouldn't come to that. If nothing attempted escape tonight, then perhaps they could ease up and not have to do this the next time. This park had to be secure before they could allow guests on the island. Geoffrey walked slowly along the fence line. He did not want to be here out in the rain and grumbled to himself about how terrible this all was. He had not taken the safety off his rifle as he felt that this was all a bit extreme. Surely zoos didn't send armed men to the lion exhibits for a little rain storm, he thought to himself. Nalani was being too cautious, and Geoffrey was paying the price of that, he thought. His boots slopped in the mud as he proceeded along the tour route; mud splattered onto his poncho and ran down the yellow plastic like tear drops with the rain. Lightening flashed across the sky, lighting up the path ahead of him. A deafening thunderclap echoed through the air, causing a cacophony of terrified animal noises to resound through the air. The various roars and bellows seemed to echo around the tour route. The path ahead seemed to go on and on without end. Geoffrey did not know why he couldn't have just driven the car along the fences. At least if he was in a vehicle, he would be dry by now. His socks began to slowly become more and more wet despite his boots. He could feel the wet fabric adhere to his feet and toes.

Another flash of lightening lit the sky, illuminating a shadowy figure and an ominous set of fiery yellow eyes in a nearby bush. Geoffrey jumped as the figure disappeared back into the darkness. Had something already gotten out of containment, he thought. A wave of panic swept over him. He pointed his flash light slowly towards the brush. All he saw were leaves illuminated by his torch. Geoffrey let out a sigh of relief and continued to walk forward. His eyes must have been playing tricks on him. A patch of leaves rustled aggressively behind him, causing him to jump. He pointed the flashlight on the end of his rifle at the moving bush outside of the enclosure. His heart began to race as he watched the bush shake. Geoffrey could feel his knees locking and the hair on the back of his neck standing straight up. There were no holes in the fence, this couldn't be a raptor, he thought. Geoffrey slowly backed up along the tour route, keeping his eyes fixed on the bush that was now no longer moving. His boot hit something hard as he proceeded to walk backwards. He took his eyes off the bush and looked to see a small rock under his boot. Geoffrey squatted slowly towards the ground, picking the rock up while making sure to keep his eyes fixed on the brush. He lowered his rifle and threw the rock in the direction of the creature. The rock cracked through a few branches before striking what sounded like a tree. A large tropical bird came flying out from between the leaves and flew high into the night sky. Geoffrey let out a sigh of relief; he was being paranoid, he thought to himself. Surely there was nothing to worry about.

Before he could turn around and continue on his way, he heard something breathing heavily behind him. The soft purring noise was a sound that he unfortunately knew all too well. Geoffrey froze, his shoulders raised slightly by his side in an unconscious effort to protect his head. He turned slowly around, the light on his helmet illuminating what was in front of him as he turned. The electric fence came into view, followed by the jungle of the enclosure behind him. When he got to the cage, he was now facing a Dakotaraptor. The raptor squinted and turned away from the bright light that was now being shown in her face. The animal's pupils constricted in the bright light and its wet, scaly face glistened in the rain. Rain drops fell off the rest of her feathered body as she stared at Geoffrey. She pulled back her scaly lips into a snarl, revealing her terrifying yellowed teeth. Geoffrey wanted to scream but couldn't find his voice. He stood there frozen in front of the dinosaur. Once the raptor had adapted to the bright light, it let out a deep guttural cry and launched herself at Geoffrey. Geoffrey fell backwards into the wet mud with a loud plopping noise. Mud splattered all over his clothes, and his rifle slid away from him along the wet ground. Sparks filled the air as the raptor hit the electric fence. Geoffrey shielded his face with his right arm to protect himself from the sparks raining down on him. The raptor clung to the fence and tried to chew on the wires fruitlessly. After a few seconds, the creature jumped back; smoke billowed from her hands and feet. Geoffrey was heavily panting; it felt as if his heart was going to explode from his chest. He slowly got to his feet as he kept his gaze fixated on the raptor. Picking up his gun, he walked closer to the fence. The animal was equally as interested in Geoffrey. She kept her eyes fixed on him and began to tilt her head as she examined the fence for an exit point. Geoffrey began to laugh as he realized he was safe with the animal trapped behind the fence. He was lucky, he thought.

"You gave me a scare there, girl," said Geoffrey as he composed himself. "Why you do this to me, huh?"

The raptor barked in reply almost as if it were trying to answer him. Geoffrey walked to pick up his gun; once again approaching the cage, he raised his rifle to the animal and pointed it at the dinosaur's head. He feigned pulling the trigger and shooting the animal. The Dakotaraptor let out a high pitch scream of alarm and rushed off into the jungle at the sight of the rifle.

Geoffrey stood there for a moment, his gaze fixated on the spot where the dinosaur once was. Had it recognized the gun, thought Geoffrey. That was impossible, she was just an animal, he thought to himself. He began to walk back along the cage line when he again heard noises coming from the enclosure. The sound of feet pattering in the mud alongside him made him feel uneasy. With each step he took, he heard an equivalent step off to his right-hand side. Geoffrey gripped his rifle and tried not to look into the cage. Walking alongside him behind the electrified fence was the Dakotaraptor. The animal was following him as he walked back to meet Nalani. Geoffrey stopped short, and to his surprise, so did the Dakotaraptor. The two turned to face each other; her pupils rapidly began to enlarge and constrict as she stared at Geoffrey. The Dakotaraptor snarled, pulling back her lip to reveal dozens of sharp teeth once again. The animal hissed and acted as if she were going to lunge at the fence causing Geoffrey to wince. Geoffrey pulled his gun on the animal, causing her to jump back slightly and recoil, but this time she did not run off. It seemed as if she was challenging Geoffrey to shoot her. Geoffrey bent down and picked up a rock from the muddy ground. Rain water and mud dripped off the rock in his hand as he stood back up.

"Go on, get out of here," shouted Geoffrey as he lobbed the rock at the Dakotaraptor.

The rock hit the ground by her feet and skidded along the wet grass. The animal let out a short barking noise followed by a loud hiss. She again jumped at the fencing, only to be repelled by the voltage. She let out a high pitch scream as she leapt off the fencing.

"That's what you get!" said Geoffrey, laughing. "You need to learn your place. Stupid lizard."

The Dakotaraptor shook her head as she recovered from the electric shock. Despite the negative reinforcement, she continued to follow Geoffrey as he walked back to Nalani.

Geoffrey grew increasingly uneasy from being stalked by the persistent predator. The electric fencing gave him a slight sense of security, but having her follow him so intently made his skin crawl. He felt her gaze piercing through him, and he could hear her matching her steps with his. It was a long way back to the meeting point, and Geoffrey did not know how much more of this he could take.

"Go away, will ya!" he shouted at the animal as he threw another rock.

The rock struck the animal on her side, but still the Dakotaraptor pursued on, watching his every move. Geoffrey reached for a cattle prod on his hip; if she wasn't going to leave him alone, he was going to make her leave him alone. He approached the fence as he drew the cattle prod. Sparks flew from the end of the long metal rod as he approached the fence. Similarly the Dakotaraptor also approached the fence, mimicking him. She placed her head parallel to the fence and was staring at Geoffrey with one large green eye. Geoffrey seized the opportunity and hit her with the cattle prod through the fence. The raptor shrieked in pain as she lunged backwards, falling onto her side. She glared at Geoffrey and growled menacingly from inside the enclosure. She once again approached the fence but took care to stay out of the range of the cattle prod. She snapped her jaws repeatedly at the man's weapon. Geoffrey poked the cattle prod between the fencing a few times, taking care not to touch the wires himself with the metal pole. The raptor let out one final set of screams and rushed off back into the jungle.

Geoffrey smiled and stood there victoriously. He walked back to meet Nalani through the light rain, replacing the cattle prod at his hip. The occasional lightning bolt illuminated the sky, elucidating the path before him. The rain was letting up now, and the storm seemed to be passing. Geoffrey could see Nalani approaching in the distance; her bright yellow poncho stood out among the dark background of trees. Geoffrey raised his hand above his head and waved at her. Nalani returned the gesture, waving her flashlight above her head. Geoffrey began to pick up his pace; he was thrilled to see another person after his close encounter. His feet splashed in the mud as he ran.

"Everything go alright on your end?" asked Nalani. "I didn't even see them on mine."

"Yes, ma'am," said Geoffrey, purposely choosing to omit his encounter with the raptor. Geoffrey did not want Nalani to know he was taunting one of the animals.

"Good, good," said Nalani. "It looks like things are clearing up; let's head back to the control room."

"Sounds good to me," said Geoffrey. "I can't wait to get out of this damn rain."

"You and me both," said Nalani, laughing.

The two headed back to the car together. As they got to the vehicle, the rain stopped. Nalani removed her soaked poncho, throwing it in the back seat before hopping into the car. The two drove off back to the visitor center to regroup with their team and discuss what they had seen.

Jayden Charles logged into his work station for the first time that morning. Typing his password into the machine, he let out a loud yawn. He did not sleep well during the thunderstorm last night. Jayden rubbed his eyes as smoke rose from the cigar in his mouth. His eyes itched and burned from the lack of sleep. He put his glasses back on his face and began to scroll through the systems one by one to make sure everything was online. As he scrolled through, an alert popped up on his screen. The words "Damage Report" flashed across his screen. Jayden opened the alert to view the IT ticket. Anger promptly swept over him when he saw that the alert was from 8 A.M. He was not on the early shift today, and it was now almost noon. This ticket had obviously been ignored by his compatriot without anyone addressing it. Jayden glared at the schedule to see Kyle was on the early shift today. It was his job to handle such things.

"Hey, Kyle, did you see this alert from the raptor paddock?" asked Jayden, audibly annoyed as he rolled his chair out from his desk.

"What, huh? Oh, yeah, I saw that," said Kyle, seeming distracted. He was typing furiously on his computer and did not even bother to turn his head when he addressed Jayden.

"Well, you were here at 8 A.M., didn't you think you should have addressed it by now?" asked Jayden.

"Listen, do you know how many other things I have to debug here? I still can't get the vehicle doors to stay locked like Nalani wanted on the tour program," said Kyle defensively. "I have a million things to do here, and quite frankly I'm not paid enough for all this work."

"Kyle, the Dakoraraptors are the most dangerous animals on this island. Any alerts from their paddock should be a priority as it would be a disaster if they were to escape," barked Jayden. "Thankfully it's just a shorted-out feeder, but this could have been way worse."

"Yeah, yeah, yeah. I hear you," said Kyle. "I'll call Dr. Harmon and have his team go look at it. Storm must have knocked out the power or something."

"Get it done, Kyle," said Jayden. "I'm tired of dealing with your crap."

"Listen, champ, if you want to do this job all by yourself, go right ahead," said Kyle in a snarky tone. "You'll be the only tech guy on this island and then maybe you'll see all the stuff I do. I'm so unappreciated."

Jayden rolled his eyes and shook his head. Any time he asked anything of Kyle, it was the same story. Kyle would complain and make excuses about why he hadn't finished even the simplest of tasks. The act was getting old, and Jayden's patience was running thin. He sat there for a moment, watching Kyle to see if he would pick up the phone. Kyle typed away at his screen almost defiantly as he seemingly ignored Jayden's stare. Seconds seemed to tick by like hours as Jayden waited. Kyle continued to type and stare intently at his screen. A large grin took over Kyle's face as he paused, staring at his screen like a proud parent watching his child getting an award. With a few more clicks of his mouse, he finally picked up the phone to contact Dr. Harmon. Jayden shook his head and cursed under his breath. He shook off some ashes from the tip of his cigar into an ash tray on his desk. Jayden took a deep breath to center himself and went back to scrolling through the alerts from the morning.

Scott began to load up his car with the things he would need to deal with the task of fixing the feeder in the raptor paddock. The feeders were placed at the back of the paddock, away from the tour fences. Dr. Harmon did not want these animals on the tour, nor did he want them near the fences when the vehicles rolled by. Reginald hopped in the back seat of the car with a tool bag as Stephen climbed into the front, placing a barrel filled with dead rats in between his legs. Within the hour, they were on their way to the Dakotaraptor Paddock. Scott pulled up along the tour route and dropped off Stephen. Stephen's job was to distract the animals and keep them focused on the front end of the paddock while Scott and Reginald tended to the feeder. Stephen grabbed the bucket of rodents and waddled off to the fence. He began to shout and bang a stick against to the barrel to try to get the animal's attention and draw them to his position. Dr. Harmon put his foot on the gas and pulled away, leaving Stephen behind. As they drove to the service entrance, Dr. Harmon looked at the shotgun in the passenger seat next to him. He hoped he would not have to use it, but he was glad to have the weapon at his side. A small blood stain brandished the floor where Stephen had placed the bucket. Dr. Harmon scoffed to himself at the thought of having to clean this up later. They pulled up to the utility bunker first to see if they could fix the problem without entering the enclosure. Scott pushed the large metal doors of the bunker open and held them for Reginald to pass through with his heavy tool bag. They walked down the long, dark utility corridor. The smell of farm animal filled the air and assaulted their noses as they proceeded down the hall. Long pipes and wires overhead led to the elevator for the feeder. Reginald approached the computer console and began trying to locate where the issue was. Scott stared at the ceiling, imagining the monsters that were just above coming through the elevator door that allowed goats and cattle into their paddock. He shuddered at the thought of having to fend off hungry Dakotaraptors. Scott gripped his shotgun tighter as he imagined having to shoot the creatures.

Reginald pulled a screw driver out of the bag and opened up a panel on the side of the console. His tongue hung out of his mouth as he quickly removed the screws holding the panel door. Once the last screw was out, he placed them into his pocket and pulled off the panel door. Reginald began to examine various wires and switches within the innards of the lift computer. He pulled away a large cluster of wiring and began to examine a set of fuses and switches. He then grabbed the ball of wires and examined them in his hands for any sign of damage before putting them back into the console.

"Everything here checks out," said Reginald, replacing the wires back into the console. "The issue has to be within the enclosure itself unfortunately."

"Damnit," said Scott. "I was afraid that would be the case."

"Should we wait for Nalani and sedate them?" asked Reginald. "I don't feel comfortable going in there with those things awake."

"Nalani is on the other end of the island dealing with a sick Triceratops," said Scott. "That means we would have to put it off till tomorrow. I don't want to be trying to sedate these things when they are hungry."

"Good point," Reginald said, swallowing hard.

Reginald closed the panel on the side of the computer; his head hung low as he let out a lengthy sigh. He jumped to his feet and grabbed his bag of tools, zipping it shut after replacing the screwdriver. The two men walked silently back to the vehicle. Scott began to wonder if Stephen would be able to adequately distract the raptors long enough. He didn't know if he had given him enough rats to hold their attention for this long. The service door for the enclosure was about five miles from the feeder. This was going to be one hell of a trip, thought Scott. He drove to the paddock entrance as quickly as he could; leaves and branches beat against the car as they pushed through the jungle. Scott knew time was not on their side. When they arrived at the service entrance for the paddock, Reginald hopped over the side of the vehicle before it had come to a complete stop. He rushed to the panel on the side of the cage door and flipped various switches to activate the automatic opening protocol. Reginald hopped back into the car as the first set of doors slowly opened. A siren echoed through the jungle as red lights began to flash above the cage door to signal that the door would be opening. Scott drove the car within the first set of open doors and sat in the vestibule; the gate began to close behind them as he waited eagerly for the second door to start opening. Dr. Harmon did not wait for the second door to fully open. Once the gate had raised high enough to allow the vehicle through, he was off.

Scott began to speed to the feeder as quickly as the terrain would allow. The tall grass and rolling hills did not allow him to go much above thirty miles per hour. His heart was thumping so fast that he felt it would beat through his chest wall. He glanced into the rear-view mirror to see Reginald clutching the the high caliber revolver at his waist. Scott began to tap his left foot on the floor as they traversed the Dakotaraptor paddock. He hoped they did not hear the warning beacons from the enclosure entrance. The vehicle ploughed out of the jungle and into an open plain. The feeder became visible just over a small set of rolling hills. Scott was finally able to get the vehicle up to a higher speed on this open ground. The feeder was out in the open, surrounded by the jungles of the rest of the paddock. This allowed it to be viewed easily by the paddock's security cameras. Scott realized he was going a bit too fast as he neared the feeder. He slammed on the brakes, causing the car to skid on the grass and past his target. Dust and blades of grass flew into the air as the car came to a skidding stop. He quickly put the car in park but took care to leave the engine running. Scott grabbed the shotgun out of the passenger seat and immediately began to open the shoulder guard of the weapon. He took the safety off and readied the shotgun to be used. Reginald similarly undid the top of his holster, so that he would have easy access to his revolver. He pulled the bag out of the back seat and headed to the feeder. This feeder was encased in an electric fence to prevent the raptors from climbing down the service elevator and attacking the workers below when the feeder was in use.

Reginald lifted a small fake rock near the electric fencing of the feeder to reveal a small key panel. He quickly used the panel to run diagnostics on the electric mechanisms; the power to the fencing around the feeder was offline. Reginald approached the electric cage, noticing that it was covered in burnt branches and vegetation. He began removing the charred branches, making his way around the rest of the cage. He tirelessly removed the foliage entwined amongst the wiring. The burnt wood smelled like someone was having a cookout. This made Reginald begin to feel a little hungry as he thought about lunch. Scott stood on watch with his shotgun. He nervously pivoted his head, almost expecting to see a Dakotaraptor every time he turned around. Scott clutched the weapon tightly; his knuckles were blanched, and his hands began to cramp. He dropped the weapon to his side to shake out his right hand. Up ahead a set of branches began to move. Scott raised his shotgun urgently and scanned the tree line for any signs of the dinosaurs.

"Reginald," said Scott urgently. "You need to hurry…"

"I'm trying, all these branches shorted out the fuses for the fence, I'm trying to reboot them," said Reginald nervously. "I'm going as fast as I can."

The bushes parted as the long snout of a Dakotaraptor made its way out through. She paused at the tree line and began to look inquisitively at Scott and Reginald. She was about a hundred yards away. Scott raised his shotgun and prepared to fire on the dinosaur should she get any closer. At the moment, she was out of range of the shotgun. What should he do, thought Scott. If only Nalani were here, she would know exactly how to handle this. Scott slowly felt panic begin to overtake him. He wondered if they would be able to handle the pack of Raptors with the limited weapons they had brought with them.

Reginald worked on a fuse box connected to the doors of the elevator within the small feeder cage. He glanced at Scott to see him pointing his shotgun at a Dakotaraptor in the distance. Reginald cursed under his breath; he was worried something like this would happen. His hands shook as he furiously re-wired the fuse box. He kept looking up into the distance at the Dakotaraptor; he wished he hadn't looked up when Scott told him to hurry. Reginald dropped a pair of wire cutters onto the metal keyboard with a loud metallic thud. The Dakotaraptor jumped but remained in place. Her gaze was fixed on them as she turned her head slightly in a curious fashion. Reginald struggled to pick up the wire cutters; his hands fumbled the tool as he tried to pick them up. Scott felt sweat begin to roll down the tip of his nose; he wiped his brow while taking care not to lower his weapon. Reginald meanwhile struggled to replace the wiring. Normally a job like this would only take a few minutes, but now it felt like it was taking hours.

"I'm done, I'm done!" shouted Reginald as he slammed the control panel shut harder than he had to.

He crawled out of the cage, hitting his head on the low hanging doorway as he exited. He rubbed his head and slammed the door shut behind him. Reginald flipped some switches on the control panel outside of the small cage, causing a slight buzzing sound to fill the air as the power to the fence returned. Reginald threw his bag into the back seat from about ten feet from the vehicle and drew his revolver. Scott slowly backed his way around the front of the car to the driver's seat. He reached with his left hand behind him for the handle of the door. As soon as his fingers ran over the handle, he popped the door open. Scott threw the shotgun into the passenger seat, slid into the driver's seat, and quickly put the car into drive. The wheels spun rapidly in place as the car slowly kicked into motion. Dr. Harmon made a sharp U-turn and sped off at full speed for the enclosure's service entrance. He was taking no chances here. The speedometer began to raise, and the car started to jerk. Scott quickly shifted gears just before the vehicle stalled out causing the car to lurch as it sped off. Reginald re-holstered his revolver and grabbed the shotgun from the passenger seat. He turned around, pointing the gun over the back end of the car. The muzzle of the shotgun bounced up and down as they drove over the uneven ground. At the moment, it did not seem like they were being followed.

When they got to the service entrance, Reginald immediately jumped over the side of the vehicle. He stumbled a few steps forward before regaining his balance. He ran so quickly to the security panel on the wall that he had to stop himself from smashing into it with his forearms. The shotgun clanged against the concrete wall. Reginald's hands shook as he opened the panel on the wall. Repeatedly gazing over his shoulder, he flipped the switches on the panel. He quickly set the cage doors to open and rushed back to the car. Scott continually used his mirrors to gaze behind them and make sure they were not followed. The first set of doors creaked slowly open; the red warning lightly flashed and the alarm sounded. Scott wished they hadn't programed the alarm to be so loud; why couldn't they mute the sound for circumstances like this, he thought. The raptors had to be hearing this, he thought. Scott pulled the car up to the gate without waiting for the doors to open fully. The hood of the car slid under the door as Scott waited for the gate to lift high enough for the windshield to pass. Dr. Harmon smashed on the gas as soon as the door had cleared the top of the windshield. The car skidded to a halt in the waiting area between the two sets of doors. Reginald held the shotgun at the ready off the back end of the car as they waited for the door to close behind them.

'C'mon, c'mon, c'mon," Scott repeated to himself as he tapped his hands on the steering wheel. He kept his eyes fixed on the rear-view mirror.

The gate began to pull down behind them, creaking as it closed. Scott's heart sank as he saw a brownish figure moving through the forest behind them reflected in the glass. He turned around and pulled the revolver from Reginald's waist. Reginald jumped as he looked back at Scott. His eyes were as wide as dinner plates, and he was heavily panting.

"Did you see something?!" screamed Reginald, hearing the animals barking to each other in the distance. "Where are they?! I can hear them!"

"Calm down, man," said Scott. "You're not gonna be able to shoot them if they come when you're like this."

"Calm?! We are about to be lunch, man!" screamed Reginald.

The enclosure-side gate slowly came to a close behind them as the second gate began to open. Scott dropped the revolver onto the passenger seat and hit the gas; the top of the car's windshield scraped against the bottom of the exit door as he peeled out of the enclosure. Once they were out of the enclosure, Scott stopped the car and put it in park. He was panting loudly and sweating profusely. This was not something he wanted to make a habit of doing. Scott had worked with some large predators during his training, but none of them scared him as much as these animals did. He was glad to be out of their domain and behind the safety of the electric fencing. Scott put the car in drive once he had recovered and drove off to the visitor's center.

The drive back was a hazy blur. Dr. Harmon felt almost as if he were in a dream sequence watching himself drive. He began to think about all the ways in which the encounter could have gone south. They would need a better plan if they were going to have to enter the enclosure again. As he drove past the Pachycephalosaurus paddock, he brought the car to an abrupt stop. Scott quickly began to reverse the car and make a U-turn.

"Woah, woah, why are we going back there, man?" asked Reginald, panic resonating through his words.

"We forgot Steve," said Scott, laughing slightly.

Reginald let out a sigh of relief. He had thought that they had to interact with the Dakotaraptors again. Dr. Harmon swung back by the tour route to pick up Stephen. He couldn't believe he had been so careless as to leave someone behind. He followed the tour route back to the Raptor enclosure. Stephen came into view as they pulled over a small ridge. He had flipped the barrel over and was sitting on it as he waited to be picked up. Scott began to honk the horn to alert Stephen of their arrival. Stephen got up and picked the empty barrel up off the ground as Scott approached him.

"I thought you guys forgot about me," said Stephen. "How did it go?"

"It went," said Reginald, nervously laughing. "We almost left your ass here."

"I tried to keep them at the fence, but two of them ran off into the jungle on me," said Stephen. "I even threw an extra rat their way to try to get them to come back, but they ignored it."

"Wait, two of them?" asked Reginald. "Doc, did you see a second one?"

"No, I didn't," said Scott, sounding alarmed. "All I saw was the one on the ridge."

"Wait, so they came your way?" asked Stephen nervously. "Did they attack you? Are you guys okay?"

"Yeah, we are fine. They left us alone. Holy shit, man!" exclaimed Reginald. "We were almost lunch for real."

Scott stared straight ahead at the road silently. He had not realized just how dangerous this venture truly could have been. These animals did not behave like any predator he had interacted with in the past. Most predators don't turn down a free meal, thought Dr. Harmon. They ignored food to come investigate. Scott felt light-headed as he realized just how close they were to potentially becoming a meal.

Dr. Bai stood over a set of incubators, eyeing his latest creation. He held a clipboard in his hand as he examined the temperature settings on the machine and adjusted some of the knobs. He scowled as he ticked off some boxes on his clipboard. Dr. Sung approached him from behind sheepishly. He looked as if he wanted to ask Jin Moon a question but decided against it. Dr. Bai always made Ernie feel uneasy. A large smile filled Jin's face as he gazed over this new clutch of eggs. He had succeeded yet again in sequencing a new species. The two were interrupted by the lab door opening; the loud hissing noise echoed through the air as the door slid open. Sir Ethan hobbled into the laboratory, his fancy shoes clapping on the tile floor as he walked. Dr. Bai placed the clipboard down onto the incubator and extended his right hand readily to greet Ethan. The two hugged as they said hello as if it had been months since they had seen each other.

"Jin, my boy," said Ethan. "What have you got for me now? You sounded pretty excited on the phone about this brood."

"This species here is thought to be another intelligent one like the Dakotaraptors," said Jin. "It's smaller but should make for an excellent attraction nonetheless."

"Ah, marvelous. Do you think they will be tameable? Maybe we can use them in shows or something," said Ethan. "Well, don't keep me in suspense. What are they?"

"This species should be *Pectinodon bakkeri*," said Dr. Bai almost triumphantly. "It's a small predator from the Cretaceous Period. Dr. Bramme tells me they are thought to be smart like the Dakotaraptor but much less dangerous because their small stature."

"Marvelous!" exclaimed Ethan. "I'm sure we can find some use for them."

"Ha-ha-ha, for sure," said Dr. Bai. "I will have to see if I can get them to express traits that will make them friendly. Like prehistoric dogs."

"I'm sure you will get it soon, Jin. You are the best at what you do after all. How do you know what this species is though?" asked Ethan. "You figured out how to identify the animals' genomes."

"Yes, yes, I did," said Dr. Bai, smiling triumphantly.

"Well, actually, Dr. Bai, it was me who . . ." interjected Dr. Sung quietly.

"I figured out how to identify which animals we were working with once our genome library had become more complete," said Jin Moon, cutting Dr. Sung off.

"Wonderful, wonderful," said Ethan. "You are worth every penny we pay you."

The men stared earnestly at the clutch of eggs under the bright yellow incubation lamp. The eggs glistened under the glow of the bulb. Jin Moon pulled a calculator out of his breast pocket and began typing away furiously. With the rate of growth of the embryos, this brood should be ready to hatch by the end of the week. They should be sub-adults by the time the park opened in July, he thought to himself. This would be just perfect timing.

Jayden sat at his desk, smoking his usual cigar. Smoke billowed from the end of it towards the ceiling as he watched the various security monitors from his desk. The tropical storm from the week prior had swung past them, dealing only minimal damage. They had gotten lucky, but it served to highlight the need for weather tracking as priority to park security. Jayden was getting ready to clock out for lunch when he happened to glance at one of the monitors, which depicted the various dinosaur paddocks. The Dakotaraptor paddock was again glowing red, indicating an error. He clicked onto the paddock with the mouse to bring up the error message. He cursed as he noted that there was an issue with the feeder in the paddock again. Jayden slammed his fist onto his desk and gazed over at Kyle. Kyle was sitting in his chair with his hands folded over his stomach. His eyes were very clearly closed as he slumbered peacefully. Jayden shook his head and took the cigar out of his mouth, placing it on the edge of an ash tray at his desk. He debated for a moment if it was worth waking Kyle or if he should just phone Dr. Harmon and handle this issue himself.

Kyle's complete lack of a work ethic made Jayden furious as he often had to pick up the slack himself. Kyle was a competent individual, but his time management skills left something to be desired. Jayden picked up the phone and held it to his ear for a minute. He left his finger hovering over the keys on the phone before finally deciding to dial the number of the veterinary unit.

"Hello," said Stephen as he answered the phone.

"Hey, it's Jayden from control. Is Dr. Harmon or Nalani there?"

"No, they are dealing with a Triceratops that is having some trouble walking," said Stephen. "What's going on?"

"The feeder in the raptor paddock is acting up again," said Jayden. "It must still be on the fritz from the storm last week. Could you all take a look at it?"

"Dr. Harmon should be gone for most of the day, but I can take a team and go look at it," said Stephen.

"Perfect, thank you," said Jayden.

Jayden hung up the phone and glanced over at Kyle again. The conversation he had just had with Stephen did not seem to disturb Kyle from his slumber. Jayden clocked out for lunch and picked up his cigar; he didn't have time for this. He rolled his chair up against his desk with a loud crash in an attempt to wake up Kyle. To his frustration, he continued to slumber as Jayden walked out of the control room. He did not bother to continue to attempt to wake Kyle. This was Sir Barnes' problem, Jayden thought. He was not about to deal with keeping Kyle honest anymore.

Stephen grabbed a group of men to help him with the feeder in the Dakotaraptor paddock. He placed a large white bucket of rodents into the back of the truck for distracting the animals. One of the men walked out of the barn carrying three shotguns in his arms bundled together. He placed them into the back of the vehicle before jumping into the backseat. The weapons clanged together as they fell into the back of the vehicle. Stephen took a quick glance at his team to make sure everyone was accounted for before driving off to the paddock. I can have this done before Dr. Harmon gets back, he thought to himself. The car rolled along the gravel, crunching its way towards the main service road. Upon arriving at the tour route, Stephen dropped off Edward to lure the raptors to the fence with a free meal. He waddled away with the heavy white bucket as he followed the tour route. Stephen drove off to the service door of the enclosure, figuring the issue was likely similar to last week. He didn't want to waste any time in getting this handled. When he got to the service door, he radioed Edward to make sure he had the dinosaur's attention. Once he got the go ahead, Stephen proceeded to drive into the enclosure.

The vehicle drove through the lush jungle on the fringe of the paddock. It was noticeably cooler under the canopy as a light breeze rushed over the men. If there weren't dangerous animals living here, this might be a pleasant place to spend some time on this hot summer day. They pulled out into the open plains section of the paddock and made a B-line to the feeder. After about twenty minutes of driving, the feeder became visible on the horizon. Stephen hit the gas as he caught sight of the small cage, trying to make up some time. The tires slipped slightly on the grass, causing the car to swerve a bit as he increased his speed. He laughed off the swerving with the men as he pulled up alongside the feeder. Stephen hopped out of the car and walked to the back to grab a shotgun. He picked up the weapons as a group and proceeded to hand the shotguns to the other two men as he walked back to the front of the car. Stephen took a knee and focused on the horizon in front of them with his gun raised and ready to fire. Adolfo walked up to the feeder with his shotgun at his side. Adolfo was a large, burly man with a thick black mustache. He waddled as he walked and hiked his pants up until they rested on his hips. He casually examined the small electric fence for issues but could not find any abnormalities in the wiring. His face scrunched as he interrogated the current flow in the wiring with a tachometer counter. He cursed under his breath as he discovered there was no current flow at all. He repeated this procedure on all four sides of the cage, as well as on the roofing. The result was the same, the wires were not holding any charge.

Darius got behind the wheel of the vehicle and sat ready to drive in case the raptors attacked. Darius was a young Puerto Rican man who looked a lot older than he actually was. Part of this was due to his height as he was well over 6'5". Darius wore an Archosauria embroidered cap, the brim of which was hanging over his back. A tuft of black hair poked through the front of the cap. Darius reclined back in the seat, his arm resting on the door of the car. He was not a marksman with a gun, so he had volunteered to be the getaway driver. As Adolfo walked around the fencing of the feeder looking for issues, he paused to open a container of chewing tobacco. Adolfo placed a large wad in his mouth and casually continued to exam the electric fencing. Adolfo approached the fake rock that hid the control panel and noted that it was already overturned. He had heard that Reginald had had to leave the enclosure in a hurry last time and wondered if he forgotten to close the lid. He let out a loud grunt as he sunk to the level of the panel on the ground.

Adolfo crouched down in front of the panel and spat onto the ground. Bits of chewing tobacco rolled off the blades of grass where his spit landed. His eyes widened as he stared at the screen, noting it was smashed. Large, spider-like cracks ran through the monitor, making it hard to decipher the typed writing on the screen. The keypad appeared to have been clawed, and the wiring was frayed. A few of the keys were missing on the keypad where the claws had made purchase into the metal. Had the animals done this, or was it the storm, he thought to himself. He began work on replacing the wiring when sounds could be heard coming from the radio in the car.

"They….Off….Not here anymore…your way! Be prepared to…"

"What was that, you're breaking up?" asked Darius.

"…into the jungle. Couldn't keep their attention…"

"I think Edward is trying to tell us they ran off. We should hurry up," shouted Darius to the group reading between the lines of the garbled message.

Adolfo swung his shotgun back over his shoulder to stop it from sliding in front of him as he began to replace the wiring to the control panel. He melted a plastic covering over the exposed wire connections with a lighter from his pocket. As he examined the keypad, he realized he did not have the tools needed to replace all of the damaged parts. He would have to try to get the fence back online without a functional keypad. They had really destroyed this unit, he thought.

The branches on the horizon began to shake, and a Dakotaraptor leapt out from the tree line onto the field about 200 yards ahead of them. The dinosaur tilted her head inquisitively as she stared at the men. Stephen shouted to the team to be ready to flee. He urged Adolfo to hurry up as he stared down the barrel of his shotgun. The Dakotaraptor remained perfectly still for a moment and then threw her head back. She began to bark and chirp loudly into the air. Stephen felt a chill run down his spine. He had a very bad feeling about this.

"Adolfo, if you can't finish this in the next few minutes, get back in the car," said Stephen, taking care not to take his eyes off the Dakotaraptor ahead of him.

"I don't think I can fix this panel now," said Adolfo, throwing his shotgun over his back again.

Barking noises and chattering began to fill the air all around them. It sounded as if there were Dakotaraptors everywhere. The jungle rang with the vocalizations of the incoming predators. Adolfo dropped a screwdriver from his hand and grabbed his shotgun. He turned his head rapidly as the noises filled the jungle, only to see a second raptor coming out of the bushes behind them.

"Stephen, we have a big problem," said Adolfo, panic echoing in his voice. He pointed to the raptor that had just appeared behind them and got to his feet.

"We need to go now!" screamed Darius. "Back in the car! Let's go, go, GO!"

The men watched in horror as the remaining six Dakotaraptors emerged around them, forming a large circle and cutting off their exits. Stephen and Adolfo jumped into the car as quickly as they could. Stephen fumbled with the passenger side door as he tried multiple times to close it. Try as he might, the door kept popping back open every time he tried to slam it shut. Adolfo grabbed the seatbelt that was blocking the passenger side door, which allowed Stephen to slam it shut. They raised their weapons over the sides of the vehicle and prepared to shoot the animals surrounding them.

The Dakotaraptors stood there, motionless. A few of them began to chirp. They all repeatedly stared at the first raptor that had emerged from the jungle. It was almost like they were looking to her for instructions on what to do next. The lead Dakotaraptor stood there, lightly cocking her head, as if she were calculating. She crouched down on her haunches, opening her clawed hands and terrifying jaws as she let out a slight hiss. As her arms spread out, so did her wings. The feathers on her back ruffled. The other animals followed suit and adopted a similar attack posture. The lead raptor screamed with their signature high pitched vocalization.

EEEK!

Her body rocketed into action as she raced forward, leading the charge. She barreled forward at the car, prompting all of the remaining raptors to do the same. All eight Dakotaraptors were now charging the car from all angles. They were reasonably far away but were closing the gap quickly. The animals snorted as their nostrils flared. Similar to a jet engine, their large nostrils took in oxygen to fuel their large muscles for the chase.

"DRIVE, DRIVE, DRIVE!" screamed Stephen, beating his hand on the side of the door.

"Holy shit!" cried Darius as he stepped on the gas.

The vehicle lurched as he hit the gas and began to slowly proceed forward. Darius stepped on the clutch peddle and promptly tried to shift the car into third gear. His knuckles were blanched white from gripping the steering wheel so tightly. His pupils took over his eyes, and he was heavily panting as he drove forward. Adolfo and Stephen kept their shotguns perched on the sides of the car, ready to fire at any animal that got too close.

Darius pushed the gas pedal to the floor with his foot, trying to accelerate as fast as he could. One the Dakotaraptors had changed its course and was now barreling towards them head-on. Time seemed to move in slow-motion as the two approached each other. The animal's sharp teeth became more and more visible as the gap between her and the car shortened. Darius was focused straight ahead at the oncoming predator. He had gotten tunnel vision and was unable to focus on the other raptors closing in on his sides. He gripped the wheel with both hands as the raptor got closer and closer.

"Man, what the hell are you doing?!" screamed Stephen as he noticed the Dakotaraptor approaching them head-on.

Darius began to let out a loud scream, almost as if releasing his own battle cry. He accelerated forward as fast as he could, barreling at the raptor going forty miles per hour. Stephen shielded his face with his arms as he braced for the impact. The vehicle rammed into the creature, hitting her with full force. Somehow the raptor managed to cling to the hood of the car with her claws and began to scrape at the hood as she tried to get her footing. He feet slipped on the bumper of the car as her tail trailed under the vehicle. She put deep claw marks into the hood with her hands, shredding the Archosauria logo. She snapped her hungry jaws at the men as she tried to climb onto the hood and into the vehicle.

"Get off my car, you bitch!" screamed Stephen as he rose in his seat with his shotgun.

Stephen steadied the weapon on the windshield of the car and fired a round at point blank into the Dakotaraptor, blowing her off the hood.

The car rocked as the wheels ran over the animal's limp body. Stephen sat down, victoriously smiling as he returned to his seat. Reality soon set in as he realized the remaining raptors were still in pursuit, and they were not happy. As they ran by their fallen comrade, the raptors seemed to glance at the body like they realized she was dead. They began to let out angry sounding screams and increased their rate of travel. Darius glanced down at his speedometer; he was going forty-five miles per hour. He looked into the side view mirror and his mouth dropped open. Not only were the animals not falling behind, they were catching up. Their loud grunting noises became more and more audible as they closed in on the vehicle.

"What the hell?! How are they so fast?!" screamed Darius.

"Dude, drive faster!" yelled Stephen.

"I can't, the terrain won't allow it," said Darius, his voice shaking as he talked.

Darius began to panic as he noticed two of the raptors beginning to flank them. One raptor ran up on the left side of the car and another on the right. They were both around the level of the tail lights and snapped at the vehicle as they ran. Darius swerved the car to the right, sliding along the grass as he turned. This effort to shake the animals failed as they quickly changed direction with the vehicle and continued their pursuit.

Stephen could feel his heart racing; sweat poured down his face as he sat in the passenger seat. His mind was blank as he struggled to think of a way out of this situation. The raptors had not only set a trap for them, but from the looks of it, were going to succeed in eating them. Stephen began to think about his life and how he had led these men to their deaths. He glanced over to his right to see a Dakotaraptor running directly alongside the car. He could see the animal breathing as it ran; her chest rose and fell quickly with each breath. He could see her nostrils flaring much like a thoroughbred race horse, sucking in vast quantities of oxygen as she kept pace with the car.

"Shoot it, Stephen, snap out of it and shoot the damn thing!" screamed Darius.

Stephen raised his shotgun to the animal and struggled to steady it on the door of the car as he aimed at the Dakotaraptor. The vehicle bounced on the uneven terrain, making it hard for him to line up a shot. The Dakotaraptor glanced over at him and took notice of the weapon. She let out a shrill scream as her pupils constricted, focusing on the gun. The animal stopped in her pursuit and skidded to a halt. Dust and blades of grass flew into the air as she stopped. Stephen turned his head to watch the animal fall behind the vehicle. He glanced over his shoulder to see her come to a stop behind some of the other pursuing raptors. She then resumed her chase, but this time was running up through the pack on the opposite side of the car. She was now trying to catch up and run along the driver's side.

"She recognized the gun, holy shit, she recognized the damn gun as a threat!" screamed Stephen.

"What? It's just a damn animal, don't be crazy!" yelled Adolfo.

"Dude, I raised my shotgun to her and she stopped running and is now trying to run up on the other side," said Stephen.

"We're gonna die! We're gonna die!" repeated Darius as he drove.

The raptor on the driver's side of the vehicle pressed forward, increasing her rate of travel. She was now running alongside the front door at top speed. Darius looked at the speedometer quickly and noticed he was going fifty miles per hour. How were these animals keeping up with him for so long, he thought.

The raptor glared at the men as she ran, locking eyes with Stephen. He felt her menacing gaze pierce through him. This was no animal staring at him;

he could feel a malice in her glare that seemed almost human. It was as if he could hear her cursing at him in her head as she pursued them. The animal opened her jaws and let out a hissing noise followed by a few barking sounds. Darius immediately turned his head to stare at her; she looked like she was preparing to pounce. The Dakotaraptor leapt into the air at the vehicle, Darius quickly turned the car to the left as hard as he could. His quick thinking caused the car to slide under the pouncing Dakotaraptor. Adolfo and Stephen followed the animal with their eyes as she sailed over the car safely and only a few feet over the tops of their heads. The tip of her feathered tail hit the passenger side of the car as she skidded in the grass just to the right of them. If they had been just a few more feet to the right, the animal would have landed in the vehicle with them.

"Oh my God!" screamed Adolfo.

Darius quickly began to turn the wheel back to the right, spinning the steering wheel like a sea captain trying to turn his ship. The vehicle swerved a bit as it struggled to gain traction on the grassy terrain. The men screamed as the car slowly regained traction and continued to speed off.

The Dakotaraptors were still in pursuit but were starting to fall behind. They had finally seemed to reach the limit of the animal's stamina to keep this intense speed. Darius continued looking into the rear-view mirror repeatedly to watch the creatures. They were about thirty feet from the rear bumper of the car at this point. Stephen grabbed the car radio and began adjusting the knobs to access the right channel.

"Control, control, do you read, over?!" screamed Stephen into the radio.

"This is control room one, we read. Over," said Jayden's voice on the other end of the radio.

"We are being pursued by raptors, open gate twenty-three. Override protocol, over!" screamed Stephen.

There was a pause on the other end of the line as Stephen anxiously awaited a response.

"I'm watching you on camera forty-five, they are too close in proximity to you. You will have to lose them for me to open gate twenty-three," said Jayden.

Darius reached over and grabbed the radio from Stephen. He glanced into the rear-view mirror to see the animals were making one last push to try to get to them.

"Man, you can't just leave us in here to die!" screamed Darius. "Open the damn gate!"

"If I open that gate, they are going to follow you out. They will kill you and then be loose in the park!" screamed Jayden.

"Dude, please!" yelled Darius almost on the verge of tears. "You have to help us."

"I'm watching you on the cameras, put some distance between you and them first and I'll open the gate," said Jayden.

Darius slammed the radio's receiver multiple times onto the base in frustration. He groaned and slammed his foot onto the gas pedal once more to try to put some distance between him and the rapidly approaching raptor pack. The animals were close, the lead Dakotaraptor snapped at the bumper of the car as it rushed forward. The vehicle lurched as Darius hit the gas, rocking all the men inside as it increased speed.

Darius stared at the speedometer anxiously, tapping his fingers on the steering wheel. Every time he approached fifty-five miles per hour, the car would begin to swerve. He could feel the tires struggling to maintain traction and sliding on the grass. The vehicle rolled over a small hill and became airborne for a few seconds before slamming down on the ground below. The men rocked violently from the impact and stared back at the hill behind them. Each of the Dakotaraptors jumped effortlessly from the hill to the ground below to continue their hunt. Darius let out a sigh of relief as he glanced at the terrain ahead of him. It was an open, flat field with short grass that would not slow him down. He began to floor it, smiling as he watched the speedometer begin to approach sixty. As their car gained speed, the animals began to fall further and further behind. Stephen and Adolfo stared behind them; their eyes fixed on the aggressive animals. Distance began to grow between the pack of Dakotaraptors and the car as Darius approached seventy miles per hour. The radio clicked on, startling the group.

"Keep your pace, gate twenty-three is open," said Jayden over the car radio.

The men began to cheer as they raced towards the open service gate. Slowly the animals began to fall out of view on the horizon. It was clear that they had abandoned their pursuit. The perimeter fence of the raptor paddock became visible on the horizon. Darius began to slow down as he approached the jungle road that led to the service gate. He sped up again once the gate was in sight and drove through it. He had to turn the vehicle hard to the left after exiting the gate in order to stop the car and avoid hitting the trees. The men stared anxiously at the open gates as they slowly began to close. Their heartbeats seemed to match pace with blaring alarm beacon that indicated the closing of the paddock. Adolfo raised his shotgun, preparing to have to fight off a hoard of angry raptors. The gates closed without incident as the men stared at them for a few minutes, as if frozen in time.

Darius turned his head to look at Stephen and Adolfo. He wiped his forehead with his arm to remove the beads of sweat that were rolling down it. Looking at the damaged hood of the car, he became fixed on the claw marks that the animal had dug into the metal logo. He shuddered as he thought about what those claws would have done to them if the animals had caught them.

"Awesome driving, man, you could work for Hollywood," laughed Stephen.

"Awesome driving? That's all you have to say?! Man, what the heck was that?!" yelled Darius.

"I had no idea..." started Stephen.

"Exactly, you had no idea! Next time we wait for Dr. Harmon! You almost got us all killed!" screamed Darius, cutting Stephen off.

"Seriously those things are super dangerous," chimed in Adolfo.

Stephen glanced down at his feet, not knowing what to say. He had clearly underestimated the Dakotaraptors and had almost gotten himself killed in the process. His good intentions had almost cost him his life. The men sat in silence for a moment with nothing but the jungle noises filling the air. As they sat there, the Dakotaraptors slowly approached the fence in front of them.

"Screw you guys," said Darius, giving the animals the finger.

He put the vehicle back in drive and began to head off to pick up Edward. His face was flushed with a crimson red. It looked as if he was almost on the verge of tears as he drove along the fence line back to the tour route.

Chapter 17

Scott was woken up by the loud screeching of his alarm clock. The sound echoed through his apartment and assaulted his ears while he struggled to figure out where he was. Confused he finally realized what was happening and reached over to his nightstand to shut off his alarm. He stretched out his legs and arms with a loud groan and sat up in bed. The morning sun had yet to rise, but the sky was beginning to brighten as night faded away. He placed his feet on the cold wooden floorboards and walked to his coffee machine. As he set the pot to brew, he walked over to the window to look out into the forests of Dionysus. His view on Dionysus was not nearly as scenic as what he had on Protogonus. Scott laid out his work clothes and proceeded to mull about his apartment as he got ready for the daily tasks at hand. He began to go over the many different jobs he had to do that day in his head as he got ready for work.

Scott left his apartment, taking care to check that he locked his door a few times before he proceeded to get Nalani. He walked down the long outdoor balcony and knocked on Nalani's door. She answered almost immediately. Scott jumped slightly as the door opened. Nalani put her safari-style work hat on as she laughed at Scott. The two walked silently over to their car, both struggling to wake up. Scott started the vehicle, yawning deeply, and drove off into the jungle towards the Pachycephalosaurs paddock. One of the animals was noted to be limping yesterday, so today Scott was off to investigate. Nalani reached for the hand-radio in the car and put the receiver to her lips as she pressed the button on the side.

"Reginald, we are on our way, over," she called into the two-way radio.

"We are at the fence waiting for you," called Reginald back to them.

Nalani put the receiver down and sat back in her seat. She pulled her hat down over her eyes and crossed her arms over her chest. Nalani told Scott to wake her up when they got there. Scott nodded in reply and focused on the road in front of him. He began to lose himself in thought as he drove. Scott was planning on calling his ex-wife later this week to solidify Erica's trip down to Dionysus in the coming months. He was excited to see his daughter again and was even more thrilled that she had agreed to see him. Scott couldn't tell either of them what Erica would see on Dionysus, so he was surprised that his wife had agreed to this plan with so much secrecy surrounding it.

He was going to start Erica off by taking her in his car to see the larger herbivores. He wanted to take her on the park tour, but the thought of having his young daughter encounter the Dakotaraptors was too unsettling. Scott snapped out of his thoughts when they arrived to the service entrance of the Pachycephalosaurs paddock. There was a large metal door in the middle of a rock face that was at the back of the enclosure. The security at this paddock was not as tight as it was for some of the other more dangerous animals. Overall these animals were not seen to be much of a threat. Scott and Nalani met a team of ten other men, including Reginald at this service entrance. Nalani loaded her tranquilizer rifle as the rest of the team readied their equipment. One of the men pressed a large red button on the side of the door. The button was one of many on the operating panel of the entryway into the enclosure. The alarm beacons at the top of the door began to howl and screech as the metal gears of the door clanked to open it. Scott pulled his vehicle out in front and waited for the door to open. He drove through, followed by another car and a large pick-up truck.

The vehicle entered a long tunnel that bore through the rock face bordering this enclosure. The rock pass was dimly lit by fluorescent bulbs that lined the ceiling. Scott hated how narrow this tunnel was. He began to feel a rising sense of dread burning in his chest as his claustrophobia began to kick in. Sweat began to accumulate on his brow, and he felt waves of nausea begin to fall over him. A light appeared at the end of the tunnel as they reached the enclosure entrance. Alarm beacons began to sound again as the electric fence began to lift. Scott felt relief almost instantly as he entered the paddock and left the cramped tunnel behind. This enclosure was much less densely forested than some of the other paddocks. Scott drove along the flat earth, kicking up dust behind the car as he went. They clung to rocky cliffs that lined the back of the enclosure. The animals tended to hang out around these cliff faces during the day in a similar fashion to mountain goats. In the early morning hours, however, they were likely to be sleeping on the soft grass field near their water source. That is where they were headed. The hope was to dart the affected animal while it slept, so as to avoid any confrontation from the rest of the herd.

As they drove through a large open field of short grass, the morning sun began to peer over the cliff face to their right. The light glistened off the morning dew hanging from the grass blades. Nalani tapped Scott on the shoulder and pointed off to their left. Two of the animals were standing at attention on either side of the sleeping herd. They were standing guard while the others slept in order to watch out for any predators. Scott turned the steering wheel to the left and began to plot a course for the herd. As they approached, the two sentinels began to vocalize. Their deep, whooping calls filled the air and caused the herd to begin to clamor to their feet. Their calls resonated through the paddock as the animals began to panic. Scott watched them begin to scurry off towards the safety of the cliffs. The animal that they were looking for became readily apparent. As the herd rushed off, one individual limped slowly behind the rest. Scott could see that the poor thing was struggling with every step. It labored to walk and almost looked like it was about to topple over each time it tried to use its right leg. The nostrils flared, and her face contorted with each step. She let out multiple grunts and cries to the rest of the herd as she lagged behind.

"That's the one," Scott said, pointing. "Nalani, I'm gonna pull up alongside her if you can dart her."

"I'm on it," said Nalani confidently as she patted her rifle.

Scott pulled the vehicle up alongside the injured animal. He watched her panting heavily as she tried desperately to join the rejoin her kin. Scott took his foot off the gas as he got close and just let the vehicle roll on its own parallel to the injured creature. Nalani shot at the muscles of the animal's tail base. It yowled as the dart hit and fell forward onto its face. Her head whacked the ground with a loud thud, leaving an indent in the earth when it hit. Nalani and Scott looked at each other and winced as he put the car into park.

They climbed out of the vehicle slowly, keeping their eyes on the injured dinosaur. Scott grabbed his medical bag out of the back of the vehicle. He placed it on the grass and slowly unzipped it to remove his stethoscope. Slinging the stethoscope around his neck, he searched the bag for a bottle of sufentanil. He wanted to give the animal some pain medication before he began to examine her obviously injured leg. The bottles clanked together as he slowly turned each of them around to scan the labels. Once he found the right bottle, he grabbed a large syringe and shoved both of the items into his pocket. Scott grabbed the still open bag by the handles and proceeded to approach the animal. The Pachycephalosaur lay on her side and wailed hopelessly into the early morning air. She appeared as if she had given up trying to run away. The men surrounded her and slowly began to close in. Dr. Harmon could see an almost sad look in the creature's eyes as it lay on the ground helpless. She threw her head around in the air several times in a circular motion as she bellowed. She was clearly feeling the effects of the sedatives. This was a condition known as dysphoria, a state of semi-psychosis where the animal would be between unconsciousness and wakefulness. Scott had seen it many times in his career. As the sedatives took effect, the animal would begin to hallucinate and sometimes behave erratically. Two men approached the Pachy from the front with large, thick blankets. Scott instructed them to get in and try to cover the dinosaur's head. Dr. Harmon had found that darkness was often calming to animals as the sedatives kicked in and would allow the drugs to take effect faster.

The two men threw their blankets over the creature's head, covering it. The dinosaur lay there, covered in thick blankets with her head poking upwards. It almost looked like a small child trying to pretend to be ghost. Scott instructed his men to get in close and pin the creature under the blanket while he gave it some pain medication. The injured Pachycephalosaur screamed loudly as the men jumped on her. Her piercing cries caused the men to wince as it echoed in their ears while they held her. Even from under a blanket, she was loud. Scott slowly approached her back left leg and laid his hand gently on her scaly skin. She kicked her left leg a few times, as Scott had startled her with the sudden, unexpected touch. He placed his hand down on her leg again and kept it there. Slowly the kicking stopped.

"Nalani, Eugene, come here," said Scott. "Try to hold the leg still while I find a vein."

Nalani and Eugene approached the dinosaur from her dorsum, where her spine was. They leaned over the creature's back and latched on to her thick, muscular thigh. Nalani could feel the animal's large muscles pulsating under her hands as she struggled to keep the leg still. The two began to turn red in the face, sweat dripping from their brows as they tried to help Scott.

Scott had a third man grab the animal's foot to extend the leg in an attempt to further immobilize it. The men were jostled about despite their best efforts to help Scott. He stared at a large vessel that ran over the dinosaur's ankle. He quickly soaked some gauze in alcohol and began to try to clean the skin over the huge vessel. The Pachycephalosaur jumped as the cold alcohol hit her scaly leg but began to calm down slightly as he continued to scrub. He pulled the cap off his needle with his teeth while he used his left hand to put pressure on the vein to distend it. As the animal moved, so did Scott. He tried desperately to line the open needle with the moving target. Scott shot his hand quickly forward to drive the needle into the vessel. The dinosaur again jumped, causing the syringe to be pulled out of Scott's hand. He tried multiple times to grab the syringe again as it flailed in the creature's skin, wiggling about like a worm attached to the animal's leg. Finally Scott was able to get a hold of the syringe as the dinosaur calmed down. Luckily the needle had not lacerated the vessel, and Scott was still able to use this vein. He slowly redirected it until a flash of blood filled the hub of the syringe. Scott pulled back on the needle and got a rush of red blood into the syringe. The blood wafted into the clear liquid in a wispy, cloud-like fashion as it mixed with the sufentanil already occupying the syringe. He lifted his left hand and injected the medication into the animal's vein. Scott quickly placed his thumb on the needle still embedded in the skin as he pulled the syringe away. He held off the vessel at the site where the needle was to prevent the vessel from swelling and forming a large blood clot at the site of the venipuncture. Dr. Harmon handed the syringe off to the other men as he lay in place. Slowly the dinosaur began to settle as the pain medication began to kick in. This was finally allowing the ketamine mixture to fully override the creature's adrenaline. Sleep was slowly but surely setting in. Scott lifted his fingers to check the vessel once more before getting to his feet.

He instructed the men to get off the dinosaur to provide as little stimulation as possible. Slowly the animal drifted to sleep under the blanket, her head dropping lightly to the ground. Scott and his team again moved in to turn the large creature over to the other side, so that he could examine her injured leg. Even asleep she winced as they flipped her bulky body. Scott hovered over her injured leg, examining it visually before he laid hands on the animal. He could see a large bruise over her right thigh encompassing much of her upper leg. The bruise disappeared under the orange feathers that ran along her back. The purple bruise blended with the greens and yellows of her normal skin coloring. At the center of the bruise was a dark purple circular knot. He placed his hand on the area, causing the thigh muscles to begin to twitch rhythmically in unison. This area was clearly very painful for her to respond this way, even while sedated, Scott thought. Her leg felt warm to the touch; there was a lot of inflammation here. Her thigh was swollen and about twice the size of her other leg. As he began to palpate, Scott felt something crunch under his fingers. This was a feeling he was all too familiar with. Instead of feeling muscle and a solid femur, Scott felt knobbed bone and crunching tissue. This poor animal had clearly broken her leg.

"Reginald, grab the mobile radiograph unit," Dr. Harmon called as he palpated the dinosaur's broken leg.

Reginald grabbed two of the other men to help him with field radiology unit. The machine consisted of a radiograph plate that contained a sensor to form the x-ray image, a portable radiation unit for generating x-rays and a computer that would display and decode the image from the radiology plate. One man grabbed two large full body gowns. The apron-like garbs were lined with lead to protect the holders from the dangerous radiation emanating from the radiograph unit.

Reginald grabbed the plate and laptop while the other two men carried the components of the radiology unit. Dr. Harmon grabbed one of the lead aprons from a park worker and put it on. Nalani donned the second lead smock. Scott reached behind him to grab the straps of the gown and wrapped them around his front to fasten them down. He placed a lead thyroid protector around his neck and grabbed the radiograph plate from Reginald. A small group of men began to focus on setting up the laptop and radiograph unit to prepare it for use. Scott had Nalani help him lift the Pachycephalosaur's injured leg as they slid the thick black plate between the animal's thighs. They rested the injured leg on top of the plate, taking care to pin the plate in the right position between the animal's legs. Her leg bent in an odd angle from the center of the thigh where there was normally no joint. Nalani grimaced as she helped Scott manipulate the clearly broken limb. Scott waited for Reginald to tell him the machine was ready before grabbing the portable radiation unit.

"We good to go?" asked Nalani as she lifted the heavy machine off the ground.

"Yup, should be good now," said Reginald. "Fire away."

"Okay, everyone else, get as far back as you can," said Scott as he approached the animal with Nalani.

Scott and Nalani lifted the heavy machine over the animal's leg and slowly began to line the tip of the radiation unit up with the plate.

"Okay, go," said Scott when he was happy with the positioning.

"You're good, doc," said Reginald after a series of beeps as he gave the thumbs up over the laptop screen.

Scott and Nalani put down the heavy radiation unit on the grass and walked over to the computer screen. Scott stepped over the thick wiring as he approached the laptop setup. He leaned over and gazed at the screen as the image began to load. The image loaded slowly in rows of pixels from the top of the screen to the bottom. Dr. Harmon took off the lead gown as he felt himself beginning to swelter in the warm morning sun.

He stared at the screen intently as he waited to see how bad the fracture was. At this point, he knew the animal had a broken leg, he just didn't know how bad the break was. Once the image began to finish populating, the resolution began to improve. Scott twisted his mouth in disgust at the computer screen. There was a very ugly fracture glaring back at him. The animal's thigh bone was in four separate pieces. The top of the femur attached to the creature's hip, ended abruptly in a sharp fracture line. Two small fragments were floating around in the animal's muscles, not connected to anything. The end of the leg that attached to the creature's knee was more or less dangling with the top portion barely touching the rest of the bone.

"No wonder it was limping so badly," said Dr. Harmon. "It's amazing she was even able to walk at all with how bad this is fractured."

"How did this happen?" asked Reginald.

"No doubt one of her mates hit her in the leg with those big ole domes they got on their heads," said Nalani.

"I think you're right, Nalani," said Scott as he scratched his head and sighed. "I can't think of any other way this could have happened, unless she fell off the rock face. Her bruising definitely fits with a high-impact injury like being rammed though."

"Can you fix it, doc?" asked Eugene as he stared over Scott's shoulder.

"Yes but not here in the field. We have to get her back to the main hospital," said Dr. Harmon. "She is going to need surgery."

"Cool! Can I watch?" asked Eugene eagerly.

"Well, not cool for her but sure," said Dr. Harmon, laughing.

The men quickly packed up the radiology equipment and began to make preparations to move the animal onto the bed of one of the vehicles that they had come with. Scott was not thrilled at the idea of surgery on an animal like this as he had never attempted a fracture repair on something so big. He tried to keep his composure, but inside he was nervous about what he would find once he had the animal on his operating table.

Scott sat in the back of the pick-up with the dinosaur as they rode back to the main veterinary office. The truck bounced on the main rode and so did the sedated dinosaur. She would groan and twitch with each bump they hit. Scott sat at the ready with a syringe of sedatives in his pocket. He had placed a catheter in the animal's back leg prior to moving it, so that he could sedate her faster should she wake up in transit. Eugene sat across from him, and the two met eyes as the pick-up jostled about. Eugene was a Korean man in his early twenties with long black hair. He had a medium build and very fair skin. He was the son of one of the R.N.A. executives that made up Ethan's board. Scott was not thrilled about the idea of having to be saddled with the responsibility of watching this young man, but to his surprise, Eugene had proven himself quite capable. He was highly intelligent and picked things up easily. Scott had found himself relying on Eugene more and more as time went on. What he had originally thought would be a burden had become a blessing in disguise.

The pick-up truck came to a halt in front of the main barn. Men swarmed out of the vehicles to gather around the injured dinosaur. Two of Dr. Harmon's men rolled out of the veterinary quarters with a large stretcher for the animal.

Moving the dinosaur out of the pick-up bed and onto the portable stretcher was hard work as she weighed close to a thousand pounds. Once she was relocated into the surgical prep room, Dr. Harmon began to bathe the animal in preparation for surgery. Blades of grass and dirt flowed off her body as rivers of water flooded onto the floor and down a large central drain in the middle of the room. Scott and his men used garden hoses to wash the animal and clear her of debris. One of the workers cleared the drain multiple times of mud and leaves that repeatedly clogged it. Once she was clean, Dr. Harmon put on a pair of latex gloves and began to scrub her limb with antiseptics. Thick green soap bubbled on her skin as he scrubbed her clean with sterile pads. A few others began to pluck her feathers at the top of the bruise until only normal skin was visible. Once they had finished scrubbing her scaly skin, Scott left the room to prepare himself for surgery. He donned shoe covers and a hairnet with a surgical mask as he headed to the prep sink. He began to vigorously scrub his hands, taking care to get the dirt out from under his nails. Pink bubbles covered his hands and forelimbs as he scrubbed his skin vigorously with the sponge. Once he was done, he held his hands above his shoulders as he approached his gown and gloves. Scott pulled a blue towel out of the surgical pack and began to dry his hands and forelimbs. He dropped the towel on the ground as he got ready to don his surgical gown. Dr. Harmon slid on the surgical gown while one of his assistants tied him into it from behind. He began to put on his sterile gloves before entering the OR. Scott kicked open the swinging surgical doors to see the animal intubated on the OR table. Men were stringing the large leg up to a hook on the ceiling to keep it sterile while others were sterilely draping the large creature. It took several large blue surgical drapes to cover the site. She was so large that her head and torso protruded out from under even the largest drapes.

Scott walked over to his surgical table and removed a roll of elastic bandage material. He unraveled the material and began to roll it over the animal's large, clawed foot. It took several rolls of the material to cover her foot. He took care not to touch her skin with his gloved hands. Scott then cut her leg down from the ceiling with a scissor and had several men who were also gowned help him lower it down. He grabbed his scalpel blade and approached her muscular thigh. Scott felt the area with his gloved hand and started his incision at the top of the large bruise. He cut down the leg to the end of her bruising, the metal blade slowly slicing through her scales. A thin incision was made through the animal's thick skin. The cut was barely visible, so Dr. Harmon made a second pass with the blade. Scott lifted the scalpel for the third time to run it down the length of the cut he had just made. As he drew the scalpel down the incision, he could feel it dragging through the creature's tough hide.

"I'm going to need another ten blade, this one is dull," Scott called to his assistant.

He removed the dull blade with a hemostat and dropped it into a bowl on his table. He then used the hemostat to grab a new blade from his assistant out of the sterile packaging. Scott re-applied the new blade with care and tried again to cut through her hide. Her skin was so tough that it had dulled the surgical scalpel with just a few cuts. Once he had made his incision through her skin, he could immediately see the bruising of the muscle tissue around the shattered bone. Scott cut between her quadriceps muscles and her hamstrings to get to the damaged femur. The muscles flayed easily apart as he ran his blade over them.

Once he got down to her bone, he dug through the damaged tissue for the bone fragments. The sharp bone edges had cut some of her muscle tissue, so Scott began to repair this prior to fixing her shattered bone. Scott began to realign the bone fragments the best he could, trying to place them how they should have been when the bone was whole. He had a surgical assistant help to hold the large bone fragments together while he reached for a large metal surgical wire. The wire was thick and wrapped tightly on a large spool. Dr. Harmon took care to wrap the wire around the bone fragments, so that they aligned as perfectly as he could get them. He twisted the wires with a large metal instrument until it was tight around the animal's femur. He then cut the excess wire with an over-sized wire cutter when he was done. He grabbed the twisted end of the wire loop and bent it down against the bone. Now that the fragments were aligned, it was time for him to place the bone plate. One of his assistants approached him to show him a quick blood panel that they had just taken on the sleeping dinosaur. The numbers looked good, so Scott continued his procedure. Scott and his surgical assistant placed the titanium plate over the length of the animal's newly repaired bone. Dr. Harmon began to set up the surgical drill, testing it out as he hooked it up. The drill whirled menacingly in his right hand as he combed through a set of screws with his left.

Scott attached the screw to the drill and lined it up with one of the holes in the surgical plate. The drill screamed as the screw delved into the depths of the bone. Blood and bits of bone fragments shot into the air as the screw burrowed into the cortex of the bone. A burning smell filled the air, and a small puff of white smoke rose from where the screw hit the bone. Scott's assistant squirted sterile saline onto the screw to cool off the bone as Dr. Harmon drilled into it. The drill jumped slightly as the screw entered the bone marrow. Scott pressed on until it hit the other cortex. Dr. Harmon repeated this process with each hole in the plate, taking care to make sure the screws were lined up appropriately.

Once the plate was on, he began to suture the animal's muscle back together over his plate. Now all that remained was the thick, scaly hide. For this Dr. Harmon grabbed a surgical staple gun and stapled the skin back together. He didn't feel suture material would work on this kind of skin since he was barely able to cut it with a scalpel. Most surgical needles would dull in mammalian skin, making suturing hard for long incisions like this. With dinosaur skin, it would be near impossible. The gun clicked with each discharge as large metal staples clipped into the animal's scales. Once the procedure was over, Dr. Harmon again employed the use of the field radiology unit to make sure his repair was sound before waking the animal up. He was pleased with what he saw on the laptop screen and proceeded to have them move the animal to recovery. Fifteen men carried the large animal into a padded room. They placed her on the floor of the room carefully while one of the men guarded the endotracheal tube extending out of her beak. Eugene waited with her, watching her mouth for signs of swallowing. Her tongue slowly began to move, and the muscles of her throat began to contract. The ET tube was pulled into her mouth a bit as she attempted to swallow it. He quickly pulled the large tube out of the animal's throat and ran out of the room. Saliva clung to the tube as he removed it. Dr. Harmon quickly shut the door to the padded room once Eugene was out and walked over to a set of monitors to watch the cameras as she woke up. The dinosaur stumbled to her feet and stood with a wide-based stance on her two legs. Her head was low to the ground as she snorted and swayed. She took a few steps forward and fell into one of the padded walls with a thud. Slowly the animal became steadier on her feet. Scott gave the order to open the recovery room door and let her out into a holding enclosure where she would remain until her staples were removed and she could be re-introduced into her herd. Nalani approached Scott, who was reveling in his success to tell him they had gotten a call from one of the keepers who was concerned about a triceratops. Scott let out a sigh and began to remove his surgical gown. He peeled off his gloves and flung them into a trash can. He readied himself to go back out into the field.

Scott and Nalani came across one of the adult triceratops stumbling about her enclosure. The large animal was limping heavily on one of her front limbs. She was panting and grunting randomly. Pools of saliva could be seen dripping from her beak. She fell over onto her side into a small tree, knocking it over with a loud cracking noise. Scott watched as she struggled to get up. Her clawed feet tore at the earth as she struggled to get off the ground. Every time she tried to get up, she would bellow and moan as she tried to put weight on her right forelimb. Scott caught a glimpse of something hanging out between her clawed toes.

"Let's get her sedated and take a look at that foot of hers," said Scott. "Nalani, can you tranquilize her for me?"

"Sure. What the hell do you think is wrong with her?" asked Nalani.

"It could be a load of different things. Right now some sedation might stop her from hurting herself, and hopefully we can get a closer look," said Scott.

"Fair enough," said Nalani as she raised her rifle to dart the animal.

Nalani hit the animal in her thigh with the first dart. She bellowed in pain from the prick of the metal needle entering her skin. Nalani quickly reloaded the rifle and shot a second dart into the dinosaur's back amongst her quills. The two sat and waited for her to settle down, so that they could approach her.

Once she was sedated enough to safely approach, Scott walked closer to examine her right front foot. As he examined the massive foot, he saw that she had a large swelling between two of her toes. Separating the digits, he could see that her interdigital space, or the space between her toes, was swollen and red. A large wooden spike protruded from the skin. Pus oozed out around the wooden object. Dr. Harmon asked Nalani to hold the toes open for him while he put on some gloves. Scott grabbed the stick and removed it. Several inches of wood were pulled out of the poor animal's foot. Blood and pus oozed out of the site as

Scott removed the branch. He cleaned the area with some diluted antiseptic soap. Nalani grabbed some sterile saline from the truck and rinsed the soap off as Scott explored the wound. He was fairly confident that he had removed all of the wood from the animal's foot. Scott grabbed an antibiotic spray from the back of his truck and began to coat the area in a bright blue antiseptic.

"Harmon? Dr. Harmon," said Jayden Charles' voice urgently.

Nalani looked at Scott questioningly as she walked away from the sleeping dinosaur and towards the truck.

"What the hell does he want?" asked Nalani.

Scott shrugged his shoulders and got into the front seat of the truck. He picked up the receiver of the radio and held it to his mouth. His left leg was hanging out of the open car door as he clutched the radio.

"Yeah, Jay, I'm here," said Scott.

"There has been an incident in the Dakotaraptor paddock with Stephen. We need you to come to control immediately," said Jayden.

"Oh, Christ, is everyone okay? Are they alive?" asked Scott abruptly as he looked at Nalani. She was equally as concerned and was buckling her seat belt in preparation for the trip.

"They are okay, but we need you here," said Jayden.

"We are on our way," said Scott.

Scott looked at Nalani and cursed. He hastily put the car into drive and peeled away from the sedated triceratops. The veterinarian in him wanted to stay by the creature to make sure she recovered appropriately, but he had to make sure his team was alright. Scott loved these animals, but to him, people came first.

Nalani jumped out of the truck as Scott pulled up to the front of the visitor's center. She didn't wait for the vehicle to come to a full stop before she exited. Her boots crunched on the gravel parking lot with each step. Scott's mind was still partially focused on the triceratops he was treating. Try as he might, Scott couldn't shake the feeling of guilt from leaving the animal to recover unwatched. This, mixed with his long day in surgery caused a knot to form in his stomach. It felt as if his heart was on fire, and he could feel a pulsing sensation rising up the center of his chest. Scott hopped out of the car and paused for a minute to stare at the mauled vehicle that they had parked next to. He focused on the claw marks on the vehicle's hood and bumper. Nalani walked up along-side him, placing her hand on Scott's shoulder. Nalani motioned for them to head inside to meet their team.

Scott and Nalani rushed down the winding hallways of the visitor center to get to the main control room. When they got close, Dr. Harmon peered through the large circular windows to see a gathering of familiar faces. Stephen was sitting on a chair near Jayden's desk with a beer in his hand. Stephen's hair was disheveled, and he had multiple buttons on his shirt unbuttoned. He was surrounded by Jayden, Jin Moon, Sir Barnes, and Adolfo. Nalani rushed ahead of Scott to prop open the door for him. Scott thanked her as he entered and walked down the small staircase to get to the control room floor. He made a beeline directly for Stephen with his fists clenched tightly by his side. He swung his arms aggressively as he walked and could feel his face beginning to flush.

"What the hell were you thinking?!" screamed Scott. "Those are the most dangerous animals on this island, and you got into the paddock with them after what happened last week! You could have been killed!"

"I thought I could..." started Stephen.

"You thought? You clearly didn't think," chimed in Nalani. "You should have waited for us."

"Now, now, now. Let's not do this. The boy has already been through a lot," said Ethan, placing himself between Scott and Stephen.

"More importantly what are we going to do about the dead Dakotaraptor?" asked Jin. "These are multi-million-dollar animals. Your man so casually killed a huge investment."

"That is the least of our concerns, Dr. Bai," said Jayden. "We could have lost people today."

"What the hell is the matter with you?" questioned Nalani. "These men almost died, and you're concerned about those monsters that almost killed them?"

Jin Moon made a face and scoffed at the notion of anything being more important than his creations. Scott and Nalani stared at him in disbelief that he would even suggest a dead dinosaur was a more pressing concern. Scott shook his head and let out a loud sigh.

"We don't have to remove the body; they will likely eat it and take care of it for us," said Dr. Harmon.

"Are you sure about that?" questioned Stephen.

"How are we going to handle feeding them?" asked Dr. Bai. "The feeder is still offline."

"We have a crane that should reach over the fence," said Adolfo. "Maybe we can hoist the food in."

"That's a good idea," said Sir Barnes. "We can do that until they, uh, cool down a bit."

"They aren't going to calm down, Ethan," said Nalani. "This is how these animals are. They should all be destroyed. Who cares about feeding them?"

"Destroyed?!" exclaimed Dr. Bai as if he couldn't believe someone would suggest such a thing. "Those animals cost more than your life, Ms. Mwangi. You are lucky that I have been breeding more on Protogonus and happen to have an adult to replace the one your man killed."

"Those animals almost ate us!" yelled Stephen. "How can you think about bringing more of them here?! Why are you so concerned about those monsters?"

Jin Moon didn't acknowledge Stephen's words. He remained focused on Nalani with an intense glare. He would not have these simple-minded cretins destroying his vision, thought Jin Moon.

"Alright, gentleman, alright," said Ethan. "Scott, could you and Nalani please take these men to their quarters? Jin and I will discuss further."

"Sure," said Nalani as she helped Stephen to his feet.

Stephen shot Jin Moon a sharp look as he passed by. Jin ignored the dirty look from Stephen and proceeded to walk off with Sir Barnes into the genetics lab. Dr. Bai placed his arm around Ethan as he guided him out of the room.

The group proceeded out of the control room door. They walked along the long gray corridor as they headed towards the back exit to get to the car. Scott tried to figure out what to say as they approached their vehicle. He wanted to know the details of the encounter, but given how shaken up Stephen looked, didn't feel like this was the appropriate time. They all got silently into the vehicle with nothing but the sounds of the doors slamming shut to break the silence of the usual jungle noises. Nalani looked over her shoulder as she pulled out of the parking spot. She proceeded down the tour route as she headed to the veterinary unit's quarters. She pulled down a small service road off the main tour route as she drove home. The forest enveloped them while they drove. Nalani checked the rear-view mirror to check on

Stephen. Stephen was finishing his beer and staring mournfully out at the tree line.

"So what exactly happened?" asked Nalani calmly, breaking the awkward silence. "Those little buggers gave you all a fright, huh?"

"It was an ambush. They set a trap for us," said Stephen. "I wanted to be useful and get something done while you guys were out."

"A trap?" questioned Dr. Harmon. "What do you mean they set a trap?"

"Yeah, they flipped the fake rock near the feeder and destroyed the console," said Adolfo. "When we tried to fix it, they were waiting for us."

Nalani and Scott shot each other a surprised look. The level of intelligence it would take to realize disabling the feeder would bring people into the enclosure was astounding. These were no ordinary animals, thought Scott. They very clearly had problem solving intelligence on a level that Dr. Harmon had not heard of outside of primates.

"How did they know to destroy the console?" asked Nalani. "Surely the console got destroyed as a coincidence in the storm or something."

"No, man, they chewed the wires and clawed the screen and key pad," said Adolfo. "I saw it, it was done purposely with intent."

"They must have remembered how we fixed the feeder last week," said Dr. Harmon, his voice cracking slightly as he realized what he was saying.

"How would they know to do that?" pressed Nalani again. "I've never seen an animal figure something like that out, let alone so quickly."

"These animals are far smarter than we thought," said Scott. "They may even be smarter than primates."

"What's worse is they recognized the damn guns," said Stephen as he chugged the last sip of his beer, throwing the now empty bottle over the side of the car and into the jungle.

"They what?" said Nalani and Scott in unison.

"Yeah, man, Stephen went to go shoot one and it stopped dead in its tracks," said Adolfo. "The damn thing even looked scared."

"We are in way over our heads here," said Scott. "I've never worked with an animal that has this level of intelligence."

Scott felt a chill run up his spine. There were many bird species that were highly intelligent, but none of them were anywhere near this level. Having this kind of problem-solving intelligence was something that Scott had never had to deal with. None of his birds or reptiles were this devious. How could they possibly hope to keep these creatures contained, thought Scott.

Back in the control room, Jayden sat at his desk as he scanned the various computer programs for issues. He had not seen any alerts but liked to double check manually to ensure the programs weren't missing anything. He let out a large groan as he stretched his arms above his head and sat back in his seat. Jayden glanced over at the computer monitors that displayed various park security cameras. Sometimes Jayden would watch the animals in their paddocks; he found it very relaxing to watch them wander about their enclosures. It was similar to watching fish mull about a fish tank. There was something very relaxing about it for him. Jayden began to scroll through the various paddocks as he tried to decide which animals to watch today. He couldn't help but feel wound up from the events of earlier in the day and was desperate for a way to relax. One of the cameras in the Dilophosaur paddocks had a perfect view of several of the animals. He watched them as they drank from a stream that ran through their enclosure. The animals would lower their heads into the water and then tilt their heads backwards as they swallowed mouth-fills of water. Beads of water ran down their necks and dripped from their feathers.

The Dilophosaurs would jerk their necks slightly with raised heads to swallow the gulps of water. Each animal repeated the process just seconds after the other. It almost looked as if they were doing the wave as one of the animals would bend over as the next one would come up. Jayden half smirked as he watched them, his cigar tilting slightly in his mouth. A small bird flew across the camera's line of view, catching the attention of the drinking animals. They all rushed off into the forest after it and left the camera's line of sight. Jayden cursed under his breath as he tried to find another paddock to view. He got to the series of cameras that lined the Dakotaraptor paddock. Initially he started scrolling through them as he had had enough of these animals for today. Something odd caught his eye as he blew past the cameras of their paddock. Jayden paused for a second and began to slowly scroll back through the different cameras that viewed the raptor paddock. He paused at the camera overlooking the damaged feeder. The remaining seven raptors were gathered around closely in a small huddle. What the hell are they doing, thought Jayden to himself.

He hit record on his computer, figuring that Dr. Harmon may want to view this footage later on.

Jayden stared at the animals as he tried to make sense of what this strange behavior was. He zoomed in on the pack to see that they were gathered around the body of the raptor that Stephen had killed. Are they eating it like Dr. Harmon said they would, thought Jayden. None of the animals appeared to be chewing or doing anything that resembled eating. Instead they stood there nuzzling their fallen comrade and each other. Jayden stared at the screen, confused at what he was witnessing. He reached over to his phone and let his hand hover over the receiver. Jayden picked up the phone and began to dial, his finger quickly dialing the number to Dr. Bramme's desk on his rotary phone. The phone rang a few times before Richard picked up the receiver.

"Hello, Richard. It's Jayden."

"Hey, what's going on?" asked Dr. Bramme.

"Can you come to control?" asked Jayden. "I got something on camera forty-three that I think you'll want to see."

"Okay, I'll be right up," said Dr. Bramme.

Jayden stared intently at the screen. He was glad he had had the foresight to record it just in case they stopped before Richard arrived. Jayden tapped his cigar into his ashtray to let flakes of burnt ash roll off the tip. He tapped his foot on the floor rhythmically as he waited. Every time the control room door opened, Jayden would turn around to look for Dr. Bramme. Finally Richard entered the room. Jayden began to wave at him to try to flag him over to the monitor quickly. Richard picked up his pace and rushed towards the monitor.

Jayden looked at the screen, only to watch the raptors run off into the jungle. He grimaced as he closed the cameras and began to search for his recording. Richard approached the desk quickly but paused when Jayden raised a finger and asked Dr. Bramme to give him a minute. He clicked quickly through various folders and pulled up the footage on camera forty-three.

"You need to look at this," said Jayden as he pulled up the video and pressed play. "I recorded it a few minutes ago in the raptor paddock."

Richard leaned in closely as he stared at the computer screen. He tilted his head slightly as he watched and got closer to the monitor.

"Remarkable," said Richard. "I need a copy of this, Jayden."

"What are they doing with the body?" asked Jayden. "I thought Dr. Harmon said they would eat it."

"They are mourning her," said Dr. Bramme, sounding excited.

"What did you say?" said Jayden. "Animals don't mourn their dead, Richard. That's something only people do."

"You're wrong, Jay," said Richard. "A lot of highly social animals will mourn their dead. Elephants do it all the time. Look at how they are nuzzling the body; it's as if they are saying goodbye. And when they nuzzle each other, it's like they are saying 'it will be okay' to one another."

"This is crazy," said Jayden. "I didn't think animals were that smart."

"Don't let Harmon hear you say that," said Richard, laughing. "This is incredible. These animals weren't just dumb lizards like we thought years ago. They are so much more than I ever thought they would be."

"Should I call Dr. Harmon to have him watch this?" asked Jayden.

"No, no," said Dr. Bramme. "He's had a terrible day. I'll show him later. Let me get a copy of that."

Jayden nodded and inserted a CD into the computer. He clicked on a few buttons with the mouse and the two men waited. The computer whirred and buzzed as it made a copy of the video onto the CD. Richard waited awkwardly for his copy of the video. He stood there in deafening silence until the computer ejected the disc with a sharp click. Jayden placed the CD into a case and handed it to Dr. Bramme. Richard took the CD and promptly rushed back to his desk.

It was early morning as Kyle entered the visitor's center. Dawn was just starting to grace the park with its light. Kyle fumbled with a large set of keys as he searched for the right one to open the employee entrance to the side of the main doors. He cursed under his breath as he tried multiple different keys on the lock. I need to label these better, he thought to himself as he struggled. Kyle could feel his face begin to flush as he tried desperately to enter the building. It was very urgent that he get inside and handle this task prior to anyone else arriving. Kyle could not afford to have anyone catch him in the act today. He had decided that Splice Genetics would be a better option than the treacherous R.N.A. for his future. He needed to make sure his plan went off without issue, so he could begin to get Splice the data what they were seeking. Kyle was confident that he could complete this act of espionage by using the back doors he had planted in R.N.A's security systems when he wrote the programs that ran them. Finally the lock clicked open. Kyle let out a sigh of relief as he walked through the door and into the main lobby. He glanced momentarily at the shadows cast by the Pterosaurs hanging above him before he began to head to the control room. A few of the geneticists walked past him to the cafeteria. There were already people here it seemed. Kyle cursed under his breath; he was sure he would be alone this early in the morning. He had thought 6 A.M. would be early enough for this act.

When Kyle got to the control room, it was pitch black. Nothing but the blue light from a few of the monitors were lighting the room. Kyle smiled as he stared at the room devoid of people. He walked to his desk in the darkness, figuring it would provide him with some cover. He quickly booted up the computers on his desk. Kyle grabbed a half-eaten candy bar resting on his keyboard and began to eat it. He hadn't had breakfast yet, and he was starving. He greedily finished the candy and stuffed the wrapper in his pants pocket. Kyle pulled out a small drawer from under his keyboard. He dug through pencils, papers, and wrappers as he searched through the contents of his drawer under the dim computer screen light. His fingers finally made contact with what he was searching for. Kyle pulled out a small flashlight and promptly turned it on. He let the light flood over the room as he scanned it once more for signs of life. Kyle walked through the rows of computers in the control room, weaving in and out of the rows of desks. He pulled the hood of his Archosauria jacket up in an attempt to hide his face. Arriving at the back of the computer lab, he reached a large staircase. He paused a second at the bottom as he stared up at the top of the stairs. Kyle walked up the long staircase at the back of the room, panting as he got closer and closer to the top. In front of him stood the main CPU unit for the genetics lab; he had made it. He could see the security cameras sweeping back and forth within the room. A red light flashed under the camera's lens. No one was in the immediate vicinity. Kyle walked around the genetics lab mainframe computer to search for any signs that he was being watched, shutting off his flashlight, so as to not draw attention to himself. He peered over the railing to the genetics lab and hatchery below. A few workers were busy at their desks, but the lab was relatively empty. No one seemed to have noticed him. I can still try this out, he thought to himself. You can do this, Kyle, he said to himself to try to calm his nerves.

Kyle rushed back to his desk as fast as his legs would carry him. He plopped down into his desk chair, which creaked under his weight. He was panting and lightly sweating from the exertion. He pulled up a window on his screen and began to furiously type away code. Kyle smiled from ear to ear as he entered the last few lines of computer coding. A window appeared on his screen and asked him if he wanted to execute the program. Kyle lifted his right hand to his face and switched his watch over to stopwatch mode. He readied himself to press execute and start his watch at the same time. He hovered the mouse over the execute button and simultaneously clicked the button on his watch and on the screen. Kyle began to walk casually towards the main genetics CPU. He knew he would not be able to run out of this room without raising suspicion when he did the final run, so he had to time himself based on his normal walking pace. Kyle would have to leave the island after he took the second round of data. As Kyle walked to the back of the control room, one of the monitors began to scream on a computer next to him. Kyle paused for a second to see what the alert was for. As he stared at the screen, he realized the alarm was telling him all the fences were now off around the park, including the Dakotaraptor paddock. His eyes lit up as he realized what this could potentially mean for him. Kyle immediately rushed back to his computer. He had heard about how these animals were dangerous and liked to attack the fences. There was no way he could risk them getting loose when he himself was trying to escape. Kyle immediately logged in and ended the program. The alarm shut off as the fences once again switched on. Letting out a sigh of relief, he began to furiously rewrite the code, so that the enclosures of all the large predators would not be affected by the security shutdown. He also began to program in a delay to the shut off. Kyle did not think it would be wise to have him exit the room with all the monitors broadcasting alerts. He had to be more discreet.

Kyle entered the finishing touches to his security shutdown. He sat back in his chair and smiled. He was rather proud of himself for this work. He once again synced up his watch and hit execute. Kyle walked back to the computer room with no issue. He stood by the door of the unit and waited for the security camera to shut off. The camera slowly came to a stop, and the red light switched off. Kyle did a quick visual screen for people before he entered the room. The coast was clear. The door hissed as he opened it, and a wave of cold air smacked him in the face. Kyle waddled over to the mainframe and quickly attached his laptop to it. Kyle typed furiously as he began to download as much code as he possibly could, hacking into the system's security to do so. His goal was to steal as much of Dr. Bai's data as possible. In doing so, he would be able to decode these encrypted files later and send them off to Splice. This would give his new employer the secrets to the technology they so coveted. Kyle would thus fulfill his obligations and become a millionaire all at once. He stared at the camera to make sure it was still off as the first part of his download finished. He would come back for the rest of the data another time. Kyle hastily exited the room and pushed the door shut behind him. He stopped his watch and looked down at the clock; it had taken him thirty-four minutes and forty-five seconds to complete the task. He let out a sigh and began to slowly walk to his desk to turn the fences back on and upload the data to his desktops. As he approached the staircase, a voice echoed behind him.

"What are you doing here so early?" asked Nalani. "You're usually always late."

"What...um...I...What are you doing here?" asked Kyle nervously as he was at a loss for words. He was not expecting anyone to accost him. Kyle thought he had gone unnoticed. His heart began to race as he tried to think of what his excuse would be.

"Dr. Bai wanted me to check on a few of the chicks that hatched yesterday," said Nalani. "Why are you sneaking about?"

"I was trying to get a head start on some of the tour programs that needed debugging and I...uh..." stuttered Kyle. "I got hungry and I...I needed something from the vending machine."

"Oh, okay, what did you get?" asked Nalani, furrowing her brow. She felt she was being lied to as Kyle was not the type to be early or do extra work.

"Well, what did I get? I mean..." Kyle fumbled for words as he kept his left hand in his pocket. Suddenly he realized he was clutching the empty wrapper from earlier. He quickly pulled it out of his pocket and presented it to Nalani like a trophy. "I got a chocolate bar, but I was so hungry I already ate it, ha-ha."

"Hmmm, alright," said Nalani. "Carry on I guess."

Kyle held his breath as he watched Nalani walk away. That was way too close, he thought. Had she seen me leave the main CPU room, thought Kyle.

No, this was impossible as she had just seemed to round the corner when Kyle got to the stairwell. Nalani would have most certainly questioned him about being in the that room if she had seen him in there. Kyle looked around the halls one more time and ran to his desk. He had to get the power back on quickly before the animals realized it was off. If the creatures escaped, he would have a lot of explaining to do.

Kyle quickly ended the program and rebooted all the security protocols. He watched as the fences slowly began to turn back on one by one. He thought to himself if he should exempt all the fences from the security shut-down like he had done with the predators. Surely people would die if the animals got out and it would be his fault, thought Kyle. He debated for a while at his desk and decided that the escaping dinosaurs would provide him with a good cover for him to get off the island. Having the staff trying to wrangle dozens of escaped dinosaurs would prevent them from realizing he was gone and that he had robbed them. Kyle smiled nefariously as he reveled in the perfect nature of his plan. He pulled up a small chat window to contact his Splice colleague.

Kyle: I did the first run, and I have half the data.

DinoRider0572: Excellent, how long until you can unlock the security on the data files.

Kyle: I am still working on that.

DinoRider0572: Hurry up! We have big plans for this technology, and we need you to get us that data.

Kyle: This isn't easy, the files were heavily encrypted by Selena Ortega before I got here. She isn't as good as me, but she's no slouch.

DinoRider0572: Let's schedule a meeting in person to discuss further.

Kyle: Excellent. And my fee?

DinoRider0572: You will get what we discussed as long as you deliver. I'm signing out. Do not fail, or you will not live to see another day.

Kyle: That's a bit much, don't you think?

Kyle stared at the monitor for a reply that never came. He swallowed hard and closed the chat room. He quickly began to close all the windows on his monitors and wiped his history. There was no way he could have anyone discovering his betrayal. Kyle pushed away from his computer screens and headed out of the control room. It was time for breakfast, and he had worked up quite the appetite.

Chapter 18

Dr. Bai stood nervously by the entrance for the Dakotaraptor paddock. He had a new raptor sitting in a metal cage that he had shipped in from Protogonus sitting next to him. His plan was to have this individual take over the pride and be the new alpha since the old one was killed by Stephen and his men. This individual was a male and was noticeably larger than the other raptors they had bred initially. He was visually more heavily muscled and slightly taller than the rest of his kin. His tail feathers were bright red, and he had similarly colored long feathers on the back of his head that stood up akin to the crest of a cockatoo. Nalani and Scott stood at the ready with their teams to introduce him to the pack. Scott knew that introductions of new animals into existing social groups could have fatal consequences. Animals would often reject new members, seeing them as rivals for food and resources. Because of this, he had insisted he be there with his team in case things went south. Jin Moon had argued with him every step of the way and insisted that things would be fine. Dr. Bai had come to the paddock out of spite. He wanted to rub it in Scott's face when everything went swimmingly according to his design. There was no way he could fail, thought Dr. Bai. Jin Moon was tired of Dr. Harmon's insolence. In his mind, Scott was not even a real doctor. How could a simple bird veterinarian even hope to understand what he was trying to accomplish, thought Jin Moon. Dr. Bai knew that everything would be fine and planned to use this as leverage against Scott for the future. Dr. Harmon was always asking way too many questions for Dr. Bai's liking. Scott clutched his rifle nervously as he watched the large raptor pace in the holding cage suspended above the ground slightly on a forklift.

The creature snorted and barked as it furiously wandered back and forth in the small cage. It was clear that he was becoming increasingly frustrated. It's calls seemed noticeably deeper. The commotion outside the paddock had caught the attention of the individuals being housed within. The remaining seven raptors were now at the fence, pacing and vocalizing in tandem. One individual paused just in front of the fence and began to stare at the forklift. Her pupils began to dilate and contract rapidly as she stared at the raptor imprisoned by the machines. She cocked her head from side to side and chirped as she investigated. She called out to it from behind the fence, attracting the red-tailed raptor's attention. The two animals began to bark at each other and chatter back and forth. Great, they are talking to each other, thought Scott, this was just what they needed right now.

"I wonder what the little buggers are saying to each other," said Nalani. "They are rather chatty today."

"Probably planning on how they are gonna eat us if they ever get out of there," laughed Stephen.

"Quiet! All of you quiet," said Dr. Bai. "Please load the animal into the enclosure."

The forklift lurched forward, causing the raptor within the cage to stumble from the momentum. The creature struggled to maintain his balance as the cage was secured into the loading bay. A series of lights on the concrete next to the enclosure entrance went from red, to yellow, and finally to green.

"Alright, let him in," said Jin Moon.

"No, wait a second!" screamed Dr. Harmon. "Wait, wait, wait! You have to let them get acquainted with him first. You can't just let him in and see what happens. Give it some time."

"Very well," sighed Dr. Bai as he lowered his hand and grunted with exasperation. "But after this is over, you will listen to me about how things are done here, Dr. Harmon."

"I'm the veterinarian and the animal expert here," said Scott. "If you want to do this safely, Jin, you have to listen to me."

"When I prove you wrong, Dr. Harmon, it will be you listening to me from now on," said Jin Moon obnoxiously. He turned to the face the cage and crossed his arms across his chest.

Two of the raptors approached the cage door and began to interact with the caged animal on the other side of the metal grate that separated them. They snorted softly and began to rub their heads against the metal door. The red-tailed raptor within the cage also began to follow suit and rubbed his head against the cage as well. They looked almost like cats in the way they rubbed against the metal in an attempt to reach one another. This was fascinating, thought Scott. It appeared as if two of the pack had accepted the new individual willingly. The remaining five were standing at a distance and did not seem so eager to accept the new pack member.

Scott began to think that maybe he had over-reacted as he watched the animals interact with each other. Possibly they were not like other social animals he had worked with, and maybe they were willing to accept another member of their species, even if they were not a member of their pack. I have to write about this later and discuss it with Dr. Bramme, thought Scott.

"Alright, that's enough," said Jin Moon. "I have better things to do. Let's open this cage and get on with our day, gentlemen."

Jin raised his hand and hit a button on the control panel on the wall of the paddock loading bay. The red alarm beacons began to flash and scream as the door began to slide to open.

"No, Jin! It hasn't been enough time!" screamed Dr. Harmon. "Nalani, Reginald, prepare the team to dart them."

"Do not dart my animals," said Jin angrily as he rushed over to Scott and his team. "You need to stand down and know your place!"

The large red-tailed Dakotaraptor walked slowly into the paddock and was greeted by the two individuals who had been standing by the entrance of his cage. They rubbed up against him like large, bipedal cats. The other five individuals in the paddock did not seem to take to this change as readily.

Hissing and barking began to fill the air as the five other raptors began to get more and more agitated by the sight of this invader into their territory. The red-tailed raptor began to hiss back and was joined by the two pack members that had accepted him. Battle lines were being drawn as Jin Moon tried to wrestle the rifle away from Nalani and Scott. He held their rifles by the muzzle and refused to let go. Reginald and some of the other veterinary team members were trying to break up the scuffle when they were all startled by a loud screeching call.

EEEK!

The red-tailed raptor leapt across the grass and tackled one of the other raptors to the ground. He began to tear viciously at his opponent's throat and raked his sickle shaped claw across his target's abdomen. He tugged at the animal's neck, ripping off chunks of flesh. Intestines began to spill out of the tackled raptor as it screamed futilely in pain. The other two raptors that had greeted the red-tailed raptor rushed into action and tackled the two opposing raptors to the left and right of the red-tailed raptor and his pinned target.

"Stop them! STOP THEM! STOP THEM!" screamed Jin Moon as he let go of the rifles and pointed at the carnage that was ensuing in the raptor paddock. "What are they doing?! NO!"

Scott and his men grabbed their rifles and immediately rushed to the fence to try to dart the raptors before they could cause more damage. Three of the five original animals were clearly dead, their innards and feathers strewn about the grass in a haphazard fashion. The red-tailed raptor and one of his cohorts had tackled a fourth individual. They began slowly pulling her apart. The poor victim screamed as the red-tailed raptor ripped her arm off with a quick tug of his jaws. He dropped the severed limb on the ground and began to snap at the dying animal's neck. The injured raptor tried to kick at the red-tailed raptor with her clawed foot when a second raptor quickly side-stepped the dangerous claw and grabbed the pinned raptor by the ankle. She used her foot to wedge the injured raptor's other leg to ground, preventing her from being able to kick. The pinned raptor struggled while the red-tailed raptor sliced her abdomen open and proceeded to pull out her bowels.

Scott fired, hitting the red-tailed male with a dart in the back of the neck. Nalani managed to hit his co-conspirator with a dart at her tail base. They then proceeded to try to dart the remaining two raptors. These animals were rolling on the ground, snapping and clawing at each other viciously.

"How could this happen?!" screamed Jin, dramatically falling to his knees in the dirt. "Shoot them, you idiots! Hurry up and shoot them!"

"I told you this needed to be done right!" yelled Scott as he stared down the barrel of his gun. "You never want to listen to anyone, you self-absorbed prick. This is your fault."

"Just shoot them," screamed Dr. Bai, almost seeming to be on the verge of tears. His voice cracking as he spoke. "Please shoot them!"

The last of the red-tailed raptor's minion pinned the last raptor of the five originals under her feet. As she was about to deal the killing blow, Reginald's dart made purchase at the base of her neck. She began to try to remove the dart and stepped off her defeated enemy. The darted raptors all slowly began to collapse and fall victim to the sedatives. Scott let out a sigh of relief as he watched them fall to the ground. He lowered his rifle and began yelling at the forklift operator to back out of the entryway. Once the path was clear, he entered the paddock with Nalani and her team. They rushed in like soldiers as they tried to assess the damage.

Scott walked along the grass towards the carnage. There were raptor body parts, feathers, and blood all over the field. The scent of fresh blood was so strong that even he was able to smell it. He covered his face with his shirt to try to mask the foul smell.

"What a mess," remarked Nalani as they approached the first corpse stepping over a pile of innards.

"See if any of them are alive and let me know," said Dr. Harmon, motioning for the men to move out. "We have to see if we can save any of them."

"What are we going to do with the attackers?" asked Stephen. "I think we should put these three down."

"We will deal with that after we sort this out," said Scott.

"There will be no euthanasia here!" screamed Jin Moon, sniffling. "You will not be 'putting down' any of my animals."

Nalani approached the first corpse. She knelt down cautiously as she placed her fingers to the animal's neck to see if she felt a pulse. She didn't appear to be breathing, and her intestines were not only laying on the grass but were chewed. Nalani felt her bloodied neck for signs of life and felt nothing. She removed her hand as she rubbed her blood-covered fingers together. Nalani happened to catch sight of her foot and noted the broken killing claw. She took her hat off and placed it to her chest. She had a history with this raptor and almost felt sorry to see her die in this violent manner. Nalani rose to her feet as she bid the animal farewell.

The team walked from body to body to try to find a survivor of the massacre. It seemed hopeless as individual after individual was pronounced dead. Scott hung his head low as he watched Eugene approach the last of the defeated five Dakotaraptors.

"Hey, doc! This one is breathing," screamed Eugene. "Come quick!"

Scott rushed over to the injured animal as fast as his legs could carry him. The raptor lay there on the ground covered in claw marks and bite wounds. A flap of skin and feathers hung off her chest and seemed to flap in the wind. As he approached, she raised her head in a feeble attempt to attack him. She was gravely injured and had lost a fair amount of blood, but he may be able to help her.

"Get the bodies out of here," said Dr. Harmon. "We will leave the three aggressors in here for now until we can figure out what to do with them. Nalani, help me load this one into the cage, and let's get her treated."

Nalani removed her belt from her waist and quickly fashioned it into a snare. She cautiously approached the injured raptor with the make-shift muzzle dangling from her hand. She slowly advanced the muzzle towards the animal's snout. She snapped a few times at her before Nalani's belt wrapped around her jaws. Nalani quickly tightened her make-shift muzzle down to close the animal's deadly jaws. The raptor shook her head a few times and then stopped. It was as if she had given up. The Dakotaraptor lay there as the men bound her legs and immobilized her. She did not have any more energy to fight them.

The men worked quickly to load the bodies into the back of a pick-up truck on the scene. It was messy work as they found themselves covered in blood and gore by trying to move the mangled corpses. Jin Moon approached Nalani and placed his hand on her shoulder. He pulled her aside, away from the rest of the group. When he was sure that no one else was in ear-shot, Jin Moon began to speak.

"I'm going to leave the care of these three to you and you only," said Jin Moon. "Design a holding paddock for them until we can figure out what to do with them."

"I think we should seriously consider getting rid of them, man," said Nalani. "They have been nothing but trouble since you brought them back to life."

"Do as I ask please," said Jin Moon as he walked away and headed to a vehicle outside the enclosure. This was the most defeated Nalani or any of the men had ever seen Jin Moon. He was usually much more authoritative, but now he seemed almost sheepish.

Scott stayed with the injured individual as they prepared to rush her back to the main veterinary hospital. Nalani rejoined the group, shaking her head as she leaned down to help lift the injured raptor. Scott was not keen on treating this animal, and part of him wondered if he should just let her pass and tell Jin Moon that she died. One less Dakotaraptor did not sound all that bad to him. He struggled internally as he debated this on the way back to the hospital. Ultimately he decided that he had to try to help this creature, even though she was dangerous. It was not her fault that she didn't know what century she was in, thought Scott. She was still an injured animal, and it was his responsibility to treat her. As they pulled up to the hospital, Scott could see the look of terror in Darius and Adolfo's faces when they caught sight of what Scott had brought back.

"What the hell, doc?" remarked Adolfo. "What are we going to do with that thing? What happened to it?"

"I'll tell you all later; let's get her inside and get her prepped for immediate stabilization and surgery," said Scott.

The men cautiously approached the injured Dakotaraptor. They slowly opened the cage door when she lifted her head. Adolfo quickly slammed the door shut and jumped back. The Dakotaraptor lowered her head and let out a soft, pitiful cry. Adolfo stared at the animal and locked eyes with it. As the two stared at each other, he couldn't help but feel sorry for her. This dangerous animal, that not too long ago was hunting him, now lay helpless at his feet. She almost seemed to be asking for help.

Adolfo again opened the cage when Darius placed his hand on his shoulder as if to try to stop him. Adolfo shrugged off Darius's hand and entered the cage. To his surprise, the animal did not react. She continued to lay there almost motionless and vocalized softly. Dr. Harmon entered the cage next and stood behind the animal's head. Slowly the rest of the men entered one by one to lift the animal, so that they could carry her inside. To everyone's surprise, she did not try to fight them and instead complicity laid in their arms as they carried her through the hospital doors. They placed her on a table, where Scott immediately began to work on trying to place a catheter. He wanted to give her some pain medication and sedation before he began to work on all of her wounds. Scott taped the catheter into place above the animal's ankle while someone held her deadly foot to keep her leg straight. He cursed Jin Moon under his breath as he made sure the catheter was working one last time. This was all his fault, thought Scott.

Scott sat on his balcony as he stared into the night sky. The reds, yellows, and oranges of the setting sun illuminated his face, and the wind ruffled his hair. He had a beer in one hand and a cordless phone in the other. Scott stared at the phone in his left hand as he chugged a sip of beer. He had told his wife, Emily, that he would be calling tonight to finalize the trip plans for Erica to come down next month. Scott tried to get the energy up to dial the phone number, but he was mentally and physically exhausted from the day he had just had. He slumped in the deck chair and took another sip of his beer. You have to do this, Scott, you can't miss another deadline, he thought to himself. He put the beer down on a small table next to him and slowly dialed the number. He sat there and listened to the phone ring, silently hoping that Emily did not pick up.

"Hello, Scott," said his wife on the other end.

"Hi, Emily, how are you?" asked Scott.

"Are you okay?" she asked. "You sound a bit rough, almost like you're getting sick."

"Yeah, yeah, I'm fine," he said calmly. "It's just been a long day, that's all."

"Oh, okay," said Emily. A long, awkward pause ensued as neither party said anything. "So tell me more about these plans to bring our youngest daughter to a remote island in the middle of nowhere."

"I can't tell you a lot of details, but what I can tell you is it's a special kind of zoo with very unique animals," said Scott. "I've been working down here with Sir Barnes for some time now, and I really think Erica will love it."

"So I'm just supposed to drop our daughter off to some butler at the airport and walk away," said Emily, clearly not thrilled about the idea.

"No, no. She will be in the care of one of my team members. Reginald Laurent will be there to meet her," said Scott. "I've worked with this guy for the last few years. I trust him."

"Okay, so she flies to this magic zoo of yours and then what?" asked Emily.

"Listen, if you don't want her to come, she doesn't have to," said Scott, annoyed. "I would like to spend time with my daughter, and I think she would really enjoy what I am working on down here."

"Okay, okay," said Emily. "I'll trust you, but Scott…don't let her down and stick her with some babysitter the whole time. She won't forgive you again."

"She will be with me the whole time," said Scott. "I promise you that."

"You've promised before," said Emily.

"This time is different," said Scott.

"We've heard that before, too," said Emily sadly.

"Just trust me, okay!" said Scott.

"Alright, I'll drop it," said Emily. "Take care of yourself, Scott. You sound exhausted."

"I will, goodnight," said Scott.

He hung up the phone and dropped it on the table. Scott grabbed his beer and chugged the remainder of it. He picked the phone back up and walked slowly into his apartment. Scott let the phone down on his bed, watching it bounce a few times on the mattress as he placed the bottle on his nightstand. He collapsed onto his sheets with a creak of the mattress. Scott closed his eyes and let out a deep sigh.

Jin Moon sat at his desk, staring at the beat-up watch on his wrist as he pondered over the events of the day. He twirled a pen in his fingers repeatedly as he contemplated what his next move would be. Jin was not used to failure, especially not a failure this big. Four of his creations were dead, with a fifth critically injured. It was possible that this animal may not survive her injuries. This was a disaster of a level that Jin could not even begin to accept. Dr. Harmon was right, these animals couldn't be on display. Maybe I can edit them to make a less aggressive batch, thought Jin Moon. He knew that these animals took about six months to reach maturity. He did not have that kind of time as the park was set to open well before then. I can't have an empty paddock on the tour, thought Jin to himself. He began to wonder what manner of creature he could place in the raptor paddock as a place holder for them until he could develop a more acceptable iteration.

"Damn it!" Jin Moon yelled as he slammed his fist onto his desk.

He repeatedly slammed his fist down on the wooden surface, causing the pen he was holding to fly out of his hand. Jin paused for a second and got up to pick up his pen. I'll have Nalani take the raptors off the tour and house them in a temporary holding pen for now, thought Jin Moon. I have to pull something from Protogonus to replace them this week, Jin said to himself. He picked up his pen off the floor and threw it onto his desk. There wouldn't be enough time to reprogram to tour audio before the island received more guests. Jin Moon walked out of the genetics lab and headed to his quarters for the night as the pen rolled unceremoniously back onto the floor.

A few weeks had passed since the incident in the raptor paddock. Nalani had followed Jin Moon's demands and constructed a small, high security paddock in a remote section of the park. She was happy to get these animals off of the main tour route. The paddock was heavily guarded and fortified; this was one step closer to euthanizing them and getting them out of her hair. Thick concrete walls with barbed wire and electric fencing on top contained the troublesome animals. Nalani figured that if they were not making money off of these creatures, the board would likely want to get rid of them instead of losing the money on feeding them. She walked up the stairs to a security tower overlooking the paddock and stared into the pit below. The densely packed forest within the paddock made the animals hard to see, unless they were near the water source, but she could tell they were watching her from down below. Nalani looked over to the adjacent security tower on the other side of the paddock and waved to Stephen. Stephen waved back and began to press some buttons on the control panel in front of him.

A crane began to lift a large steer into the air and dropped it into the enclosure. Men could be heard shouting in Spanish. Nalani watched as the steer stood in the paddock attached to the crane. The animal bellowed as it began to sense something amiss. Nalani heard the raptors begin to scream as they caught sight of the steer. The red-tailed raptor jumped onto the back of the steer and began to attack it. Another raptor did the same thing as they wrestled the steer to the ground. Nalani looked away as the three Dakotaraptors began to kill and feast on the steer.

"I hate these damn things," said Nalani as she averted her eyes from the carnage. Nalani shook her head and walked off. She was tired of these animals and all the trouble they caused. She wanted to make sure they could never leave their little box again. Nalani wanted nothing more to do with them. If she had her way, she would leave them on their own to starve in this prison she had built for them.

Sir Barnes sat in his office at the main visitor center on Protogonus. He looked out onto the holding paddocks below. Ethan very much enjoyed watching his animals go about their lives. It brought him great joy to see his creations alive and well. Opening day was coming closer. Soon he would be known as the greatest theme park owner in history. He smiled to himself as he thought about how much fame and praise Archosauria would bring him. People would forget about all of the others, and he would be known as the theme park kingpin. His name would be a household discussion topic around the world, especially once he got to expanding. He had plans of building parks all around the globe and had begun to purchase several remote island archipelagos. He was on the top of the world in this moment. Prior to his absence from the company, Ryo Sana had Arthur bring a Microraptor to one of the board meetings. This little stunt had brought in a ton of funding and essentially ended his financial woes. Ethan was interrupted from his visions by the sound of his ringing phone. He turned around and hobbled to his desk.

"Hello," said Ethan as he picked up the phone.

"Hello, Dad, how are you?" said a very familiar voice on the other end of the line.

"Melissa, my dear," exclaimed Ethan, recognizing his daughter's voice. "How are you, how are my lovely grandkids?"

"They are doing well," said Melissa. "This divorce has been rough on them, but they are very excited to come visit you next month. Those gifts you sent them were a bit over the top, as per usual, Dad."

"Nonsense, nonsense," said Ethan. "I always aim to please, especially with my family."

"Did you really do it, Dad?" asked Melissa, clear concern sounding through in her voice. "Do you really have living dinosaurs on that island? The videos Arthur delivered were a bit hard to believe."

"Why yes, my dear, of course," said Ethan enthusiastically. "Those videos were the real deal. And soon Dwight and Gregory will have tons of stories for you about these lovely animals."

"Dad, is it safe?" asked Melissa. "Greg was really excited to see the Tyrannosaurus, but that thing is terrifying. I'm scared to send the kids there to be honest."

"Now, now," said Ethan. "It's perfectly safe, my dear. I've been here for years without incident. There is nothing to worry about, nothing at all."

"Alright," said Melissa, not sounding sure about her decision. She trusted her father, but Melissa had her reservations. "I have to keep them in the house until they can come down there. Gregory won't stop talking about Archosauria. We can't have him leaking your secret to the world just yet."

"Ha-ha, that boy has always been a ball of fire, hasn't he?" laughed Ethan. "I can't wait to see them."

"Listen, I have to get to a divorce hearing. Take care of yourself, Dad, and I'll see you soon," said Melissa.

"I will, my dear, I love you," said Ethan.

"Love you, too, Dad," said Melissa before hanging up the phone.

Ethan put down the receiver and walked over to pick up a small suitcase on the side of his desk. Today would be his last day on Protogonus for a while. He was moving to Dionysus on a semi-permanent basis to be there for the opening of his park. He picked up his bag and walked out of his office where he was greeted by a personal assistant. Ethan handed over his bag and shut the light to his office. He paused for a second to stare at the room before heading off with his assistant to the helipad for departure.

Chapter 19

Time was passing excruciatingly slow; the second hand ticked by methodically notch by notch. The clock's solid black hands remained frozen in place. Erica sat at her desk, twirling her pen in her hand; her other hand was holding up her head as her long brown hair flowed over her shoulder. Her biology teacher droned onward about Punnett Squares and inheritance. Erica heard nothing but affectless chatter. Didn't he know summer vacation was only three weeks away, Erica thought. No one cared about anything he had to say at this point in the year. Erica couldn't wait for the clock to strike three. Her freedom was only moments away, and soon she would be able to see her boyfriend, Jimmy. In a few short weeks, she would be at Jimmy's father's lake house and away from the humdrum classes she was forced to sit through. They would spend the summer together before starting college. Her father wanted her to spend the summer with him, but Erica had no real interest in this. Her relationship with her father was strained at best. Her older sister, Ashley, had not spoken to their father for the better part of three years. Erica was at least on speaking terms with her dad, but they did not speak commonly. He had missed far too many important events in her life, and she felt that he did not care about her or her sister. It was always about his precious job. She couldn't imagine loving a job so much that one would be willing to forsake their family.

She let out a sigh as she tried to change her thoughts from her deadbeat father to something more pleasant. Her focus switched once again to her boyfriend and the activities they were going to do this summer. Erica began to wonder if he was the one, picturing herself in a white dress at an altar. The thought amused her for a bit. Erica never was the kind of girl to fantasize about weddings, but Jimmy was different. She met Jimmy her freshman year of high school at a school dance. He nervously approached her to ask her to dance with him; the rest was history as the two hit it off immediately. Since then the two were inseparable. A smile took over her face as she began thinking about swimming and summer sports by the lake. She was no longer in the classroom but instead was sitting by a campfire swaddled in her boyfriend's arms, the warm air from the fire caressing her body.

"Can anyone tell me Mendel's second law of inheritance?" asked Mr. Smith. "How about you, Ms. Harmon, since you seem so happy about learning today?"

Erica continued to think about what kind of clothes she was going to bring to the lake house. How many dresses would she need? Should she bring her good pair of jeans or the fancy ones? Her thoughts continued to block out the world around her and consume her attention.

"Ms. Harmon!" screamed Mr. Smith again as he smashed his hand onto the table.

"What...I, uh..." said Erica confused.

"Mendel's second law of genetics please," asked Mr. Smith as he smiled almost maniacally at her.

"Heredity factors don't blend when they are present in an individual," said Erica confidently. She had her father to thank for a good science education, even though he was barely there.

"Very good, Ms. Harmon," said Mr. Smith, sounding annoyed that she had answered correctly. "I get that you are smart, but please do try to pay attention."

"Yes, sorry, sir," said Erica, feeling embarrassed as she felt her face turning red. She hated being called on in class. The eyes of her classmates peered through her and felt like warm daggers assaulting her from all ends. Faint giggling echoed through the room.

Erica sunk into her chair as if trying to melt into the floor to escape the gaze of her classmates. A shrill alarm bell echoed through the room, signaling the end of the day. Mr. Smith hurriedly gave them their assignments for the night as they all rushed to leave. Erica shoved her books into her bag and slung it over her shoulder. Her classmates rapidly tried to get out of the room, similar to cattle rushing through a chute. Bodies bounced off each other as the students struggled to leave the classroom to get to their freedom. Erica pushed her way into the hallway and made her way to her locker. She was going to meet Jimmy in the lunchroom, so that they could walk to the bus together. This was something she had done every day for the last four years. Erica spun the dial on her combination lock eagerly as she unlocked it. She quickly shoved heavy text books into her locker and took out those that she would need for the night. Running her fingers over the books in her bag, she double and triple checked to make sure she had all the necessary texts for her homework.

Erica zipped up her bag and scurried off to the lunchroom. She sat down at her usual table and waited for Jimmy to arrive. A few of her friends passed by and waved as she sat. Erica stared at the clock, tapping her foot on the floor. Where was he, she wondered. This was the third time this month that he had not shown up on time. Erica made a face as she watched the clock tick. Slowly the lunch room began to empty as the rest of the children began to file out. Erica could feel tears welling up in her eyes as her face became flush. She sniffled and slowly got to her feet. It was now 3:30; it was very clear that Jimmy was not going to show up again. I wonder what his excuse is going to be this time, thought Erica as she threw her bag over her shoulder. She pushed her way through the double doors and began walking to the bus stop. Erica tied her hair back in a bun as she turned the corner. She pulled her bag in front of her and sifted through the front pocket for a cigarette. She pulled one out of the white box and placed it in her mouth. Holding the cigarette between her lips, she searched through her pockets for her lighter. She had to calm down before she got home. If she went home like this, her mother would ask her what was wrong, and she just didn't want to deal with it. Cupping her hand over the end of the cigarette, Erica struggled to light it. Her mother hated the fact that she smoked and would be livid if she knew that this was what Erica was doing now. Knowing this she puffed away defiantly. It was seven more blocks to the bus stop; she could easily finish the cigarette by that time and pop a piece of gum in her mouth, so her mother wouldn't smell the ash.

As the bus stop became visible, Erica took a few last puffs and put the cigarette out on the concrete. She snuffed out the embers with her sneaker and continued to the waiting bus. Pulling a stick of gum out of her bag, she quickly shoved a piece of it into her mouth. Erica took care to re-apply some perfume before getting on the bus. She put her fare into the meter of the bus and walked down the narrow aisle to an open seat at the back. Throwing her bag at the wall of the bus, she plopped down on the worn leather seat. She let out a loud sigh as she began to become lost in her thoughts. The bus ride seemed like a blur as she stared out of the window and watched the houses fly by. Erica didn't seem to remember the bus stopping at any of the stops prior to hers. It was almost as if she was teleported from school to her front door. She quickly grabbed her bag and walked off the bus to her front door. I hope Mom isn't home, she thought to herself. She wanted nothing more than to go to her room and sulk. Part of her wanted to call her boyfriend to give him a piece of her mind, and the other part of her wanted to just not deal with it and go on pretending that everything was fine.

As she approached her house, she noticed her mother's minivan was parked in the driveway. Erica walked around the front of her house to a gate on the side that led to the back door. Her hope was that she could sneak by her mother and could walk up the back staircase to her room undisturbed. She opened the gate cautiously, trying not to make any noise. Closing the gate, she pulled her keys out of her pocket and searched for the back-door key. After finding the right key, she walked through her yard to the back-door. Erica opened the door and slowly pushed it open. She squeezed through the door as soon as it was open wide enough for her to fit and gently closed it. The lock made a faint clicking sound as she turned the deadbolt over.

"Erica? Is that you?" called her mother from the next room.

Damnit, she thought. This was exactly what she didn't want to happen. Why did I have to lock the door, she thought. She was so close to sneaking in without being noticed.

"Yeah, Mom, it's me," she said, trying not to sound upset.

"Well, why are you home so late, and why are you sneaking in the back door?" said her mother as she began to head towards Erica in the kitchen.

"I stayed after to ask Mr. Smith some questions about the homework," said Erica quickly. She purposely ignored her mother's second question, hoping she wouldn't notice, and headed for the stairs.

"Now hang on a second, I need to talk to you about something," said her mother as she entered the kitchen.

"What is it?" asked Erica, audibly annoyed.

"Don't take that tone with me, young lady. Listen, your father is really adamant that you come down to see him at his new job and..."

"I'm not going, Mom!" screamed Erica. "I'm supposed to spend the summer at the lake with Jimmy and his family."

"Now listen here, don't you scream at me," said Emily Harmon. "I know how you feel about your father, and trust me, I share those feelings, but he is really trying this time. Also, I never agreed to you going to Jimmy's lake house..."

"You always say 'he's trying,' Mom!" screamed Erica. "Can't you see he doesn't care about us! He's literally never there!"

"Now your father has not been the greatest about being present, but he does care about you," said Emily Harmon. "I think it may be good for you all to reconnect."

"Absolutely not!" screamed Erica, now in tears. "I'm going to the lake, and you can't stop me! I'm over eighteen; I'm an adult now!"

"You are barely eighteen, and I am still your mother!" Emily screamed after her daughter as Erica ran into her room and slammed the door behind her.

Erica locked the door of her room and picked up her CD player. She defiantly put her headphones on and turned the music to its maximum volume, so that she did not have to hear her mother anymore. Collapsing onto her bed, Erica wiped her tears and stared at the posters on her ceiling. She collected herself after about an hour of pouting and sat up on her bed. She took the headphones off her ears and threw them onto her pillow. Erica got to her feet and walked over to her nightstand. She picked up the phone and quickly dialed the number to Jimmy's house. She listened to the phone ring a few times before it was picked up by his mother.

"Hello?" said Jimmy's mother.

"Hi, Mrs. Weathers, it's Erica. Is Jimmy there?" asked Erica, trying to remain calm.

"No, he hasn't come home yet, sweetie. I'll tell him you called," said his mother.

"Oh...Okay, thanks," said Erica, sinking to the floor.

She hung up the phone and put her head to her knees as she began to cry. This was a terrible day, she thought to herself. What else could go wrong, she thought.

The next morning, Erica awoke to the sound of her alarm clock. She smashed her hand onto the button to turn the alarm off and let out a loud yawn. She rubbed some sleep from her eyes and slowly sat up. Pausing for a second, she threw the blankets off her body and proceeded to the shower. She turned on the faucet and made a face as she remembered that Jimmy never called her back. What was going on with him, she thought. He had never behaved like this in the four years that they had dated. The water from the shower beat on her head like a small rainstorm, echoing her emotions. She turned off the water and reached for her towel. As she continued to get ready for school, she decided it was time to confront him. She had to call him out for this behavior as she was no longer going to tolerate it. Erica rushed to get ready and ran out of the door to the bus without saying goodbye to her mother. On the bus ride to school, she went over in her head what she was going to say to Jimmy. There was no way she was going to continue to date him if he was going to treat her this way. The thought of breaking up with him made her sad, but it had to be better than dealing with this nonsense. Erica grabbed her bag and rushed off the bus as it rolled to a stop in front of her school. Glancing at her watch, she noted it was 7:10 A.M. She had plenty of time to find him and have a chat before the homeroom bell rang at eight. Erica rushed to meet Jimmy at his locker. He normally got to his locker at 7:30 A.M. to get his school bag ready before eating his breakfast.

Erica counted the numbers in her head as she walked down the hall, even though she had walked this way dozens of times before. The numbers slowly increased as she got to locker number 345. He wasn't there yet; she let out a sigh of relief as she leaned against his locker and again began going over her speech to reprimand Jimmy. She had her arms crossed over her chest and leaned her head against the locker as she waited. She glanced at her watch; it was 7:28 A.M. He should be there any minute now.

"Are you looking for Jimmy?" said a voice from behind her.

"Um, yeah," she said, turning around to see a mutual classmate going through her locker behind her.

"I saw him back by the athletic field near the bleachers earlier when I was at crew practice this morning," said Amanda.

"Oh, really?" questioned Erica. "How long ago was that?"

"We finished about ten minutes ago," said Amanda. "If you go now, he may still be there."

"Thanks," said Erica as she rushed off down the hall.

What was he doing back there, she wondered. Jimmy wasn't on any sports team; he would have no reason to hang out by the field. He also was not the type to get to school early. Panic began to rush through Erica as she began to think about what and potentially who she was going to find. He couldn't be cheating on me, she thought. We have been together forever. He would never do that. Erica began to slow her pace as she realized she was almost running through the hallways.

When she got to the back door of the school, she quickly pushed them open and rushed out onto the track. She scanned the bleachers with her eyes looking for any signs of Jimmy. As she walked onto the field past the track, she caught sight of two figures who appeared to be making out. As Erica approached, the two noticed her and ran off into the locker-room. Erica was filled with anger and sadness as she instantly recognized Jimmy running off to the lockers with some other girl. She broke into a run and followed them into the locker-room. When she got to the locker-room door, she noticed that it was difficult to open. Someone was holding it shut from the other side.

"Let me in, Jimmy!" screamed Erica. "I know it's you, and I know you're in there."

She tugged on the door and forced it open. There stood Jimmy with a guilty look on his face. Sitting on one of the long benches was an attractive blonde from the cheer squad named Tiffany. She sat there almost proudly as she fixed her make-up using a small compact.

"I can explain, Erica," said Jimmy timidly. "It's not what it looks like…I…um…"

"Girl, it's exactly what it looks like," said Tiffany. "He is done with you and just didn't know how to tell you. You're so pathetic."

"You know what, I don't even care!" screamed Erica. "We are done, have fun with your whore!"

"Wait…Erica…" said Jimmy, his voice cracking.

"Wait?" asked Erica. "For what exactly am I waiting for? You're just like your father, and I'm glad you showed me this now instead of later."

"You take that back! I am nothing like him!" screamed Jimmy, upset that Erica was referencing how his parents were divorced because of his father's extra-marital affairs.

"This," said Erica, pointing at Tiffany, "this says otherwise."

Erica stormed off, slamming the door behind her. She cursed under her breath as she fought back tears. I can't believe this is happening, she said to herself over and over again. Erica felt her stomach begin to ache as her mouth filled with saliva. She was going to be sick. She rushed off to the bathroom and slammed the stall door shut behind her. Erica pulled back her hair as she vomited into the toilet. She began to sob violently afterwards and let out a scream of frustration. Breathing heavily she began to try to compose herself. She tore off a small piece of tissue and wiped her mouth. Throwing it into the bowl, she pulled off another piece to wipe her face and flushed the toilet. Erica got to her feet and closed the lid of the toilet, so she could sit on it. The home-room bell began to scream, announcing the beginning of the school day. Erica sat there alone in silence as the events of the morning began to replay in her head. She began to think of all the things she should have said. Did the last four years of happiness mean nothing to him, she thought. Sadness was soon replaced with anger. How dare he think he can do this to her! After all that talk about not repeating his father's mistakes. He was pathetic, and she deserved better. Erica wiped her tears and exited the stall. She fixed her make-up and calmly walked to her homeroom class. This was all the time she was going to waste thinking about that loser, she thought to herself.

Erica got off the bus and calmly walked towards the front door. Her mother's car was in the driveway again. She was okay, she could do this. I can tell my mother without crying, she told herself. Part of Erica felt numb, as if this was a dream unfolding in front of her. Over the course of the day, she had become progressively more and more apathetic to the situation. At times she felt like everything was okay, just to have waves of sadness hit her at random points throughout the day. Walking through the front door seemed to flip a switch of emotions in her head. As soon as she saw her mother, she broke down crying. Tears poured from her face, and she rushed to her mother's open arms.

"Baby, what's wrong?" asked her mother, concerned. "What happened?"

"I found out Jimmy was cheating on me, Mom," said Erica through sobs.

"Oh, baby, I'm so sorry," said Emily Harmon as she caressed her sobbing daughter's head. "He's a jerk, and you can totally do better."

"Mom, how could he?" asked Erica as she sobbed.

"Sometimes people do shitty things," said Emily Harmon. "You have to let their actions speak to you as they will always tell you who they really are."

"My whole summer is ruined!" said Erica. "I loved him, Mom."

"I know, sweetie, I know," said her mom as she tried to comfort her. "Maybe you should take your father up on his offer. Some good may come out of this after all."

"I'll think about it," said Erica, not completely sure she was ready to give her father yet another chance to hurt her. The thought of spending the summer alone though seemed like a far worse option than going to some zoo in the middle of the ocean.

The two sat on the couch together as Erica sought comfort in her mother's embrace. How was she going to get through the next few weeks of school, thought Erica. This was truly turning out to be a terrible senior year.

Erica walked up the stairs to her room dragging her bag behind her. She dropped her school bag on the floor at the entrance of her room. She walked over to her desk and turned on her computer. Letting out a deep sigh, she stared out of her window at the swaying trees as she waited for her computer to turn on. Her eyes caught sight of an envelope on her desk from her father that she had left unopened. Erica picked up the envelope and opened it, tearing the paper as she pried at the flap of the envelope. She reached in and pulled out a handwritten note, some plane tickets, and what looked like a concert ticket of some kind. She placed the airline tickets aside and picked up a small attraction ticket printed on glossy paper. The ticket said "Archosauria" and admit one on it. The word "VIP Admission" was printed in bold letters on the ticket. What was Archosauria, she thought to herself. Erica pulled up a search window on her computer and typed it into her browser. Pictures of all sorts of birds, lizards, and surprisingly dinosaurs came up on the screen. She searched for a few minutes to see if any of the results brought up a location. As she searched, she came up with nothing. Even searching the destination of the airline ticket led to no results. Erica stared, confused by the ticket, wondering what this ticket was for. Erica opened the note from her father and began to read.

Erica,

I would like for you to come down and spend the summer with me. I know we haven't had the best of relationships, but I want to try to use this time to make things right. I have been working on a small project for the last few years, and I want nothing more than to share it with you. I have enclosed your airline tickets, as well as your ticket for the park. I can't tell you much about the park, but I can tell you it is something everyone is going to be talking about soon. I hope you have had a great senior year, and I look forward to seeing you.

Love,
Daddy

Erica stared at the note from her father, turning it over to see if there was anything more to it. This was all so sketchy, she thought. Erica let out a deep sigh as she stared at the ticket on her desk. What kind of zoo was her father working in now, she thought. The wind blew loudly in the background, causing a tree branch to beat against the house in a rhythmic fashion. I guess I'll give him another shot, thought Erica, it's not like I have anything else going on right now. She got up from her computer and collapsed on her bed for the night.

END OF BOOK ONE

CPSIA information can be obtained
at www.ICGtesting.com
Printed in the USA
BVHW040948210122
626020BV00027B/151/J

9 781637 640760